INVITED PASSION

"And why are you dressed in so expensive a manner, and in such a drab setting as this?" Read asked Glenda, lifting his fingers to the diamond necklace. He touched it, then let his fingers stray to the softness of her skin.

Glenda could smell the lingering aroma of seawater on Read's clothes. His touch made her skin tingle. "I wanted to go to the party with my mother," she lied. "But she didn't want me to go out because of the storm." Glenda marveled at her sudden ability to conjure up tall tales. It made talking to him even more exciting.

Read continued to touch her. "Your mother is also gone?" he asked huskily. He knew the dangers of the thoughts that were running through his mind—but she was so enchanting! And the sight of her breasts from this closer vantage point was an invitation—one that might never again arise. He let his hand glide down her velvety skin . . .

BOOK YOUR PLACE ON OUR WEBSITE AND MAKE THE READING CONNECTION!

We've created a customized website just for our very special readers, where you can get the inside scoop on everything that's going on with Zebra, Pinnacle and Kensington books.

When you come online, you'll have the exciting opportunity to:

- View covers of upcoming books
- Read sample chapters
- Learn about our future publishing schedule (listed by publication month *and author*)
- Find out when your favorite authors will be visiting a city near you
- Search for and order backlist books from our online catalog
- Check out author bios and background information
- Send e-mail to your favorite authors
- Meet the Kensington staff online
- Join us in weekly chats with authors, readers and other guests
- Get writing guidelines
- AND MUCH MORE!

Visit our website at
http://www.zebrabooks.com

CASSIE EDWARDS

SILKEN RAPTURE

Zebra Books
Kensington Publishing Corp.

http://www.zebrabooks.com

ZEBRA BOOKS are published by

Kensington Publishing Corp.
850 Third Avenue
New York, NY 10022

10 9 8 7 6 5 4 3 2

Printed in the United States of America

*To my parents, Virgil F. and Mary Kathryn Cline,
with my deepest love, gratitude and devotion.*

"When love's well-timed, 'tis not a fault to love;
The strong, the brave, the virtuous, and the wise,
Sink in the soft captivity together."

— Addison

Chapter One

From the shallow draft boat moving slowly through the blue-green waters of the Caribbean, eighteen-year-old Glenda Galvez was watching the panorama of shapes and hues changing before her eyes as her half-brother, twenty-year-old Marcos, was struggling with the boat's oars. He was taking himself and Glenda, along with their mother, Rosa, to the powdery white shores of Honduras.

In the far distance, Glenda could make out the towering, bald mountain peaks that would suddenly dip low to form lush green plateaus that reached for mile after mile with virgin green forests of giant mahogany trees. Then one turn of the head and she was gazing upon pine forests cloaking volcanic mountains. She knew that to move among the pines, oaks and palm forests was to enable one to find large, beautiful orchids, begonias and many varieties of roses.

Yes, the flora of her beloved Honduras always provided a pageant of brilliance, and, somehow, it had never been as beautiful as at this moment.

"The sun. It is so hot," Rosa spoke in Spanish from

beside Glenda, suddenly breaking the spell that Glenda had found herself in. "Can't you row any faster, Marcos?" Rosa added with a deep sigh, glancing, squint-eyed at the blazing sun that was beating down on her so unmercifully.

With the jerk of his head, Marcos answered also in Spanish. "I'm sorry. My muscles. They cannot flex anymore than they already are doing, Mamma," he protested. He then quickly flashed her an apologetic half smile, revealing white, straight teeth, so contrasting against his dark skin and wide, brown eyes.

"It's okay," Rosa replied sullenly. "I understand."

Both Marcos and his mother were racially mestizos, a mixture of Indian and European. They both sported the high, aristocratic cheekbones of the Maya race, and the short, squatty build, whereas Glenda was their exact opposite.

Glenda reflected the English heritage of her true father, whom she had never known. It had been told to Glenda that this Englishman had raped Rosa Galvez those eighteen years ago after his ship had wrecked off Bay Island, where the Galvez family had made their residence.

As the story went, the Englishman had been confined to the island while repairs had been made to his ship, and his boredom had led him to take his restlessness out on this young girl named Rosa whose dark eyes had enchanted him, though she was known to be married and already a mother of one son.

After the rape, it was said that the tall, blond Englishman had barely escaped with his life, yet with only a leg wound to show for his fleeting moment of lust. Nine months later, when the golden-haired and light-skinned daughter had been born to Rosa, good-natured, understanding José, Rosa's husband, had accepted the parentage and had raised this child named Glenda as his own. How could he have not, with her hair the color of maize, the product that all Hondurans put so much value in, sometimes even almost worshipped, because of its usefulness in their everyday lives.

And, ah, Glenda's skin! It was the pale color of pink, like the inner walls of the precious conch shell that the Hondurans were always in search of, for that one rare pearl that could make them immediately rich. With her difference . . . her loveliness . . . Glenda in a sense had taken the place of that rare find. She was the pearl, the treasure of the Galvez family.

Then, after she had matured into a young adult, Glenda's hair, long, golden and flowing, framed a face that all men would always take a second, long, lingering look at with her large green eyes that were hidden only when she allowed her thick, feathery lashes to lower over them.

Her lips were full, sensuous and seductive, but not yet touched by a man's lips that could excite her in ways that she had so often fantasized about. It was her goal to meet such a man. Wasn't that what life was all about? To find a man who could make one's body become as one massive heartbeat? She had watched such love between her mother and father.

Glenda drew her mother to her side to hug her. "Mamma, I know why the heat is bothering you so," she said in a voice soft and mellow. "It is siesta time. If you were home, you would now be having your after-dinner nap. Lean against my shoulder and close your eyes. Surely you can sleep."

Glenda hadn't been one to gladly partake in this daily limp siesta . . . where it seemed that some great magician had cast a spell over the people. No. She had felt that sleeping in midday was a waste. Glenda wanted to experience everything in life and sleeping one's life away was, oh, so wastful!

She now sighed deeply, holding her eyes to the sky, inhaling the fresh aroma of the sea water. An occasional breeze from the sea gave her only a promise of coolness. Across the water of vivid blues and greens, the air was shimmering under the harshness of the sun. The boat shuddered a bit as a huge wave smacked against its side, causing warm sprays to settle on Glenda's skin and water droplets to cling to her lashes.

She reached up and unbuttoned her blouse halfway to the waist of her brightly colored, fully gathered skirt. She lifted her free hand and separated the blouse, so that the deep cleavage of her high, firm breasts was exposed. Knowing the heat of the day, these times before the "wet season," she had chosen to wear no undergarments, although she was so wont to neglect them, no matter what the weather. To wear such was to imprison her body. She liked the feel of the breezes up her skirts and the looseness of the cotton materials around her breasts. She never wore shoes. She was free, ah, so free. Would she continue to be, in this new way of life she was headed for?

Ah, Honduras! It was the Spanish word meaning "depths" because of its deep offshore waters. It was the year 1897 and Honduras's Liberal forces were in power with Policirpo Bonilla acting as president after having aided in the overthrow of the government of Ponciano Leiva. Bonilla depended heavily on foreign support and had welcomed with open arms the American Fruit Company on Honduras's northern coast.

The American Fruit Company hadn't offered only badly needed job opportunities for many Hondurans, but also better housing on its lush plantation grounds. This was the reason for the Galvez family's flight from their place of residence on Bay Island, one of Honduras's small islands off its northern coast.

All of the Galvez family but Rosa were eager to become a part of this alliance with the United States of America. But Glenda was by far the most excited of the group. She knew that it was only the beginning of her dreams come true. She had prayed for a reason to escape her humdrum life on Bay Island, and the Americans had brought an answer to her prayers.

"I already miss my house," Glenda's mother murmured softly, now leaning her full weight against Glenda. She reached with plump fingers to push a strand of wiry black hair back into the tight roll atop her head.

"Papa said the house at El Progresso is even nicer," Glenda whispered, lifting the tail of her skirt, fanning herself and her mother with it. "It even has four rooms. A kitchen, a bedroom for you and Papa, one for me and my brothers, and a sitting room. I think it sounds magnificent, Mamma."

"But Glenda, nothing in the house will belong to us. We weren't allowed to even bring our own dishes and bedding. The American Fruit Company wouldn't let us."

"It is nothing personal, Mamma," Glenda laughed lightly. "It is probably just easier for them to supply the houses with all that is needed to not have any further worries about it. Or maybe they are only making it more attractive to we Hondurans, to offer such luxuries. But it is not personal, Mamma. Don't think that."

"It's like a dict . . . a dictatorship, if you ask me," Rosa argued. "I don't think I can be happy on that banana plantation. It will never be home."

"No. It won't, Mama, but Papa feels this is a chance to get rich. The Americans are paying well to harvest the bananas. With Papa and your two healthy sons working for the Americans, it won't take long to make us rich. Then we can move back to Bay Island." She wanted to say that she never wanted to return. But she knew that her mother would not understand. This was something best left unsaid.

"Maybe you're right, Glenda," Rosa sighed. "Maybe when we're able to return to Bay Island, your *padre* can acquire more land and become, you know, at top of the social class, since wealth is based on land ownership."

Glenda's brow furrowed. "Mamma, don't let your dreams get *that* large," she said. "Only the old families, the capitalists, are among such a social class."

"Yes. I'm sure you're right," Rosa whispered. "Oh, how I miss my house. No matter how much wealth we might acquire, I will always ache for my house on Bay Island."

Glenda could feel her mother's body finally relaxing against hers, now in a half-sleep. Now able to relax a bit more herself, Glenda bent her head and blew down onto her breasts, relishing the breeze she had created against the flesh of her skin. She reached to pull her blouse more open, almost revealing the brown tips of her nipples. She wiped her long, lean fingers across each breast until the beads of perspiration were smoothed out and quickly dissipating. Her thoughts were of the house they had left behind. It had been a ranch built high off the ground on stilts, with one room, combined with eating, living and ʻsleeping quarters. The roof had been made of a palm leaf covering. The sides had been made from roughly hewn, unpainted boards, and the cooking had been done in a corridor outside the living quarters.

Glenda knew she wouldn't miss the only house she had ever been a part of. The makeshift beds made of piled straw and palm leaves had been placed side by side, affording no privacy. Glenda had learned many things while lying on her bed, pretending sleep. Listening to and watching her mother and father, she had learned of the ways man made love to a woman and the pleasures these caresses and copulations always seemed to create.

She had also learned the ways of young men, how they gave themselves pleasure with their hands in the darkness of the night, the moon's silver streamings showing shadows of the hands' movements and the shudderings of the body when the full release had been reached.

All these things had begun to arouse strange stirrings between Glenda's thighs and a need for something that she hadn't yet found in life. Something was awakening inside her . . . something akin to the attempted stolen kisses from the boys when playing street games on Bay Island at predusk.

But something told Glenda that somewhere . . . sometime . . . all the mysteries of these strange stirrings would be revealed to her. There would be a man . . . a man only for her. Ah, if only she could meet him soon. To most, her age of eighteen . . . and to not yet be wed . . . was almost a disgrace. Age fifteen was the usual age to choose the man with whom to speak your vows. And there had been one young man in particular who had begun his pursuit of Glenda when she was fifteen, but she had so far succeeded at evading him and his attempts to hold and kiss her.

Yes, Ramón Martinez, now twenty-one and still a bachelor that most girls swarmed around, was too macho as far as Glenda was concerned. She wanted virility in a man, but not to the extent that Ramón exhibited in this male-dominated society of Honduras. Ramón's first loyalty was to himself, seeking to acquire power and wealth, even at the expense of the community, so that he could elevate himself above all else.

Glenda knew that to be married to such a selfish person would be to chain herself to a life of being humble to a man that she could never love.

She shook her hair back from her face, flushing a bit when she allowed herself to think of what Ramón had come to be called because of his sexual prowess. *Caudillo*. Little dictator Ramón had many followers now, attracted by this *caudillo* who bragged of his sexual conquests to all who would listen.

"Well, I showed him," Glenda whispered. "He did not conquer me. And now that I'm traveling from Bay Island, maybe he will forget me and not pester me

14

any longer. . . ."

"What's that you say, Glenda?" Marcos yelled from across his shoulder.

Glenda's voice caught in her throat and her face turned a bit crimson. "Nothing, Marcos," she replied, glancing down at her heaving bosom, now thinking it best to secure the buttons with the beach moving closer. She sighed a bit resolutely, still letting her mind wander to subjects she never spoke of aloud. . . .

Well, maybe *her* man awaited her on this banana plantation. But she knew that he had to be special, ah, so very, very special, like her own beloved father . . . the only father she had ever known. If she would ever find such a man as he, a love so pure in heart as her father continued to feel for his woman, then Glenda knew that she would follow this man to the ends of the earth, if need be, to get to be with him.

Her gaze moved to the tall palmetto trees and the density of the tangled undergrowth that sat back away from the powdery sands of the blinding white beach. Then she smiled warmly when she saw a mule-drawn cart move from the brush and begin to make its way toward the water's edge.

Glenda began to wave heartily when she recognized her father's thick mustache and wild spray of dark hair that framed a dark square of a face. "It's Papa," she shouted, waking her mother with a start.

Glenda had missed her father's gentle ways, but knew that one day *she* would have to be the one to break away. She hoped for a future that was more than island *or* banana plantation living. She knew that she was different than even most her friends. Her color being so pale and the quickness in the way she had picked up the English language from others of English descent on the island, and then during her attendance of school, had proven to her that these different ways meant a future filled with excitement . . . adventure . . . though she hadn't yet found a way to fulfill these dreams of hers. But she would, no matter how "foolish" her mother called them.

"Papa should be happier on this banana plantation," Marcos said, flexing his muscles even more as he pulled harder on the oars. "It will be easier on him than rising every morning at three o'clock to take chickens and fresh vegetables to the market for selling."

"He should have let you or our brother Carlos go to the market," Glenda said, helping her mother to lift a small travel bag of clothes from the boat's deck to her lap.

"No. He wouldn't let us," Marcos grumbled. "Don't you know, I'd have welcomed going to town instead of working the fields all day in the hot sun? Just think of the beautiful women I could have watched."

"Yes. Women packing forty and fifty pounds of papayas, avocadoes or mangoes in baskets balanced upon their heads," Glenda scoffed. "I'm sure they would be beautiful with their rounded backs and beads of sweat on their brow."

Marcos laughed into the air. "There's even beauty in those kinds of women," he shouted. "Wouldn't any man want a wife who is willing to work so hard? It shows character, Glenda. Have you such character? I've never seen you work as hard."

Glenda straightened her back and thrust her chin

16

haughtily into the air. "You say I don't do my share of work when not a day has passed since my youth that I haven't taken your filthy breeches to scrub in the stream that passes many footsteps from our back door?" she hissed. "Marcos, from now on, you wash your own breeches."

Rosa reached for Glenda's hand and patted it. "Here now," she murmured. "Let's not let your father see bickerings between brother and sister. This is a time of hope for the Galvez family. As I have to put my yearnings for my house behind me, so must you and your brothers place your snapping words behind you." Her eyes turned to the man waiting on the mule-drawn cart. She smiled warmly. "See your father?" she added. "There *is* hope in his eyes."

The boat was guided upon the powdery sand. Marcos jumped from it and secured it while Glenda and Rosa placed their bare feet over the sides and began splashing through the effervescence of the water's edge, then onto the sand.

Glenda lifted her skirt and ran toward the cart. "Papa," she yelled. "It's so good to see you, Padre. Where's Carlos?"

José jumped from the cart, stretching his arms toward Glenda. "Carlos? He is already busy with bananas. And how is my golden beauty?" he laughed, hugging her to him when she rushed into his arms.

"I'm excited, Father," she purred. "You know how I love new ventures."

He was so short she could rest her chin upon his head if she chose to do so. Her added height made her even appear a bit statuesque next to the rest of the Galvez family. She had begun carrying herself proud and tall upon first discovery of this difference. On one of the rare times Rosa had spoken of Glenda's true father, Rosa had said, "He was such a tall person. But after being shot so severely in a leg by my beloved José, I have to wonder just how tall this man is now."

Having such a true father hadn't embarrassed Glenda. It had always excited her. She could envision this tall blond man on a magnificent ship, sailing toward America . . . the land of promise . . . opportunity. . . .

José stepped from Glenda's embrace and moved into that of Rosa's. "And how are you, my sweet Rosa?" he said hoarsely.

"I'll be okay, José," Rosa purred. "Now that I am with you, the days will be beautiful again."

José's dark eyes brightened as he moved toward Marcos with arms outstretched. "Marcos, my son, did you hear how my woman greets me?" he shouted. "Will you ever be so lucky?"

"Papa, my woman will kiss my feet if I ask her," he said, eyes gleaming. Then he burst into a fit of laughter along with his father as they clasped onto each other's shoulders, sharing gazes of mutual admiration.

Glenda helped her mother onto the cart, then hurried herself onward until she was sitting with legs dangling from the back side. She lifted her skirt, baring her legs past her knees, waiting anxiously for her father and brother to quit fussing over each other and bragging about their superiority over women. Though it was the Honduran men's way, to dominate the women, Glenda had vowed long ago that *no* man would dominate *her*. If anything, she would learn how to have full control over a man. . . .

As José and Marcos climbed onto the cart and the mule began to saunter its way toward the dense thickets of the brush, Glenda turned to her father, all eyes. "Papa, how much farther until we get there?" she asked anxiously, flipping her golden hair away from her shoulders, already missing the cooler ocean breezes. She could feel the thickness of the humidity as the cart moved into the density of scrub brush and thorny trees of the palm forest.

"Very soon. Only a stone's throw," José said, urging the mule onward with the swat from a thin branch. "I am no longer just a farmer who works," he laughed. "I soon will become a very wealthy person."

"If there's no war with El Salvador," Marcos retorted, crossing his arms angrily.

"The treaty of 1895 signed by the republics of Nicaragua, El Salvador and Honduras organized a new Greater Republic of Central America," José argued, furrowing his brow. "It is designed to keep peace."

"But, Papa, how many constitutions have been approved and then repealed?" Marcos replied. "Civil wars and revolutions have become commonplace events. Little government money is used for furthering education or building the economy. Most goes to the military." He laughed sarcastically. "And you'd better believe that won't be money wasted if el Presidente Bonilla has anything to say about it."

"Silence, Marcos," José shouted. "Your schooling wasn't meant to teach you how to belittle our government. Your words are a bit reckless. We are lucky to have this president. He has welcomed Americans onto our soil. One week's wages on the plantation amounts to more than we could earn in several months on Bay Island."

"Yes, Papa," Marcos grumbled. "Yes." He lowered his head and closed his eyes, ready to take his own private siesta.

Glenda had learned long ago that it was Marcos's way to be left alone, by hanging his head and pretending sleep, though she knew by the restlessness of his lowered lashes that it was just a game he had learned to play as even a child of two.

Glenda clutched onto the cart, swinging her legs freely into the air, forgetting her brother's words and the battles that she knew raged between the conservative and liberal factions of the government. She instead began looking . . . listening. . . .

The screams and screeches of the monkeys and birds filled the air around her. Then suddenly what appeared to be an arc of green flame soared through the air above her, taking her breath away, but soon she recognized it to be a quetzal bird, one that resembled a large parrot. She smiled warmly and looked further around her. The trees were also filled with red, yellow and blue macaws and green toucans.

Hummingbirds, scarcely larger than a man's thumb, were flitting around and into all sorts of beautiful yellow, pink and white blossoms.

Citronella, a tall, thin-leaved grass that produced an oil used for making perfumes, bent beneath the cart's wheels as the mule continued to move closer to the new "Banana Republic." And then Glenda saw it, in the clearing ahead . . . the large, sprawling banana plantation located on this flat, rich farming belt that had been named "El Progresso." She had arrived. Shivers of anticipation raced up and down her spine.

"We will go directly to our lodging," José said, then elbowed Marcos. "Awaken, Marcos. This is no time for a siesta. You soon will be with me and Carlos harvesting bananas."

Marcos grumbled a bit then opened his eyes and murmured, "Yes Papa. Yes. But you will have to show me what to do. I'm not familiar with anything but our vegetable garden and with catching fish for our supper."

"Good. Now listen carefully. I won't explain again."

"Yes, Papa. I'm listening."

"The main stem of the banana plant is annual, Marcos," José said determinedly. "It dies after bearing the fruit. After the fruit has been harvested, the stems are cut down and replaced later by new sprouts from underground. Two or three of these are allowed to bear."

"How quickly do they grow, Papa?" Marcos said, straightening his back.

"Usually in ten months. To a ten- to forty-foot height," José answered. "The average cluster of bananas weighs twenty-five pounds, but individual bunches often exceed forty pounds."

"How many workers are there?"

"Two to three hundred."

"After the bananas are picked, then what, Papa?"

"Workers clean and sort the green bananas and pack them into crates for exporting."

Glenda's eyes widened as she scooted to be behind her father. "Did you say . . . exporting . . . ?" she asked anxiously. "Do you mean . . . by . . . ship . . . ?"

"Yes. By ship . . ."

"American ships . . . ?" she said in a silken whisper. She didn't want to think of the possibilities of her true father returning to Honduras in one of his ships. She truly didn't! But . . . Maybe . . . he just might. She couldn't help feeling further tremors of excitement course through her veins. What if she could . . . meet . . . him . . . ? It would prove interesting. . . .

"Yes. Yes," José mumbled. He turned his dark eyes to her, glowering.

She could see a touch of hurt in his eyes and knew what he had to be thinking. The word "American" always sparked a deep anger inside her father. Glenda had to remember why. She even realized that her own hatred for Americans should be just as strong. But she had American blood flowing through her veins. She even looked more American than mestizo. How could she not fantasize about one day meeting one . . . of . . . her own kind . . . even . . . her true father.

She scooted to the edge of the cart, seeing the activity now all around her. There were hordes of workers in the fields on each side of her. And there were green bananas, everywhere she looked. Mule and donkey drawn carts filled with cut bananas stems were moving toward jungle paths. The rock-strewn earth path that her own cart was moving on led on into a village.

Glenda moved to her knees, balancing herself on them, now peering on all sides of her at the many small houses standing in short rows along the edge of the banana field. All were built on stilts, as most houses were that stood so close to the sea, for the grounds were known to become very wet and muddy when it rained.

"What new type of housing is this?" Rosa exclaimed, shifting her bundle in her arms. "The roofs are tin!"

"And, Mamma, see how clean and painted the outside walls are," Glenda sighed. Her eyes ventured upward. "And there is even a chimney. Mamma, you no longer will have to cook outside the house you have residence in. This house must have a cooking stove."

José laughed heartily. "Yes, my Rosa. A surprise from your José."

"Really?" Rosa whispered.

"Yes. All the company dwellings have stoves," José replied, then tilted his chin into the air, flaring his nostrils. "Don't you even smell it?"

"What?"

"Over everything is the pleasant odor of burning soft wood," José sighed. "It is the wood being burned by the women for cooking."

"José," Rosa said excitedly, "hurry. I am fast forgetting my longings for my house on Bay Island that had only one room and no stove."

"Carlos went to the company store and got supplies for you," José said proudly. "Carlos has even ground the grain and has ready for you all that is necessary to prepare tortillas and tamales for our supper tonight. We shall have a feast."

Glenda laughed throatily, oh, so loving her family. It was good now, to be together again. Her gaze traveled further down the road. Something grabbed at her heart, seeing a huge house on a hill at the far end of the village. Though a stockade fence surrounded it, she could still see enough of the house it surrounded to know that it was like no house she had ever seen before. It was of a pastel color of green and had many windows. It was not only one story, but two, and had a colorful red tile roof. Glenda couldn't help secretly wishing for the day to arrive when she might visit such a house and the people who lived there.

"Papa?" she suddenly blurted.

"Yes . . . ?" he replied, guiding the mule to a halt in front of a much smaller house.

"Whose house is that?" Glenda said, pointing to the huge, two-storied house at the far end of the road that she was now comparing to a castle in her mind.

José laughed sarcastically as he stepped from the cart, going to Rosa to help lift her onto the ground. "That is the house occupied by the most important person of this plantation," he said firmly. "The 'division manager' for the American Fruit Company lives there."

Glenda's feathery eyebrows tilted, glancing quickly around her, then back to the house. "But it is the only grand one here and it is the only one built on a hill. . . ."

José laughed again. "You've much to learn about Americans," he said. "They have the best of everything. And they say no houses can be built as high on land here on this plantation as the division manager's. If the land is flat where their house is planned, then hills are created artificially. They are snobs, Glenda, but snobs that can make us rich. Yes, the company owns it all, lock, stock and barrel. Even the fork you will be eating with."

"Have you seen these Americans, Papa?" Glenda sighed, full of wonder.

"Yes. Many times."

"And what do they look like, Papa?"

José's thick mustache worked as his lips began a slow tremble. "Golden-haired, Glenda," he murmured. "Much like yourself. . . ."

Glenda's heart began to race. Somehow . . . some way . . . she had to meet every one of these Americans, even though they had placed themselves on a hill, to look down their noses at the Honduran laborers and families. . . .

Chapter Two

The sun was quickly lowering behind the distant mountains, casting shadowed orange shimmerings along the horizon. The moisture was heavy and thick in the air, causing Glenda to stop to wipe beads of perspiration from beneath her nose.

In a low-swept blouse and brightly colored skirt, she stood gazing around her, realizing that this was the usual time of evening that afforded most the luxury of resting, leaving Glenda to now work alone in the laborers' communal garden. It wasn't because she enjoyed the chores of hoeing the weeds from between the rows of beans and maize, but for the sole purpose of being closer to the American's house on the hill, where so many happenings astounded her.

Bright rays of light were reflecting in golden hazes from each of the upper windows. Glenda had never seen kerosene lamps or candles that could cast off such a brightness. She stood as though hypnotized, resting against her hoe, as she saw movement at one of the windows. Her breath then caught in her throat when she saw the outline of a woman and knew that this had to be the American lady that her younger brother Carlos had spoken so fondly of. This made Glenda's pulse increase, and she wanted so to move closer, to get an even better look. But the high fence and the many tall stalks of maize stood in her way.

A rustling of maize leaves behind her drew Glenda around with a start. She searched with her eyes around her, suddenly feeling too alone, even a bit isolated . . . being quite a distance away from the safety of the Galvezes' back door. The many birds in the forests and the forever screeching monkeys seemed to be settling in for the night, and the incessant humming of the mosquitos was quickly a threat to all who would venture out when the sun was replaced by the crisp, clear outline of the moon.

"Is someone there?" Glenda said, almost in a whisper. She clasped more tightly to the hoe's handle, now only hearing an awkward silence around her. Then when a damp breeze lifted a few maize leaves and rustled them noisily together, Glenda let out a deep breath of relief.

She laughed softly and began to walk through the tight confines of the tall plants on each side of her, amazed at how fast night had fallen. As she looked toward the sky, a shiver ran through her. When it was dark, the sky was like a sheet of black velvet. Only an outline of the moon was visible through the storm clouds that were beginning to form above the mountains.

Small flashes of lightning began to unravel across the sky, causing a low rumble of thunder to vibrate in the ground beneath Glenda's bare feet, hastening her pace. Then she halted in midstep when she heard another rustling of leaves behind her, then another and another, causing Glenda's knees to feel as though made of rubber. She dropped her hoe as she tripped over a mound of dirt, and as she stooped to pick it up, she saw feet move before her eyes. Her mother had warned her of the dangers of being out alone . . . now Glenda understood why.

With a dryness forming in her throat, Glenda inched her fingers toward the hoe, hoping, if needed, to use it as a weapon. But she gasped noisily when one of those feet she was staring at moved to hold the hoe to the ground.

Slowly, she straightened her back and when another flash of lightning lighted the spaces around her, Glenda let a gasp of uncontrollable relief tremble from the depths of her throat. "Ramón Martinez, it is you! You scared me so," she laughed nervously. Then her hands went to her throat, realizing this wasn't Bay Island where Ramón could materialize at a moment's notice to annoy her, but El Progresso, where she had thought to be . . . free of . . . his nuisances. Had . . . he . . . followed her . . . here . . . ?

"You are glad to see me, no?" Ramón said suavely in thick Spanish.

"What are you doing here, Ramón?" she hissed, flipping her hair back from her shoulders.

"Did you think the waters of the Caribbean could truly separate you from me?" Ramón laughed, revealing smooth, white teeth against the dark brown of his skin. He squared his shoulders, exhibiting his ripples of muscles and the haughtiness in the way in which he carried himself. His dark hair hung to the collar of his white cotton shirt, and the heavy cotton

28

material of his breeches was drawn tightly over him, as though poured onto him, revealing a significant bulge pressing against his breeches' front buttons.

Glenda sighed exasperatedly. "Ramón, why did you even come?"

"Only to see you," he said, reaching for her.

She brusquely brushed his hand aside. "You have no reasons to see me, Ramón," she snapped. "I gave you no encouragement. I've told you over and over again that I have no interest in you or your macho image you flash for all to see."

Ramón grabbed her around the waist and yanked her roughly to him. "It is because of such an image that I have come," he growled, grinding his body into hers. "I no longer am called *caudillo*. My followers laugh at me. They say I am half a man because I haven't been able to conquer you."

"Ramón, you *borrico!*" she spat, squirming against his grip of steel. "You must let me go. If you force yourself on me, you will be no more *caudillo* than if you had left me untouched."

He laughed throatily. "You are wrong. I will become a leader again if I can boast of my conquest of the señorita with the golden hair." He laced his fingers through her hair and crushed her mouth to his, sinking his teeth into her lips.

Glenda began to kick and scratch at him but found that her struggles caused him to become even more aggressive. With a pounding heart, she couldn't even stop him when his hand pulled her blouse free from the waist of her skirt and reached inside and found her breasts high and firm and free of undergarment protection. With skill, he began to squeeze and

29

fondle, causing alarm to rush through Glenda, never having felt a man's hand on her body before. It was causing a strange tingling up and down her spine, something that she had never felt before and knew that she shouldn't even now. She couldn't let him continue. It was wrong. She not only hated Ramón, but, also, wasn't this the way her mother had been taken by the American all those years ago? Her mother hadn't wanted it. Glenda didn't want it. Glenda wanted her first time to be with the man she loved.

A groan rose from inside his chest and he released his lips from her. "I must have you," he whispered. "Now . . ."

"No. You cannot!" she screamed. "I do not love you. Let me go, Ramón. I will kill you if you take my virginity away from me."

He laughed gruffly, shoving her to the ground. "Yes. You are so valiant." His mouth crushed against hers again as he suddenly seemed to be all hands, wandering from breast to breast, squeezing, pinching. And when Glenda's skirt was lifted to reveal still the lack of undergarment, Ramón let his fingers move to the soft spot between her legs, where they began a gentle caress.

Glenda continued to fight him until a wave of warmth slowly began to wash over her, making her wonder about what this man she despised was causing to happen inside her. Her breath began to come in short rasps as her strength against him waned. But when she heard his low, mocking laugh as she further opened her legs to him, the spell that he had momentarily succeeded at weaving over her was quickly broken. She now realized how he had succeeded at becoming a *caudillo*. He had a way with his hands that surely no other man had. Hadn't her senses left her for a brief moment?

"You do like. Yes?" he said huskily, breathing hotly over a breast. When his tongue reached for and flicked over its nipple, Glenda began to push at his head, tossing her head back and forth on the ground, never having felt so humiliated and angry.

"No. I do not like. I hate you. I hate what you do," she shouted. Then she grew quiet and tense when she saw him reach for and began to unfasten his breeches.

"You will like my hardness inside you, yes," he said thickly, releasing his manhood from inside the tight confines of his breeches.

Glenda tensed when she glanced downward and saw his hand guiding his large throbbing manhood between her outspread legs. "No!" she screamed. "You are malicious!" Her fists hit against his chest. Her fingernails scraped the flesh of his face. But it seemed that all attempts to thwart his attack were useless. He hadn't traveled by boat across the Caribbean and by mule through the jungle to not succeed in his seduction of the woman he had been desiring for three full years now. By her having left him behind without a promise of marriage, she had in a sense stripped him of his manhood and the followers who had been attracted by the macho qualities that they had seen and admired in him.

A loud clap of thunder echoed around Glenda and the first drop of rain splattered onto her bare legs. Hope surged through her. She stared toward the sky, praying for a deluge of water to drop from the clouds,

31

hoping that Ramón wouldn't continue his sexual assault in the mud. . . .

Footsteps racing toward Glenda and Ramón caused Glenda's head to turn in the direction from which they came and just as Ramón's hard throbbing member began to push at her, she recognized the stance of her fifteen-year-old half-brother Carlos racing toward her with raised fists.

"You stupid ass. Release my sister," Carlos shouted angrily. "Ramón, you deceived me. When I told you where you could find my sister, I only did so because I thought you held her honor in high esteem inside your brain. Instead, you attack her as though she is a beast."

"Carlos. Thank heaven. Oh, Carlos, thank you," Glenda cried, sobbing hard as Carlos pushed Ramón from atop her. Glenda rose quickly, rearranging her clothes to hide her nudity, then hugged herself with her arms as a cold rain began to fall upon her. Tears mingled with the rain on her cheeks as she watched Carlos and Ramón wrestling along the quickly becoming rain-soaked ground. It was now hard to tell them apart from behind the mud that glistened from their heads to their toes. But she recognized her brother's voice when he began to yell at her.

"Leave here. Now, Glenda," he shouted.

"But, Carlos," she cried, tossing her wet strings of hair from her eyes. "I want to wait on you."

"No," he said as he yanked Ramón up and held Ramón's arms locked behind him. "I am going to guide this filth from El Progresso. I have just shown him who is true macho." He laughed throatily as he yanked roughly on Ramón's arms.

"I will get you for this, Carlos," Ramón growled. "You had me at a disadvantage."

"I guess I did," Carlos shouted above the continuing thunder and solid sheet of falling rain. "You were raping my sister. Even now your penis hangs from your breeches. I should even cut it off. That way I would be assured of you not bothering my sister again."

Glenda covered her mouth with her hands, shocked, but yet so proud of her brave younger half-brother. He did appear macho now with his arm muscles flexed and his dark square jaws set so determinedly. Though night, the bright flashes of lightning could reveal the hatred in his dark pools of eyes. But yet he looked so innocent as the rain continued to pull his wiry mass of black hair to rest upon his shoulders.

"Glenda, like I told you. You leave. Now," Carlos shouted. "And take the main road. It is quicker."

She wiped at her eyes, hating the blur the rain was causing. "But what about you, Carlos? I shouldn't leave you." She worried that Ramón might possibly regain his full strength and use it on Carlos, who wasn't as yet matured in his weight, height or muscle.

"I plan to take Ramón through the fields," Carlos replied, almost angrily. "That way will be quicker for me. Now run. Go to the road. And don't stop for anyone or anything . . ."

"Si, Carlos," Glenda said, glancing quickly toward Ramón who stood glaring at her. She thrust her chin haughtily into the air then lifted the tail of her skirt and began to splash barefooted through the thickening mud.

The lightning flashed in slivers of light around her,

helping to light her way, and when the road was reached she began to trudge through the mud that seemed to get deeper and deeper. Then a throaty scream emerged from somewhere inside her when she came face to face with a horse that was struggling just as she, with the thickness of the swirling mass of brown liquid beneath its hooves. Glenda froze on the spot, feeling the fingers of fear riding her spine. She had never seen any horses on Bay Island nor on this plantation. Mules and donkeys, yes, but never horses.

"Get out of the way," Glenda then heard a man's loud voice yell through the rain.

She finally found the strength in her legs to move aside and searched through the shreds of rain and found a fine, black, fringe-topped carriage with an American man holding the reins to the horse. He was continually flicking them angrily against the horse's mane, even almost unmercifully. Glenda then looked toward the carriage wheels and found them straining with each attempt of the horse to pull them forward.

"Your wheels. They are stuck, señor," Glenda yelled into the rain, continually wiping the wetness from her mouth and eyes.

The man in a top hat glared through the rain toward Glenda. "And so you also seem to be," he growled. "What the hell are you doing out in such a downpour?"

"Nothing I am enjoying doing, señor," she tossed flimsily back at him.

The man's eyes traveled over her full figure, then motioned with a hand. "Come. Get on the carriage with me. And if we can get this damn bastard moving, I will take you to my house to get dry."

Glenda tensed, remembering her brother's words that she should stop for no one . . . that she should hurry on home . . . where she knew safety awaited her. "I . . . don't know, señor," she stammered.

His eyes scanned over her again. "I didn't know there was an American family living here on this plantation who had a daughter your age," he shouted. "Damn it. Come on. Or your parents will eat me alive if they find that I didn't take you safely to either your home or mine until the storm passes."

Glenda's heart palpitated. This American gentleman thought she was from one of the other few American families who lived on the plantation. She smiled to herself, liking this comparison. Then she once again felt wary of this stranger of the night. "And might I ask you where your house sits, sir?" she said, making sure to not refer to him as "señor" any longer. She was glad that he had forgotten to notice her earlier reference of such. Ah, how glad she was that she had paid attention at school . . . and had learned the English language so accurately.

"The house at the far end of the road," he said, pointing. "But you know which one I mean. And where is your house? Maybe it would be easier to just drop you by there . . . ?"

Glenda's breath caught in her throat. This gentleman was from the house . . . the one she had been admiring from afar for the full week since having arrived on the plantation. She peered through the blur of rain, trying to make out his facial features, but found it impossible. All that she could tell was that he sat tall and was finely clothed, even though wet.

Then she let her fingers move to her throat, remembering his question as to where . . . she . . . lived. If he knew that she was a Honduran laborer's daughter, he would not even bother with her. How could she evade such a question?

"Sir, I do believe your house is closer," she laughed nervously. "And I've heard that it is so grand inside. Much better than any of the homes we . . . uh . . . other Americans live in. I, as well as . . . uh . . . others, have wished to see its interior. If you don't think I am too wet . . . and . . . uh muddy, I'd much prefer to go to your house this night. Then I can run on home once the downpour lets up."

"Then hop aboard and maybe between the two of us, we can get this damn horse to pull the carriage through the muddy mess," he said, offering her a hand, helping her onto the carriage seat next to him. "I've only been here a week. And I've found this jungle quite an unpleasant place to live."

"You've been here only a week?" she gasped, arranging her wet skirt around her legs, hating the way it clung, wet and itchy. She hid her muddy feet from his eyes, knowing he would soon question as to the whereabouts of her shoes if she was such a fine American woman.

"You should know that," he grumbled, flicking the reins even harder. "Everyone knows that the new division manager has just arrived to take over command of the plantation."

She flipped her wet strands of hair back from her eyes, feeling heat rising in her cheeks. She cleared her throat nervously. "Oh, yes. How dumb of me," she laughed, eyeing him out of the corner of her eyes. His suit was severe in color, being all black, but white ruffles splashed at his throat and down the front of his shirt. Though dark, she could see the blue of his eyes whenever the lightning would strike anew, and his face was long and angular. She was anxious to see the blond of his hair that her father had spoken about, but the top hat still sat undisturbed, glistening with wet droplets of rain.

Shivering, she hugged herself, relieved at least that the roof of the carriage kept the rain from drenching her anymore than she already was.

"You haven't told me what you were doing out alone and in such a storm," the man said, eyeing her quizzically as the horse continued to struggle, making a fraction of progress at a time toward the gate that was already swinging open, waiting.

"I was out exploring," she murmured, lowering her thick lashes. "That's all."

His eyes captured the bareness of her feet which she had forgotten to keep hidden beneath the seat. "And without shoes?" he said, lifting a heavy, pale eyebrow.

"I so often while in America ran through the rain barefoot," she lied demurely, envisioning just what it might be like to do so. Surely in America there would be no mud to fight. Surely in America the streets were crystal clean as well as everything else that existed there!

"Well, if you were my daughter, I would teach you the true way in which to behave," he snapped. He leaned a bit forward as he guided the horse and carriage through the opened gate. "And what might your name be?" he said, eyeing her once again.

"Glenda . . ." she said, tensing, hoping he wouldn't prompt her to speak her last name. She quickly added, "And what is yours?" Her eyes were wide and wondering as he pulled the horse to a halt in front of steps that led to a large expanse of a veranda that stretched out on all four sides of the house.

"Rayburn Turner," he said, then jumped from the carriage, cursing beneath his breath when he sank deeply into the mush of brown mud. He secured the horse's reins to a low limb of a dwarf palmetto tree, then hurried to the other side where Glenda sat staring at the mud at his ankles. Her nose screwed up, dreading having to also sink her feet into it anew.

"I'll carry you to the veranda," he said, reaching for her.

"Oh, *muchas gracias, señor,*" Glenda blurted, then covered her mouth with her free hand when she saw his mouth open in dismay and his hands drop to his side.

"I know that your parents probably made you take an extensive course in Spanish before traveling to El Progresso," Rayburn sighed heavily. "But you do not have to practice it on me. Do you hear?"

"Yes, sir," Glenda said obediently, relieved when he offered her his arms once again. She eased into them and clung loosely around his neck as he rushed up the steepness of the steps, onto the slickness of the rain drenched wooden veranda flooring.

"Though you are a bit disheveled, I'm sure Christina will welcome an American female guest," Rayburn said, sliding Glenda from his arms onto the veranda. He guided her by the elbow on toward the front door. "She seems a bit depressed. First the ship's journey . . . then seeing the isolation of this mosquito-infested land," Rayburn added sullenly.

"I'm anxious to meet this Christina," Glenda said in a near whisper. "She is your wife? *Si?*" Again she had let some Spanish slip. Oh, if only she could bite her tongue! She would be much better off if she did that instead of trying to pretend something she was not!

"Yes. My wife," he said, casting her a look of annoyance. "And, please? Try to speak in your normal English while around my Christina. She seems even more disenchanted with the natives of this land. She even is afraid to hire herself a personal maid. Too proud, that one."

A slow anger began to rise inside Glenda. So this Christina person thought herself too good for the Honduran people! Oh, how it caused Glenda's blood to begin a slow boil. But she had to push anger from her thoughts. She was just about to enter a house . . . of even . . . her own kind. While there, she could . . . she would . . . try to forget even herself that she had family of different skin coloring. She would relish the moments of being with people who had the same heritage as herself. Maybe these people could even guide her to her true father some day!

But, no. She just couldn't want to see him. He had been evil. She couldn't want to be a part of such a man. She wasn't even sure if she could be a part of this man and his prissy wife she was now becoming acquainted with if they continued to speak so lowly of the Hondurans. The Hondurans were a fine, proud people. All except for one. She would never forget what Ramón Martinez had tried to do to her. Never. She would pay him back for this. Some day . . . some way . . .

"Step on inside," Rayburn said, opening the door

39

widely for Glenda.

Glenda glanced down at her dress and the mud on her bare feet. "Shall I? Do you really think I should?" she said meekly. "I am so filthy. What will your wife think?"

Rayburn laughed hoarsely. "She will think I have rescued a small duckling from a muddy pond," he said, motioning her on with the flick of a wrist. "And if you will even notice," he further added, "I am not any better off than you are. I guess you and I will have to get used to such sudden outbursts of rain and the ensuing mud that may now linger for days upon days."

She giggled a bit. "Yes, I guess we shall," she said, remembering the wet season that had just begun. And what would this fine American gentleman think when a hurricane chose to move onto the island? He hadn't seen rain . . . until caught in the center of a hurricane.

She moved on into the house, stepping lightly, then in complete awe of all that she was seeing. The room she was now standing in was bathed by some strange bright lights. The glare even made her squint. She looked quickly toward the tables of the room. The lamps on these tables weren't being fed by candles or kerosene juices. The bulblike thing that sat glowing was of a funny egglike shape and looked so fragile that even a strong breath of air might explode it.

Then it suddenly came to her! She was experiencing one of the first of the electric inventions that had been whispered about on Bay Island. This globelike thing was an electric lightbulb! She continued to stare in amazement at the brightness. The lights were like magnets, compelling her to go to them. But would a touch from her finger bring harm to her, as it had just done to a poor moth that had fluttered against the bulb, then down to the table top, flapping its wings in desperation?

She forced her eyes to move on around her, making her insides quiver from excitement. The furniture was magnificent. It was made of mahogany, and the tables, doors, chairs, bowls, and even statues that sat boldly on the table tops were carved with different designs on each. Overhead, a strange thing was circling four blades around, whirring evenly, casting downward a faint spray of air, cooling the wetness of Glenda's skin.

"I shall tell Christina of our arrival," Rayburn said, then paused a bit, eyeing Glenda questioningly. "You look a bit dismayed by what you see. I know you said that you had longed to see my house, but it is truly not that much better than what you live in here on this plantation. And what you were used to in America was indeed a mansion compared to this relic of a house. Why would you stand with mouth so agape?"

Glenda's face turned a pale crimson, realizing just how much she was revealing to this man by staring so. She cleared her throat nervously. "I am admiring your tables," she said softly. "They have been carved much more beautifully than the ones my family has in its plantation house."

"We had these brought to us from Tegucigalpa," he said proudly. "It is the capital of Honduras. But I'm sure you were taught that before venturing by ship to this land."

Glenda's lashes fluttered nervously. "Yes. I am

41

aware of Honduras's capital," she said. "And I have heard that many beautiful things are carved and sold on the streets there. One day . . . I would . . . like to travel there and see it all." She had dreamed of such, but doubted that that dream would ever materialize. It was several days' trip by mule. Not too many ventured into the depths of the jungle unless one had to.

"I'd ask you to sit down while you wait, but I doubt if Christina would appreciate your mussing up her cushions that she has just recently embroidered for the sofa," he said, laughing a bit as he lifted his hat from his head. His fingers traveled through the thickness of his blond hair that was fringed with gray, making Glenda's heart race, remembering that her true father would have such hair . . . be nearly the same age. But he was surely still the owner of a great ship. He wouldn't be with a fruit company . . . handing out orders every day to hundreds of Honduran laborers. No. Her search for her true father would go much farther than this room.

"I'll be careful of the things in the room," she said, lifting her feet, checking to see if the mud had dried. And after Rayburn left, Glenda began to inch her way around the room, glad that the mud was now as cement, and wasn't leaving traces of her footprints behind her.

She moved to the large expanse of the sofa. It was made of wicker, with soft pillows thrown all across it. She touched one of these pillows, seeing the beautiful designs that had been sewn onto it. She had heard of such beautiful threads that could be used on materials, but she had yet to see any of this silk and satin that she was now touching. It was soft and cool. As soft as the velvet petal of a rose and as cool as a splash of rain. The designs were of assorted flowers, mainly that of varieties of roses, and there were butterflies in graceful poses. Suddenly she wanted to learn the art of embroidery. She knew that such an art had to be fulfilling to the soul.

She moved on around the room, seeing the many more designs that had been sewn onto other pieces in the room. A hassock sat at the foot of a wicker chair across from the sofa, and the designs of the hassock were of unfamiliar settings to Glenda, resembling golden blowing grasses at the foot of brown, treeless mountains. It was too beautiful a sight for which to place one's filthy feet! Then she moved to look at the wall hangings, these also of different beautiful designs sewn with these colorful threads. . . .

Light footsteps behind her drew Glenda around. Her fingers went to her throat when seeing the gracefulness with which this American lady moved toward her with an outstretched hand. As was her husband's, her hair was blond and also tinged with gray and was circled at the base of her head in a chignon. Her face was like a delicate porcelain figurine, with pink cheeks and anxiety showing in the depth of her blue eyes. Her narrow lips lifted in a soft smile as she moved on toward Glenda in her quite revealing lowcut silken dress, showing off the magnificence of her bosom, a true sign that she was aging quite gracefully.

"I'm so glad to make your acquaintance, Glenda, I believe Rayburn said your name was," Christina said in a silken purr. She secured Glenda's hand in hers and patted it with her other. "I have been so lonely

43

since having arrived. But tomorrow there has been a get-together planned to acquaint all of us American women. How nice that I am meeting the daughter of one of these women ahead of the others." The purr of her laughter matched that of her voice.

"I'm very glad to make your acquaintance, ma'am," Glenda said, curtsying a bit, having heard this was the proper thing to do when meeting such a genteel lady.

"My, oh, my, aren't you a sight though?" Christina laughed, clasping her hands together in front of her. "We must get you into something dry. I can't send you home in such a condition. What might your mother and father say to such inhospitality on my part?"

Glenda's heartbeats hastened. She was slowly getting deeper into her web of deception. What was she to do . . . ? "That isn't necessary, ma'am," she quickly blurted. "The rains have slackened a bit. I can just be on my way. Please don't bother about me."

Christina took Glenda's hand and began guiding her from the room, into a narrow hallway that led at the far end up a staircase to the second floor. "I shall not take no for an answer," Christina said flatly. "We shall get the mud washed from your feet and legs, then put on a clean dress before sending you out in this mess once again."

Glenda held back a bit, tensing even more. "But, don't you see, ma'am, once I get back outside on the road, all you will have done will be in vain. I shall get just as muddy. It is a waste of your time and your clothes."

"We shall see about that," Christina said stubbornly, tilting her chin. "We shall see if Rayburn has found help today while out before the storm. He was to go in search of a personal maid for myself, a cook and stable hand." She trembled a bit. "I hesitate to have such in my home, but if this is what is required to live decently in Honduras, I guess I can place my fears behind me."

Glenda set her jaws firmly, glancing sharply at Christina as she now moved beside her up the staircase. "And why would you fear the people of Honduras?" she said in a near whisper. "They are as you, only of a different skin coloring. These people are decent, lovable people."

Christina's face paled as she glanced quickly toward Glenda. "Why, Glenda. How would you even know? You have only recently arrived to El Progresso as I have also done and shouldn't be yet acquainted with the Honduran people. I can't believe a girl of your age would have such insight into the ways of the world," she gasped. "How is it that you do?"

"It is just feelings I have, ma'am," Glenda said. "You should never fear the Hondurans," she then added quickly. "They are fine. . . ."

"You speak as though you have been here for sometime," Christina said, interrupting Glenda. "I ask you again . . . how is it that you do have such insight into such matters?"

Glenda lowered her eyes. "I only guess, *señora,*" she whispered.

"*Señora?*" Christina gasped again, hesitating momentarily on the stairs to stare questioningly at Glenda. "Did your parents suggest you use the term '*señora*' when addressing another woman while on this plantation? It came so easily for you. . . ."

"Ma'am," Glenda stammered. "I really must be

going. Really I . . . must . . ." Backward, she began to inch her way down the staircase, watching Christina from the corner of her eyes.

"Who are you?" Christina said in a strained voice. "Whose daughter are you? Which house do you . . . ?"

Glenda was glad to place her feet on the lower floor landing. She turned to run away but found herself face to face with Rayburn and his change of clothes. He was comfortably puffing on a pipe, eyeing her with a tilted eyebrow. "What the hell's going on here?" he grumbled, then eyed Christina as she moved gracefully down the stairs.

"From what I can gather, we might have us an imposter here, Rayburn," Christina said, moving to his side, circling her arm through his. "Well? Glenda? Can you explain your strange behavior . . .?"

Fear was causing Glenda's heart to pound erratically. She felt cornered, as though captured now in a spider's web, unable to move. She glanced first at Rayburn . . . then Christina, swallowing hard. "My name is Glenda Galvez," she quickly blurted, curling and uncurling her toes on the cold floor beneath her feet.

"Galvez . . . ?" Christina barely whispered. "That isn't an . . . American . . . name. . . ."

"If you're not one of the Americans' daughters, then whose are you?" Rayburn asked, moving from Christina's side. He clasped his hands together tightly behind him, making a wide circle around Glenda. "You speak half English and half Spanish. I don't understand. You can't be Honduran. You are . . . white. . . ."

Christina stepped forward, chin tilted haughtily

upward. "Well? Are you going to tell us who your family truly is, young lady?" she said, trying to sound firm, but still having that purring depth to her words.

"My mother . . . and father . . . are Honduran," Glenda said, squaring her shoulders, displaying pride in 'family' as all Hondurans were known to do. 'Family' was foremost in their hearts. Though Glenda's true father was not Honduran, her Honduran father was true 'family.'

"So you're not of the American employees of the American Fruit Company," Rayburn grumbled hoarsely.

"No, *señor,* I am not. I am the daughter of José Galvez. One of your laborers," Glenda said quietly. "I didn't truly plan to trick you. I am sorry."

Christina lifted her skirt a bit as she moved even closer to Glenda. "But I don't understand something," she said. "If your mother and father are Honduran, how is it your skin and hair are so fair?"

"I am sorry," Glenda said, casting her gaze downward. "I wish not to say."

"Your father? Could he could not be Honduran, but American?" Rayburn said smoothly, drawing deeply from his pipe.

Glenda's eyes widened. She gasped, "How could . . . you know . . . ?"

"Your eyes . . . your hair . . . your skin," Rayburn said. "I choose to guess that somewhere along the line it would be more logical that an American male visited your mother's bed as to believe an American female could have found her way to your . . . or should I say . . . to a Honduran male's bed. You see, American men have been known to travel the high seas for many years, but not too many women have been known to do this, except in the company of their own men."

Glenda's temper flared. She stomped a foot angrily. "You have it all wrong," she stormed, clenching her fists at her side. "My mother is not guilty of any wrongdoings. It was an American like yourself. He . . . he . . . took advantage of my mother. He . . . raped . . . her. . . ."

Christina's hands went to her face. "Oh, my God," she murmured, paling even more. She reached for Glenda, then withdrew as Glenda took a wide step backward. "I'm sorry, Glenda," Christina murmured. "Truly I am. We . . . I never . . . meant to . . ."

"To what?" Glenda said, nearing tears. "To badger me? Make me feel as though below you, though our skin coloring is the same? I had looked forward to meeting you Americans. But now . . . now I . . . wish I had not. . . ."

She rushed from the house and down onto the muddy stretch of ground, stumbling, falling awkwardly into the mud. "Damn!" she exclaimed, then grew silent when Rayburn moved to her side and offered her a hand.

"Christina and I," he said. . . . "Well, we wish you to return to our house. We have an offer to make you. . . ."

Feeling the squishing of the mud between her fingers and toes and on her legs, Glenda cringed as she pushed her own self up from the ground, glad at least that the rains had traveled on toward the Caribbean. She straightened her back as she wiped her hands on her skirt. "I wish to never return to your house," she hissed, working her way through the mud away from him. She tensed when she heard him close behind her. He didn't give up so easily.

"Christina needs a personal maid," Rayburn persisted. "She encouraged me to ask if you would consider the position."

Glenda swung around, glaring. "Hah! Only because I am white-skinned," she argued. "How nice it would be for her to not have to worry about a dark skin touching her own delicate flesh when busy brushing madame's hair or helping her dress." She spat on the ground at his feet. "This Honduran will not dirty her fingers touching the American lady's flesh!"

"We both are sorry we offended you," Rayburn said softly, reaching for her. "We want to make it up to you. It has nothing to do with the color of your skin. It would please my wife to know that she was being forgiven for her careless words of a moment ago."

"I shall return to my mother, father and two brothers," Glenda said proudly, yanking away from him. "Though in one of your company's houses, it is the Galvez home because the Galvez love makes it so." She flipped her hair haughtily over her shoulders. "Good night, *señor,*" she snapped, then rushed on away from him.

When she had moved from the gate and was now a good distance away from the American house, she turned and stared in silence toward it. Her heart ached a bit, oh, so wanting to return and shout, "Yes!" over and over again, that "Yes!" she definitely wanted to be the beautiful, blue-eyed lady's personal maid. To live in such a house . . . be able to sit on such beautiful furnishings . . . and yes, to learn the

ways of the "beautiful threads" sewn onto the pillows
and pictures. . . .

Wouldn't it be too grand!

She lowered her eyes and moved on along through
the mud, wondering if she might be given a second
chance. . . . If so, could she even then say an eager
. . . "Yes" . . . ? Or was she discovering that all
Americans were alike . . . ?

Chapter Three

With the blink of an eye it seemed that the wet season had arrived in full force at the El Progresso banana plantation. Glenda stopped her floor scrubbing long enough to push herself up from the floor to go to the opened front door. She doubled a fist toward the sky and muttered soft obscenities at the low hanging gray clouds. The rain had stopped for the moment, but never long enough to enable the mud of the streets to dry . . . mud that always found its way to the floors of the Galvez house.

"This plantation is no better than Bay Island," she said aloud, then swung her skirt around and eyed this house that belonged to the American Fruit Company. It was cheerless. The walls were of unpainted boards, nothing to compare with the neatly painted white exteriors of the walls. It hadn't taken long for Glenda to realize that the paint applied to the outside of all the laborers' houses had only been done for show. Any visitor to El Progresso would think that the American Fruit Company had given their laborers the best. . . .

"Hah! The best," Glenda grumbled. "Floors that

have wide cracks from which to see the pools of mud on the ground beneath, between the stilted poles . . . cockroaches that fly and eat the food from our kitchen table . . . and mildew stench that continually curls my nose. . . ."

Rosa entered the room in her simple cotton frock with its neck swooping severely low and its sleeves rolled to above her elbow. She slumped to the floor and dipped a scrub brush into a bucket of sudsy water. "And what are you grumbling about, Glenda?" she grunted, moving both arms to push the brush back and forth. "This floor," she added. "It is dirty."

'Si, Mamma, it is dirty. This home. It is truly no better than what we left behind on Bay Island," Glenda complained, blowing down the front of her blouse. Her wardrobe didn't consist of much variety . . . three brightly printed skirts that were fully gathered at the waist, and three white blouses, two gathered elastic off the shoulder and one button-up the front. She had never owned any shoes and had urged her mother to not bother sewing her undergarments, that they were only a bother. This day she wore an off-the-shoulder blouse and a skirt of many colors of red.

"Please, Glenda. We have to make our best of the situation," Rosa grunted. She lifted her wet fingers to her hair to secure some loose locks back into the tight confines of a bun.

Glenda moved around the room, avoiding the soaped areas. "But look at the furniture," she said sullenly. "Only pieces of wood thrown carelessly together. Why, father doesn't even have a comfortable place to sit at night to smoke his pipe."

"Most other Hondurans approve of their American homes," Rosa said, splashing more water onto the floor, then moving the brush again. "They have larger rooms and . . . uh . . . privacy." She gazed upward at Glenda. "Your father and I. We have never known such privacy since before Marcos was born. We are like on a what would the Americans say . . . on . . . a honeymoon." She quickly lowered her eyes as a blush encompassed her face.

Glenda smiled warmly. She fell to her knees by her mother's side and circled her arms around Rosa's neck. "Ah, Mamma." She laughed silkily. "If you're happy then I am happy."

Rosa stopped her scrubbing long enough to give Glenda an affectionate kiss on the cheek. "Though with your father alone at night, I still have deep longings for my home on Bay Island through the day. Some days I feel such a strange, inner sadness. So, Glenda, I'm not all that happy as you suppose. But one thing I will say . . . I'm very proud of my one daughter," she murmured. Tears sparkled in her eyes. "I am glad for that reckless American," she whispered, patting Glenda on the cheek. "If not for that American those many years ago, I would not have my rare pearl to show off to everybody."

Glenda's eyes lowered. She always felt humble, to realize that her mother had never felt embarrassed to have such a contrasting daughter at her side, though many times eyes had turned and the look of knowing had been there.

"Let me have the scrub brush," she said quickly, taking it from her mother. "It is my chore for this morning. My sweet mother should not be on her knees

53

slaving so." She spied the beads of perspiration on her mother's brow and the fast way in which her pulsebeat was moving at the hollow of her throat. It frightened Glenda. Her mother hadn't appeared all that well as of late. But the humidity during the wet season could do this to a person. Glenda silently hoped that was the only reason.

Rosa moaned a bit more as she rose from the floor. "Thank you, Glenda. I guess I could go and grind some maize," she said. "We can have tortillas with sausages for supper. It seems our men are always so hungry after a day with the bananas."

"They do work hard, Mamma," Glenda murmured. "As you also do." She let her thoughts drift slowly to the American's house on the hill and the beautiful lady who appeared to have never done a day's labor in her life. The *señora's* back was straight, her fingers clean and uncallused, and her thin waist and lifted breasts were like those of a younger person, not those of a woman whose hair was fringed with gray.

Then Glenda's heart ached a bit, remembering having been asked to be a part of the beautiful *señora's* way of life. Oh! If she had only said "Yes."

Glenda's mother's shuffling bare feet moving from the room drew Glenda back to the present. She felt guilt splash through her. If she left the Galvez house to be a part of the American's way of life, what would Rosa Galvez do? Work all day alone with scrubbing and cooking? No. It wouldn't be fair.

With a quiet anger in each stroke, Glenda moved the scrub brush in wild circles, blowing air from the corner of her mouth as wisps of hair kept falling across her lips. The strong aroma of hogs blew through the opened door and up inside Glenda's nostrils, making her cringe. The American Fruit Company hadn't only offered a communal garden to all its laborers, but also the sharing of many hogs and chickens that had been brought from America as gifts, to entice their laborers to work even harder, with expectations of even more compensations.

In a pen not far from the Galvez house, the hogs rooted and wallowed in the mud. Their constant grunts could be heard all hours of the day. But they weren't only used for food, the only meat Hondurans would allow in their diets, but also the fat, skin, hair and other parts of the hogs were used to make lard, leather, brushes and soap.

When the mud wasn't the annoyance it became during the wet season, the chickens became the next hated annoyance. As it was on Bay Island, it would probably be at El Progresso. Glenda knew to expect the chickens to peck at the dusty ground around the house, leaving their ugly white droppings everywhere for everyone to step their bare feet into. But now, during the wet season, they were being kept in an out-building where they were being fattened by a steady diet of maize.

"Finally. It's done," Glenda sighed, dropping the scrub brush into the water. She rose and lifted the heavy bucket and moved into the kitchen. Though quite ugly, the kitchen did have the convenience of a wood-burning stove that burned both day and night, no matter the humidity that hung like a damp shroud in each of the rooms of the house.

A wash basin stood on a stand with fresh water from buckets on the floor next to it. An unpainted table sat in the middle of the room, where all meals were prepared and served. A narrow row of shelves had been nailed to the wall, where upon these sat the bare necessities of dishes, cups and glasses. The crude pots and pans that had been placed in this kitchen by the American Fruit Company hung from nails next to the black, soot-covered stove.

Glenda moved to the opened back door and slung the water from the bucket to land in large splashes next to the steps. She took the time to look toward the thousands upon thousands of banana plants. Some had grown to be twenty-five feet tall and looked much like trees. The long leafstalks of the plants were unrolled and reminded her of great drooping feathers.

Throngs of workers were chopping away at the banana plants with machetes. This huge, sharp, heavy knife was the Honduran's most used tool, be it for cutting the brush while traveling through the jungle, or for using while laboring. Glenda shivered a bit, knowing that in large towns, many, many miles away, the machetes had been used for even more than this. These knives were used as . . . weapons. . . .

"Glenda, it is so hot. Why don't you take a few minutes for rest?" Rosa said, scooping mashed maize into a wooden bowl. "Since getting caught in that downpour last night, you have looked a bit paler than usual."

Glenda sank a tin cup into a bucket of water and lifted the fresh drink to her lips, averting her gaze from that of her mother's. Glenda hadn't confided in anyone of her horrible experience with Ramón Martinez. Only Carlos knew, and he had promised to not tell. Wouldn't everyone believe that she had even

56

encouraged such from this Ramón whom she had been known to be around while on Bay Island, though not of her own choosing?

No. Her terrible ordeal of almost having been raped would be kept a secret. And she knew that from now on, she would be aware of all movements around her while in the midst of the long rows of maize. Ramón would never have the opportunity of attacking her again.

"I shall rest later, Madre," she finally answered. "And please don't worry about me. I am all right. Truly I am."

"But, Glenda, you do not look all right," her mother replied, furrowing her brow.

"I guess it was the lightning that frightened me the most last evening, to make me become so pale looking," Glenda murmured. "And I did get chilled to the bone." She hadn't told of being inside the American's house either. She didn't want to have to tell her mother of the comforts she had found . . . knowing that her mother would never have the same.

"You've seen lightning before," Rosa said. She began stirring crumbled pork into a cast-iron skillet over the stove, filling the air with a rich enticing aroma.

Glenda reached a hand into the bucket of water and got her fingers wet and splashed some on her brow, then down between her breasts, sighing heavily. "But the storm was much more frightening," she said in a near whisper. "I guess . . . it . . . is because this place is still strange to me."

Rosa dropped sliced tomatoes into the splattering pork. "I've told you, Glenda," she said with a furrowed brow. "You should not tarry in the maize field after dark. Only bad can come from it. If anyone knows, I should. You must remember . . ."

"Remember what, Mamma?"

"A man. He doesn't care where a beautiful woman is if he decides he wants to make her his," Rosa said sullenly. "I also was in such a place. I was tilling the soil the night the American decided I shouldn't be alone . . ."

"You never told me about where you . . . were . . . uh . . . assaulted," Glenda said, blushing a bit.

"Well, I now have told you, little one," Rosa said more firmly. "And you pay attention. When José, Carlos and Marcos come home from the fields, so must you. I don't want to have to pace the floors like I had to do last night."

Glenda placed the tin cup on a nail above where the water sparkled. "I didn't know," she said, moving to Rosa, placing her arms around her waist. "I'm sorry Mamma. I'm so very sorry . . ."

"You were such a sight," Rosa exclaimed Like a drowned puppy. Why wouldn't a mother worry?"

"I'm sorry. It won't happen again. I promise. . . ."

A light tapping on the front door facing drew Glenda from her Mamma. "Who . . . ?" she said, then went in an almost skipping fashion to the door. Hardly ever did they get a surprise visitor, and when they did, it was a most welcome one.

Glenda's voice caught in her throat when she found who the caller was. Then she managed to speak in a slow strain. "Mrs. Turner? It is you," she mumbled. Her eyes moved quickly over the American woman.

She wore a cotton frock trimmed with lovely white lace and her hair was hidden beneath the protective covering of a straw bonnet. Glenda looked on past her and saw the magnificence of the carriage that had carried Glenda to the American's house only the night before. Its wheels had once again this day sunk deeply into the mud and the sleek black horse's hooves could hardly be seen. A tiny-boned Honduran boy had lain planks of wood from the carriage to the Galvezes' front steps and was now waiting for the American woman's return, to then pick the boards back up and follow along after her.

"Glenda?" Christina said in her usual purr. "I was hoping the right house had been pointed out to me."

Rosa moved into the room, wiping her hands on the skirt of her dress. She inched her way to the door, eyes wide. She stood a bit behind Glenda, staring openly. "Glenda, who is this American woman?" she whispered shyly. "Why is she here?"

The truth was soon to be known that Glenda had done more than run in the rain the previous evening. She swallowed hard and stepped aside so that her mother was fully revealed to Christina. "Mother, this is Mrs. Turner," she said quietly. "She is the American lady who lives in that large house on the hill. She is the division manager's wife. And Mrs. Turner, this is my mother." She watched as Christina swung her hand before her, offering it in friendship to Rosa.

"Pleased to meet you," Rosa said quietly, lowering her eyes humbly.

Christina forced a smile. "I am so glad to get to meet Glenda's mother," she said. She shook hands abruptly, then let her hand drop back to her side, glancing quickly back at Glenda. "Glenda, I've come to talk with you. May I come in?" she speedily added.

Glenda flipped her hair out of her face, feeling almost a pressure around her heart when she had seen the look of distaste in the American woman's eyes when she had shaken hands with Glenda's mother. Oh, she only hoped she was wrong. Maybe she had only imagined such a look. But just in case she hadn't, she lifted her chin haughtily. "What would you have to say to me?" she snapped. She eyed her mother cautiously, not having yet explained the whys of this *señora's* presence at her house. Would her mother even understand that she had not been told all the truths? Oh, surely she would!

"I know that Rayburn tried to apologize to you last night," Christina said, clasping her hands together in front of her. "But I know that you didn't accept. So I am here to apologize also to you. I feel that I treated you very poorly while you were in my house."

Rosa grabbed Glenda's hand. "What? You were . . . ?" she gasped. "You didn't tell me. . . ."

Glenda turned and framed her mother's face between her hands, momentarily having forgotten her mother's own skills of translating the American. language. Her mother had said that she had picked it up, little by little, through the years. But she never spoke it . . . only knew how to, if ever the need would arise. "Mamma, I didn't tell you . . . because . . ." she stammered. She swallowed hard, then added. "I will later. Please understand. I will. . . ."

"That's good. I will go back to my kitchen," Rosa said sullenly, pulling away from Glenda. "You visit with the American lady. I do not wish to be a part of

60

such a visit." She moved jerkily across the floor and disappeared into the kitchen.

Glenda turned abruptly to face Christina. "Really," she snapped. "You come to my house and cause trouble? I do not understand."

"What trouble? I do not understand."

Glenda sighed resolutely, not understanding why the American woman couldn't have seen or heard the hurt in her mother's face or voice. Didn't she understand Spanish? Was that the reason . . . ? "My mother. I did not tell her about being in your house," she said stiffly.

"I didn't know that your mother would be unaware of your visit to my house," Christina said, paling. "I am sorry, Glenda. I guess I now have apologies for two things."

"No. Three," Glenda snapped back, placing her hands on her hips.

"Three? I do not understand," Christina said softly. "What third apology do you speak of?"

"It is my mother," Glenda said firmly. "You looked down your nose at my mother. When you shook her hand in friendship, it was not in sincerity. I feel you owe me, as well as her, an apology. This house may be owned by the American Fruit Company of America, but it is ours while we live in it, and it is respect that we demand. Even from you."

Christina placed a hand to her brow, panting a bit. "I didn't know . . ." she said in a near whisper. "Yes, Glenda, I do apologize. And please convey my apologies to your mother. But you must understand something. I have been in America all my life. I have never lived away from my own people. I feel a bit isolated. Already. Even though I have been here such a short time. I guess I have much to learn about you and your people."

"I can tell you in one word about we Hondurans," Glenda said, straightening her shoulders. "Pride. That is the one thing you must remember. We are all very proud people. We are from a special heritage. And even though I am white, I am also of that heritage."

"May I come in, Glenda? Have a further talk?" Christina said wiping her brow with a handkerchief she had pulled from inside her dress sleeve.

"You will find it nothing like your house," Glenda said, softening a bit inside. "But I will never turn anyone aside. You see, I am even proud of my mother and father's house, though it isn't in truth theirs." She stepped aside and gestured with an outstretched hand. "Enter. Please make yourself at home in the Galvez house." She would never, no never, admit to this American woman her hatred for the house. She was not one to grovel in pity. Especially her own.

Glenda sniffed wildly, so aware of the strong aroma of expensive perfume as Christina moved past her. Her senses reeled a bit from the sweetness of it. It seemed to be the smells of many different flowers blended into one. She then followed along behind Christina and offered a chair. She watched as Christina's gaze traveled around her as she pulled the fullness of her dress and the many petticoats up to expose tiny ankles and beautiful two-inch-heeled slippers. Suddenly Glenda wanted much more out of life than she had dreamed of before. She wanted to one day be able to dress in such a way as this

American woman . . . and smell as good. She curled her nose up, now smelling the filth of her own flesh. Bath time was after the evening meal. Oh, could she even wait that long now? What if the American woman was even smelling her unpleasantness . . . ?

She settled onto the hardness of a chair, trying to look the lady she knew that she did not represent. "And what might you want to say further to me?" she said, reaching to pull her blouse up closer to her neckline, aware that too much of her breasts was showing.

"I have come to make an offer for employment to you," Christina said, smiling warmly. "I know that Rayburn mentioned that also to you. But he said that you hurriedly declined." She paused a bit, then added, "But I believe that you did so in haste because of what had happened earlier in my house."

Glenda's heart was thumping wildly. She couldn't believe that she was actually being given a second chance. She glanced toward the kitchen, hearing her mother puttering around, and smelling the tantalizing aromas rising from the pots and pans on the stove. Doubts of ever truly leaving this way of life assailed her. Would it even be fair . . . ? It was as she had been thinking earlier. She had her mother to consider. She lowered her eyes, curving her shoulders a bit. "I don't think it is possible," she said in a near whisper.

Christina leaned forward, blinking her blue eyes unbelievingly. "And why not . . . ?" she murmured. "I don't understand. . . ."

Glenda wiped building perspiration from her brow with the back of a hand. "I have commitments," she said softly. "I just can't . . ."

"These commitments you speak of? They are to

your mother . . . ?"

Glenda's eyes widened in bright greens. "How did you know . . . ?" she gasped.

"I saw the relationship between mother and daughter," Christina said, laughing softly. "I do understand. I love my mother also as much. In fact, I now miss her so much, my heart aches at times."

"Truly?" Glenda said, straightening her shoulders once again.

"Yes. Truly," Christina said. "But you see, oh, so many years ago, I also had a commitment to myself. I had a life to lead. My own life. Don't you see? You can't live the rest of your life for family. If you have an opportunity to better yourself . . . you should do it. Your parents will understand. If they truly love you, they will understand."

"By bettering myself, do you mean by living with you and having things as you do?" Glenda snapped, anger flaring her nostrils. "You, Mrs. Turner, are looking your nose down at my family once again."

Christina paled even more. She sighed heavily. "I seem to be saying and doing everything wrong this day, Glenda," she murmured. "I am sorry. Again I am sorry. But please, realize that I am very sincere in my offer for employment to you. I will pay good wages. And if you would feel so inclined, you could even share these earnings with your family. Then I am sure they would agree to you working as my personal maid."

"Personal maid?" Glenda whispered, testing the words. Then she frowned. "And why is it that you single me out from all those others willing to take such a position on this plantation? Is it because of my

64

. . . color?"

"Not your color. It is your language. You can speak English so clearly. I believe we could have quite a time together, you and I, chatting the day away. I don't think I could bear to have a Spanish-speaking maid around me day in and out. What on earth could we even speak about? How could I tell her to even brush my hair?"

"You can't . . . speak . . . any Spanish . . . ?" Glenda said in a near whisper. "You have come to Honduras and not prepared to speak any Spanish?"

Christina lowered her eyes, blushing a bit. "Rayburn warned me. But you see, I didn't know the extent of foreigners on the plantation. I had thought maybe there would be somebody who would speak as I besides the other American women who also came on the ship." Her head moved swiftly upward, her blue eyes dancing. "And I was partly right," she quickly added. "I found you. you can speak English. Oh, Glenda, say that you will be my personal maid. Please say that you will. I will even share some of my dresses with you. We could . . . what we could say . . . play house." She laughed softly, watching Glenda's eyes sparkle in many different shades of green.

Glenda's wildest dreams were coming true! Or was this another dream? Might she awaken at any moment and find herself sweating on the hard thing that had been called a "mattress"? Her insides were a-quiver, just thinking about living in such a grand way. But then her thoughts went back to her family. She did have to win their approval. It was the Honduran way. The family had to speak as one in such decisions of the heart. "I must tell you later," she finally answered.

"And when will that be?"

"Tonight? As soon as our evening meal is shared and our family has a chance to talk? I could send my youngest brother Carlos with the message. Is that all right with you, Mrs. Turner?"

Christina reached a hand toward Glenda. "It's Christina," she purred. "My name is Christina. Please don't call me Mrs. Turner." She laughed softly. "You see, that makes me feel much older than I want to remember I am."

Glenda's gaze lowered as she felt a blush rising. She took Christina's hand and let her lashes flutter nervously. Then her gaze met and held Christina's. "Yes. Christina. I will call you Christina," she murmured.

"And I will await your response. Tonight," Christina said, squeezing Glenda's hand. She then withdrew her hand and rose. "But for now, I must return home. I hear rumblings in the sky. Heaven forbid we get more rain. I feel as though I am a sponge already, soaking it all up into my pores."

"It was so nice of you to come, Christina," Glenda said, following Christina to the door.

"I'm glad I did come," Christina said, turning to gaze toward the kitchen. "And will you give your mother my best regards? I did enjoy meeting her."

"Yes. I shall," Glenda said, moving out onto the veranda with Christina.

"And maybe you can also become my Spanish teacher?" Christina said, turning, smiling toward Glenda. "Maybe you can teach me the most necessary words to speak so that I can confer a bit with my cook that I am also planning to hire soon. The stable hand

66

has already been taken care of by Rayburn."

"I'd love to do what I can," Glenda said. "I think it could be fun. It all sounds like fun. In fact, so much so, I'm not sure it would be fair to get paid."

The small Honduran boy who had been waiting on Christina's return to the carriage lifted a hand and aided her down the stairs, onto the boards. "You will be paid. And quite well," Christina said.

"I will send Carlos. Tonight," Glenda said anxiously.

"I will be waiting. Bye, Glenda. It's been nice," Christina said and moved on into the carriage. She settled onto the seat, then flicked her wrist in a small wave as the horse began making its way through the thick, muddy paste of the street.

Glenda's heartbeat was erratic, so anxious to get the okay from family to move into the house on the hill. She turned quickly when she heard her mother move to her side. She now wondered how she would even approach telling her mother the exciting news. Would her mother even understand? Would it be as exciting to her . . . ? Would she even approve . . . ?

Chapter Four

Glenda stuffed the last of her few clothes inside a travel bag, tensing a bit when her mother moved into the room. She tied the bag's strings into a knot then swung around, holding the bag in the crook of her left arm. "Mamma, please don't look so sad," she murmured, tears burning at the corners of own eyes. "I thought we all decided that this was best for me as well as for the family. I have been promised to be paid quite well for what I will be doing."

Rosa twisted a handkerchief around her forefinger. "I do not trust Americans, Glenda," she said sullenly. "I do not have to tell you why."

Glenda placed her free arm around her mother's neck. "Mamma, these Americans are different," she sighed. "These Americans, well, they are respectable. I told you the way in which they live. And the man? You have no reason to fear him. He is happy with his wife. You have no reasons to suspect that he might try to . . . seduce . . . me. Please don't worry. And I will come home. Often. If you have trouble with keeping the laundry done, I will come home and help you. I am sure Christina will understand." She wanted to tell

her mother that not only did Americans seduce . . .
rape . . . Honduran women . . . but also did the
mestizos! But she still chose not to. She had to believe
she no longer had anything to fear from Ramón
Martinez!

Rosa moved away from Glenda in a huff, her dark
eyes flashing. "Hah! So it is now Christina instead of
Mrs. Turner, is it?" she exclaimed harshly. "You are
already on the first name basis with this foreign
woman? The next thing I will know is that you will
forget you even have a mother. This American woman
will be called mother by you."

Glenda smiled softly. She now understood. Her
mother was jealous more than anything. Her mother
never shared Glenda with anyone except the Galvez
family. And now that she was going to have to, it was
causing her to worry about losing her completely.
"Mamma, you are jealous of this woman? Huh?" she
said, once again approaching her mother with a warm
embrace around the neck. Her mother didn't smell
like the American woman, all perfumey and sweet.
Her mother smelled of harsh soap and cooking spices.
But it was a smell that Glenda would remember when
missing her mother at night.

Rosa slung a hand in the air. "Jealous? Your mother
jealous? No. Never. Don't be stupid," she shouted.
Then she clasped her arms around Glenda and
hugged her tightly to her. "But your mother is going
to miss her rare pearl. What am I going to do? I will
worry too much."

Her mother's ensuing sobs began to tear a corner of
Glenda's heart into tiny shreds. "I'm sorry, Mamma,"
she whispered, clinging. "But I must go. One day you

will understand. I am sure of it. You see, I need the experience. I do not want only to know how to scrub floors and grind maize. I believe with this American woman, I will be taught many things about America and their ways. Maybe one day I will even be able to go to America." She pushed her mother gently away from her and gazed with longing into her eyes. "Just think of it, Mamma," she sighed. "America? Would you even deny me this opportunity? Huh? Mamma, would you?"

"America? So now it is America?" Rosa shouted. Then she saw the pain in Glenda's eyes and softened a bit. She lifted a hand to Glenda's cheek and stroked it gently. "I have acted selfishly, my little one," she said quietly. "Go. Do what you must. I will say no more."

Glenda's heart began to pound in anxious anticipation. "You really do give me your blessing, Mamma?"

Her mother's eyes lowered. "Yes. I do," she whispered. Then her head swung upward. "And if you must go, please go now. I'm afraid I'm going to be a bit weepy. I don't wish to make you become red faced also by crying. Go, Glenda, go." She motioned with her hands, then rushed from the room.

Glenda swallowed back a lump in her throat, so wanting to go after her mother, but knew that privacy was what her mother needed now, to wash her grief from inside her by letting her tears fall. Instead, Glenda focused her thoughts on her own self. She reached upward with her free hand to touch her hair, hoping that it was shining and clean enough and lay in perfect enough waves around her face and onto her shoulders.

Then she glanced downward at her flimsy attire of

skirt and blouse. She could see the outline of her breasts beneath the tight confines of the blouse and the sway of her hips beneath her skirt as she moved on toward the door. Was she truly presentable enough? Would Christina truly approve?

Stopping to take one fast glance toward the bedroom where harsh sobs were surfacing, Glenda then rushed from the house, glad to be welcomed and caressed this day by the sun's rays instead of drenched to the bone by the cold of the rain. She stepped into the ooze of the mud, feeling it work between her toes and began to make her way down the road, holding her head high and her shoulders back. She was beginning a new way of life this day. Now if only it could be as she had dreamed.

A mule-drawn cart turned onto the road from the banana field, filled with large clusters of green bananas. As it moved on past Glenda, she waved to the young Honduran guiding the mule along, then sniffed eagerly. She loved the aroma of freshly picked bananas. Though pungent, it was pleasant to her. She then gazed hopefully toward the swarms of workers in the fields, hoping to get a fast glimpse of her father or one or both of her brothers. But it was too hard to distinguish one laborer from the other with their straw hats pulled low over their faces and with the machetes moving at such quick speed around them.

"But I shall see them. Often," she said in a low whisper, stepping high, lifting the tail of her skirt from the muddy grime that lay all around her. "Whenever I have the need to see family, Christina will give me her blessing and let me return home. Oh, this is a dream coming true. Can I truly have everything? All at once . . . ?"

With a determined step, she moved toward the high fence, and on through the gate, feeling the thundering of her heart against her chest. Her gaze traveled over the grounds around her. Flowers were in abundance in pots lifted away from the mud of the ground in swaying baskets hanging from trees.

Glenda went to the flowers and touched the petal of one that was orchid in color. She knew this to be a petunia, one of an herblike plant native to Honduras. This beautiful funnel-shaped flower . . . ah . . . it was so velvety. Then she touched and sniffed the other flowers that were intermingled in the hanging baskets. They were French marigolds with flower heads in colors of yellow and oranges. When she sniffed them, her nose curled. They were most unpleasant. But very charming. Glenda was reminded of her schooling on Bay Island and her studies of Shakespeare. In *A Winter's Tale*, Shakespeare had written of the marigold . . . "that goes to bed wi' the sun, and with him rises weeping."

José Galvez had made it a point to see that his three children received a certain degree of education. But Glenda had been the only one to see his plans through to the end. Carlos and Marcos? They had found that it was more rewarding to help their father than to sit behind a desk and stare blankly at books.

English and English Literature had fascinated Glenda the most. Shakespeare had been her favorite. But Glenda had always known why she had held such a devoted interest in the English language. Because she had dreamed that one day . . . she would . . . go . . . to America!

Hearing light footsteps behind her on the wide expanse of veranda surrounding the American's house, Glenda turned and smiled shyly toward Christina as Christina extended a hand toward her.

"I'm glad you've come," Christina purred. "Come in out of the heat. We can get you cooled beneath the ceiling fan."

Glenda moved up the stairs, accepting Christina's hand in hers. "Fan? What is . . . a . . . ceiling fan . . . ?" she said in a near whisper.

Christina's head tilted in a purring laugh. "My dear, you don't know what a fan is?" she said.

"I have made many fans with palm leaves," Glenda said. "But the fan you speak of . . . a ceiling fan . . . I am not familiar with."

Glenda's eyes traveled over Christina's attire. It was of a lightweight silk, cut low, but yet not too revealing at the neck, with its bodice trimmed with the familiar open work of embroidery that Glenda remembered seeing on the many cushions and pictures in Christina's house. The silken folds of the dress rustled about Christina as she guided Glenda on into the shaded room, where she pointed toward the slow-moving, four-bladed fan hanging from the ceiling in the center of the sitting room.

"There is your fan," Christina said, marveling at what little knowledge this young woman had.

Glenda stepped beneath it and felt the cool breeze moving over her. She reached a hand upward. She now remembered the fan from her one other brief visit. "Why, it sends forth artificial wind," she sighed. "It is much like the breeze from the sea. So fresh and delicious." She tilted her face to it and closed her eyes.

"I love the way it lifts my hair," she added softly.

"So you do feel a bit refreshed already, do you?" Christina murmured, clasping her hands together in front of her. Her gaze traveled over Glenda, seeing her statuesque height. She suddenly realized it matched her own, as well as the high firm breasts, and the smallness of their waists. Yes, it would be simple to clad Glenda in something more respectable than she was at this moment. Why, it even embarrassed Christina a bit, seeing the sharp point of Glenda's nipples so vividly through the thinness of her blouse. It was quite evident that she wore nothing beneath it.

"Yes. I love it," Glenda said. "It's a marvel to be able to own a fan that you don't have to place in your hands to move back and forth until your wrists ache so."

"It is from the power-driven generator in our outbuilding out back," Christina said, smoothing some hair back from her eyes, repositioning combs at each side of her head.

Glenda began to move around the room, suddenly shy of her bare feet and the dried mud caked to them. "It is the electricity?" she said, trying to keep attention drawn from her own self. She was once again in awe of everything she was seeing. The beauty of the carved mahogany furnishings . . . the embroidered cushions . . . the vases after vases of flowers arranged on tables all around the room. It was all too magnificent. And she was now a part of it all.

"Yes. It is the electricity," Christina laughed softly. "And now may I get you something to drink so we can relax and chat a bit before I show you to your room?"

Glenda flashed Christina a pleasant smile. "Yes.

That would be fine," she murmured.

"Then you make yourself at home. Please choose any chair that you feel looks comfortable to you. I will be back shortly."

"Yes, ma'am," Glenda said, moving toward a chair, making sure her feet didn't touch it when she settled down onto the soft cushions.

Her fingers trembled and her eyes glistened, so excited by all the newness, and the kindness of Christina. When other footsteps entered the room, she was unaware. She moved her fingers to her throat when Ramón Martinez moved to stand before her. "Ramón, what are you doing here?" she said, paling. "Why . . . would you be in . . . Christina's house?" She moved her back against the chair, now a bit frightened. She would never forget his hands on her and his forcefulness. She would never even forget the way in which his caresses had caused her body to begin to respond in crazy ways to his. But she had been saved in the knick of time by her brother. Oh, how she now hated Ramón!

"I am the new stable hand for this estate," Ramón said, snickering as his dark eyes narrowed into two coals. "Strange that you are here also. Why are you?"

"I am to also work here. And you? A stable hand? You know nothing of horses. All you know about are asses!" Glenda said, breathing hard now, thinking she would be better off if she would just turn and flee back to the safety of the Galvez house. She then quickly added, "How is it that you have chosen to work here, Ramón?"

"I spoke with Rayburn Turner when I heard word that he was looking for a stable hand. The first boy he tried wasn't macho enough," he said, flexing his muscles as he doubled his fists at his side. "I had no idea I would come in contact with you so soon . . . after . . . well . . . you know . . ."

"I thought Carlos directed you to the sea and ordered you from El Progresso," Glenda hissed. "When he hears you are still here, he will kill you. I know he will."

"He and who else?" Ramón laughed harshly. "He just had me at a disadvantage the other night. But next time? I will be the one to show who is the macho of the two. Your brother is too little for the likes of me. You will see."

"Ramón, you cannot work here. If you do, I can't," Glenda said, her eyes wavering. "And I must. I must."

He sauntered closer to her and bent his back to thrust his face into hers, revealing the smooth, clean line of his white teeth. "And why should you be privileged more than me?" he growled. "Is it because of the color of your skin? Because your skin is white and mine is brown? Well, paleface, I will not budge. If you can't stand to be near where I am to be, then it must be you who leaves."

Christina entered the room, carrying a tray. She gasped noisily. "And what are you doing in this house?" she directed at Ramón.

A smile tilted his wide lips upward. He straightened his back and lifted his shoulders in a shrug. *"No comprendo,"* he said smoothly. *"No comprendo."*

Christina flashed an irritated glance toward Glenda. "Doesn't he understand English, Glenda?" she asked, exasperated.

"No. Only Spanish," Glenda said from between

clenched teeth, shooting arrows toward him with the flashing of her green eyes.

Christina placed the tray on a table and crossed her arms angrily. "Will you then tell this young man to leave my house?" she snapped. "He is not supposed to be here. If Rayburn was here, he would pitch him out quite fast."

Glenda rose and moved toward Ramón. She tossed her travel bag onto a chair and gestured with her hands. "You are not welcome here," she said in thick Spanish. "The beautiful American lady wishes you to leave. Do you now understand, Ramón, stable boy? Huh?" She flipped her long blond hair across her shoulders haughtily.

"The beautiful *señora* had better get used to seeing me around," Ramón grumbled. "It is I who will be taking her by carriage wherever she needs to go. I could make it very uncomfortable for her if she treats me as lower than her."

"I will tell her that you said that, Ramón," Glenda hissed. "But for now, leave. It is I who gets to remain in this beautiful house."

Ramón took a step forward, glaring. "If you breathe one word to this American family about your dislike for me, I swear I will take a machete to both your brothers at once. Do you understand?"

Glenda's knees grew rubbery. She swallowed back a fast growing fear. "You wouldn't . . ." she said in a low whisper.

"Wouldn't I?" he laughed hoarsely. "You do one thing to cause me to have to leave this job as stable hand and I will do as I said. It is myself I am looking out for. Only myself. Only in this way can I go back to

Bay Island and flaunt my riches and also you at my side. . . ."

Glenda's insides twisted. "What did you say, Ramón? What did you say about . . . me . . . ?"

"I won't leave this plantation until I have seduced you and made you with child. Then you will have to return for all my followers to see. Only in this way can I hold my head up and be the *caudillo* that they all once claimed me to be."

"Make me with child?" she gasped. "You are sick," she then hissed. "Nauseating, you *ass*. If you so much as ever try to come near me again, I will thrust a knife into your stomach. Mark my words. I will . . ."

Christina moved to Glenda's side. "Glenda, is there some problem here?" she asked softly, eyeing Ramón out of the corner of the eye. She immediately hadn't liked this young man. There was much to distrust about him. She could tell by the shiftiness in which he looked at a person. And she could feel his eyes undressing her.

"No. He's leaving," Glenda said, stiffening as Ramón turned on a heel and moved from the room, but stopping to stare wickedly from one to the other before moving on away from them.

When he was finally gone, Glenda's shoulders slumped heavily. She did know to expect much from Ramón in the future. Oh! He would have to throw hazard into the wind at the time she was having so much good happen to her. She went and slouched down onto the chair, forgetting the mud on her feet as she tucked them beneath her.

"He is a most unpleasant young man," Christina said, sitting, pouring drinks for each of them. "Did he even say why he was in my house?"

"You don't know . . . ?"

"No. I've never seen the young man before."

"He is your new stable hand," Glenda said, watching Christina's eyes widen in shallow blues.

"God. No," Christina gasped.

"He said that Rayburn hired him. I guess it is true."

"Rayburn is usually so very careful with the young men he has around him," Christina sighed heavily. "So this young man must be all right. I guess he just didn't know that the house was not part of his domain."

Glenda smiled awkwardly. "Yes. I guess that is the reason." She wanted so to lash out at Ramón . . . reveal his true self to this gentle woman. What if he would even rape Christina? Or was his heart set on only raping . . . the white-skinned woman born to the Galvez family . . . ? Either way, it made her have a most tumultuous, uneasy feeling inside.

She eyed the glass being handed her. She took it, once again in awe at what she was seeing. It was a drink of a brown coloring and in it were floating squares of . . . what was it . . . crystal . . . ? And the glass was so cold to the touch! Her fingers even felt as though growing numb at the continuing touch of the glass. "What is this? What are those squares inside the drink?" she said in a silken whisper.

"The small squares that are colorless?" Christina said. "It is called ice. From a cold air machine we are experimenting with here in our house in Honduras. We know of a man who owns a shipping company who is needing refrigeration compartments on his ships for which to transport our bananas back to America. So

79

we are using the same principle here in our house only on a much smaller scale, to see if it can work for such a small area. If it does, then this man will be ready to convert it to a larger area. Then this man, this Peter Grayson, the owner of the *Sea Wolf*, will be quite pleased as even I am in trying this new invention since it is so hot here on this plantation."

"This is all amazing," Glenda sighed, sipping the brown liquid. "And what is this I am drinking? It has a bit of tang to it."

"I call it iced tea," Christina laughed softly. "I've so often drunk hot tea in America on a cold, blustery night, and enjoyed it, so I had to think that ice in such a drink would be even more delicious."

Glenda felt the coldness seep down her throat and into her stomach. She had never tasted anything so refreshing. "I have already learned so much from you and I haven't even been with you for one full day," she said. "It is an honor being a part of your house. Yes. Such an honor."

"I will teach you and you will teach me," Christina laughed, tipping her own glass to her lips. "I am just glad that we have the generator for which to give me the luxury of electricity while living here. You see, not even too many Americans have such a luxury. Peter Grayson, the owner of the *Sea Wolf*, is responsible for most of these luxuries afforded me. He knows me quite well and knows that I am a delicate person and would have a hard time surviving in this damp, humid climate I have found here."

Glenda emptied her glass, toying with the ice with her fingers, watching it scoot lazily from one side of the glass to the other. "This *Sea Wolf*. It is a fine ship?" she said cautiously. She was remembering her true father, wondering what the name of his ship had been. . . .

"One of the finest. I traveled from America on it, though it is not meant for passengers. It is mainly for transporting of cargo. But Peter Grayson offered his private cabin to Rayburn and myself. We were quite comfortable."

"And where did you travel from?"

"We normally make our home in New Orleans," Christina said, removing the combs from the side of her hair to shake her hair loosely over her shoulders. It was the same as Glenda's . . . golden and wavy. But the few threads of gray sparkling beneath the light of the room were witness to her age doubling that of Glenda's. "I so miss my home," Christina further stated. "It has all the comforts that one can find in America. I miss my garden . . . I miss my parties." Her blue eyes suddenly danced. She rose from the chair. "And speaking of parties, I have been invited to one. This afternoon. At one of the other American's houses." She gathered the skirt of her dress into her arms and moved to a window to stare dreamily from it. "We will embroider and get acquainted. I believe this will become an everyday happening. If so, maybe I can forget my loneliness. . . ."

Glenda lifted an embroidered cushion onto her lap, tracing the designs with her forefinger. "I would like to learn the art of this embroidery," she said. "The colors. They are so beautiful." She let her fingers settle on a strand of orange silk. "And most of what you use is so soft."

Christina turned on a heel, eyes sparkling. "You

brush my hair and help me get ready for my parties and I will promise to teach you the craft of embroidery," she said anxiously. "We can begin our lessons first thing in the morning, if you like."

"Yes," Glenda squealed. "That would be grand." Quickly rising, she tossed the cushion aside, eager to get on with her duties. "And where shall I begin? Do you want me to begin brushing your hair right now?"

Christina placed a hand on Glenda's arm, laughing lightly. "First I must show you to your room. While I am away at the party, perhaps you might want to freshen up a bit and . . . uh . . . change into some more appropriate clothes."

Glenda reached and held her skirt away from her, feeling a slow blush rising. "You do not approve of my skirt and blouse?" she said in a low whisper.

Christina's gaze moved to the travel bag. "It's not that I don't approve," she said quietly. "But maybe you'd be more comfortable in one . . . of . . . my things." She still eyed the travel bag. "And what did you bring with you in the bag?" she quickly added.

"The rest of my belongings," Glenda said, going to get the bag, loosening its gathering strings.

Christina's hands went to her throat. "All you possess in clothes is inside . . . that . . . bag . . . ?" she gasped. "Truly . . . ?"

Glenda's looked quickly downward. "The Galvez family is poor, Christina," she said. "And I don't need many things. I keep them washed out. Each day."

Feeling as though she had made Glenda feel ashamed, Christina circled Glenda's waist and drew her to her. "I did not mean to make you uncomfortable, Glenda," she purred. She stroked Glenda's hair.

"Please forgive me. I was shocked that you possessed so little, for you see, I have never wanted for anything. In my entire life. Even though I have brought quite an assortment of dresses with me, I left my wardrobe filled with beautiful ones in New Orleans. I just couldn't imagine anyone . . . having so . . . few dresses. . . ."

"Yes. I understand," Glenda whispered. She pulled gently away from Christina. "I would love to see my room now. Is it on the second floor of this house? I've often wondered how so many windows could be in one house. Is there a window for each room? That would mean that your upstairs is filled with rooms!"

Laughing softly, Christina began to guide Glenda by the elbow toward the staircase. "No. Each window does not represent a different room. God. I have enough rooms to have to worry about. And no one but ourselves to fill them with."

"Your house is like a castle to me," Glenda sighed, taking each step, feeling her heart pounding more rapidly the closer they came to the second floor landing. She glanced backwards, seeing the steepness of the stairs, then moved her eyes forward, feeling even a bit dizzy.

"A castle?" Christina groaned. "This place? All the mosquitos and cockroaches, and the hot, muggy air make this place nothing like a castle I would like to be a part of. And the stench! According to the way the wind is blowing, I smell the foulest of odors!"

Covering her mouth, Glenda giggled. "I do believe you smell the hogs. And maybe even the chickens. They are even closer to your house than ours. I can imagine how it must smell some days. But you can keep your windows closed since you have such a nice artificial wind always blowing around in your house from the magnificent ceiling fan." She so wanted to rush to her mother . . . tell her of all her discoveries. There was this wonderful fan . . . the cold-air machine that made crystal formations that cooled drinks . . . there was iced tea. . . .

Oh, there was so much to tell! But then her heart ached a bit. To tell her mother . . . would be to flaunt her luxuries to her mother . . . who . . . had nothing. . . .

"I appreciate the sausage and bacon," Christina said, stepping on the last step, then upward onto the second floor landing. "I guess I can get used to the stench. And yes, I can close my windows if it gets bad enough." She walked down a narrow space of hallway and opened a door. She pushed it all the way back and stepped aside as Glenda moved next to her. "Glenda, this will be your room. For as long as you stay here," she said, watching Glenda out of the corner of her eye. She smiled to herself, seeing the wonder in this young woman's eyes. Being herself childless, it made a slow ache begin inside Christina. Couldn't she have even had a child the age of Glenda? Rayburn had refused her this pleasure of life . . . as he had before . . . with so many other things. She sometimes wondered if he truly knew the bitterness she felt toward him . . .

Glenda stepped lightly over the scrubbed hardwood floors, looking at the furniture that was to be hers. It was similar to the carved mahogany tables and chairs on the lower floor, but there was something added in this room. A huge bed! Its headboard with its intricate carvings just couldn't be hers! It was too breathtaking. She rushed to it and moved her fingers over it, then slipped a bit and caught herself by placing her free hand on the mattress. She gasped. Had she ever felt anything so soft in her whole life? "What kind of a . . . mattress . . . is this . . . ?" she said shyly. She placed her travel bag on the floor and slowly climbed atop the bed, sinking low into it, the mattress itself almost a caress.

"That is a feather bed," Christina laughed, clasping her hands tightly before her.

"Why, it's like I am in a nest," Glenda sighed further, patting all around her, watching the mattress rise and fall with each touch.

"The feathers are goose and duck. The mattress was made in America," Christina said. "It is quite popular in New Orleans. I hope you will be comfortable."

Glenda screwed up her nose. "At least it is not feathers of a chicken," she scowled. "I've begun to hate the pesky things."

"No. They are not chicken feathers," Christina laughed.

Glenda climbed from the bed and moved on around the room, touching everything. The wall was of a rough board, but yet painted cheerfully in pale greens. The two windows were curtainless, as was the bed without a spread, but there was one item in this room that stood out even more than the headboard of the bed and the feathers of the mattress.

Moving slowly, Glenda went to a mirror that hung long and low on the far wall. It had been a while since she had seen a mirror. She hadn't even seen one since she had full matured into a young lady. Cautiously, she began to twist herself from side to side, watching herself, seeing just how badly her skirt and blouse did look on her. They had been sewn to be too small, even showing off more of herself than she realized. She blushed a bit when she saw the deep cleavage of her breasts and knew that to lean over would be to expose all of her upper self to anyone who might be watching. Then her eyes traveled to the erectness of her nipples pushing through the thin material. She glanced a bit sideways, embarrassed. Then she reached upward and began to comb her fingers through her hair. She now could understand why she caught the eye of all the Honduran mestizos. She was so different. Her hair! It was the color of maize. She flipped it back from her shoulders, proud.

"And now I would like to suggest that we choose some of my dresses for you," Christina said, clearing her throat nervously. Her gaze moved downward, seeing the bare feet. "And, Glenda? Did you bring shoes inside your travel bag?"

Glenda lifted a bare foot, then placed it back on the floor, trying to pull her skirt down to hide it. "No Ma'am. I did not. I do not . . . own . . . a pair . . . of shoes," she said quietly, blushing anew.

Christina had to force herself to not gasp again. She was aghast that someone could actually not own a pair of shoes! But she was learning much about the ways of these Hondurans. She was learning that . . . most . . . were poor. "Then, Glenda, I will give you a pair of mine," she said in her velvet purr.

Glenda's hands went to her throat. "You would do that? Give . . . me . . . a pair of . . . shoes . . . ?" she sighed. "That would be a gift I would always cherish."

"Then follow me into my room. I will let you choose from my dresses and also my shoes," Christina laughed gaily. "I have so many. Truly, you can take your pick."

Almost shyly, Glenda followed along behind Christina, barely breathing when they entered another room, next to Glenda's. Glenda's breath caught in her throat when she saw the difference in the two bedrooms she had now become acquainted with. She stepped onto a plush beige carpet that felt almost as soft as the featherbed that she had just risen from. She could even feel the softness curling between each of her toes.

She moved further into the room, seeing the difference in the furniture. It was of smooth wood of a pecan coloring and above the bed was a canopy of sorts that hung low with pale blue lace, matching the spread on the bed of also a blue-lace design. A mosquito netting was spread back to the end of this canopy, and a ceiling fan hummed smoothly, causing the pale blue satin draperies to sway gently at each window.

"It has to be the prettiest room in the whole wide world," Glenda sighed.

"No. Not quite," Christina laughed. "But I did manage to have a few of my things brought along with me on the ship. I need touches of home to make me remember that I do, indeed, have something besides this forsaken land for which to plant my feet."

Frowning a bit from the sarcastic remark about her homeland, Glenda went to touch a few porcelain vases that had been placed on different tables. They were delicate, like maybe even a butterfly's wings! Then she watched in silent anxiety as Christina moved toward a tall wardrobe and opened its door. Glenda's heartbeats consumed her, seeing the row after row of dresses. She inched her way toward them. "These are all yours?" she said in a silken whisper. She dared her fingers to touch just one. It was as smooth as the petunia petal that she had touched in the hanging basket. . . .

"That one is my velvet dress that I very much doubt I will wear while here," Christina laughed softly. "I doubt if it will ever be cool enough." She watched in silent amusement as Glenda's fingers continued to work over the dresses. Glenda's heavy sighs filled the room.

"They each are as pretty as the next," Glenda said. She was gazing upon many different colors and fabrics. Some dresses sported low necks and short, puffed sleeves, and some sported tall necks and long, narrow sleeves. Some were flowered . . . some were plain. Some were soft . . . some were of a rough-textured material. Then her gaze moved downward to all the shoes lined up against the back wall of the wardrobe. It seemed that Christina had shoes to match each dress! How could anyone ever be so rich?

"Choose three dresses and also a pair of shoes to your liking," Christina said, settling down onto a cushioned chair. She was reminded of Christmas. She loved giving gifts. Especially to one who would truly appreciate it.

Glenda whirled around on a heel, all eyes. "Truly? Can I?" she gasped.

"Yes. Any you wish."

Glenda ran her fingers over the dresses one more

time, then when she saw the gay print of one and the swooping neckline trimmed with delicate white lace, she pulled it from the closet and draped it over her arms. "This is my first choice," she murmured. She ran her free hand over the softness of the fabric and let her eyes capture each and every rosebud design of the dress. The dress was of a soft silk, its background of white, decorated by tiny, pink rosebuds, so beautiful, one might imagine they could smell them. Glenda sniffed eagerly, then smiled shyly when she realized this delicious fragrance was not the rosebuds, but that of the perfume aroma that had lingered on this dress after Christina's last wearing of it.

"That is a wise choice," Christina purred. "It will look beautiful on you. It will make your skin look as though a flower's petal itself." She settled more down into the chair, kicking her shoes from her feet. "Now. Choose another, then another," she added, content. Maybe she could grow used to this desolation. But yet, she truly doubted it. Her heart . . . ? It had been left in New Orleans.

Glenda chose two more, the excitement of the moment almost drowning her. Then once these were placed neatly on the bed, she looked down at the shoes. Would they even fit? But, yes. She thought so. It seemed that when born, this American woman and herself had been poured from the same mold.

She leaned down and chose a pair of white shoes that had a delicate strap that would fit around the ankle. But the heels! Could she even learn to walk in them? She measured them with her fingers. Two inches! And for one who had always walked flat footed, without the aid of a shoe? She turned and blushed a bit as she held the shoes out before her. "I like these," she said. "But . . . do . . . you think . . . ?"

Christina pushed herself from the chair, laughing gaily. "Do you think you can get used to wearing them?" she said.

"You read . . . my thoughts . . . ma'am. . . ."

"You speak with your eyes, Glenda," Christina purred, bending, opening the wide expanse of a trunk that sat at the foot of her bed. "And, yes, you will get used to them. In time. You will at first feel quite awkward, but persistence will perfect your walk. You will see."

Glenda crept toward the trunk and peered downward into it. Her heartbeats were beginning in energetic vigor. What she was seeing was layer after layer of lacy underthings! There were pinks, blues, tans and they looked to even be softer than the silkiest of dresses that she had chosen for herself. She watched in silent awe as Christina lifted one of these up before her eyes. It was a . . . full . . . length undergarment, with so much lace, Glenda thought it could even be worn without a dress!

"This is also for you, Glenda," Christina said, offering it to her.

"Me . . . ?" Glenda said, dropping the shoes to the floor.

"Well, I did notice that you wear no undergarments," Christina stammered, blushing a bit as her eyes wandered over Glenda again. "I think it a much wiser thing to do. Don't you, Glenda? If you want to appear the lady, you must dress the lady. . . ."

Glenda cast her eyes downward. "Yes, ma'am," she whispered. She moved her eyes slowly upward as she accepted this newest gift into her outstretched arms. "This really is to be mine?" she sighed. Then her brow furrowed, eyeing Christina suspiciously. "I do not understand. Why are you being so generous?" She could remember her mother warning her about the Americans. Could even the women not be trusted? Was there a dark motive behind these generosities? Christina didn't appear to be the type to not be trusted. But Glenda wasn't too familiar with the ways of the world, except for her own way of life on Bay Island.

"You are to be my employee," Christina said, closing the lid of the trunk. She swung around and clasped gently onto Glenda's shoulders. "Let's say this is the first of your wages, if receiving them as a gift makes you uncomfortable."

Glenda's eyes brightened. "Yes. I like that," she said. "I would like to be able to say that I have earned these beautiful things. I will be the envy of all the women on this banana plantation." She fluttered her thick lashes nervously. She could feel the tears growing near. *"Muchas gracias,"* she whispered, choking a bit.

Christina dropped her hands to her side, laughing softly. "I think I know a thank you when I hear one," she said. "Even if spoken in Spanish."

Glenda laughed also, feeling, oh, so alive. She could hardly wait for Christina to leave for her party . . . so she could play as though this was her house. And wouldn't she look the part when she changed into . . . a . . . beautiful dress . . . ?

Glenda smiled coyly as Christina handed a brush toward her. . . .

Chapter Five

Looking from her upstairs window, Glenda watched Ramón guide the sleek, black mare away from the house, carrying behind it the stately carriage with Christina as its daily passenger. A slow smile erupted on Glenda's lips, knowing that she was now free to do as she pleased in this many-roomed house. And what a relief to know that Ramón would be gone for the same amount of time as Christina! He would have been the only person who could have spoiled these daily delights of pretense for Glenda.

Her eyes lifted to the sky, seeing the heavy, dark clouds threatening overhead. A zigzag of lightning raced across the sky breaking the clouds momentarily, and then the following rumble of thunder, making Glenda tremble as the floor she was standing upon was doing. Maybe this newest storm would become her enemy causing Christina to return to her house. It could possibly spoil Glenda's leisurely afternoons of pretending to be the fair maiden of the house. She had even carried her pretense so far as to go into Christina's room and choose a different dress to wear for each afternoon. Her first full week at this house had been spent in this way. And, ah, the jewels! She had even learned how to screw the earrings to the lobes of each of her ears to let them hang gracefully until right before Christina was expected back home.

Glenda had never thought to worry about Rayburn. He had become almost as a field laborer himself, always in the fields, watching over everything, hoping to get the bananas harvested before the American ship, the *Sea Wolf's* next arrival with its empty hold, readied to be filled with the many bananas to be carried back to America.

Pulling the shutters closed on the window, Glenda rushed from her own bedroom, trying to not let guilt be a part of her adventure of this afternoon. She realized the generosities of Christina, but yet, Glenda couldn't help herself when she hungered for the feel of the other dresses that were not hers against her skin. She even loved the aroma of each. Didn't they smell just like Christina? Glenda had so wanted to open Christina's many bottles of perfumes to dab some on herself, but had known to do so would be to give herself away. There was no way to disguise smells . . . especially such sweet smells that each of Christina's bottles represented.

Glenda now felt it safe enough to venture on into Christina's bedroom. The new Honduran cook had been ordered to never leave the confines of the kitchen. It was only her duty to cook and serve the best of food to the American family . . . and . . . now also to Glenda who had been invited to share a table with them.

"I shouldn't truly go to Christina's room. It is so deceitful, especially after she gave me the beautiful clothes she has given me," Glenda sighed heavily. "But just this one more time. After today, I won't do this again. Surely Christina would hate me if she found out. And I can't afford such hate."

Tremors of excitement bubbled through her as she pushed Christina's bedroom door open and found herself being cooled by the ever gently moving blades of the ceiling fan. Glenda lifted her face to it and closed her eyes as her hair settled down her back in golden streamers. She brushed her hair from her skin with her fingers and shook it, sighing heavily. Then as the anticipation became too much for her, she first went to the small, carved mahogany chest kept on a table beside the bed. With trembling fingers, she lifted its lid and peered admiringly, even enviously, down at the sparkling jewels that lay circled beneath her eyes. There were many bracelets . . . necklaces . . . and earrings from which to choose. Her fingers went to a necklace of tiny diamonds. She held it to the window and watched each diamond's sparkle. They were casting blue and purple splashes onto the palm of her hand. "Oh, shall I ever own such a treasure as this?" she murmured, going to the mirror that was on the opposite wall.

She placed the necklace to her throat and eyed it hungrily. Then without further thought, fastened the clasp behind her neck and rushed to the wardrobe to choose the one dress that had so far been ignored by her. It was one of black velvet that even Christina had pushed to the far end, away from the others. "It cannot be that hot against the skin," Glenda scoffed. "And it is so beautiful. Who could even care if it does cause one to be a bit uncomfortable?"

Quickly, she stepped from her own delicate dress of silk. With a pounding heart, she slipped the other over her head . . . buttoned it in the back . . . then ran her fingers over its softness, admiring what she saw in the mirror. It was a plain dress with no frills or lace, but its simplicity was what Glenda most admired about it. It clung sensuously to her figure and its low plunging neckline and the smoothness of the fabric accentuated the soft curve of her breasts and her waist that nipped in narrowly, to then flare only barely at her hips. She fingered the necklace, seeing how the diamonds seemed to sparkle even more glitteringly as they hung next to the sleek black velvet.

"And now my hair," she sighed, lifting it atop her head, turning her head first one way and then another, testing it. "Yes. I shall get Christina's extra combs and place them at the sides and back of my head, and let the hair drift ever so gently from my crown." And when she had done even this, she couldn't believe the transition of herself from the plain Honduran to the beautiful, enticing woman who could have been in America even since birth!

A loud knocking from downstairs drew a deep gasp into Glenda's throat. Someone was at the door! She glanced all around her, seeing her own rumpled dress tossed so carelessly on Christina's bed and then into the mirror, seeing the dress . . . the jewels . . . the combs . . . none of which were hers. "It can't be Christina, though," she said cautiously. "She wouldn't knock. Nor would Rayburn."

She breathed a bit easier, but still felt apprehensive about going to the door, dressed so expensively. What if it was someone who would tell Christina . . . or . . .

Rayburn? But the persisting of the knocking made her aware that she may have just been caught. Would she even find herself back at the Galvez house by sunset? Or would the whole Galvez family even be sent packing back to Bay Island for the mischief that Glenda had been caught doing?

"It just can't happen," she sobbed, rushing from the room and down the stairs. "It just can't. I am too happy. Oh, if I get through this scare unharmed, I will never, no never enter Christina's room again without asking permission."

With knees trembling, Glenda moved on to the door and opened it slowly, revealing only her face to a man . . . a stranger. But there was something about this stranger that pulled a quiet gasp from deep inside her throat. She couldn't even speak. This American's handsome face and the way he stood so tall and erect, even sinewy, made a strange warmth course through her veins. She clung to the door. . . .

The man shifted nervously from one foot to the other. *"Bonjour, ma chérie,"* he said in a deep, resonant voice. "I'm here to see Rayburn Turner. Might he be here?"

"No," she said, gulping hard, wondering about his accent. It wasn't American or Spanish. "He's in the fields. With the bananas."

The man took it upon himself to push the door fully open and stepped on inside, past Glenda. She straightened her back, barely breathing as he moved on around the room as though he owned it. "Who are you?" she said in a silken whisper.

He swung around on a heel, all smiles, with gray eyes that Glenda thought looked to be bottomless.

"William Read deBaulieu at your service, madam," he said, swooping his right arm around as he bowed deeply. "But call me Read. It sounds less sophisticated. I like things simple."

Again she was speechless. His attitude was one of a true gentleman, but yet his gaze raking over her could very well be that of a rogue. She returned the sweeping look, admiring him anew. His face was angular and weathered-tan, and his nose was his most prominent feature, being straight, yet not too long. His dark hair appeared to have been mussed by the wind, making a wicked thought enter Glenda's mind, wishing that it had been her fingers that had caused his hair to be in such disarray. She had so often watched her mother move her fingers through her father's hair while making love beneath the soft splashes of moonlight. . . .

"And you must be Rayburn Turner's daughter?" Read said, squaring his shoulders as he clasped his hands together behind him. He began moving around her, eyeing her with a lifted eyebrow and a soft, playful smile on the straight line of his lips. He came to a halt directly in front of her, looking down at her from his six-foot-four height. "Can't you even talk? Don't tell me you're deaf and dumb." His expression changed to be that of a more serious nature.

Glenda's thoughts were swirling. What was she to say? She couldn't reveal the truth . . . that she was Christina's personal maid. Maids didn't wear diamonds at their throats! And since she was white-skinned . . . well . . . she could pass as Christina's daughter. . . . But no. Surely this man would mention becoming acquainted with her to Christina or

Rayburn, or maybe even both.

She took one more quick assessment of him . . . at the shirt that fit him so perfectly, emphasizing the broadness of his shoulders, though gaped open in front, showing fronds of dark chest hair. His breeches were dark and tight, revealing more muscles and even more than that . . . to . . . Glenda's wandering eyes.

Feeling a blush rising, she averted her gaze from him. "Yes. I'm Mr. Turner's daughter," she quickly blurted, then bit her lower lip, wondering what trouble she had just emerged herself into. She swung her face around, eyes many shades of green. "But don't say anything to my father," she hurriedly added. It had suddenly become important for her to drop all Spanish from her vocabulary. She had to remember to speak English . . . all . . . English. . . .

"And why not?" he chuckled. He moved to a chair and sat down. He crossed his legs and continued to watch her, now in more silent admiration than amusement. He had never seen such rare, exquisite beauty. Though dressed in black, her skin as well as her hair seemed to be glowing. His gaze moved and held on her heaving bosom. Her breasts looked even more of a velvet texture than the dress she wore and it was creating a dangerous heat inside his loins. He had to remember! This was a division manager's daughter . . . which automatically meant . . . "hands off. . . ."

Glenda moved with grace across the room, watching through the window as rain began to fall in torrents. It was as though someone had overturned tons of buckets of water and it was falling in one place. She turned on a heel, holding her chin high. "My parents would not approve of me letting a stranger into our

98

house," she said coyly. "If they knew that I did, it would mean a punishment would be inflicted." Lies! How had they formed on her lips so easily? But when one practiced deceit as Glenda was now guilty of having done, she knew that one deceitful act created another . . . then another. . . .

"Have no fear then. I won't say anything. I believe you failed to give me your name," he said suavely, bringing his fingertips together in front of him.

"Glenda," she said in a silken whisper, fluttering her lashes nervously. The strange, pleasurable sensations his nearness was arousing in her frightened her a bit. No man had ever had such an effect on her. And she wasn't sure if an American should be the one to cause her heart to leap so. It was an American who had . . . She closed her eyes tightly together for a moment, not wanting to think of her mother's warnings, then nervously fluttered them open again. Glenda knew that no dark-skinned Honduran had made her blush as she was now doing under this . . . this Read's steady gaze. . . .

"Such a pretty name. Glenda. Yes, a pretty name to match a beautiful woman," Read said huskily. He smiled in quiet amusement to himself, realizing that he was unnerving her by his show of interest and his compliments.

"*Muchas* . . ." Glenda began to say, then placed her hand to her mouth, remembering . . . English. I must speak English. . . .

"Thank you, kind sir," she quickly added, smiling warmly.

"Read. Please call me Read," he said quietly.

"It is such a funny name," Glenda giggled. "Read?

Like to read . . . a . . . book? I have never heard such a name before."

Read leaned a bit forward, lifting an eyebrow. "Oh?" he murmured. "Usually it's my last name that draws attention and comments. But you would be the one to be different. Yes . . . you . . . are different. . . ."

Swallowing hard, Glenda began running her fingers over the softness of the dress she wore. Was he going to recognize the game she was playing? Though white-skinned, could he tell in some way that her mother was dark-skinned? "And what was your last name, Read?" she murmured softly. "It seems to have left my mind."

He settled back against the cushions, laughing a bit. "It is a French name," he said. "My full name is William Read deBaulieu. My ancestors proudly carried the name deBaulieu to America, where I make my residence."

"If your residence is in America, what are you doing in El Progresso?" Glenda asked, now toying with the diamond necklace at her throat. She had seen his gaze stop and hold on the sparkling jewels. To her, it was only a reminder of Christina and how Glenda now wished that she hadn't taken such liberties with Christina's personal belongings. To him, It probably meant other things. . . .

"I've arrived with the ship *Sea Wolf,*" he said. "I'm a new representative for the American Fruit Company. This is my first journey to El Progresso. The first of many to come. . . ."

She devoured him with her eyes. A strange hunger was gnawing at her insides . . . a hunger she didn't want to feel. She still didn't know if he was truly a gentleman . . . or a . . . rogue. Her pulsebeat quickened in the hollow of her throat. "Did you say you are with the same company as my . . . uh . . . parents? And that you will be traveling to El Progresso again?" she said quietly, realizing that she wouldn't just be seeing him this once . . . but many more times. It made a delicious thrill tremor through her.

"It's my duty to see that the bananas are loaded into the hold of the *Sea Wolf* with as few bruises as possible," he said, rising. He went to a window and stared at the continuing downpour of the rain. He had been warned of the "wet season." He only hoped that the steady rains were no cause of lower-quality bananas.

He swung around, worry wrinkles crinkling at the corner of his mouth and eyes, making him suddenly appear older than his age of twenty-five. "I must speak with Rayburn Turner. Tell him of the *Sea Wolf*'s arrival," he said. "I was told that I should first check here at his residence. Where might I now look to find him?"

Glenda rose and went also to the window, now watching pools of muddy water deepening on the ground. She then peered toward the many rows of banana plants. "He's out there," she murmured, pointing. "As of late, he's been joining the laborers. He's been a bit weary from the rain and it's slowing the laborers' progress in the fields."

"I was a bit concerned about the weather while on board the *Sea Wolf*," he grumbled. "The ship tossed around a bit too much for my pleasure."

Glenda's eyes widened. "The *Sea Wolf*," she

101

whispered. "It's such a fierce-sounding name for a ship. I bet it could withstand any harsh winds and waves. Oh, how exciting it would be to one day be able to travel on such a ship. . . ." Her words caught in her throat when she realized what she had just said. With trembling knees she turned to move away from him but was stopped by his sudden firm grip on her wrist.

"What did you just say about wishing to be on a ship?" he said thickly, pulling her to him. "You had to travel by ship to reach El Progresso. What did you mean by implying you had never been on a ship before?"

Glenda's heartbeats were consuming her. She wasn't sure of the true reason. Was it because he had just caught her in her web of lies? Or was it because he was so near? Hadn't she so often dreamed of a man who could cause her heart to react so? Was this truly the . . . man . . . ?

She could smell the lingering seawater aroma of his clothes, and his touch, though a bit too tight, was warm and electric. "I truly don't know what made me say such a foolish thing," she laughed nervously, forcing a smile as his gray eyes traveled over her.

"And why are you dressed in such an expensive manner, in such a drab setting as this?" he asked, now lifting his fingers to the necklace. He touched it, then let his fingers stray to the softness of her skin.

She was becoming breathless. Never had she thought a man's touch could cause her mind to behave in such a careless fashion. But yet warning signals were flashing off and on in the deeper recesses of her mind. She could see a questioning in the depths of his eyes. Or, no. Was it more of a knowing? "I wanted to go to the party with my mother," she said, drooping her full lips into a forced pout. "But she didn't want me to venture out because of the storm." She giggled a bit. "I guess she was afraid I might melt." She marveled at her ease at conjuring up tall tales. It was even a bit exciting!

He continued to hold her by the wrist. "Your mother is also gone?" he said huskily, feeling the renewed heat rising in his loins. He knew the dangers of such thoughts that were skipping through his mind. But she was so enchanting! His loins kindled even more at the sight of her breasts from this closer vantage point. He let his hand move from her throat to one of the heaving mounds. The opportunity may never present itself to him again. Ah, the softness. . . .

Glenda moaned throatily and felt suddenly dizzy with delight. She closed her eyes for a moment, feverish with desire. But when she felt the warm wetness of his lips replace the fingers on her breast, her senses returned in a flash of guilt. She struggled to be set free, her eyes snapping. She gasped. "*Señor!* What do you think you are doing?"

Her wrist was released so abruptly, her arm fell clumsily to her side. She grew a bit frightened, seeing the dark shadows that had fallen across his face. She inched away from him, eyes wide, rubbing her throbbing wrist.

"You speak your Spanish quite well, *señorita*," he said, now chuckling a bit. "Did you learn while in America?" He moved to her and began removing the combs from her hair. "Or maybe you've never been to

America," he added, speaking slowly and surely. He threw the combs to the floor and circled her neck with both hands and jerked her lips to his. He teased her with feathery kisses. "Your hair. It's so golden, like a field of ripened wheat. It is the color of an American woman's hair. But, still, maybe you aren't Rayburn Turner's daughter after all," he murmured. "Maybe he wouldn't even shoot me if I was to . . ." He then crushed her lips to his and let his hands move upward and through her hair.

Glenda struggled, causing his arms to then circle around her back to pinion her next to him. "Señor, please. . . ." she said in soft whispers, but being besieged more by frantic passion than the lock of his arms. She could barely recall her mother's warnings now. The words were like a gray fog, swirling, then dissipating to a nothingness as he formed the steel of his body into hers.

His hands became magic to her, demanding, yet magnets, drawing her into a whirlwind of desire and reckless passion. Her head was reeling. Her skin quivered with beads of excitement. She finally gave in to his demands and the sensuous pleasure her own body was begging to have fulfilled. This was the way she had always imagined it to be. If with the one you love, the body would give you the true answer. Yes. She was. Her body was begging for release. The pressures inside her pained, yet felt delicious. She laced her arms around his neck and locked her fingers together and returned his kiss, sighing leisurely.

"When will Mrs. Turner return?" Read asked huskily, bending his head to kiss the flesh of her breasts.

She leaned her head back, with closed eyes, breathless. She suddenly felt full of the devil and didn't care. "I am alone for many hours each afternoon," she said silkily. "Christina only just left. And Rayburn? He will be so busy with worry of his bananas, he won't be home until dark."

With a trembling hand, Read dared a fresh touch to her breast and when she gasped anew but let his hand linger, he moved it on inside the bodice of her dress, cupping a full breast now, feeling his hardness rising beneath the tight confines of his breeches in unison with the stiffening of her large, firm nipple. *"Ma chérie,* I find you too lovely," he murmured, moving his lips across the hollow of her throat, then downward. "I need you. Now. And I can tell that you need me as badly. Shall . . . we . . . ? The rain. I don't care to venture out into it. But I would dare to venture to your room."

"I don't . . . know. . . ." she whispered, wishing her heartbeat would slow a bit. "Christina . . . Rayburn. They've been so good to me. I . . . don't think I should. . . ."

He chuckled deeply. "Ah, hah! Just as I thought. You are not the daughter of the Turner's," he said. "I hadn't been told of a daughter." He pushed her gently from him and held her at arm's length. "And if you're not their daughter, who are you? What are you doing here and dressed so expensively?"

Glenda lowered her thick lashes. "My true name is Glenda Galvez," she murmured.

"You are Honduran . . . ?" he gasped.

"Yes. . . ."

"But, your skin . . . ?"

105

"Does it matter . . . ?"

"I need to know why you are here," he said, eyes wavering. "That is all."

"I am Christina's personal maid . . ."

He eyed her questionably. "The dress? The necklace . . . ?"

"I was only trying them on. . . ."

"Well, I'll be damned," he chuckled. He swooped her up into his arms and buried his nose into the depths of her hair, inhaling the clean, sweet fragrance. "You're sure no one will arrive for a while . . . ?"

"No one," she replied, leaning her head on the massiveness of his shoulder.

"You do have a room of your own . . . ?"

"Up the stairs. I will direct you. . . ."

"And, you are sure, *ma chérie* . . . ?"

"You've taken my heart from me," she whispered. She lifted her face from his shoulder and gazed rapturously into his eyes, seeing pools of hungry passion. "It doesn't matter that I am Honduran?"

"I would question that fact," he said, chuckling. "But not now." He carried her toward the stairs, each step upward causing his heart to become more erratic. He had yet to meet such a complex woman who also was so beautiful? Ah! He loved the combination. He loved the daring. He brushed her cheek with a soft kiss as he placed his feet on the second floor landing.

Glenda pointed with the toe of her shoe. "That is my room," she said silkily. "Next to Christina's. . . ."

"And you're sure we can truly be alone without worrying . . . ?"

She giggled softly, almost floating above herself it

seemed. She stroked her forefinger down the smooth, tan lines of his face, once again marveling over his handsomeness. "I'm not sure of anything right now," she murmured. "The only thing I can think of at this moment is how you've hypnotized me with your charm." Feeling indeed wanton, she leaned her face into his chest and circled one of his nipples with the flick of her tongue.

He tossed his head back with a response of sheer joy. *"C'est magnifique,"* he sighed, his nerves screaming for release.

"I love your body," Glenda whispered, now moving her fingers through his dark fronds of chest hair. She couldn't believe that she was being so careless and wild. She realized that she wasn't going to be raped by an American as her mother had been. She was in joint seduction with this man of the gray eyes. . . .

With haste, Read opened the bedroom door and stood looking around him for a moment. For a maid, Glenda WAS being treated quite special. He had to wonder about it. But the weight in his arms and the clean, sweet smell of her drew him back to the pleasurable moments of only heartbeats away. "Shall I undress you, or do you wish to do it yourself?" he murmured into her ear, holding her even closer.

The full brunt of what she was about to do washed through her in hot, searing waves. Was she truly going to surrender her virginity to this American? This stranger? Would she in the end regret it? His lips once again burning the flesh of her breasts were answer enough for her. She had lost control of her senses. Her body . . . its inflamed needs were in full control now . . . guiding her . . . as though she was in a shallow draft boat . . . drifting . . . drifting . . . away from the person she had always known as "self". . . .

"Please do me the honor," she sighed silkily. Her eyes flashed in soft greens as his response was to place her gently on the bed, to then begin at her throat, to first remove the necklace. He dropped it on the floor as though it was a toy, not a rare, expensive necklace of delightful diamonds.

Chuckling, he lifted her a bit and began to release the buttons of her dress, all the while devouring her with his eyes. He didn't want to wonder about the color of her skin, having dark-skinned parents. He only wanted her soft, pink flesh revealed completely to him so that more than his eyes could caress it.

With skill, he pulled the dress from her shoulders, then her underthings, having to do no more because the frantic passion exploding inside Glenda guided her to move from the rest of her hindrances until even her shoes were kicked onto the floor.

"You are *magnifique,*" he said huskily, now tracing all her curves and dips with his hands, feeling the softness as though it was the petal of a rose, and seeing its luster, as though the quiet glow of a midnight moon was rippling across her.

He bent over her, supporting himself with his hands on each side of her, then began to taste of her honey-dew flesh. She moaned and squirmed beneath his tongue as it flicked and teased each nipple erect, causing her to almost scream out from the intensity of the pleasures he was arousing in her.

When his lips traveled lower, causing small ripples on her flesh, she felt as though she couldn't stand any more of the teasings he was inflicting upon her. She lifted her arms to him, begging with her eyes. "Why do you wait, *señor?*" she whispered harshly. "Please come to me. Hold me. Quench the fires inside me."

He refused her arms, instead moving from the bed to hurriedly shed his clothes and boots. When Glenda's gaze settled on his throbbing hardness, a sharp pang of fear pierced her heart. Could such a largeness tear her insides apart? She had seen her father place his manhood inside her mother and she had seen the size of her two brothers, but none of these compared with the size of this man. She gulped back a knot forming in her throat as he lowered himself over her.

"My lovely lady," he said hoarsely, placing his manhood against her thigh, rubbing it up and down, causing sparks to ignite inside her.

She reached her hands up and framed his face between them and guided his lips to hers, moaning when his stomach made contact with hers. As though skilled, she flicked her tongue inside the deep recesses of his mouth, tasting him, oh, tasting him. His hands molded her breasts, causing her to writhe and wrap her legs around his back.

To Read, this was an open invitation to enter her. She gasped as he plunged inside her, though not surprised when the pain cut through her like a sharp knife might do. She pulled her lips free from his and began tossing her head as he began to thrust deeply inside her. She strained her hips closer to him, working them, panting, feeling their bodies blending, becoming one molten bed of lava splashing together. The heat rose and fell as he did. The pain became pleasurable . . . sweet. . . . She was his. Body, mind

. . . and soul. . . . She ground herself more into him as she felt the urgency building. . . .

His arms encircled her and pulled her breasts to his lips. He stroked her face with his fingertips, then stiffened his legs when he felt the flood beginning inside him. He plunged. Deeper and deeper. Until his body became one mass of trembling against hers. . . .

Glenda met the explosion of his body with increased vigor. Her heart was pounding . . . her breath was coming in short rasps. Though he was spent, he was still working with her, kissing her with renewed raw passion.

She suddenly sighed. "I'm melting. I'm melting." She felt as though the warm waters of the Caribbean were washing through her in gentle, sweet caresses. But suddenly it was as though a hurricane had erupted . . . swirling . . . blinding her . . . as the most beautiful, mind absorbing flashes of color splashed around inside her head. She lifted her body and spread her legs as the fleeting moment of ecstasy captured her . . . heart and soul.

Then she was aware of his lips tracing her body once again as he moved slowly from atop her.

"*Ma chérie,* I could never get too much of you," he whispered, caressing her between the thighs. Then he tensed, feeling a wetness on his fingers. He placed them before his eyes and saw the evidence of her debauched virginity. It was blood. "Christ," he uttered. "I didn't realize. . ." He glanced apologetically toward her, his eyes heavy. "I didn't know," he whispered again. "Christ, did I hurt you. . . ?" He hadn't felt the tightness as he had entered her. He had been too carried away by the hungry desire of the flesh.

Glenda moved to her knees and circled his neck with her arms. "It's all right," she whispered. "It only hurt for a brief moment."

"But you were a virgin," he gasped. "Why didn't you tell me? I wouldn't have . . ."

Glenda's lips formed a sulking pout. "Didn't I make you happy . . .?"

He reached down to his discarded clothes and pulled a handkerchief from his breeches pocket and wiped his hands on it. "You know the answer to that," he said thickly. "I've never known such a woman before."

She traced his lips with a forefinger. "Then you do like Glenda?"

He placed his arms around her waist, growling a bit. "I adore Glenda," he said, then gently kissed her, realizing, though, that he dare not let himself get carried away again. He had to get out of there. The rain had stopped falling and it was too chancy to linger any longer.

"Can you come again?" she sighed, feeling brazen as she let her fingers move to touch his manhood, marveling over its smallness now.

"I will be here only one more day," he said, guiding her exploring fingers away from himself, indeed feeling the flames kindling once again. He moved from the bed and quickly dressed.

"Christina will be gone the same time tomorrow," Glenda said, quickly choosing one of her own dresses to pull over her head, scoffing at using the usual undergarments Christina so urged her to wear. Her body was too alive to cover it with tight underthings! She could still feel the tingling along her flesh.

"I could come," he said, stepping into his boots. "I can make some excuse to move from the loading of the ship. But if only you can agree to tell me exactly why you are here and who your true parents are."

She leaned her body into his, touching the tip of his nose with a forefinger. "It is so necessary?" she whined.

"Damned right," he growled. "I don't want to have to wonder about who might come gunning for me because I have released you of your virginity."

She giggled a bit. "And you think I'm even foolish enough to tell that I've had this rendezvous with you? An American stranger?" she said. "I am not a foolish person."

His arms circled her waist. He yanked her to him. "We are no longer strangers," he murmured. "We are perfect lovers."

"Yes, yes," she sighed.

"But, *ma chérie,* this lover has to leave," he said, pulling away from her.

"Oh, must you . . .?"

"Yes. I've got to seek out Rayburn Turner. I must get the bananas back to New Orleans as soon as possible."

"There is that name New Orleans again," she said. "I've heard Christina speak of it with such melancholy in her words."

He laughed hoarsely as he opened the bedroom door and moved toward the stairs with her beside him, barefooted. "Anyone who has been to New Orleans speaks of it in a melancholy way," he said.

She clung to his arm, taking each step with him. "And why is that, Read?" she murmured, wide-eyed.

He moved from the last step and on toward the door. "Because New Orleans is called the Paris of America because of its French charm." He opened the door and swung around, letting his gaze rake quickly over her.

"Maybe I can go to New Orleans one day," she sighed. Her green eyes suddenly sparkled. "Maybe you'll take me with you? Read? Maybe?"

His lips lifted into a small smile. "Until tomorrow, *au revoir, ma chérie,*" he murmured, then rushed away from her, leaving her with mouth agape. He hadn't answered her! But wasn't she the fool to even think that a man would pay her passage to America only because she had given her body to him . . .?

She smiled a bit, remembering the pleasure SHE had received from the union of the two bodies. She wouldn't let guilt nor shame ruin it for her. She had become a woman . . . and . . . she loved it. . . .

As she turned from the door, her gaze settled on the combs that he had tossed to the floor. With a wild heartbeat, she rushed and scooped them up, now remembering the diamond necklace and the velvet dress that had been discarded so carelessly, also on the floor, but that of her bedroom.

The squeaking of wheels drew her attention to the window. When she saw that it was Christina returning in the carriage, she rushed up the stairs and hurriedly replaced all that wasn't hers.

Then coyly, she moved to the sitting room, waiting for Christina's entrance. She put her hands to her face, wondering if Christina could see a change in her. She felt aglow inside. . . .

113

Chapter Six

The night was thick with the steady humming from mosquitoes and the half moon was a cradle in the sky as Glenda paced the full length of the back of the Taylor's veranda. She hugged herself with her arms. Though the air was sweet and heady from the aroma rising from nearby begonias and roses, Glenda's thoughts were troubled as never before in her life. It had been four full weeks now since she had seen Read and she was wondering if and when he would return. She so vividly remembered their shared secret moments together and how she had ached for him that entire night after his departure.

But the aching had been replaced by a painful doubt when Christina had come rushing into Glenda's bedroom early that next morning saying that someone had scaled the Palmetto tree's trunk outside her window and had stolen her treasured diamond necklace, along with many other valuable pieces of heirloom jewelry. They had done so, even as Christina had slept in the same room. . . .

Lifting her fingers to her hair, Glenda brushed it up and over her ears, feeling the steaminess of the humidity in her hair's thick, golden mass of waves. She hadn't been able to think of anything or anybody but Read. Could he have managed to have left the business of loading the *Sea Wolf* that night long enough to steal from the Taylors? Rayburn hadn't returned home that night until way past midnight. Read would have been the one to know that the man of the house was out. . . . Read had seen the necklace and Glenda had seen his eyes assessing its value. And hadn't Glenda even mentioned that Christina's room was next to her own?

She stomped a bare foot in rage. She hated believing that the Read she had twice become so intimate with could be capable of such a deceptive act as thievery. And hadn't he appeared as one whom had never lacked of wealth. Wasn't he even from a distinguished line of family from France?

"William Read deBaulieu," she murmured aloud, tremoring inside with the familiarity of the name, almost a caress to her heart.

"He can't have done it," she argued silently to herself. "It is all too much of a coincidence that he was here . . . that he had seen the necklace. . . ."

Then her eyes narrowed into two slits. "Maybe being a thief is how he acquires what wealth he has accumulated," she thought further.

For some reason, the thought was beginning to excite . . . not repel her . . . for everything this American man stood for . . . spelled "excitement" in her eyes.

She was relieved that Christina hadn't thought to wonder about this American whom had arrived on board the *Sea Wolf* the day before the theft had taken

115

place. But Christina would never even have reason to suspect him, because Glenda and Read's two secret rendezvous were well kept inside her in a very special corner of her heart.

The lush tropical vegetation that laced the veranda's edge rustled a bit and a sudden call from a howler monkey sent goose pimples scattering along the bare flesh of Glenda's arm. The monkey's loud, long doleful howl reminded Glenda of a dog's lonely wail, causing shivers to ride her spine. She suddenly felt too alone on this veranda. As her gaze moved quickly around her, she was seeing shadows and hearing low scraping noises that she hadn't noticed earlier.

A puma, one of the largest carnivores of the cat family, had been spied prowling around on the white sands of the beach. Even its pawprints had been seen near El Progresso, causing enough alarm for torches burning ocote pine and the resins of the Caribbean pine to be placed at each doorway of the laborers' homes. But Glenda didn't fear the puma. She feared man even more . . . one man in particular . . . Ramón Martinez.

Stepping lightly along to the front of the house, Glenda stopped to stand next to this family's torch. The orange flames were weaving and swaying with the breeze, and off in the distance, above where the fence reached, orange reflective shadows from all the other torches had changed the dark velvet sky of night to that of dancing, pale oranges.

The night was foreboding, as though some terrible deed was about to happen. It was different somehow . . . both the stifling, damp air, and the way the night noises would suddenly halt, then slowly begin again to then become almost deafening to the ears.

When Glenda began hearing a soft, high-pitched sound of great delicacy, she whirled around, recognizing this to be the haunting music being played on Christina's magnificent music box, that of which Christina had so generously shared with Glenda on occasion.

The repetitious, sparkling tune was one of almost a reprieve for Glenda, an escape of sorts from her wearisome thoughts, if even only for a short time. She let the music lead her on into the sitting room but paused before addressing Christina. In silence, Glenda studied her. It was now, as usual, when Christina was playing her music box. As the short-skirted ballerina whirled in circles atop the music box, Christina's blue eyes showed a hazy, less distinct blue behind her gold-framed spectacles that she always wore while embroidering or reading, as though clouded by some painful memory.

Upon closer observation, Glenda could see a tear glistening at the corner of one of Christina's eyes, though her fingers were busy with her embroidery. Her complexion was rosier this night and her hair was combed into a fresh chignon at the base of her neck. Traces of perspiration shone on her brow and between the deep cleavage of her breasts, and when Christina placed her embroidery on her lap and lifted a handkerchief to dip between her breasts, Glenda cleared her throat nervously and moved on into the room.

"Christina, do you mind if I join you?" she said, tensing a bit when she realized that she had startled her. The music box and its twirling ballerina seemed to always have ways of sending Christina into a hypnotic trance of sorts. Glenda had so often won-dered if this was because of some remembrances attached to the music box. . . .

Christina had said that a friend had given it to her on her departure from New Orleans. . . .

Glenda had begun to wonder if this gift giver had been a male. But surely not. Christina and Rayburn appeared to be quite devoted to one another and being childless they even seemed closer than most husbands and wives.

Dabbing her handkerchief at the corner of her teary eyes, to remove traces of melancholy, Christina forced a smile toward Glenda. "Glenda, I didn't hear you come in," she said, then scowled a bit when her gaze traveled over Glenda, seeing the apparent lack of underthings beneath the low-cut bodice of her lace-trimmed, pink cotton dress. She even sighed exasper-ately when she saw that Glenda was also barefooted. But she didn't say anything. Instead, she lifted her embroidery cloth and needle and began pushing and pulling some bright red silken threads through a square of linen fabric.

The ballerina had come to a silent halt on its round pedestal. "May I rewind the music box, Christina?" Glenda said, flipping her hair back from her face.

"Yes. Please do," Christina murmured.

"Thank you," Glenda said, anxiously lifting the music box into her hands, admiring once again the graceful lines of the ballerina and the gentleness of colors of blues and orchids in the ballerina's short, flared skirt. One knee was bent, with a toe pointed downward and both her arms were lifted above her head with delicate fingers touching, fingertips to fingertips. The ballerina's angular, serene face appeared to hold a secret in the depths of its carefully painted blue eyes, even so much like Christina's. It made a tremor travel through Glenda.

Twisting the tiny key around until it could go no further, Glenda listened rapturously to its melody beginning anew as she placed it gently back on the table beside Christina. "It is so beautiful," she sighed, moving to a chair, where her own neglected piece of embroidery work lay waiting. She placed the wooden frame on her lap and pulled her feet and legs up beneath her. "And the music can hide the night noises," she said, visibly shuddering.

She removed the needle from her linen fabric and began moving it in and out, marveling at the design that was finally taking shape. She had roughly sketched a semblance of a lone petunia on the fabric and had been given some blue cotton threads and needle, and instructions on how to use them by Christina. Glenda liked what she was doing. She was . . . creating. . . .

"I wish Rayburn would return home," Christina said in a near whisper. "I do worry about the puma's tracks they've found. But Rayburn said he had much to do tonight. And he has been expecting the *Sea Wolf*'s arrival again. I guess at night, they keep a vigil on the beach . . . waiting . . . and watching."

Glenda pricked her finger severely with the needle, not having heard mention of the *Sea Wolf* since its departure. She thrust her throbbing finger inside her mouth and sucked on it, already feeling the thundering of her heart with the thought of possibly seeing Read again.

But once again, doubts assailed her. If Read *had* stolen the jewels, he surely wouldn't return. . . .

"Did you say the . . . *Sea Wolf*. . . ?" she said, trying to hide the anxiety in her voice.

"Yes. It's due again," Christina said in a low murmur, as though such a happening was cause for sadness. . . .

"You even believe that . . . tonight. . . ?"

"Rayburn thought so. But I do worry about the puma. The tracks have been in more evidence in the powdery white sands of the beach."

Glenda resumed her embroidery work, but now with trembling fingers. Read was near. She just knew that he would be on the ship. She was foolish to believe he had stolen the jewels, but yet. . .

"You needn't worry so much about the puma," Glenda murmured, having need of conversation to pull her anxious thoughts from that of Read. "My people don't even like the torches Rayburn has forced upon them to place beside their doors."

Snipping a piece of thread in two with small scissors, Christina eyed Glenda with wonder. "My word, Glenda," she said. "Everyone should be glad that Rayburn is being so cautious. Think of the children. A big cat like the one that's in this area could devour a small child in the blink of an eye." She visibly shuddered as she rethreaded her embroidery needle.

"I'm sure if one thinks about the puma and its size, it can be a bit terrifying," Glenda said, laughing a bit nervously. "Even I became a bit frightened, only moments ago while standing alone on the porch."

Christina's forefinger pushed her spectacles back

against her nose, then she resumed with her sewing. "And why wouldn't you become frightened?" she said softly. "Neither you nor I should leave the house until the puma is hunted down and killed."

"No," Glenda said quickly, alarm quite evident in her voice, causing Christina to lift her spectacles from her nose to stare wide-eyed toward her.

Glenda smiled a bit nervously and hurriedly added, "The puma shouldn't be killed. The mountain lion has a playful nature. When it doesn't shy away from man, it will appear to want to make friends. Legend says that a child may safely sleep in the open where the puma is the only wild animal around."

"But only legend says this," Christina argued. "I know. Some laborers told the same to Rayburn. But this is now. The present. The legend your people speak of is historical, though not verifiable. Rayburn is not ready to let such a tale cause him to become reckless where lives are concerned."

Glenda's full lips curved into a pout. "I hope the puma moves back into the jungle," she said sullenly. "I would hate to see such a beautiful creature killed."

"Why do you think the puma has wandered this far from the mountains?"

"Maybe it's a female. Maybe one of its cubs strayed and the mother has come searching."

Christina's face paled as she leaned forward a bit. "Do you mean there may be more than one. . . ?" she gasped.

Glenda sighed heavily. "Christina, please don't worry," she said. "You'll see. You'll realize just how foolish. . . ."

A loud wild scream tore through the air, causing

Glenda to stop in mid-sentence. She pricked her finger again as she tensed, listening, knowing that the puma was even closer than she had thought it to be.

"Was that the . . . Puma. . . ?" Christina said tensely.

"I believe so. . . ."

"It sounded so much like a woman screaming in pain. . . ."

"That is the way the puma cries," Glenda said, resuming her sewing. She was becoming a bit concerned herself now, wondering also why the puma would continue to linger near El Progresso. It truly wasn't their way. . . .

"Each day I have reasons to wish to be back in America," Christina grumbled as she positioned her spectacles on her nose once more. "I just wonder how long Rayburn will make me stay. . ."

Something grabbed at Glenda's heart. She moved her feet from beneath her and leaned forward. "Then you are thinking of going back to America. . . ?" she murmured, realizing that if Christina did leave El Progresso, then Glenda would have to return to her old way of life. Her gaze moved swiftly around her. She was used to luxury. She was used to the electric lights . . . the wind-blowing and ice-making machines . . . her clothes . . . her featherbed. Oh! If she lost these now, life could never be the same for her again!

"If I could return to America with the *Sea Wolf*'s return tomorrow, I would," Christina said in a near whisper. "I shouldn't have even come. I was wrong. It hasn't worked out. . . ."

Glenda could see a fresh glistening of tears in the corners of Christina's eyes. "What hasn't worked out?"

she questioned cautiously.

A blush turned Christina's face a blotchy red. She brushed a strand of hair away from her brow, laughing nervously. "Nothing," she said. "It's really no worry of yours. It's something I've got to settle in my own mind."

Glenda was surprised to find that Christina worried about anything. This American-born *señora* hadn't appeared to have wanted for anything in her life. And didn't Rayburn cater so to her. . . ? But . . . had he somehow forced her to board the *Sea Wolf* to travel to Honduras with him. . . ?"

"And are you ready to learn some more about embroidery?" Christina quickly blurted, trying to ease the tension in the air.

Glenda glanced toward the door, only wanting to see Read, and see a look of need in his eyes when he saw her. He was possibly her only answer to escape if Christina did forsake her. "He's got to come," she thought to herself.

She moved her feet beneath her again and breathed more easily as she placed her back against the cushion of the chair. "Yes," she murmured. "I'm always ready to learn. It fascinates me how these beautiful threads can make such pictures on cloth."

"Show me your petunia," Christina said, lifting her spectacles.

Glenda secured the needle in the cloth then handed the framed linen material to Christina. She waited, breathless, for words of appraisal, because she felt as though she was doing herself proud.

Christina turned the embroidery work in her hands. "Yes. You've learned quite fast," she said, smiling.

"You have made sure that the material being worked is kept taut and the tension of the stitches is even. Yes, I think your next piece should be more extravagant. Your pattern you choose to sketch onto the cloth could be of more than one object."

"You really think I'm ready?" Glenda said, clasping her hands anxiously onto her lap.

"Yes. You are. Quite," Christina said, handing the embroidery work back to Glenda.

Glenda held it before her eyes as she traced the lines of the Petunia. "I will sketch many orchids onto my next fabric," she said. "And then my next, I will sketch the sun setting into the Caribbean. Just think of the effects of the oranges into the blues."

"It sounds beautiful," Christina said. "But a bit too complicated for me. The art of decorating cloth with needlework is hard enough for me at times. I'm sure the art of transferring such a scene onto cloth by quill would be too difficult for me. I much prefer using the predrawn fabrics."

"I find it more a challenge to draw my own," Glenda said, lifting her chin a bit haughtily.

"I'm amazed at your art talents," Christina said. "Have you previously drawn on canvas?"

"Only while in school. We had a short course in art," Glenda said. Her eyes grew a bit wide. "Please tell me more about the different threads and fabrics. I want to learn it all."

Christina placed her embroidery work on the table next to her and lifted her spectacles from her nose and placed them on her lap. "Well, there is a linen-ground fabric from Russia that I on occasion have acquired from a New York supplier when in America," she said. "And I get my white linen threads imported from Scotland."

"Russia? Scotland?" Glenda sighed, placing her embroidery work aside. "It sounds so exciting."

Christina smiled warmly, then continued. "Sometimes I have worked with floss silks, glass beads, and even worked jewels onto a linen twill background. These I have left at my house in America."

"What variety of things have you sewn?"

"Fine bed linen, handkerchiefs with embroidered monograms and household linens. . . ."

"Have you ever embroidered on dresses or sewn beautiful colorful skirts. . . ?"

"A few blouses. Very few," Christina said. "No skirts or dresses. I don't prefer to start on such a large project. I like to make many smaller items. And silk is extremely expensive. I'd hate to begin embroidering on a silk dress, then have to remove some stitches that hadn't stayed taut enough. It could ruin a dress that quickly."

"I will one day hope to be brave enough to embroider on a silk dress," Glenda sighed. "The pattern will be quite detailed with threads of silver and gold. I'll fill in the pattern with shaded silk and outline it in gold. . . ."

"My word," Christina exclaimed. "You do have a vivid imagination. . . ."

A sudden single gunshot exploded and reverberated through the air, causing everything else to grow silent. Glenda's hands went to her throat as her breath seemed to catch there with one large swallow. She looked quickly toward Christina, who had jumped from her chair causing her spectacles to fall from her lap and to their glass to break into tiny, sparkling slivers across the hardwood floor.

"Rayburn," Christina gasped, rushing to the door. She opened it and fled to the veranda railing. She looked into the distance, seeing nothing but dark shadows of night and the reflections of the torches against the black velveteen backdrop of the sky.

Swallowing back her fear, Glenda rose from the chair and went to Christina's side. She clutched to Christina's bare arm. "What about Rayburn?" she asked in a strain. "What would Rayburn have to do with us just having heard gunfire?"

Christina's profile was languid. She reached her free hand to cover Glenda's that still clutched to her. "He holstered a gun to his waist this evening," she said weakly.

Glenda withdrew from Christina, as though the one who had just received a bullet into her flesh. "He . . . what. . . ?" she said. "Because of the puma?"

"Yes. Where we live in America, we don't have the need to fear four-legged wild animals," Christina said. "But here, we do. He wanted to protect himself. Fully."

Glenda moved to the veranda railing to cling to it, peering into the darkness. The night chatter of the animals was slowly resuming and she could hear movement close by in the brush. She tensed, feeling her pulsebeat racing. "Someone is coming," she whispered. She heard Christina gasp noisily.

"What if it's the puma?" Christina said, turning to move back to the safety of the house.

"Stop, Christina. Wait," Glenda encouraged, seeing brief flashes of skin in the brush, moving closer. "I believe it's Rayburn," she quickly added. "And . . . he's . . . not alone . . ." Her heartbeats raced when she caught sight of three men. And . . . one. . . ? Was . . . it . . . Read. . . ?

Trembling, Glenda swallowed hard. And when she finally was able to see the full height of each of the three men, she could recognize them. Her hands covered her mouth when she whispered their names . . . "Rayburn . . . Ramón . . . and it is . . . Read . . . ," she gasped, seeing how Read was being supported between Ramón and Rayburn. His arms were thrown across the men's shoulders, and his head was hanging, bouncing, as he continued to be dragged toward the veranda.

Frantically, feeling a light spinning of her head, Glenda rushed down the steps toward him. Then she caught herself. She wasn't even supposed to know Read. They hadn't yet been properly introduced. She put caution into her steps, but had to hold her trembling fingers behind her. When she moved next to Rayburn, she found it hard to not reach for Read, to caress his brow, to try to comfort him. . . .

"What happened. . . ?" she asked, fluttering her lashes nervously, trying, oh, so hard to remain calm, realizing that Read appeared to be unconscious. But yet . . . why. . . ? There was no evidence of struggle nor blood. His dark, tight breeches and long-sleeved, cotton shirt strained at the muscles as he continued to be dragged. . . .

"The puma," Ramón said. "The puma attacked him too fast."

Glenda glowered at Ramón, forever hating him. She wanted to ask him why he continued to be around. She couldn't understand why Rayburn hadn't been able to see his uglier side. But a man wouldn't see this about another man. "The puma?" she said, once again eyeing Read with a pounding heart. "It . . . attacked. . . ?" She looked closer, relieved to see no claw marks. . . .

"The puma," Rayburn said, panting hard with his continued struggles. "It finally showed itself. After the *Sea Wolf* docked and we three were moving through the brush, it jumped from a limb of a tree."

Glenda gasped, eyes wide. "What then? Is this man hurt badly?" She wanted so badly to speak his name, let its reality be a tender caress to her heart. . . .

"William deBaulieu appears to be unconscious," Rayburn growled. "The damn puma. It managed to knock me and William from our feet. I made it okay, but William here, well, his head cracked against a tree's trunk."

"The gunfire?" Glenda asked anxiously as she hurried ahead of them on the stairs, stepping backwards letting her eyes continue to devour Read and his continued silence.

"Ramón grabbed my gun from my holster and fired at the Puma," Rayburn said thickly. "I heard a thud of sorts. I think he may have hit it."

"You think?" Glenda said, stumbling a bit as she reached veranda level. "You don't know?" She placed her hands on her hips, facing Ramón, now speaking in Spanish. "You fool. You shot the puma? Don't you know that it probably wasn't even meaning to attack? The three of you moving through the brush probably frightened the animal. Don't you remember the legend? Pumas aren't known to attack man."

128

"To hell with the legend," Ramón spat. "I do not live in the past as my family does."

"Oh, Ramón," Glenda sighed disgustedly. "You only shot the puma to look macho to the Americans. You know that. One day, the fact that 'you' come first to 'you' will get you in much trouble."

Rayburn scowled at them both. "Will you two quit arguing and help me with the door?"

Christina stood ashen inside the sitting room, watching as they all moved on inside, toward the staircase. "Is he hurt badly?" she murmured.

"I hope only stunned," Rayburn replied. He spoke in Spanish to Ramón. "Come on. Let's get him upstairs to a bed."

Glenda followed along behind them, lifting her skirt with each step taken, wondering how she was going to be able to act a stranger around the man she had lost her heart to. She watched as Read was taken into a spare bedroom, next to her own. To think that he would be so close caused her heart to become thunderous inside her. But what if he . . . died. . . ? The thought sent her gut to twisting . . . slow and agonizing twists. . . .

When Read was taken into the bedroom and placed on the bed, Glenda inched into the room. "Is there anything I can do, Rayburn?" she asked softly, blushing a bit when Rayburn began to unbutton Read's shirt, exposing his dark tendrils of chest hair to her. She could remember so vividly curling her fingers through these hairs, causing something to stir inside her.

"Go and get a basin of water and a cloth," Rayburn mumbled. "I don't think I can ask Christina to tend to him. She's not the strongest when it comes to something like this."

Glenda's knees grew a bit rubbery, knowing it would be her duty to possibly nurse Read back to health. With eagerness, she left the room and couldn't seem to move fast enough. But when she had secured a full basin of water and a cloth, she returned to the room, gulping hard when she saw that Read's shoes and shirt had been removed, and that his breeches had been undone at the front.

"What do you want me to do?" she whispered shyly.

"I've examined his head," Rayburn said thickly, rolling his shirt sleeves down. "There is a lump. Just keep bathing his face. If he doesn't come to, I'll be damned scared. I knew that we should have insisted that a doctor be brought to this isolated jungle. Now maybe the company will believe me."

Glenda dropped to her knees beside the bed and began caressing Read's face with the dampened cloth in slow swirling motions. She watched the thickness of his dark lashes flutter a bit when she moved her hands close to them. But he still refused to open them. "But he will be all right?" she asked in a soft pleading.

"I think so," Rayburn grumbled, kneading his brow. "But if he's still ailing by the time we get the ship loaded, it will be myself who will have to return to New Orleans. Not him. I will be too afraid to move him. And I will have to see that the bananas are delivered safely. While in New Orleans, I will find a doctor who will be willing to return with me. Then if anything else happens, we will be prepared."

"Can I go with you, Rayburn, if you go?" Christina said suddenly from behind him.

He whirled on a heel, seeing that she had quietly entered the room. He winced when he saw the lingering unhappiness in the depth of her blue eyes. "You wish to return to New Orleans?" he said thickly. He went to her and framed her face in his hands. "Tell me I didn't hear right. Tell me. . . ."

Glenda turned her eyes to the couple. She was seeing a strain between them for the first time. There WAS something amiss. Embarrassed for them both, she turned her gaze from them, but couldn't help but hear their further comments, though low they uttered them. . . .

"I hate it here, Rayburn," Christina said. "If it wasn't for Glenda, I know I would go stark raving mad."

"But you do have Glenda. You have companionship. That should make things easier for you. Please say that you will try a bit longer. Please tell me. . . ."

"Are you saying that you refuse to let me return with you?" Christina said, her voice breaking.

"You cannot go under these circumstances," Rayburn argued. "Don't you see? The only reason I will be going, if I AM going, would be because William deBaulieu would not be able to make the trip. Someone has to take his place. And if he doesn't return, he will need someone here to take care of him. You must stay and keep this house open and running."

"Glenda is here. . . ."

"Christina, if you leave, so must Glenda," he argued more hotly. "Don't you see? She would have to return to her people. Would you do that to her?"

"She loves her people. . . ."

131

"But she also loves her new way of life."

"Rayburn, I am returning with you," Christina said firmly. "That is that. I will no longer be dictated to by you nor anyone. And as for William deBaulieu, Glenda can stay on here at our house long enough to take care of him for the length of time it is required. They do not need me here. I will be of no help."

"Christina, please reconsider. . . ."

"Rayburn, I even broke my eyeglasses this evening," she said. "I will need to be fitted for them again. I must return to New Orleans. Don't you see? I have more reasons than one to return."

"Yes. I know all the reasons," Rayburn grumbled. "You don't have to remind me of any of them."

"I wish to be told as soon as possible if you are going to take William deBaulieu's place on the ship," Christina said. "Please be kind enough to inform me in time so that I can pack my valuables . . ."

"God, Christina. . . ," Rayburn blurted.

Christina went to Glenda and placed a hand on Glenda's. "I'm sorry, Glenda," she murmured. "But I must do what I must do. Please understand."

Tears were splashing onto Glenda's cheeks, knowing that her beautiful way of existence was coming to such an abrupt end. But hadn't her mother needed her these past weeks anyway? Her mother's health seemed to be worsening. Each day. Maybe the American doctor that Rayburn spoke of could be the answer. She fluttered her lashes nervously as she looked into Christina's eyes. "Christina," she said softly. "I'm sorry that you couldn't be happy here in my beautiful country. I tried to help. But I guess there is something more that you are seeking in America . . . something you left behind. . . ."

Glenda now knew that it wasn't a some "thing" but a some "body." She had been able to tell by the words being spoken between man and wife. It was words of lost love. . .

"Then you do understand?" Christina said, bending to whisper into Glenda's face. "And you won't mind nursing this man until my husband returns with a doctor?"

"I do understand," Glenda replied, blinking back more tears. "And I won't mind nursing this man. But I will miss you and what we shared together. I will always remember it. Always. . . ."

"And me also," Christina said, then moved quickly from the room. Glenda could hear a trail of sobs move behind Christina. Glenda eyed Rayburn for an instant, seeing the torment in his eyes, then turned her gaze back to Read and touched his hand, feeling the warmth, the coarseness of his flesh, oh, so wanting it against her body, to ease her inner despair, to cause her sadness to flow from her mind, so that she would only remember him . . . and what he could do to her. . . .

"Ramón, come on," Rayburn said, guiding Ramón from the room. "Maybe we'd best go hunt for the puma. A wounded cat is worse than a live, healthy one."

Glenda had forgotten the presence of the man she hated. She turned her gaze to Ramón and glowered. "Yes, Ramón. Go and kill the beautiful animal with the beautiful eyes. Then see if those eyes haunt you in the middle of the night."

Ramón stomped from the room next to Rayburn,

leaving Glenda and Read alone. She rose and stood over Read, raking her eyes over his handsomeness. When one of his hands moved and grabbed hers, she let out a soft, startled scream. A slow smile began to play on his lips as his lashes fluttered fully open, revealing laughing, gray eyes staring amusedly back at her.

"Read?" she blurted. "How? I thought. . ."

His forefinger went to her lips. "Shh," he said, winking an eye mischievously. "Do you want everyone to know that I am indeed all right?"

Feeling the same warmth coursing through her veins that he had an art to cause, she fell to her knees beside him, clutching tightly to his hand. "You are only fooling, Read? You aren't that hurt after all?" she said softly.

"I had them fooled, didn't I?" he chuckled quietly.

Glenda felt stirrings of many feelings for him. The exquisite sense of building desire for his lips and touch . . . and the renewed sense of not trusting him. These feelings were battling inside her, confusing her even more about this beautiful American man. "You are one with skills of deceit," she snapped coolly. "I think you are even master of such art."

He laughed a bit hoarsely. "I think not," he whispered, tracing her facial features with a fore finger. "I think the mistress of deceit is right here beside me, with the greenest eyes I've ever had the honor of looking into."

She rose abruptly, placing her hands on her hips. "And what do you mean by that . . .?" she spouted angrily.

"I believe I remember a beautiful woman in black

velvet with a beautiful diamond necklace at her throat," he said, with an eyebrow lifted. "And this beautiful woman said that she was the daughter of Rayburn and Christina Taylor? Now wouldn't that deceit be even a bit more profound than the one I am performing on the Taylor's? What would they say if they were told?"

Glenda's face paled of color. Her hands went to her throat. "You wouldn't. . . ," she gasped.

Read laughed throatily, offering his outstretched arms to her. "No, *ma chérie*, I wouldn't," he said. "If you don't tell them that I have only a slight bump to my head, and that I am using that bump on my head to be able to stay a while longer on this island to get to be with you."

Glenda fell to her knees once more, trembling. "You are pretending to be hurt, only because of me?" she whispered. "The deceit is because of me?"

"I've tried to think of a way to get to spend more time with you, but couldn't come up with a thing," he said. "But thanks to that gorgeous cat, I now have a way. You do want me to stay, don't you? And . . . alone. . . ? It seems we will be alone. . . ."

Glenda remembered the stolen jewels. Her eyes lowered a bit. "You're not going to stay in this house for other reasons, are you, Read?" she whispered. "You do have to know that if Christina goes back to America, so will the rest of her jewels. . . ."

Read pushed himself up on one elbow, his brow furrowing. "What the hell do jewels have to do with anything?" he said darkly. "Or Christina? Why would you say such a thing, Glenda?"

Glenda swallowed hard, seeing the dismay in his

eyes. Was she truly wrong. . . ? Or was he practicing deceit to even more an extent. . . ? If he was still lying, he was quite skilled at doing such. "I'm sorry, Read," she murmured. "I don't know why I said such a thing."

"The only reason I'm not returning to my duties on the ship is because of you," he said. "And we must play the game to the hilt. We musn't let Christina or Rayburn see that I am all right. It could even cost me my job. But I guess you understand. Don't you?"

She reached her fingers to his weather-tanned face and stroked its smoothness. Then she ran her finger across the straight line of his nose. "I understand," she murmured. "I understand that we will have many days together before Rayburn will have a chance to return."

"You don't mind this little game I have chosen to play on the Taylors. . . ?"

"No. As you said, I played my own little games . . ."

"Together, we will play the ultimate of games. . . ." he whispered huskily, pulling her lips to his, crushing them with heated passion. "Tomorrow. We will be together tomorrow . . . and the next day . . . and the next. . . ."

The flames of desire were flickering inside Glenda. "Yes, tomorrow. . . ." she whispered, then scorched his lips with hers as she kissed him, while a sweet, enchanted ecstasy swept through her. She would forget the jewels . . . the Taylors . . . the puma. . . .

Chapter Seven

Watching the carriage moving on away from the house, Glenda stifled a sob. With Christina's return to America, it meant that Glenda's hopes for a different future for herself had dwindled to a nothingness. When Rayburn returned from America on the *Sea Wolf*, so would Glenda return to the Galvez house.

With a doubled fist to her mouth, she clamped her teeth down onto a curved finger and rushed back into the house. Through a hazy blur of tears, she saw someone moving toward her. She wiped at the tears, then fell, clinging, into Read's waiting arms.

"Is it truly as bad as all that?" he murmured, burrowing his nose into the depths of her hair.

"Yes," she sobbed. "I love living here. I grew to love Rayburn and Christina. And now I'll never even see Christina again. Yes. I'm so saddened."

"*Ma chérie*, I am here," Read said huskily. He nuzzled the softness of her neck.

Pulling gently free of him, she framed his face with her hands, gazing rapturously into his two pools of gray eyes. She could see so much. It was as though she was seeing into his inner soul. And at this moment, she could see passion unleashing, ready to be shared with her, only . . . her. . . .

"Yes, you are here," she whispered. She responded almost painfully as he brushed her hands aside to crush his lips to hers. His tongue entered the soft recesses of her mouth and as it explored, he caused a wildness to build inside Glenda. She fit her body into his, tremoring a bit when she could feel the hardness of his manhood pressing against her thin silk dress. She slid her arms gracefully around his neck and tangled her fingers into his dark locks of hair. But when he flinched a bit, she realized that she had touched the wound that had given him the excuse to stay behind with her.

"*Ma chérie*," he whispered as he pulled his lips free. "I could never love anyone but you." His fingers cleared a path for his further caresses from his warm, moist lips, unbuttoning her dress to pull her breasts free.

A dizziness swept through Glenda as he kissed the hollow of her throat, gently, oh, so gently and when his tongue and lips found a taut nipple of her breast, she flung her head back, moaning with sensuous pleasure. Her fingers dug into his neck, pulling him even closer. She had never felt so utterly wicked. She was letting this man wholly possess her once more and in the disguise of deceit. Oh! What would Christina think. . . ? What would Christina do . . . if she ever found out that the moment her back had turned, Glenda had been capable of such reckless behavior. . . ?

Her fingers brazenly moved to the front of Read and dropped to where the hardness had grown and touched him there. When he moaned, he pulled his lips from hers and gazed into her eyes. The color of his eyes had darkened a bit from the mounting passion needing to be released. His jaws had tightened and his face had become a bit flushed from the anxiety of the moment.

When he looked at her, he could see the face of innocence in the fluttering of her thick lashes and the slight part of her full, sensuous lips. He traced her face with a forefinger, feeling its velvet smoothness and the heat of her flesh. When she vividly tremored and leaned her face into his continuing caresses, closing her eyes languidly, he eased her up into his arms. He laughed a bit hoarsely when he spied her bare feet and the lack of undergarments as her dress hiked up to her thighs.

When she locked her right arm around his neck and rested her head on his shoulder, he leaned and with his teeth pulled the dress up to reveal the soft bush of her blonde pubic hair to his eyes. With a strain to his back, he lowered his head and kissed her at the base of the soft fluff of hair, smiling to himself when he heard a soft gurgle of sorts surface from somewhere inside her throat.

"Your lips are like magic," she murmured drunkenly. "Please? Take me to bed?"

"And you're sure, *ma chérie*?"

"*Señor*, I have waited . . . I have dreamed . . . for the moment I would be with you again," she sighed. "My insides are aching for you. You are guilty of inflicting such a sweet pain inside my body."

"Then the hours . . . the days . . . will be hours to share," Read said huskily. He took the stairs quickly and moved on into Glenda's room to place her on her bed. With deft fingers, he removed the rest of her clothing, then his own, then climbed on the bed and lowered himself over her. "I need you now, Glenda," he murmured. "I can wait no longer. You have enchanted me, *ma chérie*."

She laced her arms around him and began sliding her fingers up and down the smoothness of his back, circling and scratching gently as he entered her from below. "You're sure you feel like doing such a feat as this, señor?" she giggled teasingly.

He laughed gruffly. "You know better than that," he said, working gently in and out, straining his taut leg muscles, trembling.

She lifted her legs around him and arched her body upward, meeting his eager thrusts. "I do feel like the devil maybe has possessed me to do such a thing," she murmured, feeling the urgency building in warm splashes inside her. Her heart was beating with such a rapid pounding, she was finding it hard to breath. His mouth crushed against hers in raw passion, silencing even her thoughts. All that she was aware of was him . . . his muscles rippling next to her skin . . . his mouth exploring . . . his hands teasing . . . caressing . . .

His fingers entwined in the thickness of her hair as his breath began to come in short rasps and when he began moving even faster, groaning, she felt the strange wondrous feelings invade her senses, causing ecstasy to move through her in effervescent bubbles of delight.

When they both were spent and lay breathing hard next to one another, Glenda traced his body anew, never getting enough of him. "Read, I do love you so," she murmured. "Tell me you love me. Please? Over and over again?"

"*Ma chérie*, I love you . . . I love you . . . I love you . . . ," he whispered.

His teeth captured a nipple of her breast and his fingers stroked the satin of her flesh. Then he sat a bit upright with a trace of deviltry in his eyes.

"What is it, Read?" she murmured, pushing herself up to lean on one elbow.

"I have heard of the romantic ruins that have been found here in Honduras," he said quickly, looking a boy instead of a man who had just reached the ultimate of feelings with a woman. He wrapped his arms around his bent knees. "The Mayan ruins. There have been rumors of alters and monuments being found. How many days by horseback are these ruins?"

"Are you thinking of going there?" Glenda asked, feeling an ache circle her heart. She had thought their days and nights would be spent in this comfortable house . . . in the featherbed she had so grown to love. She now doubted that he had stayed behind only because of her. Was he an adventurer? Had he devised this time off from his duties to also go exploring? Disappointment surged through her.

"It could be a venture of romance," he said, reaching for her hand, kissing its palm gently. "We could have many delicious moments alone beneath the stars. I've always dreamed of such an adventure of seeing ancient ruins of some long ao civilization. And how much more exciting than to do it with the one you love?"

"The wet season has not yet passed us by," Glenda

argued, jerking her hand free from his. She moved to lie on her side, toying with the edge of her bed's sheet. "And the jungle. It is quite dense. I'm not even sure a horse could make such a trip. None of my people use horses. We use mules."

"A mule is much too slow. We don't have that much time, I'm sure," he said, moving from the bed, slipping into his breeches, then his shirt. "We have to be here when Rayburn returns. He can never suspect what we've done. Never."

"Don't you think someone will tell him?" Glenda pouted. She was thinking of Ramón. He was the type to spread such a rumor.

"And who would? The cook? She will be happy to not have anyone to cook for. She will have a long siesta while we're away. And she is much too shy, I'm sure, to spread such a tale to Rayburn Taylor."

"There is one more person you haven't thought about. . . ," she said sternly.

"And who might that be?"

"Rayburn's stable hand. Ramón. He has eyes in the back of his head."

"It was Ramón who was also in the carriage with Rayburn and Christina, wasn't it?" he said, going to the window, staring from it.

"Yes. . . ."

He swung around, grinning from ear to ear. "Then we must make haste before Ramón returns. We will go. Now. . . ."

Glenda moved quickly to an upright position. "Are you serious?" she said in a strained voice. "We have this house for almost a week, only to ourselves, and you wish to go into the thickness of the jungle to see some absurd old ruins?"

"Silly? I thought your people's heritage would mean more to you than that," he said, laughing hoarsely.

Glenda's eyes lowered, feeling shame rush through her. "I didn't mean that," she whispered. "It's just that. . . ."

He moved to her and pulled her from the bed and into his arms. "You didn't want to share me with the ruins," he said huskily. "Isn't that what you're trying to say. . . ?"

"Well . . . yes. . . ," she stammered, lifting her eyes to his, melting as he gazed rapturously down at her.

"We will make love on one of the altars. It will be our way of sacrificing ourselves to your gods," he said, brushing some hair away from her eyes.

"You are being sacrilegious," she gasped, then giggled a bit. "And the sacrifice? How could you call what we share a sacrifice? The gods will even blush. . . ."

"Then you are game? You will take this trip with me?"

"Yes. If you truly wish, Read," she said, sighing heavily. "But what if the rains come again in oceans? What if there is even a hurricane while we are in the midst of the jungle? And what if the wounded puma finds us and kills us, thinking we are the ones who wounded her?"

Read threw his hands into the air, laughing. "Too many questions," he said. "Let's just worry about each thing as it arrives. Now you go and tell the cook to prepare us a feast that will last for several days. Have her to be sure there is plenty to drink and I will gather together some bedding and make us some makeshift bedrolls."

143

"You had better take clothes to cover your entire flesh," Glenda warned, slipping into her dress.

"And why is that. . . ?"

"It's the mosquitos. They are as large as bats sometimes in the deeper recesses of the jungle," she said, laughing lightly. "When we return, we may be just one large mosquito bite."

"*Ma chérie!* Don't say that," Read shouted.

"And I will see to it that we have one bottle of *vino de coyol* to take with us. We will drink freely of it when we reach that altar that you have spoken of," she said.

"What the hell is *vino de coyol?*" Read said, scratching his head.

She giggled lightly. "It's a live wine obtained from the sap of the coyal palm. Rayburn has several bottles in his wine cabinet. He won't miss just one."

Read drew her roughly into his arms and jerked her body into his. "*Ma chérie*, you think of everything," he said. His mouth sought hers in a tenderness that sparked the fires anew inside Glenda. But she pushed him gently away, worrying about Ramón's return.

"We must hurry, Read," she said. "If you insist on such an adventure, we must make haste before Ramón returns. Once we are gone, he will be no wiser as to whether we are inside the house or not. He isn't allowed to enter the house. Christina has made Rayburn forbid it. Ramón's leering eyes frightened her. I guess she felt as though being raped when he looked her way."

His face darkened with shadows and traces of crinkles appeared in his flesh beside his mouth and eyes. "This Ramón," he growled. "Has he ever . . . uh

. . . touched you? When you speak his name, I sense a vehemence in your voice."

Beneath the imploring hold of his eyes, Glenda felt quickly unnerved. She didn't want Read to realize that another man's hands had even so much as grazed against her bare flesh. It was important to her that this man whom she loved as her mother did her father would believe that his touch had been the first. "No. He has not," she hissed. "Ramón is a poor excuse for a *caudillo*. He shoots innocent pumas. I would never let the *pollino* get near me."

Read threw his head back in a sudden fit of laughter. "I'd certainly not want to get on your hate list," he said. He grew serious, bending to pull his boots on. "So it was Ramón who shot the cat? I thought it was Rayburn. Rayburn was wearing a gun."

"Ramón grabbed the gun out of the holster. He wanted to appear macho by pretending to save you and Rayburn," Glenda hissed. "The puma would have hurt no one."

"You could've fooled me," Read said, wide-eyed.

"The puma wouldn't have," she said stubbornly. "But now it may. It is wounded. It is scared."

"You're sure it was shot?"

"Let's pray that it isn't."

"I'll be sure to take one of Rayburn's guns," Read said, going to the lone mirror in the room. He combed his hair with his fingers.

"And also a machete, Read," Glenda said.

Read swung around. "Why a machete?"

"Many hours on this trip will be spent in cutting a path through the jungle. . . ."

"The hell you say. . . ."

"There are no roads. And hardly even traces of paths," she answered, moving barefoot toward the door. She stopped and turned her eyes to him. "And, Read? I've never been on a horse."

"What. . . ?" he gasped, moving toward her.

"Only a mule," she said, eyes wavering. "Only on a mule."

"It's simple enough," he said, smiling warmly. He took both her hands and pressed his lips into each palm separately. Then his brow furrowed. "Rayburn does have spare horses, doesn't he?" he quickly added.

"He has four. One being used with the carriage and three others that await anxiously for Rayburn's attention."

"Then be on with you," Read said, turning her, patting her gently on her bottom. "Let's leave El Progresso. *Pronto*."

"*Sí, sí, señor*," Glenda said, giggling. She felt so lighthearted and gay. Tremors of excitement kept rippling through her. Hadn't she also longed to see the Mayan ruins? She had never dreamed that she would have the opportunity, and especially with the handsome American who had stolen her heart. Suddenly leaving the American's house was more exciting . . . than staying. . . .

The two horses, both black as panthers, moved inch by inch through the thickness of the brush. The flora that surrounded Glenda and Read provided a pageant of brilliance. The epiphytes, the air plants, were piled up in sodden masses upon the trees, crowding the leaves from tip to tip. The air plants grew open, but did not draw nourishment from other plants. They drew nourishment from the air instead of from the ground, letting their fleshy roots dangle in the moist air to extract the water from it.

There were vague and random flashes of blues and greens moving overhead, the colorful birds flying free spirited from tree to tree through the lush green foliage, and the ever present chatter of the monkeys at play filled the heavy thickness of the mid-afternoon's air.

Glenda clung to the horse's reins, slipping a bit on the horse's bare back as the horse and Glenda's perspiration mingled along Glenda's thighs. She blew a wisp of hair from her mouth, not daring to let loose from the reins long enough to secure her damp ringlets of hair back into the yellow ribbon tied around her head. The skirt she had chosen to wear and the high-necked blouse were wet with steamy perspiration and the soft shadows of the jungle were welcomed.

Urging her horse onward, not liking the distance Read kept making between her horse and his, Glenda spotted a *piñuela* tree. Its fruit, similar to a pineapple, would be a welcomed treat, to help quench her building thirst.

"Read. Wait," she shouted, then glanced quickly around her, hearing how her voice had sounded as though muffled. But she knew that it was because of the thorny trees and scrub brush, appearing as though they had tentacles, reaching for her, becoming an unwanted barrier between her and the man she loved.

Read reined his horse to a stop and turned to her. "*Ma chérie?* Are you having difficulties?" he asked. In the dim lighting, his eyes were only added shadows to the jungle.

"Let's have some nourishment before resuming our journey," she encouraged, smiling weakly.

"We don't want to eat our rations all in one day," he grumbled.

"We won't," she said. "We will fill our stomachs with the fresh fruit from the *piñuela* tree. Its sweet juices will give us energy to make our way into the jungle."

"*Nous devons* not linger too long," he said, climbing from his horse.

"What?" she murmured, lifting a brow quizzically. He rarely spoke in French and when he did, she had no way in which to interpret it.

He came to her and lifted his arms to her and helped her from the horse. "I said we musn't linger too long," he said. "We must find shelter for the night." He had seen a trail of blood up ahead, but hadn't wanted to frighten her. He now knew that they were on the puma's trail . . . a puma . . . that was indeed injured. He glanced quickly from side to side, then let his gaze scour quickly from tree to tree, checking for any movements besides that of birds and monkeys. He saw nothing and hadn't heard the puma's cry. Maybe it had found a place to die peacefully.

Glenda puffed a bit and lifted her skirt to fan her face with it. She eyed Read with a deep longing. Even with thick beads of perspiration lacing his brow and with a sweat-soaked shirt clinging to his massive chest, he was still attractive and even more virile. The straight line of his nose cut through the deep tan on either side of his face and his hair had curled a bit at the tips from the clinging, hanging humidity.

"With the mountains growing closer, maybe we can find shelter beneath a cliff's overhang," she said. She wiggled her toes in the tight confines of her shoes, hating them, though knowing they were quite necessary since having to move part way through the cut brush after Read had chopped it away. The stubs left standing, pushed their way upward, almost like sharp knives.

Read pulled a knife from his pocket and cut two *piñuela* fruits from its tree and handed one to Glenda. She sighed leisurely as she settled herself down beneath a broadleaf plant and snapped the fruit in two and began devouring its inner sweetness with her teeth and lips.

Read squatted beside her and picked at his fruit with his knife, as though carving a graceful piece of mahogany wood. His gaze moved on ahead, seeing a lagoon that had to be crossed. It was ringed with mangrove and palm trees. Suddenly a pair of strange looking animals moved cautiously toward the water's edge.

"Glenda, what sort of an animal is that?" he asked, pointing with the tip of his knife.

Glenda wiped her mouth with the back of her hand, swallowing her last bite of *piñuela* fruit. "That's a Honduran tapir," she laughed gently.

"It looks like a horse," Read murmured, lifting an eyebrow quizzically. "But yet, it has a small trunk. It looks even more like a cross between an elephant and a donkey."

"Sometimes it is called a 'mountain cow,'" Glenda

said, rising. "We are lucky."

He rose next to her, wiping the blade of his knife on the side of his breeches. "Why is that, *ma chérie?*" he asked.

"Because a Honduran tapir is rarely seen. We are among the very few who will ever be able to boast of such."

"If we venture on past, will they attack?"

"No. They will run from us. That's the main reason no one can ever see them. They're scared to death of humans."

"Then we must venture on," he said, loosening the buttons of his shirt. The tips of his chest hairs glistened with droplets of perspiration.

Glenda's fingers moved sensuously inside his shirt. She smiled coyly when his flesh rippled beneath her touch. "The *zancudo* will have fun on your bare skin," she purred. "And I'd like to reserve that for my own private pleasure."

"*Zancudo?*" he questioned, lifting an eyebrow. Then he chuckled. "Oh, mosquitos," he said. "At least they're better than bedbugs. Don't you think?"

"Anything is better than a bedbug crawling onto the flesh," she exclaimed, curling her nose. "Have you had problems with bedbugs in America?"

He guided her by the elbow to the horse and helped her onto it. He took Glenda's reins and urged the horse next to his own, then lifted a leg over and was ready to move bareback on through the scrub brush. "My first night in El Progresso?" he shouted across his shoulder.

"Yes. . . ?" Glenda replied, feeling herself slipping precariously sideways once again with each step taken by the horse.

"Well, after I met with Rayburn in the banana fields, I was directed to my dwelling for the night," he said, lifting his arm to protect his face as he moved beneath low hanging limbs of a dwarf palmetto tree. "At this small one-room house, I found it with no conveniences. It stank of mildew and there was only a bed and basin of water on a metal stand next to it. Rayburn had sent a woman with bedding. And as I began inspecting the mattress for bugs and found them, I became enraged and began cursing wildly." He laughed hoarsely, glancing over at Glenda.

"So? What then. . . ?" Glenda encouraged.

"When I kept shouting in English about the bedbugs, I forgot that this Honduran woman couldn't understand English and she flew from the house frightened to death."

"Why would she. . . ?"

"Because while I was cursing, I was pounding on the mattress. She had to think I was ordering her to bed. She thought I was commanding her to have sexual relations with me."

Glenda lifted her chin, laughing merrily. "Read, I shouldn't laugh," she said. "But it is so funny. I'm sure the woman thought you were a crazy American with only one thing on your mind."

His eyes began to twinkle as he reached to run his hand up the insides of her skirt. "Well? Is it true? Yes?" he chuckled.

Glenda giggled a bit, then noticed that their horses had moved into thicker brush, becoming an obstacle for their further approach.

"I guess I have to labor a bit and save pleasure for

later," Read grumbled. He jumped from the horse and removed his machete from its leather case. Stepping high, he began swinging the machete through the scrub brush, then tensed when he saw wet droplets of blood on the ground at his feet. His breath caught in his throat when he let his gaze move cautiously around him. The puma. It was near. The blood hadn't even had a chance to dry.

"What is it?" Glenda said, sensing danger.

"The cat. It has been here. And only a short time ago," Read said quietly.

"How do you know?" she said, tensing. She knew the dangers of a wounded puma. She wondered if Read truly did. She felt fingers of fear riding her own spine.

"Blood. I've found blood. I doubt if it's from any other animal," he said. He wiped his brow with the sleeve of his shirt. "I think it's moving toward the mountains."

"We are nearing the lower mountains," Glenda said cautiously. "I'm sure we will find them once we get through this worse brush."

"What about the cat?" Read said.

"It will reach them before us. We will just have to be cautious where we choose to make our camp for the night."

Read resumed his chopping of the weeds, then drew in a deep breath as he moved back atop his horse. "We could reach the ruins tomorrow, don't you think, Glenda?" he said, flicking his horse's reins. He was beginning to feel apprehensive about this venture. His head ached . . . his throat was dry . . . and the pests of bugs were all around his head, buzzing continuously. And then . . . there was that puma. . . .

"Yes. Tomorrow," Glenda said, then smiled widely as they moved more into a broadleaf forest of Spanish cedar, balsa and rosewood, realizing that this was the beginning of the valley that stretched out around the lower mountains, their destination for this night.

A drove of white-lipped peccary, with their big low-slung bodies, resembling hogs, moved ahead of Glenda and Read, thundering against the ground with their many hooves. Their bodies left a trail of a strong, offensive scent and their yellow-curved tusks, blunted at the tips, made them a sight of ferocity.

"What the . . . ?" Read gasped.

"Peccary," Glenda replied.

"They have to be the ugliest . . ."

Glenda laughed softly. "Yes. They are ugly. But when smothered in green palm leaves over a smoldering fire, they are exquisitely delicious."

"I imagine like a pig . . . ?"

"Yes. . . ."

A sudden clearing led to a slight slope of land leading upward to meet a thick forest of Spanish cedar clinging to the mountainside. Read reached for Glenda's reins and urged her horse to a stop. "Maybe we can camp here for the night," he said, gazing cautiously around him. "Surely the cat moved to higher ground."

"Once a fire is built, we will surely be safe," Glenda said in a near whisper.

"We have no choice but to stay here," Read said, caressing his brow. "I guess the blow to my head was more severe than I thought. I have a strong need to rest."

"Then all your pain wasn't pretense?" Glenda asked, eyeing him cautiously. All she needed was for him to lose consciousness out in the middle of nowhere and with a crazed cat possibly only a leap from a tree away.

Read shook his head, as though clearing cobwebs from inside it. "I did lose consciousness for a brief moment last night," he said thickly. "But only briefly. I thought I was okay."

Glenda noticed how pale he had suddenly become, causing his eyes to appear to be laced in white. She watched as he licked his lips. "We must hurry and make camp," she said. She dismounted and guided her horse beneath the shade of a mahogany tree and secured its reins, reaching for Read's when he moved to her side.

"I want you to just sit down and relax and let me get things ready for the night," she urged, kissing him gently on the lips as she leaned her body into his. She understood when he didn't reciprocate eagerly. She truly understood that he was in pain. It showed in the glassiness of his eyes.

Out of the corner of her eyes she could see the crimson sunset lowering quickly behind the distant higher mountains. She could smell the dampness of the vegetation around her and could hear the eagerness of the animals scampering through the brush, preparing for the velvet black skies of night.

Glenda became just as eager, feeling the need to beat the black shades of night being pulled around her. And in no time flat she had a fire flickering orange flames upward and the faint aroma of coffee heating and eggs spattering in a frying pan welcomed

154

her flaring nostrils. She arranged banana slices and squares of cheese on a ceramic dish and offered it to Read, who sat with gun loaded on his lap.

"It seems you've brought much from Christina's kitchen," Read chuckled, plopping a square of cheese between his teeth.

Glenda squirmed next to him, tucking her bare feet beneath her. "Are you feeling better?" she whispered, touching his brow gently with the back of her hand.

"It seems a few swallows of your *vino de coyol* was the cure," he chuckled. "And now for a cup of coffee for a chaser."

"Chaser?" Glenda queried. "Like a boy chases a girl?"

Read chuckled, circling his arm around her waist. "No, *ma chérie*," he said. "The chaser I am referring to is a mild drink taken after hard liquor to make it easier on one's insides."

"Oh, I see," she giggled, feeling bubbles of contentment bouncing through her.

A kinkajou whistled and played in the treetops, causing Read to tense a bit. "I think I hear the puma," he whispered. "They have such a soft whistle call when not crying aloud."

Glenda cuddled. "No. You hear the kinkajou, a small animal resembling your America's raccoon," she said, laughing lightly. "It has a round, catlike head. It whistles as it plays in the treetops at night. It is quite harmless. A kinkajou is even easily tamed to be a pet."

"I still don't feel as though I can relax tonight," he grumbled. "I can't forget the wet drops of blood on the trail. I may not even sleep the night."

"I shall stay awake with you, my love," Glenda

155

sighed. "Then tomorrow, we will make our sacrifice to the gods. . . ."

She lifted her face to the cooler breezes of night. She could hear the restlessness of the horses as they stomped nervously beneath the dark cover of the mahogany tree, and only the fear of the injured puma was now disturbing the tranquility of being with Read in such humble surroundings. It had been easy to brush thoughts of Christina from her mind. And now, as the worries of what would await her on her return from this adventure with Read kept trying to creep steathily into her brain, she had to force herself to forget that one day soon, this that she had found away from the Galvez house would only be a memory. . . .

She shivered as she reached for Read's hand.

"*Ma chérie*, are you cold?"

She blinked tears away as he tipped her chin with a forefinger, causing their gaze to meet and hold. "No," she murmured. "I am very happy. I love you so much."

"And I love you, *ma chérie*," he whispered, tangling her hair between his fingers as he eased her mouth to his. . . .

She melted into his embrace, letting his kisses absorb her tears. But nothing could ease the tearing of her heart. She knew that soon . . . she . . . would lose him. She didn't think he would be one who would come courting the daughter of a Honduran laborer. He had taken her while a part of the Taylor's American house. But once dressed in her skimpy, hand-made dresses and smelling of spices and perspiration, would he then want to be near her. . . ? Kiss her. . . ? Caress her. . . ?

156

Oh, she thought not. . . .

She let him lower her to the ground, both now mindless of everything but their bodies responding to each other's. . . .

She let her hands rest in the lap of
[illegible] of swirling but [illegible] [illegible]
[illegible]

Chapter Eight

As though crystal, water droplets glistened from the tree's limbs beneath the morning's soft rays. The greens were greener and the blues bluer as Glenda glanced first at the forest being left behind her, then upward at the crisp freshness of the morning sky. All was awakening around her, in evidence by the cawing of the birds and the screeching from the monkeys. The trees seemed alive, their leaves rustling and whispering as a damp breeze moved through them.

The crushed scrub brush path was being made more accessible for Glenda by Read's horse moving on ahead. Glenda clung to her horse's reins as the flutter of her skirt lifted around her legs. She was beginning a slow ache and cursed the horse beneath her breath. She would have much preferred a mule, though not as sleek and stately in comparison to this black stallion she had become acquainted with. But a mule was slower in its movements and stood not so tall from the ground, making Glenda feel less tense with the ground so much closer to her hanging feet.

Sighing resolutely, she let her gaze settle on Read and how tall he sat on his horse. Every movement of his body was fluid . . . graceful, though the muscles of his shoulders and legs flexed with each added step of the horse. His hair blew slightly in the breeze, lifting at his collar in heavy, dark waves. When he turned a bit and shot her a fast glance through the thickness of his lashes, Glenda felt the same familiar melting inside herself. She knew, as never before, that she could never love anyone else. She would remain true and pure for only Read. If possible, she would follow him to the ends of the earth. . . .

She smiled seductively toward him, squaring her shoulders, remembering the times she had dreamed of meeting such a man. Her dreams . . . they had come true. . . .

"*Ma chérie*, are you all right?" Read said from across his shoulder. "Your eyes. They appear a bit hazy."

"I'm all right," she said. "My thoughts. They had me carried away."

"I think we've left the cat somewhere behind us, don't you?"

Glenda shivered a bit, having heard the puma's weakened cries in the early hours of morning. She had envisioned her lying in the brush, licking her wound, possibly dying slowly . . . agonizingly. . . . "Yes. I'm sure," she murmured. She hated Ramón with a vengeance. She wanted to get revenge for the beautiful puma whose life was probably now snuffed out by the ignorance of this man who claimed to be *caudillo*. But a warning tremored through her, as she realized that Ramón was capable of going to any lengths to get what he wanted. And now that Christina was gone and Glenda would have to return to the Galvez house, would Ramón pursue her with even more ardor?

Glenda clucked to her horse and urged it on next to Read's. She smiled coyly at him, once again thinking that he was her answer . . . for many things. And if he loved her as he professed, he was her means to bettering herself . . . to even . . . travel to America. . . .

Read smiled back at her with approval in his roguish gray eyes as his gaze raked over her. She hadn't bothered to button her blouse, and as the breeze entered and lifted the cotton material as though ballons being blown up, the full profiles of her breasts were revealed to him. With each movement of the horse, the breasts bounced in unison, and where the brown of her nipples met the pink satin of her flesh, the contrast in both shape and color caused the heat to rise in Read's loins.

He purposely averted his gaze upward. As the sun's rays danced and played on her full figure in golden streamers, she seemed as though phosphorescent . . . possibly still glowing from their shared moments of ecstasy at early morning's sunrise. As the skies had been filled with splashes of radiant oranges, so had their touches created such a colorful splash inside themselves. But only Read knew that it would soon have to come to an end. He would have to return to New Orleans on the *Sea Wolf*'s next voyage. Could he even say goodbye to Glenda? He was beginning to think not.

Glenda flushed a bit under his steady gaze. She forced herself to look away from him and look into the distance, knowing that they were indeed drawing closer to the Mayan ruins. She had listened intently to Bay Islanders speaking of their adventures of seeking out these ruins. In her mind, she had stored all their information . . . the directions in which to travel through the jungle . . . the hours it would take . . . and the shape of the lower mountains that swept across the valley as one would realize they were only heartbeats away from this earlier civilization's temples and statues. . . .

In a lower valley some miles away, Glenda could see the nestling of a village of straw-thatched huts. Long processions of large-straw-hatted men were trudging down the mountainside, leading strings of stubby mules laden with chickens, fruits and vegetables, on their way to the city market.

She was reminded of Bay Island and how her father had arisen at three most mornings to shoulder a yoke or hitch up his mule from which, on braided grass rings, had hung live chickens, straw hats and fresh vegetables, to sell at the market.

Glenda could remember how her mother, when younger, would pack forty or fifty pounds of papayas, wild avocados, berries and mangoes in a broad basket balanced upon her head.

When her mother hadn't been offering her vegetables to the market, she had been scrubbing clothes in a stream that passed through the heart of the city, or had been baking tortillas on a simple, outdoor, wood-burning stove.

Glenda's insides did a slow roll. She could envision such a future for herself if Read didn't truly rescue her from such an undesirable way of life. What if she were forced to wed someone like Ramón? The thought of his lips traveling across her body set her insides to feel as cold as the crystal cubes Christina had placed in the

161

tea from the ice-making machine.

"Tell me about your city of New Orleans," she quickly blurted. "Is it as beautiful as our own capital city of Tegucigalpa is known to be?"

Read chuckled amusedly. "I've never been to your city of Tegucigalpa," he said. He wiped his brow with the palm of his right hand, feeling the intensity of the sun's heat as it moved higher in the sky. The air was now shimmering beneath the harshness of the sun. . . .

"Tegucigalpa is supposed to have brilliant patchwork quilt patterns of pastel houses, perched on narrow, winding streets that flow and dip into old, little unexpected plazas at every turn," she said, eyes wide. "One can see traces of all the various peoples who have mingled over the centuries. They say no two faces are alike in coloration or features."

"Sounds interesting," Read said, clucking to his horse.

"Now tell me about your city in America," Glenda said eagerly.

"My city? New Orleans, *ma chérie*, ah, *marveilleuse. C'est magnifique*," he said, kissing the fingertips of his right hand. "If one hasn't been to New Orleans, one hasn't lived."

"Tell me. Hurry," Glenda exclaimed, clutching more tightly to her horse's reins.

"It is the 'Paris of America'," he murmured. "Because of the charm of its French quarter. It's a romantic city, a very important seaport."

"Tell me about the houses," Glenda said even more anxiously. "Are they as grand as the mansion I have been working in as personal maid to Christina?"

Read threw his head back with loud laughter. "Mansion?" he raved. He shot her a glance of sheer amusement. "*Ma chérie*, that is no mansion. Mansions are two- and three-storied houses made of stone or brick with charming balconies and with lacy iron grillwork decorating their fronts. There are paved patios, lovely gardens where flowers and greenery are in profusion and even some splashing fountains. . . ."

A long, drawn-out sigh from Glenda caused Read's words to cease to flow from his mouth. He now realized what he had just done. Painted such a colorful portrait of New Orleans before the green of her eyes that she couldn't help but have an inner longing to see it. Ah, one day she would see it!

"Such a city cannot be," Glenda said. Her heart pounded rapidly when she reached for Read's hand. "Read, you must take me. . . ." But her words were lost from his ears as he began shouting. . . .

"*C'est magnifique*," he shouted again, urging his horse to a fast gallop. "We are here, Glenda. Just look at it."

Glenda held back a bit, her excitement overshadowed by his lack of concern over the words she had been speaking to him. But she straightened her back and set her jaws firmly. If he didn't want her, she wouldn't let him realize just how much she had wanted him. Anyway, hadn't the magic of his touch . . . his words . . . caused her to forget the deceitful side to his nature? Didn't she still believe him to be a thief. . . ? Hadn't he even perpetrated such a scheme as to stay behind while Rayburn took his place on the *Sea Wolf*? Maybe she shouldn't even love him. . . ? Maybe he would deceive her even . . . over and over

163

again. . . .

She urged her horse onward, then dismounted and tied its reins next to where Read had left his horse.

Slipping on loose rock, Glenda lifted her skirt and moved to Read's side. She tensed when his arm circled her waist. She gave him a quick glance and began her usual slow melting when the excitement showed in the glimmer of his eyes and the soft curve of his lips. Oh! She could never hate him. He was a thief! Hadn't he stolen her heart? It was nonreturnable, it seemed. . . .

"This long-forgotten city until discovered once again in 1839 is called Copán," she said, moving her body next to his, leaning. "It was perhaps the greatest religious city the Maya ever built."

"It is a city built of stone," Read said, letting his gaze travel around him, seeing lengthening shadows of many tall, stone structures on all sides of him, all lavishly decorated with paintings and sculptures etched into the stone walls.

All about them also stood tall columns, called stelae, carved with intricate pictures and the dates of each of their erections. The pictures carved were those of faces and figures of animals, reptiles and people.

"And look at the pyramid," Read exclaimed, pointing. "I read about it. It is Copán's crowning glory, it seems." He held onto Glenda's hand as they worked their way through crushed stone and stray, growing wild ferns and thick, lush creepers that had managed to grow through the debris. Tendrils of ivy were weaving and coiling, having attached themselves to the tallest columns, as though reaching to the sky, in search of moisture that seemed to be only lacking in this hollowed out, devastated strip of land. As the wind whipped around the decaying stone, there seemed to be a mournful whisper, causing goosebumps to rise on Glenda's flesh.

An iguana rushing by at her feet caused her to gasp and cling more tightly to Read's arm.

"*Ma chérie*, relax," Read laughed. He watched the swooshing of the iguana's tail as it moved behind a column only footsteps away. "There are worse animals than that in the jungle. I'm sure many watched you with wide, watchful eyes through the night when you were dozing."

"Hush, Read," Glenda shivered. "We have another night to spend beneath the stars."

"If we climbed the steps to the pyramid, we would be out of reach of all animals," Read teased, stopping at the base of the pyramid, tilting his head, gazing upward. Each side of the pyramid offered sixty-two steps with carved picture symbols. These stairs were known as the Hieroglyphics Stairs, containing the longest Mayan inscription known. At the top of the stairs, ninety feet high, a temple built on the pyramid's flat upper surface overlooked the city.

"No," Glenda sighed. "I don't believe my legs would carry me to such heights as that." She giggled as he nuzzled her neck. "But we could go in search of that altar we spoke of."

"*Ma chérie*, you are quite wicked," he said huskily. He pulled her next to him as they followed the shadows of the pyramid, to find that in its longest shadow stood many smaller replicas, with each having its own temples at the top.

"What caused the downfall of the Mayan civilization?" Read asked, kicking at a rock.

"No one knows," Glenda replied. "No evidence points to disease, disaster or weather, or revolution of the common people as is so often now in our country of Honduras. Now it seems with the blink of an eye we will have a different president."

"The American Fruit Company has worried about such revolutions," Read grumbled. "Is your government pretty stable now?"

Glenda flipped her hair angrily. "Hah! No one can say. But my guess is it's time for a change. President Bonilla has been lucky to have been in power for so long," she said sarcastically.

"Bonilla is eager to work with the *Sea Wolf*'s captain and the El Progresso plantation. I'd hate to see him replaced."

"I only wish that my brothers don't ever have to fight," Glenda murmured. "I'd hate to see them drawn into any revolution, no matter the cause being fought for."

They moved, clinging, on through the rubble of monuments and the style of hieroglyphic writing inscribed on them that no one had yet been able to completely decipher. Then they found what appeared to be a long, narrow ball court surrounded by stadium-type seats where some type of ceremonial team game had been possibly played.

"Glad you came, Glenda?" Read whispered, nuzzling again.

How could she tell him how she dreaded leaving? To return to El Progresso would be to return to her old way of life . . . to say a possible final goodbye to Read. . . .

"Very," she replied softly.

"And I believe I see an altar, *ma chérie*," he whispered, kissing her softly on her lifted hand.

Glenda's heart raced as her gaze traveled around her and found the slab of stone at the base of yet another smaller pyramid. On each end, stone figures of bald, wide-snouted, short, fat men were squatting with knees bent and arms outstretched toward the slab of stone. Their stomachs protruded over a brief loin cloth and their bare breasts had been carved to appear well rounded and full of milk.

The legs of the altar had been carved in the shape of grotesque, large hawk claws, and hieroglyphic writings had been inscribed deeply at the altar's sides.

"Do you think there were many sacrifices made to the gods?" Glenda whispered, even thinking to see a faint cast of red to the flat top of the stone.

"I'm sure not the sort you and I have spoken of sharing," Read laughed hoarsely. Feeling that they were indeed alone in this city of stone, sun, and wind's whispers, he placed his hands at Glenda's waist and lifted her onto the altar. Though his head was beginning a slow ache once again, the other ache in his body was going to take precedence.

Though consumed by heartbeats, Glenda glanced quickly around her. "Read, what if someone. . . ?" she murmured softly. Her breath caught in her throat when she realized that her breasts had already been bared to him and he was bending, flicking his tongue from nipple to nipple. She closed her eyes, sighing, as she threw her head back with rapturous desire. Her hair hung long and loose down the satin flesh of her back, more golden as the sun beat down upon it.

She reached her hands around Read's neck and

drew him even closer, then lowered her back to the altar and welcomed Read's hardness atop her. As his hands explored and lifted her skirt, Glenda tensed a bit when she heard a near crushing sound of rock. When her eyes flew suddenly open, Read's mouth covered hers, muffling a scream that rose from her throat when she saw two bare-chested, bronze-skinned Indians moving quickly toward the altar. One yanked Read from atop Glenda, while the other stood, glaring downward at her.

Feeling the quick jerk of Read's body move from hers and hearing his loud shouts of obscenities, Glenda covered her mouth with her hands, watching in stark, silent fear. The one Indian, with his sleek black hair pulled back in a long braid down his back and the prominent cheekbones almost swallowing the dark coals of his eyes, held Read's hands locked behind him, while the other continued to eye Glenda hungrily as he moved around her with his rifle pointed toward her, his finger poised on the trigger.

Glenda tried to cover her breasts with her crossed arms, glancing quickly toward Read, aching for him, wondering what his next move might be. His eyes showed the intensity of his anger and the set of his jaw showed the determination he was feeling to set himself free.

"You goddamned bastards. You'd better not touch Glenda," he sneered. "If you know what's good for you. . . ."

The Indian who was moving stealthily around Glenda stopped and spat onto Read's face and uttered some crude, low guttural words that were unidentifiable to Glenda. Then instinct told her to now fear even more for herself than for Read at this moment. The Indians looked as though crazed in the wildness of their eyes and they had red paint streaked across their leather-tanned brows and chins. They wore fringe-trimmed deerskin breeches and moccasins, but their bare chests, rippling in muscles, were the focus of Glenda's attention. In the nipples of each breast, gold rings had been screwed through and were hanging, swaying on the one as he kept bending, eyeing her more closely with his each turn of the altar.

"Please leave," Glenda suddenly blurted. "Read. Please . . . do . . . something. . . ."

"Glenda . . . I . . ." he said, wrestling, straining at his wrists. His eyes darted angrily around him. He knew that the Indians would make a wrong move. And when they did, he would be ready to make his move. But he began to grow cold inside when he realized what the one Indian had on his mind. God. He was going to rape Glenda. He began wrestling even more furiously, only causing the Indian's grip to tighten. He now knew that the only thing to do was to wait until this Indian's sure weakness would show through . . . when . . . the other one was beginning to have fun on the altar. He knew that it was only human nature to be envious. The Indian would surely wonder why the other Indian would have first chance with this beautiful white woman . . . and would . . . loosen his grip while forgetting the white . . . man. . . .

Glenda began to inch to the edge of the altar, wishing to reach Read's holstered gun. But when the one Indian grunted further unintelligible language to her, and nudged her with the barrel of his rifle, she tensed and moved back to where he had originally found her.

Wide-eyed, she watched as he removed long strings of leather from his front breeches pocket. And when he placed his rifle on the altar, Glenda jumped quickly to the ground and moved to Read's side, reaching for him, but not quickly enough. She screamed as the Indian gave a hard yank to her hair, forcing her to stand beside him. She then let tears splash from her eyes as he roughly pushed her back onto the altar, all the while grumbling unintelligibly in her face.

With quick movements, the Indian stripped her of her clothing and forced her to lie with arms and legs outstretched atop the altar. If she would try to move, he would smack her roughly with the back of the hand, making her entire body feel suddenly inflamed.

Sobbing frantically, she watched as he began tying each of her ankles to the altar, then her wrists. She struggled and pulled, but to no avail, and when she saw him remove his large, throbbing manhood from the tight confines of his breeches, she cried out, hearing her voice echo in hundreds of voices on all sides of her.

"Let me go. Please don't," she screamed, doubling her fists. The leather ate into her flesh, burning, cutting. "Read, oh, Read. Please," she cried, tossing her head from side to side, feeling her nervous perspiration wetting her hair to wet, golden strands. "Read. Please save me," she cried more weakly, becoming breathless from the struggles as the Indian began to lower himself over her.

His mouth had found her breasts and his teeth were

biting her nipples to an erect hardness. And his hot breath traveling over her as his lips exploring caused Glenda's breath to catch in her throat. She strained even harder to move her body from his touches. "No!" she shouted. And when his lips moved to hers and he let his wet, hot tongue make entrance into her mouth, she swallowed back her fear and clamped down with her teeth, feeling a sudden taste of salty blood move down the back of her throat.

Gasping, she heard his loud howl of pain and watched as he pulled quickly away from her and jumped from the altar dancing around, groaning as his hands covered his blood-filled mouth, where from it a tongue hung limply, bitten in two.

The sight sickened Glenda so, she felt a bitterness rising into her throat. She swallowed and swallowed, still tasting his blood, then out of the corner of her eyes, with tears almost blinding her, she saw a streak of movement . . . heard the thunderous explosion from a gun . . . and listened to the instantaneous throaty gurgle of a man's last breaths on this earth.

"Read!" Glenda screamed, over and over again. "No. It can't be you that's been shot." When soft hands caught the thrashing of her head and held her gently still, she knew that it was an Indian who lay stilled for eternity.

Glenda wiped her eyes free of tears and looked around her and saw both Indians sprawled across the ground. She hadn't heard the thud of the gun's butt against the one Indian's skull. Read had succeeded at defeating them both!

"The Indians must have made their home in one of these ruins," Read crooned, holding her to him as he bent on bended knees over her.

"It was so horrible, Read," she cried.

"I'll get you free. Quickly. I'm sorry it took so long, *ma chérie*," he said softly. "But I had to wait for the right moment. I'm damn sorry you had to even be touched by that savage. But now, we must hurry and put this behind us. Where there's two Indians, there's surely more."

"The gunshot. It was surely heard. . . ."

"Yes, *ma chérie*," Read said, glancing frantically around him as his fingers worked with the leather.

"Oh, Read, are you all right?"

"Yes. I'm lucky spittle is all I received from those savages," he chuckled. "I'm surprised they didn't shoot me. Right away."

Glenda moved quickly from the altar, rubbing her throbbing wrists. She could see where the leather had cut into her flesh. Then once more she glanced downward and shuddered when she saw the Indians' lifeless forms. Then her gaze settled on the Indian who had been in the process of raping her. He had come . . . so . . . close. . . .

Sobbing, she gathered up her clothes and hurriedly pulled them on, then leaned into Read's embrace, feeling drained, as they moved together, nimble-footed, toward the waiting horses.

"We're lucky the damn savages didn't steal our horses first," Read grumbled, helping lift Glenda onto hers.

"We're lucky to be alive," Glenda murmured, watching him throw his leg across the horse's back.

His eyes grew shadowy. "You are all right, aren't you, *ma chérie?*" he asked huskily. "The Indian. Did

172

he. . . ?"

Glenda averted her gaze from him, lowering her lashes almost shamefully. "No. I am all right. . . ," she said disdainfully.

"I needed to know if he hurt you in any way. Are you truly capable of traveling by horseback away from here?"

"Yes," she said. Then her eyes lifted. Her gaze traveled over him. "And you? Are you?"

"I am fine, *ma chérie*," he murmured. Then he lifted the horse's reins. "But we neither one will be unless we travel away from this place. We must get into the thickness of the jungle quickly. We must lose ourselves there so we can't be found by friends of these Indian savages."

Glenda's gaze moved to the sky. The sun had lowered a bit beneath the unraveling mountains in the distance. "It will be dark before we can even blink an eye, Read," she said, worrying aloud. "I hate another night in the density of a jungle. It's even darker there."

"Come. Follow me," Read said. He shouted to the horse and thrust his knees into each of its sides.

Sighing wearily, Glenda did as she was bade, suddenly feeling dirty all over. She reached up and wiped at her mouth, still tasting the Indian on her and knew that she had to find a lagoon to bathe in before letting Read near her again. She couldn't let him taste the savage's blood . . . sweat . . . or . . . She forced her mind to blank out the worst of her thoughts. . . .

Watching on all sides of her, Glenda followed for what seemed miles upon miles until Read led the way into the fresh greenery of a palm and oak forest.

Glenda could smell the damp pungence of the air and feel the moisture that had been kept sheltered by the low limbs of the trees. She inched her way along now, bending when Read would bend, when low limbs would threaten to knock them from their horses, and when a soft blue of water came into view, Read shouted with glee.

"We've found ourselves a spot to camp for the night," he said, jumping from the horse, securing its reins on a lower limb of an oak. He moved to Glenda and helped her dismount and then walked her to the water's edge, where they could see their reflections looking back at them from the clear, rippling pools of blue. Freshwater fish were swirling to the top and a turtle swam slowly by, revealing only the shine of its shell and the curve of its head above the lacy edges of the water where green moss met wavy splashes.

"It is quite peaceful here, Read," Glenda sighed, letting her shoulders droop wearily. Then she glanced quickly around her. "Do you truly feel we will be safe here?" she murmured.

Read swatted at mosquitos, cursing beneath his breath. "The only enemy here that I can see and feel is these damn mosquitos," he grumbled.

"You think the Indians won't follow?"

"I'm sure if there are any more like the savages we left to rot beneath the rays of the sun, they stay pretty close to the Mayan ruins. We're lucky the whole damn bunch didn't jump out on us while we were there pondering our fate."

Glenda shivered a bit. "I'd sure like a fire to warm myself with after my bath," she sighed heavily.

"You're going to bathe?" Read said, eyes wide, then

glanced toward the water, seeing just how tempting it was. He lifted his brows with anticipation, thinking of Glenda's flesh next to his beneath the safe cover of the water.

"Yes," she said, lowering her lips in a heavy pout. "The Indian. I must wash him from my skin. I do feel so filthy."

Read hugged her to him, burying his nose into the depths of her hair. "I'm so sorry, *ma chérie*," he murmured thickly. "I should have protected you more than I did. But I didn't think there was anyone within yelling range from where you and I were."

Glenda's hands reached his neck and caressed him there. "Read, it is not your fault," she purred. "Please. Don't fret so about it. I am all right. You are all right. That is all that matters now. Now, will you please build a fire while I undress?"

Read pushed her gently from him and held her at arm's length. "We can't have a fire tonight," he said softly. "The stars and moon will have to be our light. You see, a fire's smoke is a sure way for an Indian savage to track us."

Glenda swallowed hard. "I didn't think . . ."

Read kissed her gently on the tip of the nose. "And if you are worrying about being cold after climbing from the water, don't. I will be there to warm you. Have no fear about that."

Giggling, Glenda reached and began to unbutton his shirt, then lowered her fingers to his breeches and had them quickly unsecured. "Then what are we waiting for?" she said, laughingly jerking his shirt away from his shoulders and down the full length of his arms.

175

"You wench," Read growled, stepping from his boots, then his pants. "I'll show you who's boss here." He grabbed her by the wrist and playfully yanked her to him and smothered her with kisses all the while his hands were busy at disrobing her until she stood nude next to the throbbing hardness of his manhood.

"Read, what if. . . ?" she gulped, remembering the last time she had worried . . . to find that she had true reason to be. . . .

"We're safe. The forest is our cover," Read said thickly, lifting her into his arms, stepping into the water's edge, then moving deeper . . . deeper . . . until he was standing with only his head visible and hers also, while she continued to cling around his neck. She suddenly felt feverish with desire as one of his hands moved to cup a breast, then moved on downward between the deep vee of her softness. She tensed a bit, remembering the Indian . . . but then relaxed, sighing heavily as he devoured her with his lips, causing many splashes of color to move through her brain. She moaned with enchanted ecstasy as his fingers began moving inside her, drawing her legs apart, probing, tickling. . . .

Then giggling, she pulled herself free from him and began swimming to the deeper part of the lagoon, watching breathlessly as he suddenly disappeared beneath the water's surface. Though the water was a clear, crystal blue, she couldn't see him. She began to swim in slow circles, eyes wide, then gulped deeply as he pulled her beneath the surface of the water and pressed his body against hers as he pulled her along with him as he swam. She clung, soaring with wild, sensuous pleasure as his hands began to explore and caress once again, moving easier now as the water moved against them.

When his teeth caught the nipple of a breast and chewed, she felt as though she might explode with building, consuming needs. And as he pushed her above the water along with him, they both panted for air, then dove beneath the water once again and joined their bodies, clinging, and as he began to move inside her, she strained her hips to him, responding with complete wantonness . . . sheer joy . . . moving with him as their heads surfaced just as both their passions were spent in blazing, fiery passion. . . .

"Oh, God," Glenda murmured, never feeling so alive than at this moment. "Oh, how I love you. Read, how can I ever stand you leaving me? You are my life. You are my existence. . . ."

His lips sealed hers with ferocity. With a moan of ecstasy, she felt tears forming at the corners of her eyes and returned his kiss, while his fingers were eagerly exploring over her once again. "*Ma chérie*," he whispered, drawing his lips away momentarily. "I also love you. You are *magnifique*. Ah, so beautiful. So desirous. . . ."

He lifted her into his arms and carried her from the water as her head rested leisurely on his shoulder. Once securely on land, he reached for an orchid whose plant had attached itself to the bark of a tree, with its roots dangling wildly into the air. Its white flower was opened and looked almost like a butterfly. He offered it to Glenda and watched as she placed it in her hair above her ear.

"You have just given me the Holy Ghost flower," she whispered, touching his lips with her forefinger, tracing the perfect shape of his mouth.

"Why do you call this orchid a Holy Ghost flower?" he queried, trembling beneath her touch.

"The early Spaniards found one of the first orchids," she said, smiling sweetly. "They thought it looked like the Holy Dove which flew down at the baptism of Christ. They then named it the Holy Ghost flower."

"It's as beautiful as you are," Read said huskily, kissing her again, imprisoning her against him. His mouth forced hers open and his tongue became as a snake, coiling, striking, causing hot, fiery desire to shoot through her anew. Then her eyes flew widely open when she heard movement in the brush. She tensed when she heard some crushing of dried twigs close to her. She pushed at Read, mumbling.

"What the hell. . . ?" he blurted, drawing away from her.

"Read, I heard a noise," she whispered tensely.

He laughed nervously. "You are imagining things," he said, reaching his fingers to entwine in her hair, drawing her mouth to his once again. But she shook her head fearfully.

"I know I heard something," she said. "Read, please check it out. I don't think I could bear anymore surprises this day. Or this night. If someone is lurking near, you must find out. Now."

"All right," he grumbled, placing her gently on the ground. "And I guess that means get my clothes on?" he said further, eyeing her with a raised eyebrow.

"Yes. And me also," she said, looking cautiously from side to side. She had her clothes on in a flash and watched as Read stepped into his breeches and then his boots. She clasped her hands nervously in front of her as she watched him move cautiously through the brush, moving scrub brush and thick palmetto leaves aside. Then his gasp threw caution into the wind, causing a sense of panic to rise inside Glenda. She covered her mouth, frozen to the spot.

Read motioned with the wave of a hand. "Glenda, come here," he said hoarsely. "I think we've . . . found . . . our cat. . . ."

Glenda's heart raced. "The puma?" she gasped. "Is it alive, Read?" she asked anxiously, running to Read's side. Then her heartbeats faltered as she caught sight of the huge, lovely puma lying on its side, dead. Its long, slender body of fawn gray hairs, tipped with reddish browns and grays were matted with dried blood, as were its white throat and long legs. Covering the opened wound on its abdomen was an assortment of insects devouring its flesh.

Glenda turned her head aside, feeling as though she might retch. She covered her mouth with her hands.

"It's been dead only a short while," Read said, stooping, touching the puma between the base of its ears. "It's still warm."

Hope rose in Glenda. "Maybe it's still alive," she said, shooting Read a look of pleading. "Check to see if there's a heartbeat. Maybe we can do something."

Dark shadows crossed Read's face as he rose to go to Glenda. He gently took her wrists. "*Ma chérie*, the cat is dead, don't . . ."

"But we heard movement in the brush," Glenda said, eyes wide.

"The cat didn't make the movement," he said quickly. "Believe me. It's been dead longer than that. . . ."

Feeling renewed fear rising inside her, Glenda's gaze traveled around her. "Then . . . what. . . ?" she barely whispered.

A noise beside them drew them both around with a start. And as the brush separated, they both gasped in unison. . . .

"Why it's . . . it's . . . a puma cub," Glenda whispered. She glanced from the dead puma back to the cub, suddenly knowing. Ramón had, indeed, shot himself a female puma . . . the parent of this tiny, lone cub.

Glenda fell to her knees with her arms outstretched. "Come here, sweetie," she cooed. "I won't hurt you." She smiled softly when the cub raised a furry paw and swung it in her direction and let out a low, raspy hiss, trying to act as ferocious as possible.

The cub was quite small, perhaps two months old, only a bit larger than a full-grown alley cat. It was of a lighter brown than that of its dead parent, with large, brownish-black spots on the body, and dark rings on its short tail.

Read moved slowly toward the cub. "So this is what was stirring in the brush," he said quietly. He bent to lift the cub but fell backward onto the ground when the cub bounded on past him and went to its mother and began licking her face in slow, even strokes.

Glenda wanted to laugh at Read's awkwardness but was too saddened by the sight of a dead mother beyond responding to her child. She watched further as the cub stretched out next to its mother, as though challenging these two humans to take one step closer.

Read pushed himself up from the ground, brushing his breeches of damp, clinging leaves. "The cub might

180

be young, but it's smart," he said. He moved to Glenda's side, looking further around him. "And I have to wonder if there's more than one. The average number of cubs born to a puma is three."

"Why don't you search the underbrush while I try to get the cub away from its mother," Glenda said, inching her way forward. "The poor thing. It must still feel the warmth left in its mother's body, thinking her to be only asleep."

"What will you do with the cub once you do get it away from its mother?" Read grumbled, placing his hands on his hips.

"I truly . . . don't . . . know . . ." Glenda murmured. "But one thing for sure, it can't stay by its mother's side forever. We've got to think of a way to keep it alive. One dead puma is too great a loss. We don't need two."

Read scoffed. "Maybe more if there are more cubs hiding from us," he said. He began moving through the scrub brush, lifting limbs, pulling vines away from tree trunks, shaking the underbrush, but finding nothing.

When he straightened his back, he found that he had moved out of Glenda's eye range, but shrugged and continued with his search, planning to not go too far. . . .

Glenda moved stealthily toward the cub with her arms outstretched. A low growl surfaced from inside the cub's throat and his green eyes narrowed. But when Glenda saw the size of what once would be treacherous fangs, she laughed to herself and pulled the wrestling cub into her arms.

"You don't even have large enough teeth to chew

with, much less bite with," Glenda whispered, holding the cub tightly to her as it continued to wriggle frantically in her arms.

"Now, now, little one," Glenda further murmured. "I won't hurt you. I want to comfort you. You are soon to feel the greatest loss of your life . . . that of your mother." Glenda's gaze traveled to the dead puma and a sadness struck deeply inside her. "It's because you still see your mother and feel her presence that you won't relax in my arms, isn't that it, little one?" she suddenly blurted. "Well, we'll take care of that problem."

She carried the cub to the water's edge and settled down onto the ground, not even able to see the dead puma herself. She still held tightly to the cub and could finally feel the fight waning in its limbs. Glenda held it to the softness of her bosom, hoping the warmth of her own body would give the cub a sense of stability . . . well-being. And as the cub began to nuzzle its nose into the softness of her blouse between the deep cavern of her breasts, and began to purr lazily, Glenda knew that she had won. She reached for and placed a paw on the palm of her outstretched right hand and laughed about how much larger it appeared to be in comparison with the rest of its body. And as its claws began to ease in and out, circling at the tips as they would make contact with Glenda's flesh, Glenda was the one who had been given a sense of well-being, feeling almost a mother herself . . . realizing the cub had just as much as adopted her. . . .

"Read? Come here. Quickly," Glenda shouted. "The cub and I! We've become friends." She clung to it, feeling a strange warmth coursing through her as the cub looked up into her eyes with its own green eyes, so wide and full of trust. Glenda lifted the softness of its face to hers. "You are so beautiful, orphaned little cat."

She felt the soft fur caressing her cheek and heard the cub's steady purring, then realized there was no way she could set the cub free again. It would be hers. All . . . hers. She knew enough about pumas to know that it would take the cub a while to be able to develop enough skill in hunting on its own to be able to stay alive. Yes, the cub had adopted her . . . and she was willing.

"Read? Where have you gone to?" Glenda shouted again. She placed the cub next to her chest and rose from the ground, suddenly afraid. She had yelled twice for Read . . . and twice he hadn't answered. She listened for noise in the scrub brush and peered through the fast falling shadows of dusk, but hearing or seeing nothing.

She swallowed nervously as she began walking in a small circle, afraid to move away from the lagoon, knowing Read would remember having left her there if he had managed to get himself lost in his search for other abandoned cubs.

"Read! Can you hear me?" she shouted again, now trembling. She held the cub more tightly to her, letting it ease her tensions. Its warmth was comforting her. She stroked its head between its ears and kissed the tip of its nose, still watching . . . still listening. . . .

Read hastened his steps. He hadn't meant to wander so far. But in the thick underbrush, it all looked the same . . . tangle after tangle of creeping fingers of vines. Glenda's shouts drew his quick attention, suddenly worrying about having left her alone. A dead animal could attract all sorts of live animals . . . and Glenda was right there, also an innocent prey.

He didn't bother to respond verbally. He saw the quickness with which night was falling. His heart raced his feet as he threw himself through the tangle of the brush and when he caught sight of Glenda standing beside the glistening waters of the lagoon, with intense relief he began to laugh hysterically. He had truly expected . . . oh, God . . . he wouldn't let himself think further about what could have happened to her. Instead he ran to her and embraced her and her arm full of cub, kissing Glenda passionately . . . wetly . . . all over her face. . . .

"Read, what happened?" Glenda murmured as he pulled from her. "Where were you?"

Read lifted his eyes to her. "I didn't realize I had gone so far," he said. "I'm sorry, darling."

Glenda lifted a hand to his face and smoothed her fingers across it. "Read, I was frightened," she said. "Don't leave me again. Please?"

"*Ma chérie*, I won't. I became just as alarmed." He eyed the way in which she was holding the cub. There was a possessiveness in the manner. . . .

"Did you find signs of any more cubs?" she asked, caressing the cub's fur, loving its closeness and the way in which it was cuddled in the curve of her arm.

"None," he said. "I imagine there was only one cub after all. I'd bet a hundred bucks that this one cub managed to stray from its mother and ended up somewhere around El Progresso. This had to be the reason for the larger cat's prowling so close to where humans lived."

"Do you really think so?"

"Yes. And I think we are now the prey for all animals that frequent this forest," Read said, moving toward the horse. "As long as that dead cat has flesh on its bones, it's going to attract every animal on four legs. And night is when most hunt. We have to put many tracks between us and that dead cat."

"Read, I'm taking the cub with me," Glenda said, eyeing Read with wide, pleading eyes. The green of her eyes matched those of the cat. . . .

"I feared as much," he grumbled, jerking his horse's reins free from a limb. He stopped and stared at her with a furrowed brow. "Then what, Glenda? What can you do with it? You surely aren't thinking of keeping it."

"I am," she said, clutching the cub closer to her. "It is now mine," she said stubbornly. "It's only a baby. We cannot turn it loose to become another animal's evening meal."

"Glenda, this cub will one day become a large, dangerous cat."

"Yes, it will become large. But not dangerous. I will make sure it is loved. It will remain as tame as it is at this moment."

"That's impossible, Glenda. . . ."

"No. Nothing is impossible," she argued.

Read jerked Glenda's horse's reins free and offered them to her. "Whatever," he sighed exasperatedly. "But for now, we've got to leave this place. Come on."

Glenda glanced toward the horse and remembered

how clumsily she rode on its back. Then she studied the cub and wondered how she could even manage to carry it. With one hand, she lifted the tail of her skirt, smiling wickedly. It wouldn't hurt to wear a shorter skirt in the presence of only Read.

So with one jerk, she had ripped the cotton of her skirt from her knees down, all around, until she had enough material for which to make a small traveling sack for her cub. Laughing lightly, she wrapped this around the cub, leaving only its head exposed.

She mounted her horse, then placed the cub in its travel sack on her lap, tying one long loop of cotton material around her waist, feeling secure that neither the cub nor the travel sack were going anywhere until Glenda was ready for them to do so.

"Glenda, I hope you know what you're doing," Read grumbled.

"The cub is female. I noticed while placing her in the sack," Glenda said, taking her reins. "So the cub is no longer an 'it.' She is named Nena, Spanish for baby girl." She paused, then added, "and, yes, Read, I know what I am doing."

"Are you even prepared to travel all night?"

"All . . . night. . . ?"

"Yes. We must travel straight through to El Progresso."

"Why, Read. . . ?"

"Many reasons," he grumbled. "Indians . . . animals. . . ."

"I understand, Read," Glenda murmured. She eyed him trustingly. She didn't have anything to fear while with him. He had proven that he was more macho than Ramón could ever be. . . .

Thoughts of Ramón drew her attention back to her orphaned cub. What would Ramón do. . . ? What would he say. . . ? Would the cub . . . even be safe. . . ? She shuddered, thinking about it. . . .

Chapter Nine

Drained of most all their energies, Glenda and Read emerged from the jungle drooping, like wilted flowers, almost numb from lack of rest, food and water. Nena cried weakly from the confines of its travel sack, and Glenda licked her parched lips thirstily. She looked toward Read and could tell that he was as tired, but knew that being the man he was, he would never admit it. She smiled, proud.

She tried to speak but felt the dry soreness of her throat and refrained from doing anything except to urge her panting horse on toward the tall fence that surrounded the American house she had become a part of. There she would find food . . . water . . . even . . . her featherbed. . . .

When she slumped further over her horse, Read managed to move to her side and secured her reins, to now guide both their horses through the opened gate, only heartbeats away from a comforting shelter.

As Glenda glanced toward the house, she forced her shoulders back, seeing her older brother Marcos sitting on the steps, with his head hung between his hands. A chord of fear played at her heart. Marcos wouldn't be there unless something was the matter with someone else in the Galvez family. She tried to speak once again but only a whisper would emerge from her throat, and she was glad when Marcos's head swung up and his gaze found that he was no longer alone.

"Glenda," he blurted, jumping from the steps, racing toward her. "Where have you been?" His eyes traveled over her and Read, seeing the disarray they were both in. He reached and assisted Glenda from her horse, wondering about the puma cub, but not yet asking about it. He had too much on his mind.

Glenda was glad to be dismounted from the slick, perspiration-covered back of the horse. She stood, swaying next to Marcos. She held onto Nena's travel sack with one hand and placed her other to her throat, swallowing hard. "I must have a drink," she managed to whisper raspily. She eyed Read as he dismounted and when he came and offered his arm, she slinked along with him on up the stairs and into the house.

Read leaned into her face, his eyes a dark gray from worry. "Are you going to be all right, *ma chérie?*" he asked. "The horses. I feel they've been abused long enough. I must water and feed them. But first I have to know you are all right."

Glenda reached a free hand to his face, feeling the stubble of his dark whiskers, yet loving them. She loved everything about him. She always would. Oh, were their goodbyes truly so close? "I am all right," she whispered raspily, feeling the ache in her parched, dry throat. "But you? You do look so . . . so . . . tired. Your head? Does it even hurt from the strain of the trip?"

He laughed amusedly. "The knot on my head is gone and so is my headache," he said. "The head wound served its purpose. Now we can forget about it."

"Read, I'm so glad. . . ."

"Then I can leave you now while I see to the horses. . . ?"

"Ramón can. . . ."

"To hell with Ramón," he spat. "I have to be sure the horses are given proper care. I don't need Rayburn down on my ass about them when he returns. He has enough reason to see to my demise. . . ."

"I'm sorry," Glenda sighed, lowering her lashes. "It seems I've brought much confusion into your life."

"*Ma chérie*, you'll never know the pleasures you've brought to me. Never," he said, then kissed her feverishly before turning to leave.

With a pounding heart, she watched his exit, then hastened toward the kitchen, knowing that she should ask Marcos about his reasons for being there, but first feeling more the need of water to quench her growing thirst. She didn't feel she would last another minute without some wetness down her throat. . . .

"Glenda, where have you been?" Marcos stormed, following her into the kitchen, where she now stood gulping water from a glass. His gaze once again settled on the small puma, wondering about it.

Sinking down onto a chair, Glenda panted wildly, feeling a slow aching in her stomach, realizing that she had drunk much too much . . . much too quickly. "Read and I . . . well . . . we, uh . . . went exploring the Mayan ruins," she blurted. "We ran into some trouble," she quickly added.

His gaze traveled over her. "I gathered that," Marcos said. "And what are you doing with this puma?"

"Will you get Nena a bowl of milk? You'll find the milk in the cooling machine in the pantry," she said, pointing.

Marcos's eyes widened in all browns, covering a wide expanse of his dark face. He scratched through his coal black hair confusedly. "Nena? Cooling machine?" he stammered.

"I've named the orphaned cub Nena," she said, sighing heavily. "And the cooling machine? It is a new invention of the Americans. Go into the pantry. You will find an upright box with a door on the front. Open it and feel its coolness seep out onto your skin. And once you have gotten over the shock of seeing this invention for the first time, you will find a glass container of milk in it. Please. Pour some in a bowl for my poor little Nena."

She began to slowly unwrap the travel sack, watching with a warm heart as Nena jumped from it and began to explore the dark corners of the room. Then Glenda's mind began to clear a bit. She knew that she should rush out to where Read was . . . offer him a cold drink of water . . . but knew that he would see to his own needs as he was so kindly seeing to the horses. She had a sudden need of her own. To find out the reason behind Marcos's being there . . . waiting for her . . . looking as though he had lost his best friend.

When Marcos came back into the room and offered the bowl of milk to Nena, which she heartily accepted with fast slurps from her tongue, Glenda rose and went to him. "Marcos, you were here for more reasons than wondering where I had disappeared to," she said, grasping onto his shoulders, forcing his gaze upward to meet hers and hold. She was always reminded of his shorter height, when so close to him. "Tell me. Is there trouble in the Galvez family? Is that why you are not in the banana fields laboring. . . ?"

Tears sparkled in the corners of Marcos's eyes. His white teeth shone in contrast to his tanned face as he choked back the words. "It's Mamma," he murmured. "She is ill."

Something grabbed at Glenda's heart. She had worried about her mother before having left the Galvez house to be a part of another way of life. And now? To find that she was indeed ill? Guilt began to move through Glenda in crazed splashes. She tightened her hold on Marcos, also feeling shame for not having asked him the minute she had seen him there, waiting. "How ill? Tell me, Marcos," she said, weaving a bit now, realizing just how weak she was from not having taken time to get nourishment while on their journey back from the ruins.

"She just lies and sleeps," Marcos said in a choked whisper. "Papa doesn't know what is the matter. But she speaks of you . . . asks for you . . . when she does awaken for short spells."

Glenda spun around, catching her head between her hands when she saw flashes of many colors race before her eyes. "I must . . . go . . . to her. . . ," she gasped. She fell against a chair, then down onto it. "But first, Marcos, get me something . . . anything . . . to . . . eat. Go back into the cooling machine. Get whatever you can find. Something I can eat quickly. And while I'm eating, please go to Read. Take him some food. He's surely as hungry and weak as I."

When she had cheese and milk for her nourishment, Glenda consumed these speedily, quickly reviving the strength in her limbs and brushing the aggravating fuzziness from her head. She lifted Nena into her arms and went outdoors to Read. She knew this might be their last goodbye but didn't allow herself to think about it. Her family . . . her mother needed her. She moved on into the stable, where Read stood stroking a horse with a brush. She looked quickly around, glad to see that Ramón had deserted his post. She wondered where he might be causing troubles at this moment. But she was relieved that it was she who didn't have to face him.

She went to cling to Read's arm, feeling the usual gush of warmth surge through her when his gaze moved to capture hers.

"What is it, darling?" he asked, dropping the brush to grasp onto her shoulders. "You're even paler than moments ago. What's the matter?"

"Didn't Marcos tell you when he brought you nourishment?"

"No. Tell me what. . . ?"

Her eyes blurred with tears. She was afraid to leave him. She didn't want to leave him. But she had no choice. Her family needed her. She had to keep telling herself that. Was her mother even ill because of her daughter's departure. . . ? "I must go to my mother. She needs me," she quickly said, watching him, hoping that he would understand. "That is why Marcos was here to greet our return. I must go to her.

193

Please tell me it's all right. That you understand. If you do not, I cannot leave you."

Read wiped at his mouth with the back of a hand, fearing this sudden goodbye. But yet, it wouldn't be forever. He hadn't yet asked her to return to America with him. He would. As soon as she felt free to do so. He wove his long, thin fingers through her hair, stopping at the base of her neck, caressing her there. She bent her head backwards, almost in a swoon. Though tired, she was never too tired to enjoy the touch from the man whom she adored.

"Yes. It's all right," he said huskily. "You go on and see to your mother. I understand. I know of the needs of family. I also am loyal to my family when needed."

"Are you sure you do understand?" she prodded, leaning her face close to his, breathing heavily as his lips glazed her own. "You will be . . . alone . . . if I leave. . . ," she murmured further.

"I'm a big guy. I can take care of myself. I always have. No reason to think I can't now," he laughed. "Go on. Please." His gaze moved to Nena. "And take care of our baby puma," he said, teasing.

Glenda smiled widely. "If you are able to tease, then you really understand," she said, rising. She motioned with her head toward Marcos who had just entered the stable. "Come on, big brother. I think we can leave now." She took a few steps backward, watching Read, longing for him, feeling strangely inside that she just may never see him again, but then again, knowing how foolish such a thought was, and hurried, barefoot, from the stable.

Nena's claws sank into Glenda's arms as Glenda forced her bone-weary legs to run at a steady pace down the dirt road. The sun beat down upon her, and a slight rumbling of thunder in the distance drew her face to the sky. Dark clouds were moving in like waves on an ocean and she knew that the wet season was about to resume with one big blast. As the earth trembled beneath her feet, she tensed, then caught sight of the small dwelling where her mother lay, waiting. She looked back at Marcos who tarried behind. His short legs never could carry him at the pace Glenda's carried her.

Breathing harshly, she rushed on up the steps and through the door, stopping with a start when some unknown girl moved into the living room with a scrub brush and a pail of water. Glenda stood, breasts heaving frantically, as she looked on around the room, seeing that nothing had changed. The odds and ends of furnishings were still there. The only thing that was new . . . was . . . this girl . . . whose eyes were wide with wonder and whose face was lovely, square, and brown. "Who are you?" Glenda murmured, clutching on to Nena, who was wriggling, trying to be set free.

The girl spoke in thick Spanish. "Carlita Galvez," she said, dark eyes wide. Her drawstring blouse hung low over her shoulders, revealing the swell of her two bronze breasts, and her brightly colored, flowered skirt was gathered thickly at her tapered waist. She was much shorter than Glenda and tiny and frail.

Glenda's voice caught in her throat. "What did you say?" she gasped, paling.

"Marcos is my husband," Carlita said, tilting her chin haughtily. "And who are you? Why are you, a white person, in my house?"

Once again, Glenda was aware of the weakness of

her stomach and legs. She flipped her hair across her shoulders and sighed wearily. "You are married to my brother?" she said in a near whisper. "You feel you can call this house yours because you are married to Marcos? How? When. . . ?"

Dropping her scrub brush to the floor, Carlita's gaze faltered. "You are Glenda?" she murmured in a bare whisper. Her gaze raked over Glenda in a quiet wonder. "You are . . . white . . . skinned. . . ?"

"Yes. I am Marcos's sister," Glenda snapped angrily. "And, yes, I am white." She eyed her mother's bedroom door. She inched toward it. "I have come to see my mother," she then quickly added. "Marcos. He told me that Mamma is quite ill."

"Yes. Rosa is quite ill," Carlita said, setting her water pail onto the floor.

Glenda swung around, anger flashing in her eyes. "Don't you know how to show respect to my mother?" she hissed. "Rosa Galvez is Mamma Galvez to you. Do not speak of her by her first name. Show respect for my mamma while sharing her house and family!"

Carlita cast her eyes downward, clasping her hands together in front of her. "Yes, ma'am," she murmured weakly.

Glenda glanced quickly downward at Nena, then back to Carlita. "Carlita, go and make sure the back door is closed and then close this front door," she ordered. "I have to turn Nena loose and I don't want to have to worry about her running from the house. She is not yet that acquainted with life to be turned loose in the jungle or on the streets of Bay Island. And when you get the doors securely closed, find something to feed to my kitten."

"A puma? You will keep it in the house?" Carlita gasped.

"Yes. Now do as I have asked of you. . . ."

"Yes, ma'am," Carlita replied, turning on a heel, rushing from the room. When she returned and closed the front door, Glenda placed Nena onto the floor and smiled quietly when the cub's four paws began to get tangled as Nena began to slip and slide on the hard wood of the floor, only having recently become acquainted with such a surface.

Glenda eyed Carlita with a sharpness once again, guessing her to be only fifteen, and wondering how Marcos had managed to find someone so quickly. And why hadn't Glenda been summoned to observe the marriage ceremony? Anger moved through her in flashes . . . at Marcos for marrying without having told her . . . and for marrying someone so young! Yet, it was the custom. Just because she, herself, wasn't yet wed at age eighteen, didn't have to mean that all girls hesitated to exchange vows with a man. And wasn't Marcos so truly lucky? Carlita was beautiful. Her back hadn't yet become curved from carrying heavy baskets of fruits and vegetables. And now that she was settled into the family so quickly, where only the men labored in the fields, possibly Carlita's beauty would remain intact. "Unless . . . children . . . come in twos and threes," Glenda thought further to herself.

With a pounding heart, Glenda moved on into the bedroom, stopping, putting her hands to her face when she saw her mother lying so quietly with her hands resting atop her like a dead person lying in a casket.

A lump rose in Glenda's throat as she gazed

intensely at the white rosary beads clutched tightly to by her mother, sparkling beneath the rays of many candles' soft glow positioned on a table beside the bed. The gentle aroma from a bouquet of roses swam through the air in sweet, quiet strokes, and Glenda looked further through her blur of tears at her mother's hair and how it had been brushed and the way her face had been cleansed to shine like velvet.

It was then that Glenda's feelings changed for Carlita. Only Carlita could have taken such care of this beautiful Rosa. . . .

Sinking to the floor on her knees beside the bed, Glenda lifted a hand to her mother's folded hands and circled it over them. Glenda could feel a steady pulsebeat in the wrist and could see the steady way in which her mother was breathing. She swallowed hard. Her mother was much too pale and had shed a few pounds. She was so ill, she seemed to be sleeping her life away. . . .

Nena scampered into the room, slipping halfway across the floor, bumping into Glenda's thighs. Smiling, Glenda lifted Nena with her free hand and placed her on her lap, stroking her fine, sleek fur while watching her mother for any sudden movements. Then when she heard footsteps behind her, she swung her gaze around and glowered at Marcos.

He fell to his knees beside her. "I see you have met my wife," he whispered with lowered eyes.

"Marcos, when did this happen?" Glenda whispered back.

"Shortly after you left. I knew Mamma needed help. I questioned many of my friends in the banana fields. This one friend told me of his beautiful sister. I did not know just how beautiful until I saw her. When I did see her, I thought to do more than ask her to come and help around the house. I asked her to live with us. Be my common law wife."

Glenda's cheeks quivered, then a smile broke out. "Did you say common law wife? You aren't married to her by a priest?" she murmured softly, glancing toward her mother, not wanting to disturb her by discussing family problems at her bedside.

"Yes. Our free union is based only on the consent of the two of us. This way, if I grow tired of her I can find me another one just as beautiful."

Glenda's smile quickly faded. "Marcos. That is shameful," she gasped.

"But it is true," he said, laughing awkwardly.

"I think I could like her very much," Glenda said, glancing toward the door, catching glimpses of Carlita as she busied herself scrubbing the floor. Glenda now felt guilty for having snapped at Carlita. She was there because she loved Marcos and because she was willing to be a part of the Galvez family and the burdens of illness that she had readily accepted.

"I think I like her too much also," Marcos sighed heavily. "I think I maybe might have to get a priest's words spoken over us after all. I think I would like to have babies by this sweet *señorita*."

"How old is she, Marcos?"

"Fourteen."

"I thought so," Glenda whispered. "She's so young, Marcos. You are twenty-two."

Marcos's face became all shadows. "And what do you think you were doing with that man with the funny name of Read? And how old is *he?*" he said, glowering.

Glenda's face flushed. "I never . . . asked . . . his true age," she stammered. Then she set her jaws firmly. "But what does that even matter?"

"What matters is that you spent the night with him, possibly even two, I do not know. I only came searching for you this day. Did you agree on such a common law bond with him?" His gaze searched her finger for a ring. "I know you did not wed. There is no ring, and no priest has yet come to El Progresso or I would have heard about it."

"No. We spoke no vows of any sort," Glenda said quietly. "Don't worry about it. I am old enough to take care of myself, big brother."

"You are?" He glanced down at Nena. "And you think you can even handle a puma such as this? What will you do when it decides to take a bite of your finger? Huh? And what do you think Father will do when the puma kills its first chicken? Huh?"

Glenda giggled a bit. Her fingers worked through Nena's fur. She knew that in time, Nena would be the size of its mother and would have dangerously long teeth and claws. "I will worry about that when the times comes," she said softly. "Now? I will be this kitten's mother."

Her gaze moved back to her own mother. "And about our mamma," she said in a silken whisper. "What can we do? She just lies there. All the while we talk, she just lies there. Why doesn't she respond to our nearness? She . . . just . . . lies there. . . ."

"This is what I told you," Marcos grumbled.

"Rayburn has gone to America to get a doctor for El Progresso. Maybe when he returns, this doctor can come and take a look at our mamma and tell us what we can do to help her get well once again."

"But what if she quits breathing by then?"

"Marcos, she just can't," Glenda gasped softly. "Mamma. She has to get well. If not, I will forever blame myself."

"You cannot, Glenda. Mother was sick before you left. There was nothing you could have done, even if you had been here."

"She wouldn't have had to work so hard. . . ."

"Like I told you, little sister. I found Carlita quite fast. She's taken all the load off our mamma. Mamma didn't have to do anything. Then one day, Mamma just climbed into bed, closed her eyes, and they've only been open a few times since."

"What about food. . . ?"

"I believe she is slowly starving to death. We haven't been able to get her to eat anything. . . ."

"I've heard of deaths caused by melancholia," Glenda whispered. "Maybe she misses her house on Bay Island."

"Damn!" Marcos exclaimed. "This house we are now living in has that Bay Island house beat. Mamma now has a kitchen with a true stove. She has many rooms. . . ."

"Still. I saw Christina Taylor missing her home in America. I saw her almost sink into a sort of melancholia. Maybe this is what is wrong with Mamma. She did tell me of her empty feelings through the day. She did tell me that she missed her home of twenty years. Maybe we should move her back to Bay Island. See how she reacts. . . ."

"It does not make any sense, Glenda," Marcos grumbled.

"We have to try it, Marcos," Glenda said, pushing herself up from the floor. She tensed when a continuing roll of thunder echoed around the house. She rushed to the window and stared toward the huge banana fields. The laborers were scattered through these fields, as far as the eye could see. Glenda knew that a storm wouldn't even drive her father home, which had to mean that he wouldn't return for many hours. She felt an irresistible impulse to move ahead with her plans. Yes, her papa was the spokesman . . . the head of the house. But what had he done to help his Rosa become happy and well again? Nothing . . . it . . . seemed. . . .

Swinging around, Glenda's eyes shone. "You and I, Marcos," she exclaimed. "We will take it upon ourselves to return Mamma to her home of twenty years. Once there, we will remove the boards from the windows and doors that you and Papa nailed there upon our departure. We will take Mamma to the room where her children were born and where her memories of young love hang heavily in the air."

Marcos rose to his feet, his mouth agape. "Are you crazy?" he gasped. "We cannot do this. Not without Papa's consent. His word . . . his voice . . . is authority here."

Glenda returned Nena to the floor, then clasped Marcos's hands in hers. "Don't you see, Marcos?" she pleaded. "Papa's word hasn't made Mother well." She straightened her back, lifting her chin haughtily. "It is I who am now in authority here. I will take all responsibility of Mother's welfare. It appears too much time has been wasted already. The change has to take place now."

Marcos jerked his hands free, his dark eyes flashing. "You seem to forget that it is I, the next in line in the Galvez family, who should be the one handing out orders," he grumbled. "You make me less macho in the eyes of my Carlita, by ordering me around."

Glenda swung her arms in the air. "You worry about who is to look macho and who is not, while it is our mother who deserves your worried thoughts," she said.

Marcos glanced quickly toward the still form of his mamma. He swallowed his pride quickly. "I'm sorry," he murmured. He fell to his knees beside Rosa and bent over her, kissing her softly on the lips. "I'm sorry, Mamma," he murmured again. He rose and whispered harshly to Glenda. "What about the doctor you spoke of? Why not wait. . . ?"

"Marcos, to wait might mean to lose Mamma," she argued. "Perhaps later. The doctor can see her later."

"And the storm? It is violent. How strong is your bravery? Eh? As strong as your words?"

"Yes!" she snapped, flinging her head back stubbornly.

"Yes, yes," Marcos grumbled.

"And, Marcos, I have seen crates you've brought home from the banana fields," she said. "Bring one into the house. I feel it's a better way to carry Nena by boat. She'll hate having only cracks to see through, but at least the hungry waves of the ocean won't grab and take her from me."

"You and that puma," Marcos grumbled further. "It is not good that you have brought it into our house. No good will come of it. You'll see. And you haven't even revealed to me how you happened to come by it."

His words of warning shot shivers through Glenda, hoping he was wrong. Her Nena would bring her good fortune. Somehow . . . some day. . . . "When we get settled back at Bay Island, I will tell you the story," she said. "But for now, Marcos, please hurry?"

He moved away from her, still grumbling. She looked downward, blushing a bit when she caught sight of her attire. She had simply forgotten about having ripped her skirt partially away, standing now with almost her knees exposed. She felt eyes on her and turned and saw Carlita watching her. Her face flushed a bit. She had to change clothes but suddenly remembered having taken all that she possessed to the big American house on the hill.

A pang of loneliness surged through her with remembrances of that house. She longed to be there . . . to be sharing the featherbed with Read. Ah, how she could so vividly remember his fingers through her hair, his lips on her breasts. . . .

She shook her head to clear her thoughts. This was now. She had her mother to think of and a storm to move ahead of.

Rushing to the sitting room, she took the scrub brush from Carlita and threw it into the bucket of water, causing the water to splash in large bubbles around her.

"I need your help, Carlita," she said quickly. "Though you are shorter and tinier than me, I need to borrow one of your skirts. I . . . uh . . . damaged mine."

Carlita's gaze traveled over Glenda, covering her mouth with a hand to hide a few springy giggles. . . .

"And then you will be left here as Marcos and I leave with our mamma," Glenda continued, almost frantically when she heard roar after roar of thunder.

Carlita's giggles dissipated quickly. Her eyes grew dark and wide. "What do you mean. . . ?" she gasped noisily.

Glenda proceeded to tell her plan . . . urging Carlita to understand . . . that it was she . . . Carlita . . . who would have to explain to José Galvez why his Rosa was no longer in his bed. . . .

The shallow draft boat rose, fell and rose again with the angry waves of the Caribbean. The crests of the waves were shimmering from blues to whites as the whitecaps then would crash and tumble against the boat's side, making the boat shudder ominously.

Glenda clung to her mother as she lay with her head in Glenda's lap, still in a deep sleep. Nena spat and hissed, reaching a paw through a crack of the crate she was in as the rope that secured it beneath the seat creaked and snapped with its each movement.

"It'll be all right, Nena," Glenda urged, covering her mother's face with her hands as a spray of water splashed over the side of the boat. "Maybe soon I'll have you where you won't have to fear anything again. Little one, so far life has been a bit rough on you."

Marcos shouted from across his shoulder. "You still so brave, Glenda?" He continued to struggle with his paddles, sinking them deeply into the water, flexing his muscles as he then pushed and pulled all over again. "We should've at least waited for the storm to pass. The rains. It looks as though the clouds will open at any moment, and then what shall we do?"

"Just keep rowing, Marcos," Glenda shouted over the loud crashes of the waves. She glanced behind her, seeing the shapes of houses forming on the horizon, a bobbing mass it seemed, except that it was she who was riding, high then low . . . then high. But, thank God, Bay Island was now closer than El Progresso.

"Papa will be angry. He will shout above the roof-tops when he sees what we have done," Marcos yelled, coughing a bit when the wild salt water entered his mouth and nostrils, burning his insides.

Glenda tensed when she heard another shuddering of the boat as a huge wave smacked its side. She grabbed for her mother and the blankets that had been wrapped snugly around her. She was also beginning to fear for this boat and passengers. And, oh, wasn't her stomach a mass of ripples, sometimes even worse than those of the ocean on a calmer day of the dry season?

Water droplets were now clinging to her lashes, making everything around her become as a blur. And when a slippery mass of seaweed splashed and clung to her hair, Glenda fought it and threw it back to the sea, now becoming consumed with trembling fear. She had forgotten her full night of travel with no rest. She was just beginning to feel it in the lethargic ache of her bones and the spinning, dullness of her head.

"Row, Marcos," she shouted. "Harder. Harder. . . ."

"Never again will I listen to you," Marcos yelled, gasping, groaning. The seat beneath him was slippery from the wetness and his hands were beginning to feel numb from grasping the paddles so tightly. Each movement of the paddles through the water now was a major chore. But he would make it to shore. So much depended on his making it. . . .

"We're almost there," Glenda encouraged. She looked toward the sky. The gray clouds were swirling and dipping and an occasional streak of lightning zigzagged downward, appearing to move on into the ocean in golden-white sprays.

In the distance, from where the boat was traveling, Glenda could now see the fury of the wind in the way the palmetto trees' crowns of large leaves were whipping around. And just as the sky opened and let its water loose from its storage house, Marcos guided the boat onto the powdery sands that lined Bay Island.

Glenda continued to hold her mother's head on her lap until the boat was secure, then sighed deeply as Marcos bent and lifted Rosa into his arms and began to run toward the houses.

Breathing hard, Glenda untied and grabbed the crate that held her orphaned kitten and rushed with it, barefoot, behind Marcos, ducking her head as the rain became a driving force, and the wind an obstacle almost too much to challenge. The swell of the sea as it broke onto the shore was deafening. With each step taken, Glenda could hear the roar, over and over again, and the feel of the warm, wet sand oozing between her toes.

But Glenda trudged onward, wiping at her face with her free hand, watching on all sides of her as she began making her way down narrow rows of thatched-roof houses that were perched high on thin stilts. And when the Galvez house came into view, she raced on ahead of Marcos, climbed the rickety stairs to the porch and with all the strength she could muster had the wooden planks ripped from in front of the doorway.

Gasping for air, she pushed the door widely open and stood aside as Marcos fell past her and soon had Rosa stretched atop her own makeshift bed of palm leaves and straw.

Glenda looked slowly around her, hating it. She had left her dreams behind her . . . at . . . El Progresso. She was now back at the beginning. Where her life had begun. And where it would probably end. Even if Read would come for her now, it was meant for Glenda to stay loyal to family ties while needed.

Placing Nena's crate on the floor, Glenda hesitated at opening it. The walls crawled with cockroaches that had taken occupancy, and a rat scurried around a corner, causing goose bumps to scatter across Glenda's flesh. The smell was that of mildew, and the damp, humid air hung heavy and unpleasant.

Then Glenda eyed her mother. Her mother came first. Lifting the wetness of her skirt above her ankles, she moved to her mother's side. "We must get these wet clothes removed from Mother and fast," she said flatly to Marcos. "Go to the wardrobe and bring one of Mother's dresses she left behind." Her gaze moved quickly to Marcos. "But shake the dress out first. It seems cockroaches have decided they like our house."

"Yes, Glenda," Marcos grumbled, moving quickly away from her. "You think Mamma wished to come to this . . . this house. . . ?" he laughed sarcastically. "I think you are wrong, little sister. I think you are wrong."

Lifting her mother's head, Glenda removed her mother's blouse, then pulled her skirt down, revealing the wetness of her mother's underthings. Glenda ignored Marcos's presence and hurriedly removed the rest of the clothes, quickly replacing them with a dry, warm, snug dress. Glenda fluffed up the straw around her mother and pulled a blanket up to her neck, then stood, stretching as Marcos was in the process of removing the boards from all the windows of the house.

"And now you, my sweet Nena," Glenda said, sighing heavily. "This is your new home. And when I set you free from your cage, you can get your first try at hunting game for yourself. There is a rat that needs taking care of." She giggled softly and watched as Nena jumped from the crate and began scampering around, sniffing, hissing when Marcos turned on a heel too quickly, scaring the cub.

"I don't think Nena likes men too much," Glenda giggled heartily. "I think Nena is only a woman lover. Aren't you, Nena?" Glenda went to the cub and lifted it into her arms, placing its face to hers. She rubbed the fur against her cheek, thinking of Read, wondering how he was, what he was doing, and oh, so missing him.

"Now we wait," she said. "And when the rains stop, we will get a fire going and soon have some warm broth ready to force down Mamma's throat when she awakens. We will make her well. Marcos, we can do it. I know it. And when she senses that she is home, she will awaken. My prayers will make it happen."

"God has forsaken our mamma," Marcos grumbled, settling down in a corner, pulling his knees to his chest. "Possibly God has forsaken us all. I know Papa will follow Mamma and will forget the riches he had thought to make on the banana plantation. His dreams? They will go out with the tide. Just as quickly as that."

Glenda went to a window and watched the continuing raging storm, feeling suddenly so cold. She had to get out of her cold, wet things. She began to unbutton her blouse as her thoughts dwelled on her dreams. Read had been a dream. She swung around, frowning toward Marcos. "And when the rain stops, you must return to El Progresso, and not only to see your Carlita and work as a laborer, but also to do a chore for me as well," she said quietly, tears burning at the corners of her eyes.

"What else does my sister demand of me? Huh?" Marcos grumbled.

"You must go and tell Read what has happened to me," she said. "You will have to explain about our mamma. He will understand." Then another thought struck her, like a bolt of lightning that had gone astray. She shivered once more. "And you musn't let Ramón Martinez know that I have returned to Bay Island. . . ," she said in a strained whisper.

Marcos pushed himself from the floor and sauntered toward her. "And why not? Isn't a mestizo good enough for you now that you have tasted the lips of a white man?" he said furiously.

"Not that particular mestizo," Glenda snapped.

"I didn't know you even thought of him. One way or another, Glenda," Marcos teased, widening his mouth into a white, toothy smile.

"Marcos, it is not a laughing matter," she said between clenched teeth. She then rushed to the wardrobe and grabbed one of her own thin cotton dresses that she had also left behind with the hopes of finding a new way of life. "And I did," she murmured to herself. "Oh, what a life I had for a little while. . . ."

211

at the bed and again placed with the index of reading
a new way of life." And I tried," she murmured
hoarsely. "Oh, where has I just got a little while . . ."

Chapter Ten

"A full week," Glenda said in a subdued voice, grinding maize between two stones. "Read hasn't come, nor has he questioned Marcos about me or Mamma's welfare." She flipped her golden hair back across her shoulders, feeling the steaming temperatures of mid-afternoon beating into her skin. She blew down the front of her low-cut, drawstring blouse, watching Nena panting, sprawled in a deep sleep beneath the opened window.

"And you, orphaned kitten, you should be free in the wilds of the jungle, to scamper and play with your kind," Glenda said further. "But fate has dealt us both blows. I am no longer free . . . as you are not also."

A weak voice spoke from across the room. Glenda's heart warmed when she glanced quickly toward where her mother lay in a skimpy, cotton attire, wet with beads of perspiration bubbling all over her bronze flesh.

Glenda wiped her hands on her skirt and went to her mother's side. She fell to her knees and lifted her mother's head to place a tin cup of water to her lips.

Her mother's recovery was slow, but she was recovering. There was a renewed shine to her mother's eyes and she accepted food and water as she had refused to do her last days at El Progresso.

"José?" Rosa whispered thickly, licking her lips. "Where is he, Glenda?"

"He's out working the garden, Mother," Glenda replied softly, now caressing her mother's brow with a cool, dampened cloth. "Do you want me to get him for you? He never strays too far from the back door."

"No. I just needed to know that he's near," Rosa said, smiling. "I fear his going back to El Progresso. He won't, will he, Glenda?"

"Papa has forgotten becoming one of society," Glenda murmured, moving the cloth to her mother's neck, lifting her heavy, dark hair as the cloth worked beneath it. "Dreams are for fools. We all learn that in time." Her heart ached every time she let her thoughts wander to the short time that she had been afforded her own dream. . . .

Rosa's breath began to come in short rasps as tears wetted her cheeks. "The dreams of your father's. I have spoiled them," she said, turning her eyes from Glenda.

"Mamma, your dreams and Papa's weren't the same. Feel good that Papa loved you enough to return to Bay Island to be with you."

"I feel so selfish," Rosa murmured further.

"You are not selfish," Glenda demanded. "You didn't like El Progresso. And because you were weak and run down from an unknown illness, it was easy for melancholy to set in. Lots of women your age suffer from melancholy. . . ."

"I was always so strong as a young woman," Rosa cried, moving her gaze to Glenda. "Like you. You are so strong, my daughter. I owe you my life for taking it upon yourself to bring me home, no matter what your father might have done when he found out."

"Papa was too concerned about you to be angry with me," Glenda said, smiling, remembering how her father had eyed her so questionably upon his arrival to Bay Island. It had been a daughter . . . who had questioned his authority . . . ? He had expected possibly Marcos . . . or Carlos . . . but never, no never, his daughter Glenda!

But it was then that he had been reminded that Glenda was truly not his . . . but an American's . . . who had also had such reckless, daring ways. A captain of a ship . . . possibly . . . even . . . a pirate . . . ?

"We must all remember," Glenda quickly added. "Carlos and Marcos. They are still chasing their dreams. They are still at El Progresso. Carlita is now the woman of that Galvez household."

A trail of voices outside the front door drew Glenda to her feet. Always . . . oh, always . . . she would hope that a voice outside her door would be recognizable to be that of Read's. He surely hadn't brushed her from his mind so easily!

Smoothing the gathers of her skirt and wetting her lips with a quick flick of the tongue, Glenda crept to the door and inched it open, now also hearing heavy footsteps on the front stairs of their house. With a thumping heart, she opened the door more widely just as one of the visitors stepped onto the narrow spaces of the thatched-roof porch.

Disappointment coursed through Glenda's veins, yet she was eager in a way, for it was Rayburn Taylor, with his tall thinness, and dressed impeccably in a gray, pinstriped suit, with a diamond stickpin at his throat. His golden, gray-fringed hair was windblown from the sea voyage and the straight lines of his face were laced with perspiration.

Forcing an eager smile, Glenda moved to Rayburn with an outstretched hand of welcome, then stopped in mid-step when a gentleman of what appeared to be good breeding stepped onto the porch next to Rayburn. Glenda eyed him carefully. He was short and balding and the swell of his stomach showed that he had lived a good, well-fed life. He dotted his brow continuously with a handkerchief and his hawklike nose and eyes were his most prominent of features, though the lace trim of his white shirt worn beneath a dark coat, and his black satchel being carried in his left hand could most certainly draw one's speculative attention.

Glenda resumed her offer of friendship, smiling widely as Rayburn took her hand and bowed as he gave it a generous kiss.

"It's so good to see you again, *señorita*," Rayburn said, returning her hand to her own graces. He placed his arm around the shorter man's rounded shoulders. "And may I introduce Doc McAdams to you," Rayburn added, gesturing with his free hand.

Glenda flushed a bit under this Doc McAdams's assessing stare. . . .

"And, Doc, this is the daughter of the ailing Rosa," Rayburn said politely. "This is Glenda. Glenda Galvez."

Glenda offered a hand, tensing when the doctor's damp, pudgy fingers of his free hand made contact with her flesh.

"And how *is* your mother, Glenda dear?" Doc McAdams said in a shrill voice.

"She's faring well enough now that she's back home," she murmured, releasing her hand. Unconsciously, she wiped it on her skirt as something turned inside her head. . . . If Rayburn had returned to El Progresso . . . then did it mean that Read would be returning to New Orleans with the ship's return? The sudden knowledge of this possibility sent stabbing pains through her heart, making it begin a slow, agonizing ache.

She so wanted to question Rayburn about Read . . . but couldn't. Wouldn't he suspect her true motives . . . ?"

"And how was Christina when you left her at New Orleans, Rayburn?" she quickly blurted, hoping the conversation would lead naturally to Read.

Rayburn's blue eyes clouded a bit. His face shadowed as he murmured an answer. "She's fine. Just fine."

"Well, enough of small talk," Doc McAdams cackled. "Show me to the patient. Then I'd like to return to El Progresso. I like the cooling machine. Damn interesting invention, that."

"Right this way," Glenda said, stepping aside. Doc McAdams entered first, then Glenda slowed Rayburn's approach. She placed her hand on his arm. "I do appreciate this gesture of friendship, Rayburn. It is so kind. But I do believe my mother will be all right. She just needed to return to her home and her old ways of doing things."

Rayburn's thick brows furrowed. "I hold myself responsible for my laborers and their families," he said hoarsely. "When I received word that you and your mother and father had returned to this island and why, I had to bring the doctor to your mother."

"Who told you?" Glenda asked cautiously.

"Why, Ramón did. My stable hand," Rayburn said, moving on into the house.

Fear and anger caused Glenda's hands to circle in tight fists at her side. She now knew that Ramón knew of her whereabouts. But she should have known she wouldn't have been able to keep it a secret for long. He was to never leave her be. She knew this now. Then something compelled her to swing around, and when she did, she saw Ramón standing cross-armed at the foot of the stairs.

"How . . . ? Why . . . ?" Glenda stammered.

"Rayburn wouldn't want to paddle a boat as he wouldn't want to do anything else a macho lad like myself can perform," Ramón laughed, baring his smooth, white teeth to her.

"Oh! Ramón! How I hate you," she hissed. "And you be sure to return with Rayburn to El Progresso. Bay Island is a much pleasanter place without the likes of you!"

"Si, si," Ramón mocked, then laughed shrilly into the air.

In a huff, Glenda hurried into the house where Doc McAdams was already down on his knees examining Rosa. He had loosened her bodice even more than it already was, revealing the loose flesh of her breasts. He poked, probed and pounded slightly where bone

217

could be found, then listened to her chest through the first stethoscope that Glenda had yet to see.

Nena moved quickly into the room in playful leaps and bounds, stopping abruptly when she saw the strangers. The fur at her neck hiked and she opened her mouth in a loud hiss.

"My God. What have we here?" Rayburn exclaimed, stooping, holding his arms out to the puma.

Something grabbed at Glenda's heart. She had forgotten about Nena.

"Damn cute," Rayburn chuckled, patting Nena as the puma cautiously sidled up next to him. Then Rayburn's brows raised. "Where did you find the cat, Glenda? I didn't think any pumas would be on this island."

"Well . . . I . . ." Glenda stammered.

"And, by the way," Rayburn continued. "Did anyone ever find the puma Ramón shot? I forgot to ask William deBaulieu. And now that he's on his way back to New Orleans, I won't have the opportunity to ask him."

Glenda's knees grew rubbery and she saw hazy spirals of colors spinning before her eyes. "Did . . . you say . . . Read . . . I mean . . . Mr. deBaulieu has . . . left El Progresso?" she stammered, feeling a bit of nausea rising in her throat. Read had left. And without seeking her out . . . or sending word of his departure? Shame engulfed her. Shame for having given of herself so freely to a man who obviously hadn't loved her. . . .

"Left today. There were no bananas ready for shipment, so the ship returned the same day it arrived. It mainly made the trip to return me and Doc McAdams here to the plantation."

"And . . . how . . . was . . . Mr. deBaulieu . . . feeling . . . ?" Glenda murmured, putting her hands to her throat, hoping her distress didn't show in the depths of her eyes. She knew that Read's head wound had healed, but it was a way to move further into the conversation about him. Rayburn was . . . not . . . aware that Read hadn't been ill as he had professed.

"Poorly," Rayburn said, lifting Nena with him as he rose. "In fact, damn poorly from what I could gather. That's why I encouraged him to return to the states. Though Doc McAdams here is good, there's experts in all fields of medicines in America. William has to get his dizziness checked out. Damn tricky business, these problems with the head."

Further sense of shame raced through Glenda . . . but this time for having doubted Read. He apparently had been ill all along and had kept this knowledge from her to keep her worries free of him. Apparently in the end, he had been too ill to come to her, and if the ship had arrived and left so quickly, he hadn't had time to send word to her. Hope sprang forth. He surely did love her. . . .

"And when will the ship return to El Progresso?" she asked cautiously.

"In a week's time," he replied. "But without William deBaulieu. It seems he's going to be out of commission, shipping-wise, for a while."

Teetering a bit, Glenda moved to a chair and eased onto it. Gathering her skirt around her legs, she whispered, "What did you say about Mr. deBaulieu? What do you mean . . . ?" She knew that her face had paled and hated seeing the knowing in Rayburn's eyes

219

as he reached a hand to her brow, touching it lightly.

"Are you all right?" he said thickly. "You have paled so. Is it even the heat?"

Laughing nervously, she gently brushed his hand away, then leaned to scoop Nena onto her lap. "I'm fine," she murmured. "Just fine."

Rayburn straightened his back, running a finger around the inside of his collar, pulling it a bit away from his neck. "I can understand that heat," he grumbled. "The climate here is quite muggier than even the hottest days of New Orleans."

Glenda stroked Nena's fur nervously, wishing to speak again of Read but knowing to do so would be to draw too much attention to her frets about . . . an . . . American . . . man. . . .

Doc McAdams grunted a bit as he pushed himself up from the floor. He removed the stethoscope from around his neck and circled his chubby fingers about it. "As far as I can tell from the paleness of your mother's eyes and skin, seems your mother's a bit anemic," he said. "Hasn't she been eating well?"

Glenda's gaze moved from Doc McAdams to her mother. "She has just recently begun to eat well again," she said. Then she added, "What is this anemic? What does it mean for my mother? Is it . . . serious . . . ?"

"It's new in my studies," Doc McAdams said, reaching for his satchel. "You see, though my age doesn't reflect it, I am quite new at doctoring. But Rayburn here has faith in my knowledge of the necessary elements needed to do doctoring at El Progresso."

Glenda lifted Nena to the floor and settled herself next to her mother's makeshift bed. She smoothed her mother's hair back from her face, then stroked a cheek gently. "This anemic you speak of, Doc McAdams," she said in a disquiet manner, casting him a frown. "I asked before. Is it serious? I do not need to know your qualifications as a doctor to find your answer to such a question. I trust Rayburn's choice of doctors."

Opening his satchel, then dropping the stethoscope into it, Doc McAdams answered almost indignantly. "Anemia? I believe your mother's particular form is partially due to diet, causing a deficiency in hemoglobin," he said, closing his bag with a loud snap. He rested it on the swell of his abdomen as he further spoke. "Possibly she needs more iron in her diet. Possibly something is impairing her digestion of iron. If not treated correctly, yes, it can be quite dangerous as you can see by the lifelessness of your mother."

"I thought mother was only suffering from a form of melancholy," Glenda murmured, swallowing hard. "She was so unhappy at El Progresso. She's improved since having returned to her home of twenty years."

"Anemia causes slight feelings of loneliness and could even cause homesickness to increase inside one's self," Doc McAdams said.

"But, she . . . is . . . better," Glenda persisted.

"That is because you've managed to get your mother to eat again," Doc McAdams argued back. "But she must follow my instructions to fully recover."

"What? Tell me," Glenda said, rising. "Mother must fully recover. She must."

"I will prepare some medicine and send it back to your mother once I am settled in my quarters at El

Progresso. She shall have it by sunrise tomorrow."

"Medicine? What sort of medicine?" Glenda asked, shooting her mother a fast glance.

Doc McAdams placed his satchel on the floor then began to swab the perspiration from his brow with his handkerchief. "Hundreds of years ago, the Hindus in India prepared a medicine known as *lauha bhasma,*" he said. "They roasted sheets of iron and then ground them into a fine white powder in oil or milk. This was their treatment for anemia, which they recognized only as a disease causing severe weakness. They used iron because they wanted to give the patient the 'strength of iron.' So this is the preparation similar to what I will make and send to you."

"Iron?" Glenda gasped. "My mother will be taking actual iron, from iron sheets, into her body?"

Doc McAdams laughed hoarsely as he lifted his satchel. "It is not as bad as it sounds," he said. "It is now scientifically used by all doctors. But I must urge you to increase green and yellow vegetables in her diet. I saw your fields of maize. Surely she gets plenty of that vegetable."

"Until she grew ill," Glenda murmured. "You see, we use maize in most foods we prepare."

"Liver is also high in iron," Doc McAdams said, sauntering toward the door. "I smelled . . . uh . . . I mean I saw the hogs. When butchering, feed the liver to your mother."

"Yes, sir," Glenda said, lifting her skirt a bit as she escorted the doctor and Rayburn to the door.

Rayburn bent and kissed her affectionately on the cheek. "I'm going to miss you, Glenda," he whispered. "It seems my world is suddenly without my two favorite women."

Glenda giggled a bit bashfully. "Rayburn . . . really
. . . ," she said, fluttering her lashes upward at him.

"I had hoped having you around would cause
Christina's loneliness to lift, but it seems there was
more to her loneliness than I wanted to let myself
believe," Rayburn said, letting his voice trail off to
another mere, sad whisper.

"Rayburn . . . I . . ." Glenda said, reaching for
him, but he made a quick turn on his heel and placed
an arm around the squatty Doc McAdams's shoulder
and let his voice boom, to hide his brief show of
emotion. "Come, Doc," he said firmly. "We must
return to our banana plantation." He forced a merry
laugh. "By the show of beads on your brow, I'd say
you are in need of my cooling machine's sparkling
gems called ice." He turned and gave Glenda a fast
wink, then moved on along the road, toward the
sea. . . .

Glenda's teeth and fists clenched when she saw
Ramón make a quick exit from beneath the lazy shade
of a dwarf palmetto tree to follow along behind the
two dignified Americans. When he cast Glenda a
wide, white-toothed smile from across his shoulder,
her hate for him reflected in the flash of her eyes and
the firmness of her set jaw. She recoiled a bit when his
sardonic laughter trailed along after him as he made a
turn in the road and was lost from Glenda's sight.

Angrily, Glenda was reminded of her hate for
Ramón, then in her next breath was sadly reminded
of her love for Read. With rounded shoulders, she
stepped back inside, into the shadows of her house
and fell to her knees beside her mother. With tender-

ness, she began to bathe her mother's face with a cool, dampened cloth. She choked back a sob when she found her mother's dark eyes silently studying her. . . .

"Glenda, what is it?" her mother finally spoke, breaking the silence. "The doctor. He will make me well. You shouldn't fret so. That is the reason for your sprinklings of tears, is it not?"

Glenda flicked tears from both eyes with brisk movements of a forefinger. "Yes, Mamma," she murmured. She couldn't tell her mother that the *Sea Wolf* had carried her heart away as part of its cargo . . . for wherever Read traveled . . . so . . . did her . . . heart. . . .

Being a part of another lonely night, Glenda strolled along the sandy beach, in a form of melancholy herself. Two weeks had passed with her doing her chores in a half daze. Her thoughts never lingered long on the duties at hand, but would always stray to those of the sea, wishing she could become a mermaid for a short while in her life. If half woman . . . and half fish . . . she could travel without even the aid of a ship to the shores of America, where she could search out this seaport called New Orleans. Wouldn't she cause such a stir when once arrived there splashing and eager to be taken ashore where Read made his residence . . . ?

Giggling a bit, Glenda struggled with Nena's added pounds in her arms. The orphaned kitten was growing in leaps and bounds and her spots where quickly fading. "And not only your spots are leaving you, but also your milk teeth," she said, now rubbing noses with Nena, who was purring contentedly. Glenda had found two teeth on the floor two separate mornings and had known Nena's adult teeth had become the victor, pushing the milk teeth out of the way as they had come through in all their glory. Her orphaned cub was changing into an adult much too quickly. Glenda knew that soon a leash would be required when taking these nightly strolls. She knew that the muscles in her arms were insufficient to continue to be able to cradle and love what had become not only of her baby, but also . . . her . . . best friend. . . .

An involuntary shiver ran through Glenda when the sea breeze lifted her skirt to a soft fluttering around her ankles. A warm spray of water settled in gentleness onto her upturned face as she lifted her eyes to the dark velvet canvas of the sky where stars were twinkling as though winking at her. "Ah, and there's the moon," she whispered, seeing its arched tiny sliver peering from beneath one, single cumbersome cloud. "Are you peeking down at Read also with your rivulets of dancing shadows? Is he . . . even . . . watching you? Is he . . . even . . . thinking of me . . . ?"

Glenda kicked through the dampened sand with her bare feet, now looking out into the sea. This had become her nightly vigil. Trying to separate the shimmering of the lights from distant El Progresso from those that might be surfacing from a ship moving inland from the sea to drop anchor at El Progresso.

Glenda knew that the *Sea Wolf* was due to return. She had learned the timing of the harvesting of the bananas to that of the arrival of the cargo ship, which

was only one, the one with the fierce-sounding name
. . . the *Sea Wolf*. She knew that this ship was her
only connection with the man she loved. She had to
believe that one day he would return.

"But . . . will he come . . . for . . . me . . . ?" she
whispered, bending, rubbing her cheek into the softness of Nena's mane. "Or will time cause him to forget
me, to then find another? Will he choose a more
proper lady . . . one with a proper upbringing . . .
from a distinguished family like his own?"

As the one cover of cloud rolled gently away from
the moon, the moon's bright, steady beam reflected
onto the water as though hundreds of electric lights
had been switched on beneath its surface, causing the
crests of the waves to glisten, even almost hauntingly.
As these crests began to build into higher, curling
whitecaps, they became like thunder as they crashed
and tumbled onto the sandy beach, only inches from
where Glenda's toes played in the sand.

She now stood still, gathering the fury of the sea all
around her, watching a storm building in the far
distance as sparks of lightning ignited the sky in awe-
some streaks of heaven-made power.

A trembling raced through Glenda as Nena spat at
the noise and show of force in the sky. "I guess we'd
best return home, orphaned little one. Storms have a
way of traveling quite fast from across the sea," she
murmured, drawing Nena closer. Glenda smiled
warmly as the cub burrowed her nose against the
cotton of her blouse, taking comfort in the soft swells
of Glenda's breasts. "I wish you could always stay as
sweet and innocent," she sighed, turning to make her
way back to her home, where the loneliness of her bed

awaited, where only restless dreams had become her every-night companion.

She had missed the American's home in El Progresso and all the comforts she had found there. She missed even more than that. She had grown to love the pastime of embroidering and the evenings spent sharing this with Christina.

Glenda had found a hidden talent . . . that of sketching . . . as well as embroidering. But now that she had returned to Bay Island's way of life, she had no fine linens or expensive brushes for which to practice her talents. The sand had become her drawing board where she had left many designs fingered into the sand, where usually beside these, she would, with slow strokes from her forefinger, print Read's name for her to see . . . to touch . . . for above all else . . . he was what she truly missed most.

Kicking aside wet clusters of seaweed that had just been carried to her feet, and stepping high to miss some of the sharpest appearing seashells that had just been washed in from the deepest recesses of the sea, Glenda rushed onward, not wanting to be the victim of this latest storm blowing toward her much too quickly. The wind was now whipping her skirt angrily around her and her hair was becoming a mass of wild, blowing tangles.

Almost breathless, she moved between tall stilts that held up the main fishing pier for the small village. For a brief moment, she felt protected from the wind and splashing water, but the offensive rotting fish odor making rise from the piles of discarded fish heads and scales on all sides of her, was cause for her to dash from the shelter to this time find other than the weather to dread.

Stopping abruptly in mid-step, Glenda's eyes narrowed into two green slits when she found Ramón standing there with a wide, toothy grin, reflecting the white of his teeth in such contrast against the dark brown of his face. His eyes were two dark pits, yet staring a hole through her.

"Ramón, what are you doing here?" Glenda hissed, glowering. Her troubled glance flitted around her, soon realizing that the darkness of night and the fast approaching storm had sent most scurrying for cover, leaving only Glenda and Ramón and the innocence of an orphaned puma cub to face one another, as though duelists, ready to choose weapons to use on one another.

"You do not own the beach," Ramón growled. "I have a perfect right to be taking a stroll." He laughed menacingly, flinging a hand in the air. "Can I help it if I find a beautiful, 'pale-faced' woman also alone?"

"Why aren't you at El Progresso plantation?" she said icily. "Surely your duties to Rayburn can't afford you the luxury of moving so casually from the banana plantation to this island. What if Rayburn would need your services? Ha! Then you'd see how quickly he could hire someone else to take your place."

Ramón strutted closer to Glenda, smiling mischievously. His white cotton shirt was unbuttoned to his waist, revealing tight, kinky chest hairs and two taut nipples, and the coarse material of his breeches showed the swell of his thigh muscles and also that of his manhood. "Rayburn's occupied. For the full night," he said, reaching to lift a lock of Glenda's hair from her shoulder. When Nena spat and swung a paw at him, Ramón flinched and dropped his hand to his side.

Gritting her teeth, Glenda took a step backward. "You keep your hands to yourself, Ramón Martinez," she hissed.

He laughed crudely. "And if I don't? Is kitty cat there going to get me?" He poked at Nena with a forefinger, teasing, tormenting.

"Stop that," Glenda said, spinning on a heel, rushing on away from him. But when she felt the tight squeeze of Ramón's fingers around a wrist, causing her to stop with a jerk, she kicked and squirmed angrily. "Ramón, why do you continue to pester me so?" she fumed angrily. Lightning was now dancing overhead in colorful splashes, and a sprinkle of rain settled on Glenda's cheek. She was remembering another night . . . another storm. Ramón had tried to rape her then, but had failed. Would he . . . try . . . again . . . ? Would . . . he . . . fail . . . again. . . ?

"You won't get away, Glenda," he growled, jerking her, causing Nena to jump from Glenda's arms, to stand with curved back and angry-faced, hissing as he watched Ramón's continued show of force. "And maybe you won't even want to, when you see the gift I've brought you."

"You? A gift? Hah!" she mocked angrily. "Never. Never would I accept a gift from you."

With his free hand, Ramón reached behind him and pulled something from his rear pocket. Then he dangled a diamond necklace before Glenda's eyes, in his own way of bargaining with her. "Not even this?" he mimicked with a mocking tone. "The American lady. She was quite upset to lose such a treasure. No?

229

A treasure I stole to place only against the satin of your flesh."

Glenda's free hand went to her throat, remembering the one day she had privileged herself to wear this particular necklace. Her heart thumped wildly. She had thought . . . Read . . . responsible for the theft when all along it had indeed been Ramón who had scaled that palmetto tree and stolen Christina's jewels as Christina had lain so peacefully, trustingly asleep. "Ramón, it . . . was you . . . ?" she finally gasped. "You . . . ?"

He laughed hoarsely, still dangling the necklace in the air. When lightning flashed, it reflected in glittering purples and blues onto the magnificent stones. "Yes," Ramón bragged. "I have many more, too. And I will give you a different one each time you meet me. Or you can have them all at once if you will agree to speak your vows with me. You could flaunt your riches for the other island women to see. You could brag that it was *I*, Ramón, the main *caudillo* of Bay Island who presented them to you . . ."

Jerking even harder now, Glenda began to rage. "You aren't only a fool, but a thief," she shouted. "No woman wants a fool or a thief to speak of in the same breath when speaking of her man." She knew that she wasn't altogether speaking the truth. She had thought Read guilty of thievery and hadn't she loved him still? But she knew that no matter what . . . she would always feel the same about William Read de-Baulieu . . .

"If you won't accept my gifts, then I will offer them to other women," Ramón said, stuffing the necklace back inside his rear breeches pocket. "But what you won't agree to willingly, I will take." He drew her roughly to him and crushed his lips to hers, ignoring the frantic pacings of Nena as she watched, and the steady rumblings of thunder around him as the rain began to fall in soft, cool droplets.

Glenda squirmed and kicked, grumbling beneath her breath. And as Ramón wrestled her to the floor of the beach, she found herself suddenly pinioned beneath his body of steel. When Nena came bouncing forward and placed her face in Glenda's, Glenda shouted at her to leave, afraid that Ramón would tire of Nena's nuisances and possibly cause him to harm her. But Nena squatted with head tilted, silently watching as Ramón forced Glenda's skirt above her waist and her blouse above her breasts, revealing to him all that was necessary to receive his pleasures for the night.

"Ramón, when Rayburn hears that you've stolen from him and that you've raped me, he will kill you," Glenda said, squirming still. His hands were holding each of her wrists, but his tongue and lips were making quick assaults from her lips, to each of her breasts.

"You won't tell anyone," he grumbled, flicking a tongue around a nipple, causing it to draw taut in response. "If you do, I will kill that stupid cat of yours."

"You wouldn't. . . ."

"I would. I killed its mother. Why wouldn't I kill the cub? You will have to see its death one day anyway. When it begins killing chickens and causing all sorts of disturbances, even the gentle people of our village will demand its return to the jungle or its death."

231

"No!" Glenda screamed. Then she felt panic rising sharply inside herself as Ramón felt secure enough now to let a hand stray to explore between her thighs. "Ramón, you must stop! Now! Return to El Progresso. Surely Rayburn sees your absence . . ."

"Like I said," he said thickly, showing the beginning of sexual excitement, "Rayburn is occupied. He is busy loading the ship's hold with bananas. He won't even miss me with the entire plantation's laborers crowding around, passing the bananas amongst themselves as they see that the bananas are handled gently."

Glenda's pulse raced. Her back drew up tightly, as though it was a rope, ready to snap. "Did you . . . say a ship . . . ?"

Ramón left a trail of wet kisses from breast to breast, then to her stomach, as his fingers tried to arouse her to responding. "Yes. The *Sea Wolf*," he grumbled. "It arrived. Today . . ."

Glenda felt a renewed energy as she thought of the ship and to whom it could carry her. She now knew how she could finally get to be with Read again. Hadn't she known all along that was a part of the plan . . . ? To seek him out? Hadn't she always said that she would travel to the ends of the earth to be with the man she loved . . . ?

Her breath came in shallow gasps as she slowly dug the fingers of her free hand deeply into the sand. Circling her fingers, she secured a hand full of wet sand, then waited for Ramón to lift his face from his laborings, and when he did, facing her . . . leering, moving his free hand to the buttons of his breeches, Glenda raised her hand and pressed the sand angrily into his face, even grinding it in with force. He yelled and began spitting and spewing, forgetting his hold as his hands worked frantically to scrape the sand from his mouth, nose and eyes. . . .

Laughing, Glenda wriggled herself free from beneath him. "Seems I'm even more macho than you, Ramón," she said, repositioning her blouse and skirt in place. "And I'm not even . . . a . . . man . . ."

Laughing still, she bent and scooped Nena into her arms and began to run through the falling rain and the gale force of the wind that had just begun to whip around her.

"I'll kill the cat," Ramón shouted, still half blind from the grinding of the sand between his eyelids. "You'll be sorry . . ."

Glenda tensed a bit and drew Nena closer to her. But remembrances of the ship and the plan forming inside her brain gave her cause to not worry any further. "You won't have the chance," she yelled across her shoulder. "Nor will you ever have the chance to corner me on the beach again. . . ."

Chapter Eleven

The storm had drifted farther out to sea and Glenda was rowing her shallow draft boat toward the moored *Sea Wolf*. The dark sky was filled with the dancing reflections from the ocote pine torches on the shore, and the loud voices from Rayburn and the laborers reverberated across the rippling water's surface, causing Glenda to cease rowing, welcoming the chance to rest her arms a bit. She knew that the ship was still being loaded with bananas and that it was too soon to move onto land, knowing that the chances of being caught were much too great.

A soft paw reaching to touch Glenda's bare foot drew her attention to Nena. She scooted from the seat and pulled the sealed crate next to her, looking through the wide cracks into eyes that matched her own. She lifted a finger to the softness of Nena's mane and gently caressed it. "When we get safely—*if* we get safely into the ship's hold to hide—only then can I give you your freedom once again, orphaned little cub," Glenda whispered. "And even then, I'm not sure if we'll be safe or if we'll be able to get drink and food enough to last this full journey. I have only two arms and you almost fill them both."

Nena purred contentedly beneath the tender loving touch. Glenda had much to sort out in her mind and was relieved to sense trust from her puma, knowing how important this was in the months to come when Nena could become a bit too much to handle.

"As you have had to do, I am also leaving my mother behind," Glenda whispered further. Her sadness was deep, remembering the confused look in her mother's eyes when Glenda had knelt at her mother's bedside and had whispered in the dark of her need to flee to America, to search out the man she truly loved.

Glenda hadn't told her mother of the second attempted rape by Ramón Martinez, as she hadn't told even of the first, nor had she told her mother of Ramón's threats to kill Nena. Glenda knew that if she did linger on Bay Island, he *would* complete his threats, by both raping her . . . and killing her orphaned cub.

By traveling to America, Glenda was solving many problems. But leaving close family associations behind was her only building regret. She had wanted to linger on Bay Island long enough to be sure her mother recovered her full strength. "But Father is there to now look after you," Glenda said, returning to the seat, securing both paddles to resume rowing onward. "I have to believe that Papa's presence is even more important than mine. My life? It has no meaning since my last goodbyes to Read. I *have* to go to him. I . . . *must* . . ."

Feeling an achiness in her arms, not used to laboring over boat's paddles, Glenda began to breathe in short gasps. The air had become cold since the storm, and patches of sea water kept finding its way to Glenda's face, causing a chill to ride her spine. She licked her lips, tasting the saltiness, and tossed her damp hair from her shoulders, hating the steady splash of the waves against the sides of the boat.

As the boat rode high on the water, then low again, Glenda lacked the feeling of equilibrium and worried about the larger ship and how this sense of queasiness in both her stomach and head might even double, possibly even triple. Would she even be able to stay confined to the hold of the ship, where only bananas would be stored?

"I have to make it," she said determinedly, sinking the paddles deeper into the water, steering her boat toward the shore out of viewing range of the *Sea Wolf*'s crew. "No one must find me on the ship. I do not trust woman-hungry sailors. They could possibly even be more threatening than . . . Ramón. . . ."

The whiteness of the beach was an illumination of brilliance beneath the rays of the moon that had just emerged from behind the shadows of a cloud, aiding Glenda in the mooring of her small boat. When she stepped her bare feet into the effervescence of the water's edge, she shivered a bit, then went on her way until she had the boat secured as far in onto the sand as she could drag it.

"And now for you, Nena," she whispered, lifting the crate into he arms, then the travel bag that had been used only for food. She had hoped to steal what water was needed from the huge barrels of fresh water that Read, when speaking dreamily of his adventure of the high seas, had said were stored in the hold of the ship. Her only worry was for Nena. Could the pork sausage she had managed to steal from her mother's kitchen last until she reached America? For herself, Glenda had brought mainly a variety of fruit and cheeses to survive on, knowing that in no way could she choose to eat a steady diet of the green bananas that would be aboard the *Sea Wolf*. Her stomach was going to ache enough as it was, having the waves to ride. She didn't need the unripe, green bananas as well.

Nena began to toss and turn inside the crate, creating havoc in Glenda's aching arms. "Nena, please," she whispered. She looked toward the dark coils of underbrush and listened to the restless stirrings of the night life in its hidden depths. She suddenly understood her orphaned cub's sudden restlessness. Nena sensed her call of the wild . . . . her nearness to the jungle, where she had roamed and explored with her mother before the fatal gunshot wound. Glenda even felt a tremor of guilt for having this animal caged, but knew that at this age and size, Nena wouldn't last a full night among even its own kind.

"I'm truly sorry for what Ramón has caused your life to become," Glenda whispered further to Nena. "But as I am having to do, we must accept our life's plan . . . be it good . . . be it bad."

She tensed when she caught the sound of Ramón's voice drifting her way with the wind. He had returned to the north shores of Honduras ahead of her. While still on Bay Island herself, she had watched from the dark shadows as he had begun rowing into the darkness of the night across the trembling waters of the Caribbean. She had hoped he wouldn't make it, that a huge whitecap would slap against the side of the boat and dump him into the bottomless sea. . . .

Creeping stealthily now, Glenda worked her way into the tangle of the underbrush and moved beneath the protective covering of the palmetto and mahogany trees until she was close enough to where the ship was moored to be able to see the swaying fire of the torches that had been thrust into the ground along a path where the clamoring activity of the laborers moved along with the green bunches of bananas.

Rayburn was standing tall and erect, legs spread a bit, while one hand rested on a holstered gun at his hip. His eyes moved with the men while in a quiet conversation with a man of less than Rayburn's height and much less likeable facial features. This man also stood with a hand resting on a holstered gun, but was full-bearded and dressed in full black, almost looking the devil with such an untrusting glint to his dark eyes and set to his jaw.

"Is this the man who took Read's place?" Glenda wondered to herself. She shivered uncontrollably, hoping to not come face to face with him once on the ship if he was the new representative for the American Fruit Company. He looked evil . . . a man . . . to surely not be trusted.

Hunkering, Glenda continued to watch and wait until the laborers had returned to El Progresso, leaving only Rayburn and the bearded man conferring alone. The torches had been carried away with the laborers, leaving the remaining activity to be directed beneath the moon's soft glow. Glenda moved to the edge of the underbrush, barely breathing, watching Rayburn, then the ship. Then to her relief, Rayburn and the bearded man retreated along the path that had been cleared to lead an unencumbered way to and from El Progresso. From earlier experiences, Glenda knew that she had approximately one hour before the ship's departure. Rayburn and the American representative would share a final cigar and glass of port and exchange a few bawdy jokes while the ship's crew would secure the cargo for its days of travel to America.

"Oh, let there be room in the hold for me and Nena," she prayed. "Let them leave a small lantern burning as Read said they occasionally did for the sailors who would sneak a quick drink of port from the kegs that were carried aboard for the ship's captain."

The thought of her being in the dark for the days it would take to travel to New Orleans unnerved her, with the fear of having to avoid being discovered by a sailor even less than her fear of the darkness.

Breathless, she waited a while longer, and when she could tell that the activity had died on the deck of the ship and it appeared that most sailors were in a cluster at the helm of the ship, too absorbed in laughing, drinking and shouting obscenities jokingly to one another, Glenda knew that the time had arrived to make her move. Smiling a silent thanks toward the sky, she watched the moon hide its face behind a heavy shroud of dark clouds.

"It is now or never, orphaned cub," she whispered, then ran a quick sprint across the sand and once she reached the gangplank that led to the ship, she hurried with weak knees and a pounding heart. She glanced quickly around her, relieved that the men were still in their group, huddling even, and when the word "whores" reached Glenda's ears, she understood their guffaws and ignorance of what was happening only a few feet from where they stood. Glenda had to wonder if most men thought disrespectfully of women. Read hadn't appeared to be that way. But then, she would also remember her true . . . American father . . . and how he had been . . . .

Remembering Read's spoken details of a ship's body, Glenda rushed down one flight of stairs, then another until she stood, breathless, inhaling the familiar odor of freshly picked bananas. It was so overpowering in the closed surroundings that Glenda's nose twitched and her throat burned. Would she truly be able to spend days and nights in this ship's hold? She did suspect one thing. If she succeeded in this adventure, she would probably never wish to eat or even see another banana!

Nena growled and spat from her closed interior. "Patience, Nena," Glenda murmured, feeling her way around in the darkness. "It won't be long now. I hear the rumbling of the ship's boiler. The men are readying for departure."

She moved her fingers across the row after row of velvet-skinned bananas, feeling their cold clamminess, then ventured onward, wondering where the water barrels and kegs of port were kept.

"But I cannot light the lantern myself," Glenda murmured to herself. "It would arouse suspicion." Instead, she continued to grope in the dark, relieved to find many empty spaces for which to make hers and Nena's home while on their secret journey. She even found the perfect corner in which to hide when she would hear footsteps approaching on the stairs that led down into this hold. Even now, she felt that this

4 BESTSELLING HISTORICAL ROMANCES BY YOUR FAVORITE AUTHORS CAN BE YOURS, FREE!

Kensington Choice brings you historical romances by your favorite bestselling authors including Janelle Taylor, Shannon Drake, Rosanne Bittner, Jo Beverley, and Georgina Gentry, just to name a few! Each book is filled with passion, adventure and the excitement of bygone times!

To introduce you to this great club which is part of Zebra Home Subscription Service, we'd like to send you your first 4 bestselling historical romances, absolutely free! And once you get these 4 free books to savor at home, we'll rush you the next 4 brand-new books at the lowest prices available, as soon as they are published.

The way the club works is that after your initial FREE shipment, you will get our 4 newest bestselling historical romances delivered to your doorstep each month at the  preferred subscriber's rate of only $4.20 per book, a savings of up to $8.16 per month (since these titles sell in bookstores for $4.99-$6.99)! All books are sent on a 10-day free examination basis and there is no minimum number of books to buy. (And no charge for shipping.) Plus as a regular subscriber, you'll receive our FREE monthly newsletter, *Zebra/Pinnacle Romance News*, which features author profiles, subscriber benefits, book previews and more!

So start today by returning the FREE BOOK CERTIFICATE provided. We'll send you 4 FREE BOOKS with no further obligation: A FREE gift offering you hours of reading pleasure with no obligation...how can you lose?

*We have 4 FREE BOOKS for you
as your introduction to
KENSINGTON CHOICE!
To get your FREE BOOKS, worth
up to $24.96, mail the card below.*

FREE BOOK CERTIFICATE

Yes! Please send me 4 Kensington Choice (the best of Zebra and Pinnacle Books) Historical Romances without cost or obligation (worth up to $24.96). As a Kensington Choice subscriber, I will then receive 4 brand-new romances to preview each month for 10 days FREE. I can return any books I decide not to keep and owe nothing. The publisher's prices for Kensington Choice romances range from $4.99-$6.99, but as a preferred subscriber I will get these books for only $4.20 per book or $16.80 for all four titles. There is no minimum number of books to buy and I may cancel my subscription at any time, plus there is no additional charge for postage and handling. No matter what I decide to do, my first 4 books are mine to keep, absolutely FREE!

Name _____

Address _____ Apt. _____

City _____ State _____ Zip _____

Telephone ( ) _____

Signature _____

(If under 18, parent or guardian must sign)

Subscription subject to acceptance. Terms and prices subject to change.

KF0998

was the place to position herself, until the ship was out to sea and the men were busy with their chores of keeping the ship moving as smoothly as was possible through the waters of the Caribbean.

"Just a short while now, Nena," Glenda whispered, settling down into a corner, placing the crate next to her, smoothing Nena's mane with the tips of her fingers. "Once the ship is out to sea, I will let you free for short intervals. But I can't let you free at all times. The men might surprise us one time too many and find you romping and hopping around. They might even be as Ramón and only think of killing . . . not loving . . . enjoying . . . you."

She grew silent, listening to the footsteps overhead. She tensed when Rayburn's voice was heard from the shore, shouting his farewells. The noise from the boiler room began in earnest and the clanking of the anchor being lifted from its watery grave made Glenda's heart begin to beat nervously. It was finally becoming a reality. She was going to be able to seek Read out. Oh, if he wasn't too ill to be happy for her surprise! Didn't Rayburn say that he was experiencing dizzy spells? Might he even have . . . died . . . ?

She shook her head angrily, not wanting to think of such a possibility. Read was strong. And hadn't he even said that he had faked the injury? She couldn't understand how an injury that had been faked could cause so much trouble. Yet . . . there had been those headaches while on their journey to the Mayan ruins. Oh, she was so confused! But she would soon have all the answers to her questions . . . her doubts. . . .

"But, *Mamma?* I already miss you," she whispered to herself.

Hearing approaching footsteps overhead, then seeing the flickerings of a lantern being carried down the stairs that led down into the hold, Glenda quickly clamped her hand over her mouth, afraid that if this man approaching would even hear her breathing, he would discover her and would indeed get her in much trouble! Would he toss her overboard, or worse yet, would she be used as an object of ugly pleasurings by the dirty-minded sailors? She could even see their eyes now . . . watching her . . . leering . . . as they would take turns with her body. She then wouldn't be fit for Read . . . or . . . any other man.

She hunched her shoulders against the hardness of the outer wall, watching the lazy flickerings of the lantern casting shadows on the ceiling as the man moved through the cargo, inspecting it. Glenda tensed, feeling her gut twisting, waiting for him to make the one turn that would expose her to him. Then she sighed with relief when he stopped and retreated his steps where he then went to the far end of the small cargo area and anchored the lantern on the wall. Glenda could hear the splashings of a liquid being poured, then could hear him thirstily gulp it down, and waited to see what his next move might be. To her further relief, this man moved back up the stairs and slammed the cargo door shut with a loud bang, leaving the soft flickerings of the lantern for Glenda to use and feel more secure with her surroundings.

"Nena, it still isn't safe," she whispered. "When we hear the scramblings cease and know the men are in their bunks for the night, only then can I feel free to set you free," Glenda said, placing the crate even closer to her, then the travel bag next to it. She quickly opened the travel bag to secure a finger full of sausage for Nena, to ease her soft pleadings.

Smiling then, Glenda began to creep around the corner from which she had been hiding, then stifled a scream when she saw two rats scamper around the next corner. "Damn!" she said quietly. "I had thought to expect such. But . . . not . . . so . . . large. . . ." She turned and eyed Nena mischievously. "Yes, orphaned cub," she murmured. "You will be having assorted meals while aboard this ship. We will make the ship's captain wonder where his rats disappeared to."

Laughing softly, she moved on around the bananas and began to explore. The corners were dark and foreboding where the lantern's light didn't reach and there was no other cargo besides that of the bananas. Where the lantern flickered from the wall, having been secured by brass moldings on all sides to keep it from pitching onto the ship's deck to cause a sudden fire, Glenda saw the many barrels that Read had spoken of. She went to one and ran a finger over the perspiring rim, then tasted the liquid that had moved onto her finger. "Yes, fresh water. Just as Read said," she beamed. "At least Nena and I won't lack for something with which to quench our thirst."

Lifting an eyebrow inquisitively, she fingered the dripping wetness of a keg of a different size and shape. She thrust this finger between her lips and tasted the tart sweetness. "Yes, Read also knew of this port," she laughed softly. "There's enough to get the whole crew drunk." But she knew the dangers of that. She wished to be able to dump this particular keg, so no man could drink from it to dull his senses.

"But as long as I keep my ears open and make sure to keep hidden when the men come for their tastes of this port, I will be safe enough," she murmured, tensing when another rat scampered at her feet. She shivered, hoping Nena would be able to do her work soon. No more sausage would be required this night. Surely not. And hadn't Glenda worried about the meat spoiling before the trip had come to an end anyway? The rats were the answer. This would even give Nena the chance to learn the craft of hunting. And since her adult teeth were pushing their way through quite thickly, Glenda knew that Nena indeed could rid this ship of its ugly, two-eyed, long-tailed creatures!

Afraid of discovery, Glenda went back to her corner and settled down onto the dampness of the flooring. Though night and a cool wind was whipping around on top deck, the tight enclosure of the hold was sweltering. Glenda looked toward Nena and saw that she was sprawled in her crate, half asleep, yet panting wildly. Even Glenda felt the need to gasp for air as the pungence of the bananas continued to attack her keen sense of smell, and the tropic, sultry air caused her body to become many salty beads of perspiration.

Loosening the waist of her skirt and the drawstrings of her blouse, to expose her breasts, which heaved heavily with each breath taken, Glenda eased her head back against the ship's side wall and let the gentle rocking of the ship lull her into a fitful sleep. In her dreams, she was lying in a bed of many live, pale orchids, and Read was there, caressing her with the dark brown of his eyes. When his tongue began to nip at her flesh, she sighed leisurely until his teeth began to sink in and drew pain to the surface. . . .

Glenda's eyes flew open wildly, still feeling the pain; then she screamed when she saw a rat scamper away, screeching, into the hidden folds of bananas. Feeling a warm liquid on her ankle, where the pain had changed into a nervous, steady throbbing, Glenda's fingers reached, touched, and discovered what the wetness was. When she placed her fingers before her eyes and saw the blood, she gasped noisily, becoming even a bit sickened, when she realized that it hadn't been Read inflicting pain in her dream . . . but the teeth . . . of . . . a rat . . . in real life!

Knowing the filth of a rat and the dangers of infection, Glenda pushed herself up from the floor and limped, sobbing, in the direction of the barrels of water. She knew what haste was required to cleanse her wound. She didn't want to arrive to New Orleans all filled with fever and maybe even minus a lower limb. God! She wanted to go to Read bright-eyed and loving. She wanted to share a bed with him . . . but not a sick bed. . . .

The sound of the cargo door suddenly lifting caused Glenda's heart to become erratic. She was midway between the water barrels and her hiding place. She felt desperation rising inside. She was going to be caught. With one hand, she clutched at her skirt that was hanging only on the fullness of her hips, and with the other, began to reach to secure her breasts beneath her blouse, but she was much too late. The heavy-bearded man with the glint in his dark eyes and the guns holstered at his waist was already eyeing her in disbelief.

"Well, I'll be damned," the man said gruffly, stepping from the lower step. He moved toward her in a cautious stride. "I was right. It *was* the scream of a female that I heard moments ago. A female stowaway."

Glenda clung to her skirt and covered her bosom as best she could, inching back away from him. "Please, sir," she murmured, flinching when a fresh stab of pain grabbed at her wound. She almost lost her footing when the ankle gave way to the pain.

"Rayburn didn't warn me about anything like this," the man chuckled, moving closer to her. His eyes had become two dark coals, searing her flesh, as his gaze raked her up and down, stopping at her breasts. He licked his lips hungrily and took it upon himself to reach for and secure a full breast in one of his hands.

Glenda jerked free from him and managed to turn the corner that led to where she had thought she could stay hidden. But she had become careless . . . . "You do not dare touch me further," she hissed, backing up against the outer wall. "I am a friend of Rayburn Taylor. He would cut your heart out if you defile me."

The man tilted his head back in a fit of laughter. Then his gaze began raking her anew. "Tell me more funny tales," he laughed wickedly. "If you were a friend of Rayburn's like you profess, you wouldn't be traveling below deck in the rat-infested hold. No. You would have been given the captain's quarters." His fingers dared her again, but withdrew when she snapped at him with her teeth.

"Rayburn wouldn't have understood my reasons for wanting to leave Bay Island," she hissed. "Traveling in this manner was the only way." And she knew this to be a truth. To tell Rayburn that she had such a desperate need to see . . . to be with . . . Read, would have even been cause to have explained Read's deceit of Rayburn. No. She couldn't have told all. Only she and Read knew the truths of their special times together.

Nena suddenly let out a loud mewing sound and spat angrily from behind Glenda, sending waves of alarm through Glenda's brain. For another reckless moment, she had forgotten her cub. She forgot her worries of her breasts hanging freely, but instead used the hand that had so desperately tried to keep them hidden, to pull the fullness of her skirt out away from her, to try to hide the crate and its contents from this man's probing eyes.

One shove from the man and Glenda was sent sprawling to the floor next to Nena. With a wild heart, she scooted to the crate and wrapped her arms about it, eyeing this man vehemently.

"What . . . the . . . ?" the man blurted, scratching his head quizzically. "A puma? Why would you . . . ?"

"It is my orphaned cub," Glenda said anxiously. "Please. You must not make plans to hurt her. She is tame. She will harm nothing or no one."

The man laughed raucously. "You're a big bag of surprises," he said, bending, reaching his fingers through the crate, gently touching Nena's mane, which caused her to turn into a purring machine. "Baby puma, did you say?" he said, lifting a heavy, dark eyebrow toward Glenda.

"Nena. Her name . . . is . . . Nena."

"And yours?" he said thickly, his gaze moving from breast to breast.

"Glenda. Glenda Galvez," she said in a near whisper, slowly lifting her fingers to the drawstring of her blouse, finally managing to hide her breasts.

"Spanish . . . ?"

"No. *Mestizo* . . ."

"You look American . . ."

She blushed and lowered her eyes. "My father . . . my true father . . . was American. . . ."

"The hell you say," the man said, rising. He offered her a hand and helped her to her feet. "George. George Boyd," he further stated.

Glenda was leery of this man's change of personality. Was he trying to catch her off guard . . . or . . . what . . . ? She staggered a bit and found herself suddenly encircled by his arms. When his lips bore down upon hers, Glenda began beating her fists against his chest, but became helpless when he drew her to him and held her pinioned there. She didn't like the way he was moving his lower body. It was as though it was unclothed and he was moving inside her. She could even feel his hardness. . . .

"I could make the voyage a comfortable one for you," he murmured into her ear as his lips began wetting her face in hot kisses. "I have my own cabin. It could be fun, especially if you come willingly. I'll even take proper care of your cat."

"I'd rather stay here with the four-legged rats," she snapped angrily, wondering how she could have for one careless moment thought that he could be trusted. She dropped a hand to her ankle, feeling renewed stabbings of pain. Fear raced through her. How could she have even forgotten the wound. . . ?

"*Señor,*" she quickly blurted. "Please step aside . . ."

He laughed, spreading his legs a bit and placing his hands on his hips above his jutting guns. "So you can go topside and be accepted so greedily by all the passion-hungry sailors?" he said quietly. "Lady, you don't know what you'd be getting yourself into."

"No," she said weakly. "I do not wish to go topside. I wish to have water to bathe my fresh wound." She lifted the tail of her skirt and revealed the rat's teeth marks to him.

His shoulders relaxed as he fell to his knees to examine the wound. "My God, you've been bitten," he said.

"I know I've been bitten. By one of your ship's rats," she said between clenched teeth. "Now, please. I need to bathe the filth from my wound."

In one swoop, George had Glenda in his arms and was climbing the stairs and had her quickly in the close confines of his personal cabin. He placed her gingerly on the bed and before she could even question his true motives, he was cleansing her wound with a clean cloth and fresh water, and once that was done was applying some strange ointment on the wound.

"What is that?" she said, leaning on one elbow.

"My wife encouraged me to bring this homemade concoction of hers with me to the jungle," he said, screwing the lid back onto the jar. "She feared all sorts of insect bites."

"Your wife. . . ?"

His face flushed. "Yes. I'm married," he said. "But I'm sure you think me a bastard for grabbing at you like I did, now knowing that I have a faithful wife."

"If she's faithful, yes, you are a bastard," Glenda

said. "But having taken care of me in such a proper fashion can help erase such thoughts from my mind."

"I'll be honorable the rest of the voyage," George said, lighting a pipe. "I'll even give up my cabin to the injured mestizo maiden. That is, if you can forget my lousy behavior of moments ago and not mention it to Rayburn. You see, I don't make doing that a habit of mine. But you are so damn beautiful. Any man would temporarily lose his senses about him . . ."

Glenda blushed a bit, then spoke. "It is true that I do know Rayburn and I won't speak of your behavior to him. In fact, I doubt if I will ever have the opportunity of even seeing him again," Glenda sighed, tensing when her ankle began to ache anew. "And, sir, I do truly appreciate your kindness." Then her eyes flew widely open. She began to move from the bed. "My orphaned kitten," she cried. "What if someone. . . ?"

George turned on a heel and headed for the door. "I'll get your cat," he said from across his shoulder. "She can also share my room. . . ." He laughed a bit raucously. "Wait until the guys back home hear that I shared my cabin with two lively cats. . . ."

Chapter Twelve

Looking into the far distance, Read was watching the dark cover of night change to that of a vivid display of lightning. Had he had ever before seen such an array of designs of light in the heavens?

"Ah, yes," he remembered to himself. "When with Glenda, our one night together before reaching the Mayan ruins. . . ."

He swallowed hard, not wanting to remember. Then he watched lacy clouds drifts across the moon, not able to keep himself from wondering if Glenda could be also observing these many moods of this restless night. Was she a dreamer as he had just recently become? Was he even a part of her dreams? Ah, Glenda, his love, his only love. She was only a few days away by way of ship, but to Read, that was the same as the wide expanse of the continent's reach, because he knew that he had to forget her.

Leaning against the balcony's railing that overlooked the courtyard of his Creole house, he tried to focus his thoughts on the quiet splashing of the fountain below him and the flickerings from an oil lamp casting soft shadows on his private place of tropical luxury.

The large fan-shaped windows of his house looked down onto this courtyard which held banana trees, oleanders and parterres of flowers, where palm trees and live oaks took preference over all. The air was sweet with the heady fragrances from the variety of these flowers, and the twanging of a guitar from somewhere in the distance made one remember that they were a part of the French Quarter of New Orleans.

Read ran his fingers through his hair, wishing his sister Harriett would hurry a bit more for her preparations of the ball they were planning to attend together. He needed to fill his mind with gaiety, if even only in the presence of his younger sister, as he needed to help fill her mind with something besides thoughts of the husband she had recently lost at sea.

Read began to pace the small square of the balcony with his hands clasped firmly together behind his back. "Harriett and I share the same sort of loss," he mumbled aloud. "She the man she loved, and myself, the woman I shall always love."

But although he and Harriett shared such a similar loss, he knew that the circumstances were in no way the same. Though lost to him, Glenda was quite alive and probably already the wife of Ramón Martinez.

"I'll never understand," Read grumbled, now kneading his brow. "Glenda just couldn't make love so sincerely with me while at the same time knowing that she had agreed to marry this Ramón, who had been even accepted by family. Yet Ramón explained to me how important the Honduran family's decisions, as a body of one, ruled the direction a daughter's future would take."

Taking even longer strides, Read lost himself

further in his thoughts. Hadn't Ramón even said that Glenda's mother's welfare, possibly even her life, depended on Glenda behaving like a Honduran woman? Hadn't Ramón said that was the reason for Glenda's mother being filled with melancholia, because she had heard about Glenda having been . . . with . . . an American man? Hadn't Glenda even rushed to her mother's side, leaving Read alone, as though he ceased to exist. . . ?

"Oh, damn it," Read growled. "I had no choice but to leave El Progresso. I had no choice but to refuse to make any more trips on the *Sea Wolf*. I had to leave Glenda to live in the way it was meant for her to live. It is her people's way."

He had hated having to lie to Rayburn again, having feigned further dizziness from a blow on the head that had truly only been a slight scratch. But there would have been no easier way to leave the plantation without having caused raised eyebrows . . . and . . . questions. . . .

He doubled a fist and pounded it against the palm of his other hand, once more remembering Glenda's words of vehemence when having spoken of Ramón in Read's presence. This continued to haunt Read. Glenda had spoken so hatefully of Ramón, but all along having the knowledge that he was to be her husband!?!

"William Read? Are you out here on the balcony in one of your ugly, solemn moods again?" Harriett said abruptly from behind him in her soft, sweet voice.

Swinging around, Read could only see her silhouette against the backdrop of oil lamp flickerings in the room behind her. It was a silhouette of loveliness, so tiny and uncondescending, with the many layers of her petticoats beneath her silken dress the only thing to give her an air of added weight, and, oh, so graceful she was with each movement taken.

Harriet moved on out to add to the shadows of the balcony. Being shorter than Read, she had to tilt her head back a bit to gaze up into his eyes. She placed her white-gloved hand on Read's arm, so gentle was the touch, it was as though a butterfly had landed. "William Read," she said in a near whisper. "I do wish you would confide in me. Since having returned from El Progresso, you rarely even join in a conversation with me anymore. And since father and mother's departure to France, I would appreciate a voice besides that of myself and young David to fill the empty spaces in this house. . . ."

Read eyed her affectionately for a moment, seeing why the men were in eager pursuant of this young, twenty-two year-old widow, though a mother of a frisky four-year-old son. With her dark eyes, always so wide and appearing to be full of wonder, and her dimpled cheeks, he could even himself hardly take his eyes from her. She could be the answer to any man's dream. Yes, he was proud to say that she was his sister.

Smiling widely, Read placed his hands on Harriett's bare shoulders and held her at arm's length. "I am sorry. I hadn't realized I had been acting so withdrawn. But though our family's wealth leaves us with no financial worries, I am restless. I seek another ship in which to ride the seas. I need adventure. The card games I play on my most restless of evenings haven't taken the place of being aboard a ship, where one feels the excitement of danger when the waves of the sea grow angry and begin battle with the ship."

Harriett lowered her eyes, hiding the pain in their depths. She hated the mention of the sea and how the ships would do battle with the thrashing of the waves. Hadn't she lost her own Jason in such a battle? Hadn't twenty fishermen lost their lives at once on that one stormy day? "Please, William Read," she sighed laboriously. "The sea. It is my enemy."

Read drew her into his arms and held her. "I'm sorry. I didn't think," he murmured. "But you do have to forget. The sea and the river is why New Orleans prospers. The men have to be a part of it. This is how they keep food on the table. Though Jason didn't have to fish for a living, since father offered him a position at deBaulieu Gambling Palace and would have had all the money he would ever need to make both you and David happy, he had to prove his worth as a man. As I also must do."

Harriett moved from his arms and eyed him warmly. "I do know what you say is true," she said. "I just have to be reminded. I do understand the importance of the sea. I do understand your restlessness. But, William Read, you were a part of the best ship that makes anchor at New Orleans. The *Sea Wolf*. You've never given me the true reason you refuse to board it again. I do not understand this."

Read's eyes wavered. He didn't wish to speak Glenda's name aloud. Not even to his beloved Harriett. Saying her name would make Glenda too real again. And he had to forget her. "Now, *ma chérie*, how can I speak of the *Sea Wolf* when my sister stands so lovely before my eyes?" he said, forcing a soft laugh. "No one at the ball will be lovelier than my sister," he said further, admiring the way her bosom filled out the lowcut bodice so well to curve downward to a small, tucked waist. A diamond necklace against her throat matched the strand of diamonds that had been wound through and over the thick clusters of black curls that had been upswept at the nape of her neck.

"The first waltz? Will it be mine?" he quickly added, knowing how she still withdrew a bit from the crowd. Though being widowed now for many months, she hadn't let herself think on beginning a search for a new man, for which to share her bed. She still said that "many months" to her was still too short a time to forget the man she would have even herself died for.

Harriett tilted her head back further, in a feathery laugh. "William Read, you always flatter me so," she said. She let her gaze meet his again and caressed his cheek with the soft tip of her gloved finger. "And, yes. The first waltz will be yours."

"It looks as though you are finally ready to go," Read said, sweeping his gaze over her anew.

"Except for tucking David in," Harriett said, furrowing her delicate brow. She smoothed the lapel of Read's black waistcoat. "He misses his father. Will you become him tonight? Will you again see to David's nightly prayers?"

"You know that's become my favorite moment of my day's end," Read said thickly, circling his arm around her waist, guiding her into the parlor.

"I know you're unhappy, needing adventure to put spark into your steps, but I'm glad you're home, at least until mother and father return from their long-awaited voyage to and from our homeland of France," Harriett said. "I guess I'm selfish. I guess I expect too much from my older brother."

He drew her closer to him. "No you don't," he said. "And I'm more than happy to play 'Papa' for David for awhile. But you do realize the day will come that you will have to begin accepting invitations from available gents. New Orleans is full of them. And most quite well to-do."

"Ha!" she scoffed haughtily. "Only because the turn of the dice has been good to them."

"Yes, I guess most do love a good cigar and a deck of cards," Read chuckled. "But this can make a man even more interesting. Don't you think?"

"Read! Really," she said, lifting her chin haughtily. Harriett had found the atmosphere of the deBaulieu Gambling Palace quite stimulating. The red velveteen drapes and furnishings, the many sparkling chandeliers with their luster of electric lights reflecting as though diamonds downward on the many true diamonds worn by both men and women had set her heart to racing the first time her father had taken her there at age twelve to show what the deBaulieu family monies were invested in. She had been surprised, though, when Read had wanted something different in life besides that of the fancy roulette wheels that circled endlessly into the wee hours of the night, and the beautiful women that clung to the men who were handsomely attired in dark suits that frequented the blackjack tables.

Though only a representative for the American Fruit Company, the job afforded Read the pleasure of sailing the Caribbean. Would she ever discover the reason for his change of heart where the *Sea Wolf* was concerned? She had seen such a sadness . . . longing . . . in his eyes since his return to New Orleans. Could it even be because of . . . a woman . . . ?

Read laughed amusedly at his sister's forced shock. But he knew that it was because she wanted to appear the "proper," genteel Southern lady at all times, though it had been discovered that she had been meeting Jason secretly on the waterfront many months before their wedding date had been set. It had even been whispered that Harriett had been with child on even the day her vows had been spoken. The count of the months by calendar hadn't confirmed this because she had managed to give birth to a five-and-one-half-pound baby "prematurely," so the doctor had said, in her seventh month. The size of the baby had been the cause for no alarm, for wouldn't a "premature" baby be as small?

Guiding Harriett by an elbow through the parlor, Read could feel comfortable in his surroundings. Though his parent's house, he always felt he could boast at it being his. He had liked his mother's choice in decorating, with the old rosewood and mahogany pieces of furniture, high-backed chairs covered in dark leather, standing against vermilion brocade and gilded panels, and a large, ornate chandelier hanging from the center ceiling, with its Cupids and shepherds holding up gas globes.

The house had been close-shuttered against prying eyes, and flowering oleanders, with their sweet-smelling red and white flowers, grew in large jars in various corners of the room.

Many sets of double glass doors led from the parlor to other rooms of the house. Read opened one of these and moved in behind Harriett. With a touch of sadness, he followed the dim lighting from a gas-lighted wall sconce to the bed, seeing how it reflected downward onto a smaller replica of Jason Garner, the father who would never again be able to creep into this room to stand proudly over his son, to wonder about what the future might possibly hold for him.

"Shhh," Harriett said, with a forefinger to her lips. "David's already fallen asleep. He had quite a time romping in the courtyard this afternoon and watching the goldfish splash in the fountain."

David's light spray of hair lay in golden masses across a feather-pillow and his pale skin showed touches of a sunburn at his high cheekbones. "Seems he's lacked the sun until you brought him here," Read grumbled softly.

"Not really. It's his skin. It is so fair. He is his father's son. Jason always had a fresh burn to the skin. And to keep David's mind from wandering to . . . to his loss, I let him do as he wishes," Harriett said, bending, smoothing a loose lock of hair back from David's eyes. "If he wishes to play in the sun, he shall do so. Whatever he wishes for, will be his."

"*Ma chérie*, do not spoil him," Read said thickly, drawing her up next to him. "A spoiled child in one's youth can be less a man after growing into adulthood."

"Playing in the sun can spoil him, William Read?" Harriett said, wide-eyed.

"No. It is not that. It is the way you said that whatever he wishes for will be his," Read said gruffly. "You cannot let life be that easy for him. He has to learn to fight. . . ."

"William Read, he is only . . . four. . . ," Harriett gasped.

"Well, this is no time to argue about my nephew's future," Read laughed awkwardly. "I am your escort for the night and I say it's time to go."

"You've been escorting me all over New Orleans as of late," Harriett laughed lightly. "The beautiful women might shy away from you, thinking I am your wife."

Read glowered a bit as he led Harriett back into the parlor. "I doubt if that matters much, *ma chérie*," he said, not caring about chasing beautiful skirts at this time in his life. His thoughts were only on one woman, and until she . . . Glenda . . . faded, he knew that to even attempt loving another was an impossibility.

Harriett eyed Read suspiciously as he lifted her satin-lined cape around her shoulders. . . .

The Orleans Hotel ballroom glittered with lavishly dressed women in handsome gowns. Their rich perfumes overpowered even the most exquisite of blossoms that had been garlanded at the ceiling, from corner to corner.

The orchestra performed a steady flow of waltzes to which most complied by whirling incessantly beneath the prisms of crystal chandeliers that bathed the crowd with golden light. But Read had successfully escaped to the rear veranda for a breath of air and the pleasure of a fine cigar. He felt confident that Harriett was being well taken care of. Her fluttering lashes and full, dark, lustrous eyes had worked magic on many of her admirers, and to Read's relief, he could see the old sparkle of teasing whenever a man would approach her.

Pacing a bit, avoiding conversation with all who would approach, Read once again watched the sky.

He clasped his hands tightly behind him, puffing leisurely on the long, slim Cuban cigar. The sky was his only connection with Glenda now, even seeming to shorten the span between Bay Island and New Orleans. It was as though he should be able to reach up and gather this black velvet canvas into his arms and while doing so, pull Glenda within arm's reach. . .

"William Read?"

Reaching up to take the cigar from between his lips, Read turned abruptly to find Harriett and a female friend at his side. He smiled a bit amusedly, realizing what Harriett was up to. Though she was the one in more need of a companion at this particular point in her life, it was she who was playing Cupid.

"Ma chérie, what have we here?" Read chuckled, bowing quite gentlemanly as this young thing with lustrous dark eyes and sylphlike figure at Harriett's side curtsied while blushing toward him. . . .

"Annabelle Porter from Savannah, Georgia," Harriett said, giggling lightly. "Annabelle, William Read, my bachelor brother."

Annabelle's lashes fluttered nervously as she reached her delicate hand toward Read. "I've heard much about you," she said in a heavy Southern drawl.

Read's brows lifted. "Oh?" he said, eyeing Harriett quizzically. "All good, I hope," he said further, lifting her hand to brush his lips against it. With her pure profile and Patrician lines, and with hair the color of a sunset, all coppers and reds, he knew that he should be impressed. But no one could stir his heart as Glenda had done. He returned her hand and hid his behind him.

"Annabelle is in town visiting relatives, William

Read," Harriett said, looking from Read to Annabelle, her true intentions revealed in the anxious tremble of her lips.

Read knew that it was expected of him to ask Annabelle to dance, but he thought better of the idea. So instead, he chose the next best thing expected of a gentleman friend. He flipped his cigar acrosss his shoulder. "And, Annabelle, have you been shown the wonderful food being served at this ball?" he asked, offering her the curve of his arm, laughing a bit to himself when he saw Harriett and Annabelle exchange quick glances of victory.

"Why, no, I haven't, William Read," she drawled sweetly in her Southern drawl. "Have I the honor of being escorted by you to the dining table?" She smiled coyly, slipping her arm through his.

"If you so desire," he said, then winked over his shoulder at Harriett as he and Annabelle began moving through the huge crowd until they stood before a long, narrow table which offered cornets of sugar-coated almonds, squares of *massepain,* a kind of sponge cake, and *langues-de-chat,* a sort of lady finger. *Petits pâtés aux huîtres,* little patties filled with oysters served piping hot, as well as other patties filled with a luscious, well seasoned meat, were also offered as well as huge silver platters of chicken salad with fruit cake.

Annabelle's free hand went to her throat. "My, oh my, it does look inviting," she sighed.

Read moved his arm free from hers and reached for a plate. "And which would you prefer?" he asked, desiring to be anywhere but here with this young lady. He looked anxiously around him, wishing for an escape. But the hour of the night was his only reprieve. It was growing near midnight. It was then that he would return Harriett to the house, then seek a sort of release in the only way that he knew how. He had found this house on Dauphine Street that knew of the ways of a man. . . .

"William Read, I do believe I don't think I wish to fatten myself with any of these delicacies," Annabelle said, turning with a quick flutter of her skirts as a gentleman bent and whispered something in her ear.

"Oh? You do not. . . ?" Read said. He cleared his throat nervously as he began to feel a bit awkward as even Harriett approached him. He eyed her questionably when he saw the flush of her face and the look of stargazing in her eyes.

"William Read," she murmured, reaching a hand to his arm. "I wish to beg your forgiveness about something."

He placed the dish back on the table and instead lifted a glass of champagne to his lips. He took a quick swallow, then said, "What's going on, Harriett? What's to forgive?"

Harriett lowered her lashes, flushing a bit. "It's Annabelle's brother here. Terence. He has asked if he can escort me home," she said quietly. "And Annabelle will have to leave at the same time. She promised her parents that her brother would see her home safely, unless. . . ." She stood quickly on tiptoe and whispered into Read's ear, asking that he take Annabelle home, so that Harriett could be alone with Terence. And since it was Harriett's first true interest in a man since Jason's death, Harriett had thought Read would quickly comply. But he didn't. Instead, he grumbled a flat "no" in his sister's ear and watched the growing fury in her eyes.

"Then, Terence and Annabelle, I'm ready to leave the ball if you are," Harriett said, with a haughty tilt to her chin as she moved on away from Read, leaving him to stand there, laughing to himself, glad to see the vitality returned to his sister, but hoping she wouldn't be too anxious to please this first man since Jason. But he had approved of Terence's appearance. He did look to be a likeable chap with his carefully combed, sandy-colored hair and a keen set to his jaw, showing a personality of determination and solidness. Yes, possibly this chap of broad shoulders could be the answer for his sweet Harriett. But Read wasn't ready to spoil the rest of his evening's plans to cater to his sister's further whims. She was old enough and skilled enough to take care of herself. . . .

With haste, he swallowed the last of the champagne and returned the empty glass to the table, then between brief acknowledgments from one person to the next, he weaved his way through the crowd until he found himself standing alone on Orleans Street, where gas lamps flared dimly in the fog, and houses stood shoulder to shoulder, each with their balconies of ornate ironwork casting shadows, blue and lacelike, on the streets below.

Read chose to move by foot instead of carriage, finding it difficult on the uneven cobblestones. Wagons and carriages passed by him with creaking wheels, and the hooves of the horses resounded hollowly into the night.

The twanging of guitars surfaced from cabarets, and a man's voice could be heard singing a song of the bulls. And as had been done for as long as Read could remember, the voice of a watchman cried out the hour and called the message that all was well.

But all was not well with Read. He was lonely. He was tormented. But this loneliness didn't mean that he was ready to become responsible for a "proper" young lady. He wanted someone to bed up with that he wouldn't have to look back at and wonder about once he said his goodbyes. He needed someone he would find on Dauphine Street, where many beautiful women waited to be chosen from a lovely lacework balcony, already in flimsy chemises, flaunting their better qualities for any man who would pay the right price.

Hurrying his pace, Read found himself standing beneath this balcony where a particular pair of full, dark, liquid eyes persuaded him to choose her. With a glint in his eyes and a slight tilt to his lips, Read counted out many green bills and swung them in the air above his head, seeing the acceptance in the fling of this girl's head and the flick of the wrist as she disappeared through double glass doors and soon had him by the hand, leading him up a narrow staircase until the privacy of a room had been found.

"You are quite generous, my friend," the girl said as she began unbuttoning Read's shirt.

His gaze moved quickly over her, seeing so much beneath the thin, lacy covering. She had beautifully rounded limbs and her face was oval and with that of delicate features, though dark in coloring, looking a bit Spanish. His hands reached beneath the chemise and cupped each of her well-formed breasts, causing the familiar heat to rise in his loins. "You look worth fifty dollars, *ma chérie*," he said thickly, parting his legs a bit as her fingers moved deftly on the buttons of his breeches.

"Marissa warm your blood," Marissa said, smiling, revealing wide, white teeth, now touching and teasing his hardness with the continued skill of her fingers.

Feeling the pounding of his heartbeat, Read quickly finished disrobing himself, then lifted Marissa into his arms and carried her to the one main piece of furniture in the room . . . the bed. He laid her there beneath the soft caressing of a single candle's glow on the table next to the bed. Above where Read was now positioning himself over Marissa, a gentle breeze blew in, carrying with it the slight fragrance of flowers of the night, causing Read to remember Glenda and their times together in the jungle, surrounded by orchids and all sorts of blossoming flowers, making him ache even more for her. But he had to forget. He had to. . . .

"*Ma chérie,* my blood is already boiling," Read murmured, lifting her chemise over her head. Smelling the sweetness of her perfume made him forget the other passing fragrance of the night. He let his lips travel to all her hidden curves, while she expertly kept her fingers active on his body. She wasn't Glenda, but . . . he . . . could close his eyes . . . pretend. . . . Damn. Couldn't he ever put her completely behind him? For one brief moment there, he thought he had succeeded. Then her face would materialize before his eyes, ah, so beautiful . . . so alluring. . . .

When Marissa shifted her body and began exploring his body with her lips, nipping at his rippling flesh with her teeth, he lay back and enjoyed, sighing leisurely when he felt the warmth of her mouth begin to work where no other woman's mouth had been before.

"Woman, what you're doing," he said thickly, tossing his head, stiffening his legs as the pleasure built inside him. It was as though someone had poured champagne over him and had intoxicated his every pore and nerve ending. It was a sweet euphoria as she mounted him and began working her body with his. It wasn't long before he felt the great splashes of waves engulf his brain, until his shudders ceased and he lay spent and free, if only for the moment. . . .

"You come and ask for Marissa again? *Sí, señor?*" Marissa asked, climbing from atop him, pleading with her eyes.

Having heard her speak as Glenda had . . . in part Spanish . . . made a renewed ache course through his veins. He rose from the bed and dressed, all the while avoiding eye contact with this skilled woman of the night. Damn. Would he always feel guilty after enjoying the pleasures of the body with someone besides Glenda? Why had she worked her way into his blood in such severity? No other woman had. And though she had, it was useless. Damn useless. He flinched when Marissa, still nude, quickly, teasingly fit her body into his, tracing his facial features with the smoothness of her forefinger.

"Tomorrow night, *señor?*" she murmured. "Marissa be here tomorrow night. Marissa can show you many new tricks with her body. Fifty dollars again, *señor? Sí?*"

Read wriggled himself free of her while reaching for the door knob. Without answering, he rushed from the room and traveled in the dark, shadowy streets until he reached the river front. Lighting another cigar, he stood aside and watched the growing activity on the banana wharf. Being familiar with the comings and goings of this biggest banana port in the world, Read knew that the *Sea Wolf* could be due within the next couple of hours. He knew that an hour or so before the ship was due to arrive, a small army of men invaded the wharf. The crowd was usually made up of American laborers, Greeks, and sailors from all sorts of tramp ships, needing to put in an idle day's work, with Italians and Negroes predominant.

Though the hour was late, Read could see old Negro women moving among the men with tignons tied about their heads, offering sandwiches and candy. It was a time of gaiety, before their time of hard labor, and Read felt a bit out of place. He turned and headed back to the loneliness of his bed. . . .

Chapter Thirteen

The ship's heaving and pitching awakened Glenda with a sudden start. Trembling, she leaned up on one elbow, glancing quickly around her, having momentarily forgotten where she was. Then she remembered. The slapping bang of the water against the ship's hull and the creaking of its mahogany timbers were cause for remembering and alarm. As the ship bucked and rolled, so did Glenda's stomach.

Moaning, she scooted to the edge of the bunk and began to rise from it when suddenly she was tossed like a rag doll onto the damp, moisture-laden deck. The throbbing of her ankle began anew, reminding her of why the haziness of her mind. She had been scourged by an infection-inflicted temperature and had lain limp for the entirety of the trip. Her heart jumped, now remembering her orphaned cub. What had George Boyd done with Nena?

Though still sprawled clumsily on the deck and threatening to be tossed further around, she clung to the bunk, looking desperately around her. What she saw beneath the dim lighting from a porthole and a yellowed overhead skylight was a small cabin with paneled walls with unlighted lanterns on two of these, and a built-in bureau with a metal rail about its top opposite where she sat. She peered further through the semidarkness and discovered what appeared to be a topless trunk at the other opposite wall.

Above the loud howls of the wind and the banging of the water, Glenda caught the sound of a furious scratching. Her heart raced. The scratching was surfacing from the topless trunk. "Nena?" she said in a strained sort of way. "Nena? Are you . . . in . . . that . . . ?"

Not able to put weight on her ankle, and even more afraid to try because of the continuous tumbling of the ship, Glenda began to scoot her way across the deck, curling her nose from the combined stench of mildew, stale pipe tobacco and rancid seawater. Sweat beaded her brow with each added movement of her limbs, and she realized the weakened condition she was in. She couldn't even remember having eaten anything since her departure from the hold. Had Nena even been neglected . . .?

Another heave of the ship and Glenda found herself tossed against the sharp edge of the trunk. She groaned a bit, then pulled herself to a sitting position and looked down inside the trunk, relieved to see Nena safely inside her crate, though cramped and at odds with her surroundings.

"My orphaned cub," Glenda sighed. "Does the storm frighten you?" Nena's eyes were wide and she was panting from the sweltering heat of the small cabin's humidity.

"I'll get you out of that crate, but Nena, you'll have to stay on my lap," Glenda said, lifting the lid from the crate. "One toss across the room could knock the wind from you."

Grunting a bit because of her weakness and the weight of Nena, Glenda managed to lift Nena from the crate and onto the curve of her lap. Appearing to not understand the dangers of the moment, Nena circled up into a ball and began a contented purr while Glenda held to her with all her might. When a wild wash of seawater rushed beneath the closed cabin door and bubbled up next to Glenda's feet, her heart began thundering and her eyes grew wide with added fear.

She scooted as far away from the drifting water as was possible and huddled against the outside wall with uncontrollable trembles rippling along her flesh. She listened hard, now alert to the fearful shoutings from the ship's crew on the outer deck. She didn't recognize George's voice among the men and wondered if he was possibly with the ship's captain or tucked safely inside the captain's private cabin. She did wish for him to be safe. She owed him much for having taken such proper care of her and her beloved Nena.

Then through the added sea noises and men's shouts, she heard one extra loud bellow from the ship's crew. Glenda tensed and drew Nena even closer to her when she heard the desperate words, "Man overboard . . . man overboard . . . !"

Glenda closed her eyes tightly and trembled even more, trying to not envision a man floundering in the turbulent waters of the sea. But the added terrified shouts and scamperings along the ship's deck made her quite aware that someone *had* lost their footing and had been swept away into the rising, splashing hungry fangs of the sea. Was it even more than one man? Who might even be next? She kept her eye on the door, hoping it would not fly suddenly open, to fill this cabin with water, to even carry her and Nena back with it, to also become an unwilling part of the sea. She quickly closed her eyes and waited . . . and waited . . . until the shouting died away and slowly the pitching and heaving of the ship gentled to only a rocking and swaying.

Dry-mouthed, Glenda tried to rise from the floor, but felt her ankle give way beneath her, so decided to give Nena her so sought after freedom on the deck, then determinedly scooted her way to the bunk and pulled herself atop it.

Panting, she leaned her back against the wall of the ship, hoping above all else that no other storm at sea would threaten her arrival in America. Her life had so changed since she had that first time rowed with her family from Bay Island. Yes, that's where her adventure had begun . . . by way of the Caribbean. Would it end also there?

Nena pounced up onto the bunk next to Glenda and began to rub against her, purring. Glenda wrapped her arms around her and cried softly. "Orphaned little one, I suddenly don't feel so brave," she whispered, then was jolted a bit when the door flew open with a bang.

Not recognizing the man standing there in the gray shadows of "after-storm," Glenda sidled more up against the wall. "Who . . .?"

"Ship's captain," the man grumbled, lighting a lantern, then closing the door behind him. "Captain Thompson to you," he said, turning on a heel, offering a hand.

Glenda's hand went shakily forth. When the firm

grip of his fingers circled around hers and she saw the wide expanse of his shoulders and also the forceful features of his chiseled face, she was suddenly no longer afraid. He appeared to be a man of steel and surely in complete control of his banana-carrying ship. But then she remembered the shouts of "man overboard." Where had the captain been then?

"How'd you fare through the storm, Missie?" he grumbled further, dropping his hand from hers. He stood over her, appearing a bit washed out by the sad look in the depth of his gray eyes and with his clothes hanging from his broad expanse of body in wet, limp blues. He began combing his fingers nervously through his thinning hair, waiting for her response.

"I'm fine," she said cautiously, wondering if he be friend or foe.

"And yer cat?" Captain Thompson said, forcing a laugh.

"Fine as well," Glenda said, stroking Nena's fur.

"I've a bit o' bad news to bring to ye, missie," Captain Thompson said, lowering his eyes a bit.

"News? What sort of bad news . . .?"

"George. George Boyd," he blurted, wiping his nose roughly with the back of his hand.

A cautious fear rippled through her veins. George Boyd? The man who had been so kind? What . . .? "What about him?" she said, swallowing hard. Somehow, she knew what to expect the answer to be . . . Hadn't she felt his absence . . .? Oh, no! Surely . . . not. . . .

Captain Thompson clasped his hands tightly behind him and began pacing the floor with shoulders slumped a bit. "Rarely have we lost a man in such a way," he grumbled, then quickly drew his hands from behind him to smack a fist into a palm of his other hand. "The damn storm. The damn, damn storm. . . ."

Glenda brushed Nena from her lap and tried to rise from the bed, feeling weakness reach from her ankle to move even around her heart. She fell back, panting, hating her tears for creeping from the corners of her eyes. "He's dead . . .?" she whispered. "He was the man . . .?"

Captain Thompson whirled around, with a deeply furrowed brow. "Yes. Overboard. We . . . couldn't rescue him. The waves. They just swallowed him. He was there one minute . . . then . . the next . . . he was gone."

Glenda hung her head in her hands. "No," she sobbed. "He was so kind. He is why I'm recovering from the rat bite. I know it."

Captain Thompson touched her gently on the cheek. "I'm the only one besides George who knew you were aboard," he said. "I'll see to it that no harm comes by ye. And now that the sea's calmed, we should soon be seein' the bright torch lights from shore."

Glenda lifted her eyes to his. "Many thanks, captain," she said. Then she remembered that she still could not maneuver on her own. "Captain, when we do reach New Orleans, what can I do? It is impossible for me to walk. And being so helpless, where can I even go?"

He patted her on the crown of the head. "I've a daughter yer age," he said. "I'll take care of ye. Never ye fret. Though a stowaway, I'll see that good is done by ye."

Glenda smiled, sighing heavily. "Thank you," she said.

"Now I know ye can't get up to bolt lock yer door," he said, gesturing toward the door with a nod of the head. "But no fret. As I said, no crew knows you're here. An' I'll keep a watch on yer door. Just you stay in this cabin. The men's been through enough recent torments, they don' need tha' of a lady's skirts to worry 'bout."

"Yes, sir," Glenda gulped. She huddled further down onto the bunk, now full of worry about Nena's safety. If she couldn't fend for herself, then how could she even for her orphaned cub . . .?

The excitement building inside her had caused Glenda's ankle's throbbing to be erased from her mind. She had managed to hop on one foot across the deck and was now peering through the small porthole as the shoreline grew closer. Was she truly so close to New Orleans . . . the place where her beloved made his residence? Was she actually going to be able to be a part of America, where her true father also resided? Though the journey's last leg had been as though a nightmare, Glenda now worried that she was dreaming and might awaken at any moment.

She placed her nose against the cold glass of the porthole, silently cursing the moisture beads that clung to its outside, yet able to see enough as the ship's boilers ceased to vibrate the flooring beneath her feet, while the ship eased on in next to a wharf.

Butterflies seemed to be fluttering inside Glenda's stomach as she caught sight of the throngs of men crowded onto the wharf that jutted away from the land where many lanterns hung, flickering, swaying gently with the breeze. The faces of the men took on all sorts of shapes and colors. Glenda knew that more than Americans had come to greet the ship's arrival. She could even see mestizos among the faces and felt a sudden pang of homesickness, realizing just how far she had traveled, and being away from her homeland for the first time, ever. But then she was reminded why she had decided to do such a daring feat as this. She would surely soon be with Read . . . be in his arms. He just couldn't be as ill as Rayburn had said. Surely Rayburn had been wrong!

The rattling of the anchor's chain and the slight jerk to the ship as the anchor hit river bottom made Glenda aware that her journey's end was a reality. She could remember Read saying that New Orleans lay just northwest of the great delta of the Mississippi River, the natural sea outlet for the Mississippi Valley, so she knew that she was now moored in the waters of the Mississippi River. She wondered how the river would differ from the sea that she had known since childhood. . . .

She watched in further delight as the gangplank was lowered to the wharf and the ship became a hub of activity. She was glad that she had been rescued from the hold by George Boyd. If not, she could have just been discovered and possibly trampled by all who were causing such a loud commotion as they moved to and from the hold while the bananas were being quickly unloaded from the ship.

"I guess my departure will come later," she whispered sadly. She knew that the bananas had to take precedence over all else. They surely would begin to ripen more after having been in the sweltering heat of the ship's hold. But as she peered even more strongly toward the bananas, she noticed they still held their original color as when first harvested. The green bundles of fruit even gave a vivid touch of color to the wharf, and the emerging slow fog circled the lantern flares in moisture-laden colors of purples and blues, sparkling like miniature rare diamonds.

Glenda's neck and shoulder muscles began to ache the more she watched. She began glancing toward the closed door, wondering when she would be released from her self-imposed prison. Being closed up in such small quarters for so long now, with only Nena as a companion, Glenda was tired of the foul odors and the lack of anyone to have conversation with.

She then glanced toward Nena, already in her crate, ready for transporting. "Where will the captain take us?" she worried aloud. "Can I even trust him? Does he truly have a daughter of my age . . .?"

She leaned her cheek against the window, drowsy from the long, unnerving wait. And after what seemed to be endless hours, she was startled to a sudden awareness of a noise outside the cabin door. It hadn't been steady footsteps, but that of a strange mute dragging along the ship's deck and a tap-tapping of some sort.

Placing her hands to her throat and huddled against the ship's outer wall, Glenda watched the cabin door slowly open. Her eyes grew wide when she saw this tall, slim figure of a man in the dim lantern's light. He was so tall, he had to stoop a mite to fit his full figure beneath the low ceiling of this cabin's interior. He was impeccably dressed in a gray waistcoat and pants, and a maroon cravat at his throat

277

exhibited the magnificence of a diamond displayed amidst its gathers.

He stood leaning on a cane, eyeing Glenda with sparkling green eyes beneath a thick layer of gray hair. Glenda immediately thought though many years her senior in age, oh, how handsome he was, with his feathery lashes, full lips and kind smile as he began to speak. . . .

"So you're my ship's stowaway, huh?" he laughed amusedly.

His eyes raked over her anew, making Glenda more than a little uneasy. She knew the disrepair she was in, with her gathered skirt and drawstring blouse filthy and wrinkled from many day's wear, and her hair tangled from lack of a shampooing and brushing. Her fingers subconsciously went to her blouse, fingering the drawstrings, even aware of how much of herself was revealed to this man for lack of undergarment worn beneath both skirt and blouse. For the first time ever, she felt a deep desire to look more "proper." Wasn't this a man of breeding? Wasn't this a man of riches? His words suddenly sprang to the surface of her mind. He . . . was . . . the . . . *Sea Wolf*'s owner!

As he began to move across the room, Glenda's gaze lowered. This ship's owner had only partial use of one of his legs! She could tell by the stiff way in which it was held as he maneuvered the other one so normally. The dragging noise she had heard outside the door had been his lame leg . . . and the tap-tapping had surfaced from the cane having made contact with the ship's oak flooring.

"Here now. Can't you explain your presence on my ship?" he said good-naturedly, cocking an eyebrow.

"You're the first of a kind, you know. I've had plenty of male stowaways, but never a female."

"I'm sorry for any inconvenience I've caused you, sir," Glenda said, rising, flinching when standing caused her so much pain. She watched him now with a strange pounding of the heart. As they now stood, almost face to face, and with the lantern's glow more directly on his face, Glenda had the feeling that she had seen this man before. His eyes. That's what it was . . . and . . . the lips! They were as her own! As though looking into a mirror, except that he was a man . . . and she . . . a woman! What could cause her to feel even a strange closeness. . . ?

"No. No inconvenience," he said. "But I'm glad your presence was kept from my ship's crew. It could have been bad for you. Either way . . ."

Glenda swallowed hard. "Either way. . . ?" she gulped. "What do . . . you . . . mean. . . ?"

"Some men feel a woman's presence on a ship is bad luck, or some could have wanted . . . eh . . . let's say . . . something else from you."

She cast her eyes downward, blushing a bit. "Oh, I see," she said softly.

"No cause for alarm though," he laughed, reaching to tilt her chin upward with a forefinger. "The voyage is over. You are safely in New Orleans. And may I inquire as to the reason for your chosen travel?"

Glenda's eyes searched his face, wishing her heart would relax. But she was thinking. . . . Oh, how wrong and foolish to . . . be . . . thinking. . . . But, could this . . . be . . . her. . . ?

"Why?" she whispered, then almost choked on the words when she added, "To . . . search out my . . . father. . . ."

He dropped his hand, then draped it over the other that was still steadying the cane beneath the full weight of his body. "Oh?" he said quietly. "And what makes you think he's anywhere near here?"

"I'm not sure. But I will find him," she said. She had neglected to tell him that she also was searching for her beloved, for now, it seemed, only one thing was uppermost on her mind. How could she tell him that her heart was telling her to suspect that this man . . . this ship's owner with the green eyes . . . and . . . lame . . . leg could easily fit the description of the man she had thought and wondered about since that first moment to know to question about her difference in skin, hair and eye coloring from the rest of her Galvez family. . . .

"Well, miss, you can begin your search by being introduced to this man who is nobody's father," he chuckled, extending a hand. "I'm Peter Grayson. I would like to offer my services to such a beautiful lady in distress."

Glenda's breathing quickened. Peter Grayson! *The* Peter Grayson whom both Christina *and* Rayburn had spoken of so often? Why hadn't she at once remembered that, yes, if this man who stood before her was the *Sea Wolf*'s owner, he was also Peter Grayson!

She accepted his hand and circled her fingers around it, feeling the secure warmth that it held. "I know of you already," she said, straightening her back.

His eyes raked over her breasts, so high and firm and heaving with each thunderous heartbeat. . . .

How could she find out. . . ? Surely there would be a clue. Was he her father? Wouldn't it be too easy for her to find him so quickly? Surely she was wrong!

She was glad when his gaze moved to her face and held. He laughed quietly. "How do you know me, young lady?" he said. "Did the ship's captain speak of me?" His lashes cast dark shadows over his eyes as he lowered them. "Or did George Boyd?" he added thickly, then watching her again. His hand moved back to his cane, but not before Glenda's eyes widened, seeing the silver wolf's head being used as a handle. It had an almost frightening appearance, the way the teeth were exposed and the eyes . . . so wild . . . and terrifying.

Glenda looked Peter's way again, wondering if this man's personality was also like that of a wolf. . . .

"Sir, while at El Progresso, I heard Rayburn and Christina Taylor speak of you often," she quickly blurted, realizing he had seen her studies of his cane. Little did he know that she was wondering more about the cane than just its design. She had to know why . . . the cane. . . ? Couldn't that be the clue she was searching for?

Peter turned abruptly and went to stand over Nena. "And, what have we here?" he said. "Captain Thompson said something about a cat. But I didn't expect a cat of this size."

Glenda was even now more full of wonder. Why, he had completely ignored her mention of Christina and Rayburn! Why. . . ? She eyed him more quizzically, then replied, "Nena is my orphaned cub, in no way a typical housecat. I rescued her from the jungle after her mother had been cruelly shot and killed."

"And you expect to keep it?"

"I'd like to try. . . ."

"I guess my courtyard could do," Peter grumbled, bending, getting a better look, laughing when Nena lifted a paw and spat angrily at him.

"What did you say about your courtyard?" Glenda asked, all a-flutter inside if what she was thinking could be true. Was he going to take her and Nena to his house? Wouldn't she then truly find out about his background. . . ?

He swung around, smiling. "If you will honor me with your presence, young lady, you can come to my house until you've recovered from the wound you received on my ship," he said.

"Do you really mean it?" she gasped, feeling a bit weakened from all the building excitement.

"I feel responsible," he said quickly. "Though a stowaway and not supposed to be a part of the ship's crew, I still hate it like hell that a rat on my ship actually chose to taste of your young flesh."

"You are too kind, sir," Glenda said. Then she eyed Nena wonderingly. "But I do have my orphaned cub to think about," she quickly added. "You see, I am its adopted mother." She swallowed hard, again thinking to have possibly found her father. But surely not. After all the years of wondering about him, he just couldn't materialize this easily on her first arrival to America's shores.

"A huge, private courtyard adjoins the rear of my house," Peter said. "It has an eight-foot-high plaster wall on its three sides and its gate is locked from inside. Since I'm known for my riches, these precautions had to be taken. So your cat will be safe . . . if you feel it could be okay there."

Glenda's eyes wavered. "Is there any shelter from

the hot sunshine of the day . . . or the damp, sometimes rains of the night?"

Peter laughed brusquely. "You'll find New Orleans
not so temperamental in spirit as your tropics. But, we
will see if we can arrange for your room to be on the
lower floor so you can see to your cat's comfort."

Glenda's brow furrowed. He was being too kind.
She had to wonder why. Trust? This word had become
one of precaution to her. And if he was the man who
had raped her mother all those years ago, could he
even have plans to rape . . . her . . . daughter. . . ?
"Oh, if he only knew who I was," she fumed to herself.
"If he is the man . . ."

She was suddenly feeling the long-remembered pangs
of occasional hate she had held for the man who had
been the rapist. It had been that way off and on through-
out the years. But, then, there had been those moments
of longing, with such a deep desire to see him . . . even
possibly grow to love him . . . because he was her father.
Shouldn't one love their father . . . regardless. . . ?

"Now you just stay put while I go get one of my
ship's crew to carry you to my carriage," Peter said,
moving toward the door. "And surely Christina. . . ."
He swung around, weary-eyed as he so obviously chose
to not complete his words. Instead, he said, "I'm sure
your stay will be made comfortable." He again placed
his back to her and was soon gone from the cabin,
leaving Glenda to stare openly after him.

"He did briefly mention the name . . . Christina
. . ." she whispered. "It can't be the Christina I know.
Will I soon be introduced to a second Christina?" She
hopped to the bunk and settled atop it, waiting
anxiously. She hadn't expected her journey's end to be

that of such pleasantness. She wasn't going home with the ship's captain! She was going home with the ship's *owner!* She could not even thank the rat for having singled her out. For if not, she would not be receiving such special treatment. She would be as a rat, sneaking down the ship's gangplank and scurrying, scared, into the dark hollow pit of night.

The door opened again and Glenda shifted herself on the bunk, smiling weakly toward the young sailor who sported a wild spray of rusty hair.

"I'm here to take you ashore, ma'am," he said in a slow, Southern drawl. As he bent his back to scoop her into his arms, his eyes took the liberty to devour her deep cleavage and what lay on its either side. His freckles became a bit pronounced as a flush swept his face. "Sure don't know how your bein' on board was kept such a secret," he said, laughing nervously. "I'd have liked to have made your acquaintance. You're quite beautiful, you know."

Glenda laughed silkily as she draped her right arm about his neck. Her opinion of sailors could quickly change if all were as gallant as this lad and Captain Thompson. "Why, thank you, sir," Glenda replied. Then her eyes went to Nena and an anxiety crept through her. "And my orphaned cub? Who will take her to the carriage?"

The young sailor's hazel eyes grew wide. "Your . . . what . . . ma'am?" he said, tilting a brow.

Again Glenda laughed, amused at his innocence. How had he managed to become a part of a ship's crew? Would his innocence fade away with his youth? "My puma. My Nena," she answered, pointing with her bare toes. "Will her crate be removed along with me? I'm afraid to get separated from her."

A bow-backed sailor appeared at the cabin's door, then moved on inside. Without even a nod of "hello," he secured the strings of Glenda's travel bag over one arm, then lifted Nena and her crate and moved on out ahead of Glenda and the accommodating young sailor.

"There. Your question is answered," the young sailor said, moving to, and across, the outer deck. His muscles strained as he began to carry Glenda down the gangplank. "I'd sure like to know your name," he quickly blurted.

"Glenda. Glenda Galvez," Glenda murmured, now seeing so much more than the small spaces of the porthole had allowed her. There wasn't only this one wharf that she had been observing, but a harbor lined with many more such wharves. In the dark shadows, she could even see the cold-appearing bodies of warehouses snuggling next to the other along this water's edge.

The crowd was thinning, but still, many were lugging the bunches of bananas to load into boxcars lined up on a train's track. It was all so new to Glenda! It was all so . . . so . . . overwhelmingly . . . exciting. . . !

"You don't look Spanish," the young sailor said as he stopped at the grand, black carriage. "But you speak as though you are. . . . And your name is also. . . ."

"Yes. I am," Glenda said, lowering her lashes a bit. "But I am also . . . American. . . ."

Peter Grayson seemed to appear from nowhere as he suddenly moved to open the carriage door. "Deposit your fair cargo in there, my lad," he said, gesturing with his free hand.

Glenda hung to the young sailor's neck a brief moment longer. "I didn't get to ask *your* name," she said, smiling sweetly.

"Tom. Tom Andrews," Tom answered, returning her smile, then placed her gently on the plump, velveteen cushions of the carriage's interior.

"Thank you, Tom Andrews," Glenda beamed, waving as he sped away. Then almost bashfully, Glenda drew her skirt around her legs as Peter also entered the carriage and closed the door behind him. One tap of his cane against the front wall of the carriage and Glenda felt movement of wheels beneath her.

In awe, she gazed at the plushness around her. A dim light from a lantern on a side wall sent rivulets of golden along plush green velveteen cushioned seats on either side of the carriage's interior and fringed shades bounced at the small windows of each door.

She glanced a bit sideways, seeing how the wolf's head shone on the handle of Peter's cane, then upward, seeing how his green eyes appeared to be that of a cat's as he sat silently studying her. She wanted to in turn study him further, still wondering about his familiarity, but was forced to turn her eyes from him since his steady gaze was so unnerving to her. She forced her thoughts elsewhere, though hating the trembling of her fingers that she chose to clasp tightly together on her lap.

The horse's hoofbeats echoed hollowly along the cobblestone street that was void of passersby due to the late hour of the night. Glenda inhaled deeply. As so often at night while a part of El Progresso plantation, it seemed to be the same here in New Orleans . . . the air was so sweet with the breath of flowers.

Had she found another paradise such as Honduras? Could there be such a place to match the tropical display of orchids . . . roses. . . ?

The further they moved away from the wharves, the more prominent the houses appeared at the sides of the street. Though darkness was as though a shroud, a large oil lamp swung on tall posts lighting enough of the surroundings for Glenda to get her first true look at New Orleans. How could she actually be seeing anything as grand? The American's house at El Progresso had been a mansion in her eyes, but even it now seemed small in comparison to what she was now witnessing in even an abundance!

The street was overhung by wrought iron balconies, and, ah, weren't these balconies so charming with their lacy ornate grillwork? The houses stood shoulder to shoulder and flush with the sidewalks. Their windows had been close-shuttered for privacy. Then as the carriage moved onward, leaving the profusion of houses behind, Glenda saw trees whose outer branches hung down over the street like green, leafy tents. The branches were gnarled and twisted and long streamers of Spanish moss laced their way from limb to limb . . . tree to tree. . . .

Blossoming magnolia trees at the side of the street welcomed the carriage's approach, and when Glenda heard the horse being commanded to a halt, her heart thundered inside her. What would she find awaiting her in this man's house. . . ? this stranger who didn't truly appear to be that much of a stranger, though he had chosen to keep his words and thoughts to himself for the entirety of this carriage journey?

"We have arrived," Peter said, reaching to open the

carriage door. "Due to the lateness of the hour, I, personally, will direct you to your room. Then tomorrow, you will be . . . uh . . . introduced around. . . ."

"Thank you," Glenda murmured.

"Henry, my coachman, will carry you to your room as I direct him," Peter said. "And then we will also see to your cat's safety."

"Again, thank you," Glenda said, feeling deeply affected by his kindness. Surely he could have never had a roguish turn to his character. Surely this man could never have raped an innocent mestizo while in the midst of her wifely duties, working in a garden. . . .

Peter climbed from the carriage, laughing softly. "You don't have to be whispering 'thank you's' to me with every turn of your head," he said. "I have told you. I feel responsible for you. I should be whispering thank you's to you for not dying while aboard my ship from that damn rat's bite. My reputation is very important to me."

"I shall do nothing to dirty your name," Glenda said softly. "Not if I even find you to be my father," she thought to herself. She liked this man with the wolf's head cane. Something deep inside her told her that she would always like him, no matter what. . . .

Peter smiled, then directed his coachman to carry Glenda into the house, and then the cat. . . .

Glenda clung to this man's neck, hoping that one day soon she could move on her own. She had always been so strong . . . so self-sufficient . . . she didn't like depending on anyone, for anything. And wouldn't this weakness in her ankle slow her finding of Read?

She had to smile a bit to herself, hearing the heavy

pantings from this little man with the black outfit, topped with a tall, black silk hat. She glanced upward at his face, seeing mostly nose, as it was widened, purple-veined across the narrowness of his face. His dark eyebrows hung shaggily over his squint of eyes and his tongue licked thirstily as he carried her on inside this house that had appeared to be as all other balconied houses that Glenda had seen. But once inside, her breath was taken clean away from her when she saw the richness of its decor and remembering what she had left behind.

The heavy door on solid brass hinges had opened into a foyer that led into a large drawing room brightly lighted by a chandelier of crystal that had places for fifty candles, but yet, had been wired for electricity. Where the white plastered walls weren't graced with fading family portraits, tall and wide bookcases were filled with volume after volume of different-sized books. Old rosewood and mahogany pieces of furniture were placed beside various overstuffed chairs and one large sofa was positioned in front of a six-foot-high and six-foot-wide brick fireplace. Flowers and greenery were in profusion in the room and double doors led from the room out to the courtyard.

"Henry, we'll go by way of the courtyard to the room I feel will do for our little stowaway here," Peter said, moving on ahead, maneuvering his stiff leg gracefully.

Glenda clung even more as Henry followed along. Then her breath caught in her throat when she found herself being carried into a part of the world she thought she had left behind. She was being carried over a blue-gray flagstone walkway, but all else was as though once again in the tropics. The large courtyard, surrounded by the tall wall Peter had spoken of, exhibited all forms of blossoming flowers and trees. Wisteria swayed with the gentleness of the breeze, causing some purple petals to fall noiselessly to the flagstone. Palm trees circled a trickling fountain that had lights reflecting from somewhere beneath the water in strange colors of blues and purples, and this water showed even moving streaks of orange! Then Glenda laughed, realizing these were fish darting about.

Following her gaze upward, Glenda found herself looking up at the tall walls of the house and a balcony that extended across the whole end of its second floor. Glenda craned her neck a bit, seeing a sudden flutter of skirts in the shadow of this balcony. The stance was familiar to her, but yet, how. . . ?

"Over here," Peter said, opening a door. "I think this will do." He entered and soon had the room bathed in a soft lamp's glow.

Again, Glenda was made to be in awe. This room that was graciously being loaned her was one of magnificence! The bed she was being placed on was as soft as the one she had so short a time become acquainted with while in El Progresso. Its spread was more grand being that of a soft, blue velvet to match the long, graceful draperies at the room's one window. The furniture was of a richly carved mahogany, possibly having been carved in Honduras and brought back to America to show off to all Americans who hadn't yet had a chance to travel to Glenda's beautiful country.

A gilt mirror was above the dressing table and all sorts of fancy bottles filled with colorful liquid sat in mirrored trays next to another electric lamp.

"It is so breathtaking," Glenda finally murmured,

placing her hands to her throat.

"When we have occasional overnight guests, we make sure a lovely female gets this room," Peter said, looking suddenly bone-weary as he leaned heavily against his cane. "And there is fresh water on the stand beside your bed for which to freshen yourself."

He stepped aside as Nena's crate was carried into the room and opened. Glenda reached her arms out for Nena, who was too busy stretching her limbs to want to be cuddled.

Glenda laughed softly, seeing a bit of concern in Peter's eyes as he looked at Nena, then the room's furnishings. "I hope Nena won't cause any problems," she murmured, remembering the sharpness of her claws and her playful, frisky manner.

"The courtyard . . ." Peter said.

"Yes. The courtyard will be as though home for Nena," Glenda replied.

"There are no trees close to the walls," Peter reassured, turning to study the outdoor area. "I don't believe your cat can escape. And nobody will let it free. I will give strict orders." He once again stared at Nena and then the expensive oak flooring of the room. He smiled a bit awkwardly toward Glenda, then spoke again. "How does . . . uh . . . well . . . your cat relieve itself. . . ?"

Glenda smiled widely. "Sir, you don't have a worry there," she said. "Your fountain's water? Your pond? It will disguise all my cub's, well, can you call it, necessary habits?"

"Eh?" Peter said, furrowing his brow.

"It is perfect," Glenda said. "In the wild, pumas seek out water. It hides their smells from all other animals while hunting. Nena will feel your pond is the same as one of Honduras's lagoons."

Peter laughed hoarsely, kneading his brow. "Oh, I see," he said amusedly.

"But while on board your ship, Nena didn't have such a pond," Glenda said, lowering her eyes. "I'm afraid . . ."

Peter went to Glenda and touched her cheek softly. "It will busy my crew. Don't fret. They need busy hands to free their minds," he said, laughing. "And now, Glenda, I must retire. My life is a full one. I will be up at the break of dawn. You will be seen to. Don't fret about that either."

"Many thanks," she whispered.

"More thank you's?" Peter laughed, then disappeared through the door, leaving the door open a crack as Nena brushed past him to romp freely around the courtyard.

Glenda had a deep, peaceful, contented feeling about her. She so wanted to explore, but the resumed aching of her ankle made her know that to discover what was inside the beautifully designed bottles on the dressing table would have to come later. Maybe the morning would bring her an improved condition. It had to. She had to begin her search. Tomorrow. Read. Oh, where was he. . . ?

A soft tinkling of music drew Glenda's sudden attention. She scooted to the edge of the bed, breathless, recognizing the haunting melody of the song. Her heartbeats swelled inside her as she placed her feet to the floor, then hopped, one-footed, to the door's facing and leaned against it, listening intensely. She hobbled out onto the flagstone pathway and looked upward at the balcony, seeing an opened door and shadows from movements inside the room from which it led, now realizing this was where the music originated.

"It has to be Christina's music box," Glenda whispered. "Christina Taylor? Rayburn's Christina? Is this truly the Christina whose name was spoken only briefly by Peter Grayson?"

As the sweet incensed breath of night caressed her upturned face, Glenda whispered further. "Christina. . . ?" Then she hobbled back to her bed . . . wondering . . . "How? Why?"

Chapter Fourteen

Throwing the shutters back to the morning's awakening, Glenda got her first daylight glimpse of this new world she had so bravely ventured to. A wagon was passing by, creaking under the weight of cabbages, carrots, lettuce and red, shiny tomatoes and an old Negro woman with a striped tignon on her head and a basket in the crook of her arm filled with pink roses went sauntering along beneath the tunnel of live oak limbs.

Glenda stretched leisurely, feeling, oh, so alive. Even her ankle had decided to cooperate. She was at least able to place her weight on it, though limping still. A soft purr of a voice behind her drew Glenda around with a start. Her eyes widened and her pulse raced, seeing Christina standing there so tall, thin and beautiful.

"Christina. . . ," she gasped, looking Christina up and down, never having seen her look so glowing and at peace with the world. Her blond, gray-fringed hair was in a chignon at the nape of her neck and her face was still that of a porcelain figurine with eyes the color of the morning sky. Her dress was of a fine silk, low in front, and thickly gathered at her waist, and rustled voluptuously as she moved across the room with arms outstretched.

As though she might a daughter, Christina drew Glenda to her and hugged her warmly. "When Peter told me who our late-night houseguest was, I could hardly believe it," she purred softly. "The dark shadows of night didn't afford me a close enough look."

She then held Glenda at arm's length, looking her up and down speculatively. "But it is you. You are actually here in New Orleans. What has brought you on such a long, dangerous journey? And are you even all right? Peter told me about your unfortunate accident . . . an accident that brought you to our house. If not for the rat, I would have never known you had set foot on these shores."

Glenda's green eyes held much confusion in them. Why was Christina. . . ? What would Rayburn. . . ? "Yes, I am all right," she stammered. "But, Christina, I am at a loss in my mind as to why . . . you . . . are here. . . ."

Christina stepped away from Glenda and went to sit on the corner of the bed. Her eyes had a faraway look in them. Glenda could remember seeing such a look many times while attending Christina's needs at El Progresso. But there was a difference this time. This faraway look held happiness . . . contentment. . . . Not sadness.

"Glenda, there is so much I have to admit to you," Christina murmured, lifting the skirt of her dress from around her ankles. "I know what you must be thinking about me. I know you must have many questions as to what has happened to my and Rayburn's . . . marriage. . . ."

Glenda limped to the bed and sat down beside Christina, all eyes. She was feeling quite self-conscious as to how she appeared. She still hadn't been shown to a place to take a bath, nor did she have a change of clothes. She knew that she not only looked terrible, but also smelled badly as well. But that had to be put behind her for the moment. She wanted to know the answers to many questions . . . questions that only Christina could supply her with.

"Yes, Christina, I am surprised to find you living here . . . with . . . another man," she said quietly. "And Peter Grayson? I thought he was not only *your* friend, but Rayburn's as well."

Christina reached for one of Glenda's hands and cupped it with one of her own. "Glenda, our marriage hasn't been a true marriage for some time now," she confessed. "You see, we were childhood sweethearts. We got caught up in something that we didn't understand." She cast her eyes downward and blushed a bit. "You see, when we got married, it was because I was with child. . . ."

Glenda gasped noisily. "A child. . . ?" she said. "But I thought you had said that . . . you . . . didn't have any children."

Christina's eyes lifted and looked across the room, focusing on an inanimate object. "I didn't carry the child full term," she whispered. "But you see, Rayburn and I were married by then. We just decided to continue on with our lives from there and tried to make one another happy. But I couldn't seem to adjust to a loveless marriage."

"And then Peter Grayson. . . ?"

Christina's other hand covered Glenda's. "Yes. Peter. We met several years ago at a ball given by the American Fruit Company," she said. "We have . . . been . . . lovers since. . . ."

"And Rayburn. . . ?"

"He only recently found out. Just before we were to leave for El Progresso. You see, I put up such a fuss about leaving, he suspected there was more to it than my not wanting to move to the tropics. He had me watched. He found out about me and Peter."

"Then . . . what did he . . . do. . . ?"

"He begged me to stop seeing Peter. He said that he loved me. That he would do anything to make me happy. So I agreed to make the break with Peter. Go to El Progresso with Rayburn. But once there, I was miserable. I pined for Peter. His arms. His lips. I hated the sweltering climate of the tropics. I hated the mud. The torrents of rain. I hated everything about it except for our relationship, Glenda. . . ."

"I heard the music from the music box last night, Christina. . . ."

"Yes. That was Peter's parting gift when I left for El Progresso. I only played it at El Progresso . . . when Rayburn . . . was gone. The music box drew me close to Peter's memory. . . ."

Glenda swallowed hard. "I'm so sorry about all of this, Christina," she said. "I'm sure even now it is hard on you, knowing that you have more than likely broken Rayburn's heart."

"Yes. I do worry. Much," Christina said, releasing Glenda's hands, to rise and pace the floor. She swung the skirt of her dress around in a silken flutter, then faced Glenda with a fixed determination. "But, Glenda, if you ever love a man as I love Peter, you know there is nothing that can keep you apart. Nothing. You would follow such a love as I have found in that man to the ends of the earth, if need be. You will one day. . . ."

Glenda pushed herself up from the bed, teetering just a little bit on the soreness of the ankle. Her face had become flushed. "Christina, I have . . . found . . . such a man," she blurted. "He is here in New Orleans. He is the reason . . . one of the reasons I have given up my family to travel to a land I have never known. I want to see the man I love. An American. I do understand how you feel about Peter Grayson. I do. . . ."

Christina had paled a bit. "You have fallen in love with an American?" she gasped. "How? When? You weren't acquainted with that many Americans while a part of El Progresso."

Glenda hesitated a bit, not sure if she should reveal her love's name to anyone else. But she just had to! She had kept it well hidden for so long now. Wouldn't it even be grand, speaking of his name to another other than the four walls she had used as a sounding board so often? She limped across the room, to stare out into the courtyard, seeing Nena snoozing lazily beneath the shade of a palm tree. So far, her orphaned cub seemed well enough with the world. But why shouldn't she? Her Nena had to feel as though in the jungle again. Surely! All that was missing was her mother.

She pivoted on her good foot, again conscious of her attire as Christina's gaze was sweeping over her. She fingered the drawstrings of her blouse and spoke. "You knew him," she said. "He works for the American Fruit Company, just the same as Rayburn."

"Who?" Christina said softly. "I can't imagine . . ."

"William Read deBaulieu," Glenda said quickly, watching Christina's expression of wonder.

"William . . . Read. . . ?"

"You know. The man whom Rayburn left at El Progresso for me to attend to after he had become . . . uh . . . ill after a fall against a tree after a . . . puma . . . jumped from a tree and frightened him. . . ."

Christina sighed heavily and smiled. "Oh, yes. How could I have forgotten?"

"Well, Christina, Read and I became quite acquainted in your absence," Glenda admitted, blushing anew. "It was then that I knew of my deep love and devotion for the man. Then when he left El Progresso and Rayburn told me that he may not return for some time because of his further illness, I just had to come to him. Seek him out. But I'm afraid for Rayburn or Peter Grayson to find out about our relationship."

"Why your concern, Glenda?"

"Well, you see, uh, there is something about Read's accident that wasn't quite true," she said quietly, turning her back to Christina, going to the window, gazing out once again.

"What are you trying to say?"

"Well, the accident he had?" she murmured. "It wasn't all that bad. It's quite a long story, but I feel he has become trapped in his lies and can no longer find his way clear of them." She swung around, pleading with her eyes. "But please keep this to yourself. I don't want Read to come to any harm. And I so ache to see him. How can I? Even when? Do you know of him? Where he can be found?"

"I know of a deBaulieu family. But I haven't mingled much to know the details of who might live in their Creole house. You see, I am sort of a branded woman since I live so openly with Peter, and his not being my legal husband."

Glenda went to Christina and took her hands in hers, pleading further with her eyes. "Can you see if you can find Read for me? Maybe even bring him to me when Peter Grayson isn't home? Oh, Christina, it would mean so much to me. Can you? Please? You know the ache of a heart when without the one you love."

Christina's eyes wavered a bit, then they grew bright. "Yes. I will try. I need to get away from this house anyway. I will find your Read for you. I will bring him to you. Peter is gone most afternoons."

Glenda's heartbeats began to go wild. She wanted to dance around the room. She wanted to shout. But instead, she hobbled once again to the bed, suddenly again feeling the darn aching in her ankle. She leaned and rubbed it, all flushed and excited, trying to not think about Read not being able to come to her. He just wasn't ill. He wasn't!

"Christina, you just don't know what it will mean to me to see Read again," she said in a near whisper. "I have, oh, so dreamed of being with him again. And maybe I will today? It will be a dream come true. Tell me. Can dreams come true? Can they?"

Christina stared from the open door, out onto the courtyard. "Mine has. To be with Peter is all I asked for in my prayers even. I feel that Rayburn's own prayers will take care of him. And dreams? They are for lovers." She swung around, beaming. "Yes. Your dreams will come true."

Glenda's face turned to that of serious wonder. She began to fidget with the tail of her skirt. "Christina, there are more reasons than Read that I have come to this new land," she murmured, casting her eyes downward.

Christina settled down on the bed beside her once more. "And what else caused your escape from your home land? A man's love wasn't the only reason?" she asked soothingly, having seen the distraught look in Glenda's eyes.

"No. There were two reasons. Read is one. And my true . . . father . . . is the other. . . ."

Christina leaned a bit forward, remembering Glenda's confessions of "family" when they had talked those long hours while at El Progresso. Yes, Glenda had said that her true father was American. "Glenda, America is quite a large place. Don't get your hopes up that you may some day find your father. He may even be dead. You know that was a long time ago."

"Yes. It was a long time ago. But to me, it was as only yesterday that for the first time I realized I had a father besides the one who fed and clothed me. I have had this compulsion to find my true father. All my life, it seems. I must at least give it a try."

"And what did you say about your true father? Didn't you tell me that he had been a ship's captain?"

"Yes," Glenda said in a low murmur. Then she rose, forgetting her wound, determination suddenly taking over. "He was. But that doesn't mean that he will still be. He may even be rich. Own . . . many . . . ships. . . ."

"Glenda, you must put this behind you," Christina said, going to Glenda to grasp onto her shoulders. "You have been lucky enough to have arrived safely to the city of your love. Place this other anxiety behind you. It is an impossible task you are putting upon yourself."

Glenda shook herself free. "Christina, I have to ask you something," she said quietly.

"What is it? What can I help you with?"

"Peter Grayson. How well do you truly know him? How much of his past do you know?"

Christina's face paled. "Glenda, you do not believe . . ."

"Christina," Glenda said even more forcefully. "How did Peter Grayson come by his lame leg? Has he ever told you?"

"Glenda. . . ," Christina gasped noisily. She began pacing the floor like a nervous cat, suddenly feeling a bit trapped.

"Christina, you do know how he received the wound, don't you?" Glenda said, stopping Christina with the force of a hand on her arm. "Lovers do not hold many truths from one another, if it be true love they share. Tell me. How did he get the wound?"

"It was . . . because of another . . . woman," Christina said in a near whisper. "Many years ago. Before he and I ever met. . . ."

Glenda felt pinpricks of anxiety race up and down her spine. Maybe. . . ! "And where . . . what city . . . did he receive his wound, Christina. . . ?"

"He did not say, Glenda," Christina said, suddenly

setting her jaws firmly. "And I do not like to speak of it. I am reminded of another woman who had taken his mind from him. I am reminded of another woman who was wed to another while she and Peter made passionate love. When I think of him, I only want to think of him as always having been mine."

Glenda's heart plunged. Her mother had said that she had been raped. She hadn't said that she had participated in the act. She had been raped. Was Peter not the man she sought? Her shoulders slumped heavily. It would have been too simple. But she persisted. "What did Peter do before he became an owner of many ships? He has told you that, hasn't he?"

Christina's eyes wavered. "Yes. He has told me. He was proud of his exploits. He was a ship's captain. Many years ago. He traveled the seas. . . ."

"The Caribbean. . . ?" Glenda said anxiously.

"Yes. Even there. . . ."

"Did he ever mention . . . Bay Island. . . ?"

Christina teetered a bit, shock registering on her face. "Did you say . . . Bay Island. . . ?" she whispered, settling onto the bed. "That was where you made your home, wasn't it, Glenda?"

"Yes. And so did my mother . . . those many years ago. . . ."

Christina hung her face in her hands. "Oh, God," she said. "Oh, my God."

Glenda fell to her knees before Christina and took Christina's face away from her hands. "Christina, you do know now, don't you. . . ?" she said firmly. "Peter. It *is* possible that he is my true father. . . ."

"Glenda, before, when you had mentioned being from Bay Island, I didn't even think about having heard Peter mention having been there those many years ago. Now, with you bringing the past to the present, I do remember. I don't know why I didn't think about it sooner, and why I hadn't thought to question Peter about it, especially since while in El Progresso myself, I was so close to the island . . . that he has spoken of in his past."

"Christina, could . . . he . . . be. . . ?" Glenda said thickly. "Do you think . . . he. . . ?"

"Glenda, I don't know," Christina said, lifting a hand to Glenda's cheek, caressing it gently.

Glenda's eyes grew a bit hazy. "But, if so, either he is lying about my mother, or my mother has lied to me. All those years. She said she had been raped. . . ."

Christina let a few trickles of tears stream from her eyes. "Sweet little thing, you are so troubled," she murmured. "Either way, you will be confused as to how to feel. But I must say something. Please don't hate me. I don't wish to turn you against your mother. This is the thing I would wish not to do."

"What are you trying to say, Christina. . . ?"

"It's about Peter. Peter, the Peter I know, would never rape anyone. He is the gentlest man. He's never taken anything by force in his life. If he got shot by a woman's husband, it was because the woman had first participated fully in the relationship. . . ."

Glenda pushed herself from the bed, feeling something twisting at her insides. Her mother? Her sweet, gentle mother? Could she have been unfaithful to her man? To such a man as José Galvez? José Galvez was the kind, gentle man. Surely not Peter Grayson! She swung around, glaring. "You have to be wrong. My

304

mother . . . wouldn't. . . ," she shouted. "Surely this Peter Grayson is a changed man from those years ago. Surely you didn't know him as he truly was. . . ."

"I guess we neither one will ever truly know," Christina said, rising. She went to Glenda and drew her into her arms. "Sweet thing, please try to not let your thoughts torment you now, especially with your loved one so near. You want to be bubbling when he arrives. I am going to see to it that he comes to you. This very afternoon. Surely I can find him and tell him you are here, asking for him."

"But my . . . father. . . ?"

"I will talk to Peter. I will tell him. . . ."

"He will surely throw me out onto the street," Glenda pouted.

"Would you rather I didn't reveal our suspicions to him so suddenly?"

Glenda swallowed hard. "Maybe we'd best wait," she said. "Let's be a bit more sure. If I have waited this long, I can wait a bit longer."

"You are right, Glenda. This is your best decision."

"It will be hard. But I feel that I should wait. . . ."

"All right," Christina said, setting her jaws firmly. "The next thing to do is get you to a bath and then let you choose clothes from my closet to look lovely in when your Read knocks on your door."

Glenda felt a surge of warmth flow through her. "Again? You are ready to do this again for me? After doing such at El Progresso? Christina, you must be an angel sent directly from heaven to treat me so well."

"You have become very special to me," Christina purred. "And you do not know how happy I am to see you. I do grow bored, being confined to this house in such a way. One can do only so much embroidery. . . ."

Glenda jumped at the words. "Embroidery?" she exclaimed. "Oh, Christina. Do you mean maybe I can even resume embroidery work with you? I so loved it. I felt as though worth something when I created on those sheets of linen."

"Yes. We will spend our free time together, embroidering, and you can even sketch the designs freely while here. We have all the tools at our disposal here in New Orleans. Whatever you will need, I will send someone to fetch from town."

"Christina, pinch me. I so fear that I am asleep and will wake up and find myself on my makeshift bed on Bay Island. . . ."

Nena scampered into the room, purring and scraping against one, then the other. Glenda leaned down and patted her mane, then hugged her. "And my Nena, Christina," she said. "Isn't she so beautiful? And to think Peter has agreed to let me keep her here. I do agree. He is a kind man. . . ."

"The puma," Christina said, bending, also petting. "Peter told me she was here. But how. . . ? Why do you have her. . . ?"

Glenda smiled warmly, now feeling as though she didn't have to keep any secrets from her very special friend. "It is a long story. . . ," she murmured.

"Tell me. While I take you to the bathroom and introduce you to some warm suds and soap that smells even better than the magnolia blossoms that flank our front walks. . . ."

Glenda laughed and followed along with her, feeling oh, so alive, and knowing, just knowing that not only had she found Read, but also that she had found her father. She had to brush her doubts of her mother's infidelity from her mind. She just had to. . . !

Read's world had become too much that of "sister" and "nephew," almost drowning him in the domesticity of escorting Harriett and David to wherever entered Harriett's mind at her first dawning of each day. It was time for Read to make his break and approach Peter Grayson . . . say that his "illness" had passed. Peter owned more ships than the banana-carrying *Sea Wolf*. It wouldn't be the same to board another ship now, knowing where the *Sea Wolf* could carry him, but Read had to brush the thoughts of returning to El Progresso from his mind. And hadn't George Boyd already taken his place aboard the *Sea Wolf*? To represent the American Fruit Company? Would George Boyd also have found a brief escape from reality in the arms of a beautiful Honduran wench whose passion surmounted even that of a raging storm at sea? Would it even be Glenda, though now possibly even wed to that mangy weasel who called himself Ramón?

Such a thought caused Read to thrust his knees angrily into his horse's side, to now travel at a full gallop along the cobblestones of Bourbon Street. His horse competed with horse-drawn carriages, other horses, wagons filled with fruit and vegetables being pulled by mules, and old Negro women ignoring the dangers of the traffic as they lumbered along with baskets of flowers balanced on their heads.

Read tried to ignore all these passersby, but when the fluid movement of a well-dressed lady making her way beneath the shadows of the lacy balconies of the Creole houses and buildings drew his quick attention, he reined his horse to a halt and stared with a pounding heart. Wasn't she as tall. . . ? Wasn't she as well proportioned. . . ? Couldn't her face reveal to him that Glenda had somehow made her way to New Orleans. . . ?

"If only she would remove the scarf of baby lace from around her head," he whispered. "If I could see the hair. . . ."

Then the lady lifted the skirt of her dress to step down onto the street and glanced quickly from side to side, giving Read a full look at her face. Something grabbed at his heart, but not because he had just seen Glenda. It was Christina Taylor. Though having only met her briefly while at El Progresso, hers was a face he would never forget. Even now, it was hard for him to believe she was in her forties. She was so exquisite. And he knew she must be the same in bed. Hadn't rumor spread of Peter Grayson's female companion having completely bewitched this man who had never wed because of a brief encounter with a Honduran maiden those many years ago. . . ? He had taken many lovers since, but had never been able to put this woman of his past completely from his mind. . . .

"Will it be the same for me?" Read thought further to himself. "Though I have lost Glenda, has she captured and stolen my heart from inside me? Will I ever . . . get . . . it wholly back to offer to another?"

He urged his horse onward, not wanting to have to speak to Christina should she notice him there. Seeing

Christina would always be a reminder of Glenda. And how was Rayburn even faring now that he had lost his pride and joy to another? Hadn't he even fought for her? Or had he thought more kindly of Peter than to cause him the laming of another leg, knowing that one irate husband's vengeance was enough for this man who had been so respected until he had openly accepted another man's woman into his house as well as his bedroom.

"But none of that is my concern," he argued to himself. He knew that Peter Grayson was a kind-hearted, gentle man, though quite staunch where business was concerned. From Peter Grayson's struggling days, he had built his wealth from captaining one ship, to owning many.

"As I might possibly do," Read thought further. "By God, if I love the sea more than that damn gambling palace of my father's, why *not* invest in a ship?"

His determination drew him closer to the wharves, where along the waterfront many buildings and warehouses lined up, crowded next to one another, almost the same as the steamboats and paddlewheelers that lined the wharves. In one of these taller buildings of brick covered with stucco, and roofs covered with slate and tile, Peter Grayson ran his empire.

Read's black stallion pranced on by the fish market where some fish hung on hooks and others were piled high in baskets, and where sea-gray shrimp lay spread on counters of the makeshift wooden stalls. Though high on horseback, Read could see that some crabs had escaped and were moving around on the sidewalk.

Next to the fish market, there were the butchers' stalls. Slabs of bloody beef lay sprawled on the counter tops and furry, disemboweled rabbits hung upside down, blowing eerily in the wind.

The flower market was happily welcomed by Read, changing the aromas in the air from that of death to that of sweetness. Potted plants sat arranged on the sidewalk, some of those being roses, ferns, and even little trees filled with blood-red peppers.

Further on up the road, an old Indian woman wrapped in a colorful blanket sat along the walk selling baskets striped red and green and the hustle and bustle of the crowded walkways and streets were of different nationalities being spoken. There was the rapid trilling of the French, the soft slur of Italian, and the easy droning of Negroes' voices. But above all this, Read was aware of the seagulls circling overhead with their strange, echoing cries, and the slap-slap of the water against the shore, knowing that he had just reached Peter's eight-story establishment.

Again he reined his horse to a stop and dismounted. After securing the reins to a hitching post, he straightened his back while taking care to check his appearance. One glance downward assured that his beige cotton shirt, unbuttoned halfway to the waist fitted neatly into the waist of his snug, dark brown breeches made of coarse fabric, and his brown boots shone as though mirrors from a fresh waxing.

Nervously, he combed his fingers through his dark, thick hair, then hurried on his way, handling a mahogany rail along the staircase until the upper floor had been reached. A long, dark hallway afforded Read many doors from which to choose, but knowing Peter's, from past dealings with him, he strolled on toward the door that had painted on its glass the tall, gold letters of PETER GRAYSON, LTD.

Upon entering, a bespectacled secretary greeted Read from behind a small, solid oak desk strewn with paper.

"Yes. May I help you, sir?" she asked politely, though not rising.

As always when near a woman, Read's gaze quickly assessed her. Her business outfit of white shirtwaist blouse was worn impeccably beneath an oval, pinch-lipped face framed by a gathering of dark hair pulled severely into a tight bun at the nape of her neck. Her voice was nasal and high-pitched and she appeared to have no showing of breasts.

Read cleared his throat nervously as his gaze moved to the closed door that separated the skimpily furnished, dull, outer office from the plush, sun-washed inner office that overlooked the daily activities of the waterfront. "Mr. Grayson, please," he finally said.

With a forefinger, the secretary pushed her spectacles back further on her nose. "Is Mr. Grayson expecting you, sir?" she said, again nasally.

"No. I haven't spoken with him for some time."

"Then, I'm sorry, sir. Mr. Grayson is quite a busy man."

Read's brow furrowed with an angry, growing impatience. "Miss, I. . . ."

Peter opened the door abruptly and stepped across the room with the aid of his cane, smiling, extending his free hand toward Read. "Hey, there, William," he said light-heartedly. "Heard of your mishap in Honduras. Is your head farin' better?"

Read clasped Peter's hand firmly and gave it a generous shake. "Aw, nothing to fuss about," he laughed awkwardly.

"To hell you say," Peter said thickly, dropping his hand to his side. "Heard it lost you a job on my *Sea Wolf*."

"That's the breaks," Read said.

"Sherry, my secretary here, give you a rough time?" Peter said, winking at her, causing her to giggle approvingly.

"You could say that," Read grumbled.

"Well, she has her orders," Peter said. "If she sent everyone in my office who came in off the waterfront, I'd be doin' more visitin' than work. Come on. Let's go have some coffee. And Sherry here just bought some cakes fresh from the oven. They're just drippin' with honey."

Read followed along after Peter. "Can't turn down an invitation like that," he chuckled. "I left the house without breakfast. If I'd have stuck around, for sure Harriett would have asked me to escort her and David somewhere, as though that's all I was put on this earth for."

"Your sister is still widowing it, eh?" Peter asked, laboring toward the door.

"She met someone last evening," Read replied. "But he's only visiting relations here in the city. I'm sure nothing will come of it."

"Damn attractive, your sister Harriett."

"Oh? You've even noticed with such a beautiful wench you now have at your disposal?"

Peter's pale, thick lashes hid the annoyance in his green eyes and ignored the reference to Christina. He closed the door behind Read, then made his way to his desk where he sat down on a leather, high-backed chair behind it. He gestured with his arm. "Sit. Make yourself at home. Enjoy refreshments, then tell me what's on your mind," he said, now pouring coffee from a silver pot into two ceramic mugs, which Read heartily accepted, then also a square of steaming cake, where butter and honey melted together on top.

Read sat comfortably against the back of the plump, overstuffed brown leather chair, devouring first one cake then a second, washing the sweetness down with generous gulps of coffee. When he was finished, he accepted a Cuban cigar from Peter and then a light, with them both now hazy-eyed with pleasantly filled stomachs and the private pleasure of men when they had the taste of an expensive cigar on their tongue.

Read's gaze took in his surroundings. Not only was Peter's taste for cigars expensive, but also for furnishings. The desk was a magnificent solid oak piece where upon it could be found a sterling silver wolf-head's paper weight, stationery with an embossed wolf's head as its letterhead, and a sterling silver letter opener, also with a wolf's head as its handle.

A richly carved mahogany case offered the well-kept supply of cigars, and the desk top was profusely littered with figured papers and an inkwell sat opened and half-emptied.

At the far end of the room, a leather sofa was flanked on each side by matching chairs and above this, tall and wide expanse of windows stood curtain-less to the view of the hustle and bustle of the waterfront.

An oriental rug was only partially hidden from view by more chairs, oak end tables and pot after pot of green, flowering plants.

"You've got quite a layout here," Read chuckled, gumming his cigar.

"It wasn't always this way," Peter grumbled, placing his fingertips together before him. "I started at the bottom to first be a deckhand, then moved my way up to captain, then to ownership. It was rough sailin' at first, so you could say." He chuckled even further, puffing leisurely on his cigar.

"My plans are to not start at the bottom," Read said, leaning forward. He flicked ashes from his cigar, then watched the smoke spiraling upward from its tip as he added. "No. What I'd like to do is buy a ship. Maybe even one of your, if you need one taken off your hands. I'd like to buy it *and* be its captain. All in one stroke."

The chair squeaked noisily as Peter also leaned forward. "By God, man. Did you say what I think you said?" he replied quizzically. "You're thinkin' of goin' into business? I thought becomin' a part of a ship's activities like you did when you became an employee of The American Fruit Company was only a stubborn tactic on your part to show your father that you didn't have to stay glued to the roulette tables like a common gambler, like he'd have you to be to just keep you at his gamblin' palace, to watch over things. Is there more to it? Did you fall in love with the sea? Eh? Do you wish to court it as I did for so many years?"

Read settled back against the chair once more and thrust the cigar between his lips. "Guess you could say that," he said. He wanted to say, "If I can't court my lady love, then the sea it will be." But no one knew of his feelings for Glenda. No one but . . . Glenda . . . herself. . . .

Peter leaned his elbows on the desk, lifting an eyebrow as he continued to puff on the cigar. Then he said, "You sure you want to jump into this thing so quickly?"

"I enjoyed your *Sea Wolf*," Read replied. "So will I more my own ship."

"But what I'm trying to say is that the position you gave up on the *Sea Wolf* is available again," Peter said, leaning against the chair once more, but looking anything but relaxed.

"What's that you say?" Read asked, straightening his back. "George Boyd just only began. Why would he no longer be taking the voyages for the American Fruit Company? It was not an unpleasant job." His gaze lowered. He removed his cigar and turned it round and round between his fingers. "The islands," he said quietly. "They have much to offer. Much more than bananas. . . ."

"Yes. I know," Peter said darkly. "I've also . . . been . . . to the islands."

Read's gaze lifted and he eyed Peter closely. He knew what was on his mind . . . a love affair that apparently would continue to haunt him until he was lowered into his grave. "Oh, God," he thought. "Will it be the same for me. . . ?"

"But back to the decision you must make for your future," Peter said, coughing a bit nervously as he ground his cigar out in an ashtray. "There is a position open on the *Sea Wolf* again. And let me tell you, the American Fruit Company is a mite unhappy about this last voyage of my ship."

"Oh? How's that. . . ?"

"George Boyd didn't quit as the fruit company's

rep," Peter growled, fingering his silver wolf's head paper weight. "You see, a storm at sea . . . well . . . it claimed his life. . . ."

Read's hands clasped tightly to the chair's arms. "What. . . ?" he gasped. "You mean . . . he. . . ?"

Peter's face became all shadows as he kept his eyes lowered to the desk. "Overboard," he mumbled. "Swept overboard and never another sign of him after that."

Read pushed himself quickly from the chair. He crushed his cigar in an ashtray then began pacing the floor, kneading his brow. "God," he grumbled. "Damn it." He felt a deep remorse for the loss of the fine gentleman's life and even a bit strangely guilty, wondering if his playacting with his "head injury" made him a bit responsible for this man's death. Had Read continued traveling with the *Sea Wolf*, then George Boyd would have not been aboard the ship to be swept overboard.

He swallowed hard, suddenly realizing had it not been George Boyd, might it have even been himself? Suddenly the sea had lost its glamour.

"So? Want the position left vacant by George Boyd?" Peter said, rising, letting his cane help him to move and stand to gaze from the window. He had seen many a man grabbed by the hungry, devilish fingers of the sea and taken to its depths. Then there had been the times when the sea had been serene, like an angel's heavenly outspread wings. . . .

Read slumped back down onto the chair, his shoulders slouched and his legs spread widely apart. "God, Peter, I don't know. . . ," he murmured.

Peter's soft laughter drew Read's brows upward. He

watched as Peter began to talk, laughingly. "But there is a much lighter and brighter end to the latest *Sea Wolf* voyage," he chuckled amusedly, kneading his chin with his free hand.

"Can there truly be?" Read questioned.

"Yes. Quite," Peter said.

"Well, then, what. . . ?" Read prodded.

"A stowaway," Peter chuckled further.

Read's expression lightened. His face broke into a soft smile. "A stowaway? On the *Sea Wolf?*" he said, laughing quietly. "How? Who. . . ?"

"She was found with the bananas in the hold of the ship," Peter chuckled further.

Read's laughter faded away. "She. . . ?" he gasped. "A woman? On the *Sea Wolf?*"

"Damnest thing you ever did see," Peter said. "Her and her cat. . . ."

"Cat. . . ?" Read said even more softly. "What . . . cat. . . ? A house cat. . . ?"

"No. No ordinary house cat," Peter said, now roaring with laughter. "Our female stowaway had a puma with her. Can you believe it? A goddamned puma. In the hold of my ship."

Read's face paled and his heartbeat was thundering wildly. He rose from the chair and went to Peter. Weak-kneed, he said, "This stowaway. Tell me. What'd she look like. . . ?" he stammered.

"I'll do you better than that," Peter laughed. "Her name's Glenda. Glenda Galvez . . ."

Read's fingers went to his hair. "God! Glenda. . . ," he whispered.

Peter eyed Read closely. "William, what is it. . . ?" he said softly. "You're . . . you're pale as a ghost."

Read clasped his fingers to Peter's shoulders. "This . . . uh . . . stowaway," he said cautiously. "You didn't . . . uh, harm her in any way for traveling unasked on the *Sea Wolf*, did . . . you. . . ?"

"God, man," Peter stormed. "You know me better than that. Why, William, I even took her to my house. . . ."

"Your . . . house. . . ?"

"Christina even knows this young lady. She's seein' after her. . . ."

Read swung around on his heel, ignoring Peter's confused questions that were being left behind. Instead, he raced down the stairs and onto his horse, only heartbeats away from seeing . . . kissing . . . holding Glenda once again. She surely didn't wed Ramón Martinez! If so . . . why would she be in New Orleans. . . ?

"Only to seek me out," he shouted. "Me. She's come to *me*. . . ."

His horse's hooves thundered across the cobblestones, in a race with his heartbeats, it seemed. . . .

Chapter Fifteen

The cooing of the pigeons under the eaves and the click of their red claws on the tiles of the roof serenaded Glenda as she paced her room nervously. Could it be true. . . ? Was Christina truly going to deliver Read to her in possibly only moments. . . ?

She inhaled deeply, enjoying the fragrance of her skin. The leisurely bath in the fancy bathtub with its magnificent gold faucets that poured both hot and cold water from them, and the fancily shaped bars of soap in pinks and blues which held fragrances of all flowers combined, had been an experience she would never forget. And then the fancy bottles on the dressing table that she had been admiring! When opened, didn't such overpowering, heady fragrances swirl upward into the air, causing her senses to even become a bit giddy? What fun it had been to splash the cold, oily liquid onto her flesh!

She sniffed each wrist, smiling. Would both her appearance and luscious smell cause Read to throw her to the bed and make passionate love to her. . . ? Ah, how she remembered the skills he possessed. No other man could ever cause her to become so wanton

. . . so daring. . . .

Relieved that her wound was almost fully healed, she felt the strength to whirl around the room, almost becoming that ballerina atop Christina's music box. She loved the dress she had chosen from Christina's many. Its green silk matched her eyes. It was cut very low and clung sensuously to her figure, displaying the splendid whiteness of her high, firm breasts and the smallness of her waist. The fully gathered skirt worn over yards and yards of crinoline was bedecked with bead embroidery in a design of tiny, pink roses. And Christina had quite deftly pinned matching live roses on each side of Glenda's head, lifting her golden, thick mane to hang voluptuously down her back.

Diamonds sparkled at her throat and ears, reminding her of another time . . . other diamonds. She felt guilt pangs, remembering even more. While in El Progresso, hadn't she been so wrong to sneak Christina's lovely dresses and jewels? She now knew that Christina would have shared anything. It had been Glenda's for only the asking. She knew this now. She did not . . . then.

"And, Read," she murmured aloud. "How could I have suspected that you would steal anything from anyone? Oh, I've learned so much. Trust, oh, how I should have trusted you more. . . ." She swung around when she heard footsteps approaching. She tensed. They were not heavy footsteps of a man. When Christina opened the door and stepped inside, heavy-lidded, Glenda's heart sank. Christina either had not found Read . . . he was too ill to come to her . . . or he hadn't cared enough to come. She just couldn't believe it was the latter. They had made such passionate love together! But yet, there still was this knowledge that he had left El Progresso . . . and . . . he had not returned.

Her heart began a slow hammering. Maybe he *had* left for Bay Island by way of another ship other than the *Sea Wolf* at the very same time she was traveling toward New Orleans. Maybe unknowingly . . . their paths . . . had . . . crossed. . . .

She went to Christina and clasped onto her hands. "Christina, what is it?" she said tremulously. She saw the uneasiness in Christina's eyes and how pale she was, though having had to have walked some distance beneath the rays of the sun.

Christina eased Glenda's hands from her own and reached to untie the scarf of white lace from around her head. "It is a lovely day for a stroll," she murmured, turning her back to Glenda.

Glenda eyed her speculatively. Christina had to know that the loveliness of the day was the last thing on Glenda's mind. She swung her skirt and many petticoats around and stepped to Christina's front. "Christina, why are you delaying? Did you or did you not succeed at finding Read?" She felt suddenly awash inside. She knew that if Christina had carried good news with her, there would be absolutely no need for small, idle talk. Christina had failed . . . surely . . . failed.

"In a way. . . ." Christina murmured with further wavering eyes.

"Christina, please," Glenda cried, circling her fists to her side. "I cannot stand this suspense. Tell me!"

"Glenda. . . ," Christina began but swung around, open-mouthed, when the door crashed suddenly open and Read stood there red-faced and panting. His gray eyes, clouded with feelings, told it all as his gaze swept over Glenda. . . .

"*Ma chérie*, it . . . *is* . . . you. . . ," he murmured. He went to her and drew her quickly into his arms. He buried his nose in her hair, clinging tightly, murmuring still. "God, Glenda. My sweet, sweet Glenda. You've come. You love me enough to stow away on the *Sea Wolf* to search me out. I love you, darling. I love you so deeply."

Glenda forgot Christina. She didn't even hear Christina as she moved swiftly from the room, closing the door behind her, leaving Glenda and Read to their passionate embraces. Glenda was almost ready to give way to tears with such a rush of happiness coursing through her veins. She seductively twined her arms around Read's neck and met his kiss with an unleashed fury, becoming almost wild with the building sensuous pleasure rising with the demanding heat of his lips that felt to be on fire with raw passion. She trembled as his hands traveled over her from her cheeks, downwward, causing her to catch her breath when his fingers found the heaving of her breasts.

She returned his caresses, feeling the thickness of his dark hair, his angular, weather-tanned face, and his straight, long nose. She opened her eyes and found his gray eyes watching her, full of desire. She pulled her lips free and smiled sweetly as she traced his nose with her forefinger. "I can't believe it's truly you, Read," she purred. "Darling, how can I even be so lucky? And . . . you . . . you are quite well. . . ."

As he held her at arm's length, she felt her heart beating furiously. He was so handsome in his beige shirt opened almost to the waist and his tight breeches revealing his mounting desire for her.

"It is I who am the lucky one," he said huskily, letting his gaze rake over. "*Ma chérie*, you've never been more beautiful. More . . . desirable. How is it that you've chosen to come? Is it truly because of your love for me?"

She gave him a downcast look through her lashes. "Yes. You are the main reason," she said quietly.

"Then there is another?"

"Yes. . . ."

"What. . . ?"

"Do we have to talk about it now, Read?" she murmured, touching his lips, trembling, feeling their softness, their warmth. "I've dreamed of this moment. Please let's not spoil it by talking."

He drew her close, then tenderly kissed the soft hollow of her throat. She threw her head back, moaning with ecstasy, then entwined her hands through his hair and guided his lips to her breasts. While he leaned over her with his searching lips, Glenda reached behind her and soon had her dress lowered, exposing the full flesh of her breasts to his feasting eyes.

His fingers traced them as though memorizing them, then his mouth lowered and his tongue became as a snake's, flicking, from one to the other, causing Glenda's insides to become alive, on fire with reckless desire.

Then with a fierceness, he was kissing her again, his fingers digging roughly into her flesh as he held her close. The exquisite sensations were causing her mind to begin a slow drifting, as though in a boat, floating.

His hands then went to her face, framing it. She could see the fire burning in his eyes. "Darling, undress fully," he said hoarsely, then kissed her tenderly on the tip of her nose. He stroked her cheek with his fingertips as she yielded to the sensuous tone of his voice and the heat of his caress.

"And even the diamonds?" she whispered.

He chuckled amusedly. "And even the diamonds," he said. "I have a use for them myself."

Her eyebrows arched, but she was too feverish to question anything he might do or say. She had always said that once she found the true man of her dreams, she would follow him to the ends of the earth. Oh, how glad she had followed him at least to this place called New Orleans!

She draped the diamond necklace across the bed and let her earrings drop to the floor, all the while, her eyes were full of him. She was ready to share the ultimate of feelings again. Quite boldly, she moved her fingers to his breeches and began unfastening the buttons and was glad when he took it upon himself to slide them over his hips and onto the floor, to casually step out of them.

She laced her fingers through his chest hair, then nibbled a nipple as he also removed his shirt. And when they both stood nude, assessing, admiring one another, it was then that Read scooped her up into his arms and carried her to the bed.

"*Ma chérie*, how I've missed you," he said thickly, placing feathery kisses across her face before lowering her to the bed.

"Why *did* you leave El Progresso?" she whispered, breathless, as his lips continued to move over her. Her body had never yearned more for him. He caused, oh, such sweet pain between her thighs. . . .

"This isn't the time," he mumbled. "*Ma chérie*, this moment is ours . . . only ours. We will not let anyone's name spoil it." He gently lowered her to the bed, then his mouth bore down, exploring, seducing. . . .

"And now the diamonds," he said. He took the diamond necklace and began pulling it across her body in a slow motion, causing her flesh to tremble from their icy, cold touch. She closed her eyes, sighing as he followed behind the cold diamonds' caresses with the hot quick flicks of his tongue. And when Glenda felt the diamonds moving across the rippling flesh of her stomach, and then lower, she began breathing harder and by instinct lifted her hips and welcomed the touch of the necklace being pulled across her lower flesh. Read continued playfully, pulling the necklace up and down. Glenda's breath began to come in short rasps and beads of perspiration laced her brow. She began tossing her head, moaning from the intense pleasure, and when Read finally stretched atop her, and surrounded her with his strong arms, she twined her arms around his neck and kissed him sensuously . . . demandingly . . . as he entered her from below.

Read's heartbeats were thundering against his ribs. He nibbled Glenda's ear lobe, then a breast, as he moved his body energetically in and out of hers. As his thrusts grew wilder, so did the movement of her hips against him. His mouth found hers and pulled all her passion from her, into him as he tasted her sweetness. He felt the urgency building, a frantic heat in his loins. And as his nerves were screaming for full release, it began happening. He could feel it from his brain as it moved downward . . . downward, leaving a scorched path inside him until he was consumed with mind-reeling spasms of delight, so glad that she was surrendering herself fully, responding blazingly, at the same time.

As his shudders subsided, Read moved only enough to lie by Glenda's side. He gazed rapturously at her velvet skin and touched it anew. "Yes. You are real," he chuckled. "You are no mirage."

"As you are not also, my love," she purred, feeling as though her Nena, being stroked. Then her comparisons made her rise on one elbow. "Nena! Did you see her in the courtyard?" she exclaimed excitedly.

Read drew her to him again and held her close. "Yes. I saw our orphaned cub, *ma chérie*. She is magnificent. She has grown so. And how did you get her safely here? How did you even get yourself safely here?"

She sighed laboriously as he set her free. "It wasn't all that trouble free," she said softly.

"Tell me. What problems did you encounter?"

Wide-eyed, now sitting cross-legged and with her hair streaming, loosened and flower free around her shoulders and over her breasts, she told all, from her goodbyes to her mother in the darkness of the night to this moment she was now sharing with him. She decided against telling him of Ramón's attempted rapes of her body. To do so might even give Read cause to doubt her pure, true love for him.

"A damn rat?" he blurted, rising, pulling his breeches on. "But I don't doubt it. The rats almost run the ships. There are usually more of those four-

326

legged creatures on board than there are a ship's crew."

"But my wound. It is almost healed," she said, thrusting her foot out in a fluid movement. When he bent and kissed it, she was suddenly hungry for his lips all over again. She gracefully locked her hands behind his head and guided his lips up the full length of her body, gasping when he kissed her on her most private spot. The wetness of his tongue flicking there made her moan with an almost savage ecstasy. But not feeling as though she could bear such added intensity of pleasure, she urged his lips on upward until their tongues intertwined and she had her legs coiled and locked around him.

"I only just pulled my breeches on," he laughed hoarsely.

Her fingers lowered to him and soon had his manhood released. "It isn't required to remove one's breeches," she said huskily, hardly even recognizing her own voice. Feeling the hard warmness of him, she guided him inside her and bucked and rode with him until once again they lay spent, moving from each other's embrace.

Read secured the buttons of his breeches, then lay on his back, staring at the ceiling. "And do I even have rights to your body, *ma chérie?*" he whispered harshly.

Glenda tensed. "Read . . . what do you say?"

He lifted her ring finger, seeing it void of a ring. But would Ramón Martínez even have the means to fit her with the usual showing of having exchanged vows? "I have to believe that your seeking me out has to mean that you have wed . . . no . . . other?" he said.

He watched her closely, seeing a slow flush envelop her face.

"Do you think me a whore?" she gasped. "No. I am not wed to another." Then she covered her mouth with her hands. No. She did not consider Christina a whore, and Christina was guilty of infidelity.

Read laughed heartily as he drew her back into his arms. "The damnedest . . . sweetest . . . sexiest whore, if you want to label yourself as such," he said, kissing her, then cuddling her. She was free . . . still free. . . .

"Well, mister, I am *not* a whore," she said stubbornly. "And, no, I do not belong to another man. How could you even think this? I love you. Only you. And you have to know this. Tell me you do."

He combed his fingers through her golden locks of hair, lifting it from her flesh. "Yes, *ma chérie*, I do know," he sighed.

She flung herself from his arms, glaring with her wide, sensuous lips formed into a pout. "Then why?" she said. "Why would you even think. . . ?"

"Ramón. Ramón Martinez," he blurted, watching her pale to colorless before his eyes.

"Ramón?" she gasped.

"So you do know him. . . ."

"Yes. He is a land rat," she fumed. "And you know that I know of him. I spoke vehemently of him when he shot Nena's mother. I told you then how horrible a person he was."

Read's brow furrowed. "Yes, *ma chérie*. I remember."

"Then why would you think I would exchange vows with . . . with. . . ." She couldn't finish. He had her lips sealed with his for another brief moment. Then he drew away from her, gently pushing her hair from her face.

"Darling, he said that you and he . . . well. . . ," he began.

"He and I . . . what. . . ?" she said weakly.

"That a marriage had been planned. That it was expected . . . by . . . family. . . ."

Glenda jumped from the bed, flailing her arms angrily into the air. "Damn!" she argued hotly. "That beast. That grime. That . . . that . . . menace to all women. Not only does he attempt raping me twice, but then he lies to you to cause you to leave me." She swung around, arms tightly to her side. "That is the reason you left El Progresso and refused to return on the *Sea Wolf*, isn't it? Your head wound. It wasn't your head wound. You had said it was healed."

Read went to her and clasped onto her shoulders. "Rape?" he growled. "That bastard . . . attempted. . . ?"

She swung her head back a bit, tears near. "Yes! Yes!" she exclaimed. "Twice. You see, he is not only a liar, but also an animal!"

Read moved from her, gathering his clothes and putting them on in quick, angry jerks. "Damn him," he grumbled. "I should have known. . . ."

"Yes! You should have," Glenda stormed, crossing her arms angrily.

"I'll kill him. Somehow I will manage to kill him," Read grumbled further as he pulled his boots on.

"He is in Honduras," Glenda sighed, pulling her own clothes on. "We are here. Let's just push him from our minds. We've found one another. That's all that . . ."

A light tapping on the door startled Glenda to

silence. She secured the last button of her dress and rescued the diamonds from the floor just as Christina's whispers surfaced from behind the closed door. . . .

"Glenda. It's Peter. I see him approaching by carriage," Christina said. "Your friend. He must leave. I don't think Peter would approve."

Glenda swung around, wild-eyed. "Read. . . ?" she whispered.

"Christina is right," he said, straightening his hair with a brisk combing from his fingers.

"But, Read, when. . . ?"

He drew her into his arms and kissed her briefly. "Darling, I'll be in touch. Soon," he said, tilting her chin, so their gazes could meet and hold. "Now that we're together again, I will be sure. . . ."

His words were cut short as Christina tapped, more persistently, on the door.

"Until later, my love," Glenda said, opening the door, blushing a bit when Christina looked from one to the other, also blushing.

"Come. To the back," Christina said, lifting her skirt to rush off. "I have the key to the back gate."

Nena came bouncing toward Glenda, ignoring Read's presence. Glenda stooped to pet her as she watched Read move from sight through the opened gate. Then when Christina returned, she gazed, worried, toward Glenda.

"Thank you, Christina. For telling Read where he could find me," Glenda said warmly, still feeling tremors of her body, from the shared, passionate embraces.

"Glenda, I didn't tell Read," Christina said cautiously. "I began to tell. . . " She then caught herself before finishing. Suddenly she felt it of no importance to tell Glenda of the young woman and small child that she had seen leaving the deBaulieu house. She didn't want to be the one to tell Glenda that it appeared that Read was married and also the father of a young son. But how *did* William Read find Glenda. . . ?

Glenda rose, feeling the tension flowing between her and Christina. "Yes. I remember now," she said. "Before Read's arrival, you were about to tell me something. . . ."

Peter's smooth voice broke through the tension. "Glenda, Christina. How are you farin'?" he said, laughing as Nena chose to play at his feet.

"We're fine, aren't we, Glenda?" Christina said weakly. She didn't like keeping things from Peter. Their relationship had been that of truth. She didn't want to lose this. . . .

"Yes. Fine," Glenda said, lowering her eyes. Her fingers went to her hair, knowing the disarray it had to be in. Would he . . . suspect. . . ?

"Good, good," Peter exclaimed, squatting, petting Nena. His brow furrowed. "The damnedest thing," he added. "William Read deBaulieu came by today." He eyed Glenda quizzically, seeing the rumpled dress and the . . . yes . . . the guilt in her eyes. He chuckled a bit, suddenly knowing. . . . "And would you know, strange as hell how that man rushed from my office when I told him of my *Sea Wolf*'s female stowaway and her cat. . . ."

Glenda and Christina exchanged quick glances and strolled away on into the parlor, smiling coyly at one another.

"Let's not tell him any more," Glenda giggled. "Let him guess and wonder about it. You see, I thought he'd be angry. But he's not. So why not tease him a bit?"

Christina smiled smugly. "Yes. Let's. It won't be the same as hiding something from him . . . especially if he has already guessed. And it's not something Peter and I do. Speak of other lovers," she said. She went to the liquor cabinet and poured Peter a glass of brandy and handed it to him as he entered the room, kneading his chin. . . .

Hoping to catch a glimpse of Read, Glenda was strolling along the streets of New Orleans with Nena restrained by a leash. Glenda held tightly to the leather strap, understanding Peter's cautions by offering her this gift for Nena. Even now, Glenda was made to feel uncomfortable beneath the steady stares of all whom she passed. In some eyes she could see fear, and in others, a cold contempt. This she could not understand. Couldn't the people see the gentleness of Nena's eyes and the relaxed way in which she sauntered along with her furry paws lifting so casually, one after the other, as Glenda kept Nena at her side?

But there was no doubting the confusion they were stirring as horses neighed fearfully and as people would step out into the street to avoid going near this mountain lion that had lost all her baby spots and milk teeth.

But Glenda lifted her chin haughtily into the air, not truly caring. All she cared about now was seeing Read again. It had been several days now since their passionate embraces. Glenda had wanted to ask Christina where his house might be so she could go to it, seek him out, but her pride had held her back. She had already made her sacrifices for him. Hadn't she left her strong family ties behind because of him? It was now his turn to prove his love for her.

She smiled to herself, having seen such a change in Peter since his discovery of Read's interest in her. Christina and Glenda had agreed to not speak of Read's and Glenda's feelings for one another to Peter, and the intrigue of the situation had prompted Peter to begin watching Glenda in a special way. At first it had set her nerves on edge, but then it had begun to slowly change to that of a soft glowing inside her, to know that he cared in some way for her and he wasn't yet even aware of the possibilities of her being his daughter.

"In time," she whispered. "You shall know. In time. When it is right that you know."

So often she had wondered how he would react to the news. Even though Christina had persuaded him to let Glenda remain as a houseguest for as long as she pleased, she had to know that he was thinking her stay was only temporary and that one day she would be no longer a part of his life. But a daughter? Even one who had materialized from his long ago past? How would he take her sudden interference in his life? Would he order her away . . . or would he draw her to him . . . to love . . . to hold . . . to cherish. . . ?

Tears sparkled on an eyelash as she swallowed back a lump in her throat and forced herself to become involved with her surroundings other than those people shying away from her and her sweet, gentle, orphaned cub.

With her free hand, she lifted the skirt of her light-weight, blue-flowered silk dress as she inched her way around a man at work at the sidewalk's edge. He was fully bearded, revealing only the iciness of his stare, and his clothes were crumpled and filth laden, as were the other men's who were working along with him.

Christina had warned her of these men. She had told Glenda that the open street gutters were cleared every day by prisoners from the jail. Glenda shuddered a bit, looking on past the men, seeing why they labored so hard. Between the sidewalk and road, there were deep ditches, lined with cypress wood. Water stood in these ditches at all times. Dirt, trash, and sewage were dumped into the drain in front of the houses. This filth is what the prisoners were required to clear up.

Glenda hurried on past, now looking down long, dark passages that led into sunlit courtyards where flowers grew and festoons of vines clung to walls. In open windows and doors, women were gossiping and parrots screamed from hanging cages.

Further on, men and women lined the curb, bargaining, and Negro men picked and strummed on their banjos at the doorways of saloons that smelled of stale beer. But the breeze moving from across the Mississippi River carried with it a crisp freshness that caused Glenda's direction to change. She was feeling the lure of the water, thinking maybe that was where Read would surely be. Hadn't he talked of loving the sea? Would this muddy Mississippi River have the same attraction for him?

The hustle and bustle of the river bank greeted her

as she made a turn around a bend. The wharves were lined with steamships and paddlewheelers and most in the process of being loaded and unloaded with various sizes and shapes of cargo. Some women with wide-spread skirts held out by many crinolines walked arm in arm with handsomely attired gentlemen escorts to and from the fancier paddlewheelers, and the shrill series of whistles being played on a calliope filled the air with a sense of gaiety. Though not a passenger, Glenda could still feel the thrilling excitement that seemed to be like bubbles bouncing in the air around her.

Urging Nena on with a gentle jerk to the leash, Glenda chose to stand beneath the low, gnarled limbs of a live oak, to silently observe all this that was new to her. Had it been only a short while back that she had known only the white sandy beaches where only crabs and seabirds were even occasional inhabitants, and the only sounds were those of the surf. . . ?

She held the skirt of her dress away from her, remembering also her Bay Island attire of flimsy skirts and blouses worn with no underthings to pester her. The stiff stays of the steel and whalebone corset Christina urged Glenda to wear dug continuously into her flesh, and, oh,.how she hated shoes that kept her toes from freedom!

"Glenda. . . ? *Ma chérie*. . . ?"

Read's voice drew her around with a start, causing her heart to begin pumping wildly. When she saw him, so tall, so dark in his half-buttoned cotton shirt and tight, coarse breeches, she became all a-flutter inside. She took a step forward to meet his quickening approach. "Read. . . ?" she said silkily. One moment he wasn't there, then another, only . . . footsteps . . . away. . . .

Read drew her into his arms and spoke in a subdued voice. "Darling, I've missed you so. . . ."

"Then . . . why. . . ?" she said as she pulled from him and gave him a troubled glance.

He fell to a knee beside her and stroked Nena's mane, all the while devouring Glenda with his eyes. "If you weren't at Peter Grayson's. . . ," he said huskily, furrowing his brow. "It's almost impossible for us to meet there."

"But, I have nowhere else to go," she said. "I have no means."

Read gave Nena a last brisk pat, then rose to pull Glenda away from the crowd. "I have something I want to show you," he said, noticeably beaming. "It's something I've just made my own. I only moments ago signed the papers." He laughed heartily, throwing his head back. "I can't believe it, but I am now the proud owner of my own boat!"

"You're the owner. . . ?"

He began to walk at a faster clip farther down the river bank where fewer and fewer ships and paddle-wheelers were moored. Then suddenly they arrived to a place where only one paddlewheeler stood peacefully alone, void of any passengers or crew coming or going from it. Read went and stood on the grassy bank with arms outstretched, proud. "Yes. I am the owner of this pleasure boat. Bought from Peter Grayson. I plan for it to be directed down these muddy waters of the Mississippi where it will travel free from crushing waves of the sea."

He turned abruptly on a heel, eyeing her anxiously.

"Well?" he said, gesturing with the swing of his left hand. "What do you think?"

Glenda stood with the soft whisper of wind lifting her hair and skirt of her dress and with the sun warm against her flesh. She looked at the magnificent three-decked paddlewheeler steamboat which had to be one hundred feet long, painted with lively red with white trimmings on its elaborately carved woodwork, and the promenade decks behind fancy railings appeared to lead into many rooms, of what were most surely plush grandeur. "Why, I believe it's the grandest boat I have ever seen," she sighed. "Even much more than the *Sea Wolf* with its fierce temperament and reputation."

Read laughed with delight, circling his arm around her waist. She moved fluidly next to him as he led her toward the boat's gangplank. "I believe my boat's reputation will not be on the same level as that of the *Sea Wolf*," he chuckled.

"And why not?" she asked softly.

"The *Sea Wolf* is a cargo ship, while my boat is only for passengers and even more for pleasure."

"What sorts of pleasure?"

"Whatever my passengers choose," Read chuckled. "Be it in the privacy of their staterooms, or in my traveling gambling casino, the pleasure will be found on my boat as none other that travels from Saint Louis to New Orleans."

"Saint Louis. . . ?" Glenda said, walking cautiously onto the gangplank ahead of Read as he assisted her by balancing her by her waist. Nena trudged on behind, a silent partner in the adventure.

"Saint Louis is quite a city," Read said, now

holding her hand, as she stepped onto the deck. "I'll take you there some day. And on my boat." He lifted Nena's rump over a step and then down onto the deck.

Glenda waited for Read, then silkily laced her arm through his and followed along beside him smelling the aroma of fresh paint and hearing the gentle splashes of the river's muddy waters against the side of the boat.

Steps led on upward to an uppermost deck where the breeze of the day was most prominent as its whisperings lifted Glenda's hair and caressed her face. She tilted her face to it, wetting her lips, then once more followed beside Read until all the boat's plush staterooms, salons and gambling rooms had been shown to her in their splendid grandeur of red velvet draperies and matching chairs.

"And now my own private stateroom," Read said, opening a door into a much larger, much plusher room. Its furnishings, extravagant with oak trim and cushioned red leather, and paneled walls, lustrous from a fresh waxing, showed the expense that had been used to make this newest owner proud.

Glenda's gaze fell immediately upon the bed that stood out from all the rest of this room interior. It was by no means a bunk as was found on most ships and boats, but a bed twice the size of any she had slept on. Its bedspread was of a cool-appearing white silken material and many plump, silk-covered pillows were arranged at the head of the bed.

"If you wish, I'll secure Nena's leash at the outdoor railing," Read said, brushing his lips briefly against Glenda's cheek.

Glenda glanced quickly at Read, then the bed, then smiled slowly and knowingly back at him. "Yes. Please do, Read," she said, already kicking her shoes from her feet. She stretched her toes leisurely when free, then let Read sweep her into his arms after closing the door to secure them absolute privacy. She laced her arms around his neck as his lips found hers in utter sweetness. As always, when with him, her senses reeled. Ah, such a delicious feeling of euphoria. She moaned a bit when his lips pulled free and he gazed rapturously into her eyes.

"You do like my boat, darling?" he said, reaching to tease the flesh of her face with his fingers tracing her features.

"I would have thought a ship would have been more to your choosing," Glenda said, leaning into his forever moving fingers. "The sea. I thought you would want to be a part of the sea. The sea is all things . . . colors of blues and greens always intermingling . . . so crystal clear and beautiful. But this river? Read, it is so muddy. . . ."

Read laughed gruffly. "Yes it is a mite," he said.

She pulled free of him and stood with her full lips curved in a half pout. "Then why?" she said. "Though a ship doesn't have the glamorous rooms this boat does . . . or the lure of the gambling tables . . . it does have an excitement not to be matched. . . ."

"I've recently decided that the sea is too dangerous for a man who wishes to put family first in his life," Read said, going to her, taking a hand. "If one has a wife to think about, one doesn't wish to worry about the angry waves of the sea. . . ."

With a wild heart, Glenda threw her arms about his

neck. "Read, oh, Read," she sighed. He hadn't actually said this wife was to be her but she knew it to be true. Who else. . . ? She took the initiative and covered his lips with hers, trembling, having never been so alive . . . so happy. . . .

She giggled as he lifted her into his arms and took her to the bed. When he stretched out beside her, slowly releasing her dress from her shoulders, she reached with her teeth and nibbled freely on one of his earlobes.

"Damn," he growled. "I've never seen you so fully dressed." His fingers were clumsily trying to free her breasts from their tight confines, but feeling the urgency of his needs, chose to lift her dress to explore below.

"Wouldn't it be simpler if I were to climb from the bed and get myself fully unclothed before we proceed?" Glenda whispered, feeling as though her body was encased with exquisite sensations threading their way to her heart. She hated thinking of having to take the extra time required to shed herself of her encumbrances. She wanted him now. She wanted him next to her . . . in her . . . forever and ever. If she were to climb from the bed, would some magic of the moment be lost. . . ?

"*Ma chérie*, it would be a good idea," he laughed. "And, darling, I will already be possessing you with my eyes if you will give me the pleasure of watching you."

Almost dizzy with desire, she moved slowly from the bed. As her fingers began to work with the buttons of her dress, her heart pounded with a strange excitement, enjoying this feeling of being on exhibit while

340

his eyes never left her. Something inside her drove her to teasing him as she licked her lips slowly with her tongue and let only a small portion of herself at a time become exposed to him.

She smiled wickedly as she lifted one breast free, then the other, slowly moving her fingers around each nipple until they were erect with need of his lips.

"God. . . ." Read gasped, flushing. The heat in his loins was driving him wild, but he had more of a need to watch this seductress who was his, always just for the asking. Something told him that he had better wed her quickly, or possibly some other gent might see her worth and take her away from him all that quickly!

He placed his hand over his swelling manhood, feeling it pushing against his breeches that held it inside, and slowly began to release the buttons, knowing that he couldn't wait much longer, no matter how enjoyable the show.

A noise on the outside deck drew Glenda's quick attention to the door. There was something familiar about the strange mute dragging along the ship's deck and a tap-tapping of some sort. Her hands flew to her mouth, now remembering! She knew these were sounds of Peter Grayson's approach. The dragging noise was from his lame leg and the tap-tapping was his cane aiding him along.

Before Glenda had a chance to cover her half nudity, Peter had swung the door widely open, where the full frame of his body cast shadowed images all around him.

"Peter. . . ," Glenda gasped, stepping backward, teetering a bit. What she saw in his eyes was not the

341

look exchanged between father and daughter. He was openly lusting after her. She now knew the wrong of not having disclosed her suspicions to him. But yet, there was Christina! He loved her! Why would he lust after any other woman, if he loved her? She lowered her eyes, now thinking to be wrong about the way his eyes had assessed her. She reached for her clothes and nervously began to work them on her. . . .

Read's anger flashed in hot splashes through him. Red-faced, he quickly secured the buttons of his breeches and moved from the bed. He went to Peter, glowering. "Goddamn it, man, what do you think you're doing?" he said hotly into Peter's face.

"I was checking to see if things satisfied you aboard this boat that is now yours," Peter said icily. His gaze moved from Read to Glenda. His eyes were blue steel, cold and angry. "I see you're managing. And even with my special houseguest, William?"

"Nothing about her is yours," Read grumbled, securing his shirt tail neatly inside the waist of his breeches.

"I didn't wish to imply. . . ," Peter said, leaning heavily on his cane.

"And didn't you see Nena tied outside the door?" Read shouted. "You knew Glenda was here. You knew to expect. . . ."

Fully clothed, Glenda rushed between Read and Peter. She placed a hand on each of their arms, then looked from one to the other with softness in her eyes. "Please," she murmured. "Please don't argue. . . ."

"But, Glenda. . . ," Read said, still fuming.

"Later, Read," Glenda said. "We can . . . talk . . . later." She moved toward the door, eager now to be free of both men and their grumblings about her. Yes, Peter had to have known what he would find in Read's cabin and Read had to know the embarrassment having just been brought upon her. If he truly was thinking to make her his bride, he'd best do it soon! She suddenly felt as . . . though . . . a whore. . . .

"But, Glenda. . . ," Read persisted, clasping fingers around one of her wrists.

She swung around, eyes wavering. "Read, please. I must leave. Please understand," she said. When he did set her free, she feared that she had been set free from more than just a physical embrace. Why would she feel there was something else being lost between them? Had the discovery by Peter caused excitement of the chase to have lessened for Read. . . ? Or was . . . he . . . jealous. . . ? Oh, once again, she was so confused.

She hurried to Nena and released her leash from the railing and made a fast escape from the boat. She glanced quickly toward the grand black carriage waiting for Peter, then determinedly went and spoke to Henry, the coachman.

"Please lift my Nena up to sit beside you, Henry," she stated flatly.

"Yes, 'mum," Henry answered. "Whatever you say, 'mum."

Glenda watched until Nena was secured, then very boldly climbed inside the carriage and waited in grand style for its owner. When he did arrive, she smiled coyly at the etched confusion across his face. He hadn't expected her, but she now realized why she had chosen to face him again so soon. She would use Read's possible jealousies of Peter to draw the proposal from Read much more quickly. Though Peter was surely her father, he didn't know yet. Glenda knew to not tell him now. She had other plans that included him, though wicked and wrong they were. She knew that she had the power to draw a halt to whatever might come of it at any time she would choose. She would play her cards right. She would flirt with Peter, but yet not enough for him to know it was on purpose. When it was revealed to him that she might be his daughter, she had to be sure his respect for her was still intact.

"But Christina," Glenda worried to herself. She couldn't erase Peter's look in his eyes from her mind when he had discovered her in Read's stateroom. Had it been . . . lust. . . ? Did Peter have other women besides Christina. . . ?

"What a pleasant surprise," Peter said, closing the carriage door. "I thought I may have angered you too much by breaking up your . . . tête-à-tête. . . ."

The wheels of the carriage began creaking along and Glenda clung to the seat, feeling the bumpiness of the wheels making their way across the grassy slope of the river bank. She was relieved when the gentle flatness of the street was reached.

"I wasn't angry, just a bit humiliated," she said tersely.

"It was wrong of me," Peter said, taking her hand, brushing his lips against its palm. "I shouldn't have."

She jerked her hand free. "No. You shouldn't have," she said. "A woman . . . has . . . her rights to privacy."

"So William is the man who has caused stars in your eyes, eh?" Peter said quietly.

"We've known each other since El Progresso," she confessed.

"I take it that you've been . . . uh . . . intimate many times before."

Glenda's eyes flashed in many colors of green. "Peter," she gasped. "How can you. . . ?"

His gaze lowered. His hand worked with the wolf's head of his cane, nervously fingering it. "Sorry," he said. His eyes searched her out again. "I am glad I found you this afternoon," he added.

"Hah. I bet you are," she snapped hotly.

"Glenda, I'm not speaking or thinking of the incident on the boat now," he said.

"What then?"

"It's your cat," he said, thumping his cane nervously on the carriage floor.

Glenda's eyes widened as her back stiffened. "What about my . . . Nena. . . ?"

"It's causing quite a stir. . . ."

"Stir? What do you mean by this word 'stir'?"

"Complaints are arriving at my office. Almost hourly, it seems," he said quietly. "I've been asked that your cat be removed from the premises."

Glenda's heart sank inside her. "You've . . . been what. . . ?" she gasped.

"The city of New Orleans doesn't like having to worry about a mountain lion in its midst," he said. "I guess you may have to take it to the country."

"The . . . country. . . ?"

"Yes. Christina owns a large estate out in the country. It's in joint ownership with her . . . uh . . . husband. No one can complain about the cat there."

"How far out in the country is this house?"

"It isn't just a house," Peter chuckled. "It's a mansion. One of Louisiana's finest. And how far? Not too far by carriage."

"I will feel so alone."

"I will urge Christina to accompany you there," Peter said blandly. "She can stay a few days with you. She's longed to return. This will give her a fair chance."

Glenda's plans to flirt with Peter in Read's presence had suddenly gone awry. Would she even get to see either one of them again after having to move so far away?

She grumbled aloud.

"Eh?" Peter queried with a tilted eyebrow.

"I said 'Good Lord,' " she exclaimed loudly, then scooted to the window and stared from it, pouting. She was watching the Creole houses move past her outside this window, slowly and leisurely, affording her time to enjoy their beauty anew. But when she saw a familiar figure securing reins of a horse to a hitching post before one of these houses, Glenda's heartbeats grew erratic. It was Read! His horse had managed to move at a faster clip than this carriage, and who . . . was that . . . lovely lady moving from this one Creole house toward him. . . ? She was so tiny, perfect, and lovely with her dark hair hanging in heavy waves across her shoulders. . . .

"Oh, God," Glenda groaned to herself as she saw this beautiful lady stand on tiptoe to embrace Read as he in turn embraced her. Then when a small child ran from this house and changed places with this lady in Read's arms, Glenda bit her lower lip until the salty taste of blood circled her tongue.

Not able to bear anymore, Glenda turned her head away, oh, so needing to cry. When Read had spoken of family . . . of a wife . . . he hadn't been speaking of Glenda. He apparently already had a wife. And . . . a . . . son? He had played her for a fool . . . over and over again. . . .

She licked her lips, clearing them of the lingering taste of salt, then cleared her throat nervously before she spoke. She glanced over at Peter, relieved that he hadn't witnessed the same as she, though he surely knew that Read was wed, but just hadn't wanted to reveal such a disturbing truth to her.

"Peter," she said, trying to force some strength into her words. "This mansion. Can I be assured of my privacy once there?" Then she quickly added. "You know, because of my orphaned cub?"

"Yes. Completely. . . ."

"Will you promise to tell no one I have gone there?"

"No one?"

"No one," she said flatly. "Absolutely no one. . . ."

He eyed her quizzically. "If that's what you desire," he said. "I will leave it to your discretion who you will and will not tell."

"Thank you," she murmured, turning her eyes quickly from him so he wouldn't catch the sparkle of tears in them. She felt deceived and by the only man she would ever love. But she wouldn't let this deceit grow. Read would never get the chance to feed her lies again. She would stay hidden at Christina's mansion if need be. Then in time, maybe she could forget Read, and if not, she would return home on the *Sea Wolf*. . . .

Chapter Sixteen

Christina's skirt gave a loud swish as she entered the room where Glenda stood watching from opened French doors as Nena romped free and clear around the large expanse of grounds of Christina's fashionable estate.

"She seems happy enough," Christina said, moving to Glenda's side.

"She is. And how could she not be, with your artificial lake and lagoon, the trees from Europe, Asia and even my own lovely Honduras. Ah, and the exotic flowers and vines from the Orient. She has to think she is in animal heaven." She paused thinkingly. "But she's growing much too quickly. That is what's worrying me so," she then sighed.

"The wall around our estate is tall enough," Christina said. "Rayburn's father had it erected during the Civil War to discourage slaves from running away."

"I realize the wall is sufficient. But it's Nena herself. You see, when she thinks she's playing, she inflicts hurt on my skin."

"Her sharp claws?"

Glenda swung around, sad-eyed. "Yes. And also her teeth. And when she pounces playfully at me, she practically knocks me from my feet."

"So what is the answer?" Christina said. She went and settled onto a velvet-upholstered chair. After securing her gold-framed spectacles on her nose, she lifted her embroidery and began leisurely working on it.

"I truly would hate to say goodbye to Nena," Glenda said anxiously. She went and eased herself onto a chair next to Christina, where she lifted her own embroidery onto her lap. "But maybe I should consider returning her to the jungle where she can romp and play with her own kind." She lowered her eyes. "You see, I think I've outlived my usefulness to Nena. She is no longer in need of a mother . . . but of a companion . . . possibly one to mate with."

"You really believe so, Glenda?"

"If not now, soon," Glenda sighed, beginning to draw designs on the linen with the aid of a needle and her beloved beautiful threads.

"Are you yourself lonely for your mate?" Christina murmured, lifting her eyeglasses from her nose.

"I mustn't let myself even think of William Read deBaulieu," Glenda said stubbornly, pricking her finger with the needle. Not wanting to stain her lace-trimmed pale green silk dress, she thrust her finger between her lips and sucked.

"I should have told you about the woman and child that I saw leave William Read's house," Christina said, resuming her embroidery, not wishing to make eye contact with Glenda after her clumsy confession.

"You . . . saw. . . ?" Glenda gasped, leaning a bit forward.

"Yes. The day I went in search of Mr. deBaulieu for you," Christina said. "I saw this woman and child leave his house. . . ."

"Oh, Christina, why didn't you tell me," Glenda argued. "It would have kept me from behaving so foolishly."

"I began to tell you. That's when your William Read arrived. When I saw how happy you were to see one another, I felt that it would surely work out somehow."

"Yes! He makes love to me, then returns to his little family and makes love to her," Glenda grumbled. "Yes. He had the best of two worlds. Marriage and another woman freely giving her body to him."

"I'm sorry, Glenda. . . ."

"I truly don't wish to talk about it," Glenda sighed heavily. She eyed Christina carefully. Since having arrived to this mansion in the country, there had been another change in Christina. As now, dressed in her many yards of silk and gathered bodice, low and comfortably revealing, she looked much more relaxed than she had while in El Progresso or in Peter's Creole house in New Orleans. But then all Glenda had to do to know the reasons why she was to remember how Christina had spoken so dreamily of "home" . . . a home she had known since age eighteen when she and Rayburn had wed and had moved into the Taylor mansion, to share it with the Taylor family until Rayburn's parents had moved on to a smaller estate many miles from this original plantation of all Taylors past.

"And you, Christina?" Glenda suddenly said. "Do you miss Peter. . . ?"

Christina's cheeks quivered a bit as she smiled nervously. "That is a foolish question," she replied.

"But you do seem content. . . ."

Christina paused from embroidering and looked slowly around her. "This house. It holds so many memories for me," she said. "This room? Rayburn and I . . . well . . . we were content while sharing this room." Her lashes lowered over the soft blue of her eyes. "That is, until I . . . met . . . Peter. . . ."

Glenda's gaze raked around the room, not even yet truly believing she was a part of such splendor. The day the carriage had arrived with Glenda and Christina at the Taylor plantation, Glenda had become speechless when she had seen this huge, white house with its lovely, fluted Corinthian columns and exquisitely simple detail. But it had been upon entering the house that her breath had been taken away. The interior was elegant and elaborate and the rooms were of monumental size with their ceilings rising many feet and French windows and double doors of tall and impressive beauty.

Also to marvel at was a preponderance of ornate plaster scrollwork, fine marble mantels and curving stairs of amazing symmetry with handrailings of gleaming mahogany. The drawing room was double and was furnished with crystal chandeliers, mirrors in ornate frames that reached from the floors almost to the ceiling, and expensive furniture, some being that of Mallard, Seignouret and Seibrecht.

And this room Glenda was now sharing with Christina, with its soft splashes of sun settling in through the windows, was a room filled with silk-covered sofas heaped with velvet pillows, seventeenth-century French and ancient Chinese tables and white silk damask-covered chairs. There were numerous paintings on the walls, first-edition books on shelves, and a showcase of crystal beakers.

Yes, she could understand how a man and woman . . . any man and woman . . . could be happy with such surroundings. She lifted her embroidery and busied her fingers again. "After you did meet Peter, what then, Christina?" she asked.

"It is so hard to explain," Christina replied sullenly. "You see, Rayburn had been a part of my life for so long, to not be with him was as though a part of me was missing. Like a puzzle whose one piece . . . was . . . lost. . . ."

"And when you were with Peter. . . ?"

"Not even Peter has been able to fit that last piece of puzzle into place," Christina said softly. "Though he and I share such a torrid love affair, it is the gentleness, the peaceful shared evenings in this house that I miss."

Glenda's gaze raked around her once more, seeing the wealth that had to be involved in the ownership of such possessions that belonged to the Taylors. "I don't understand. . . ," she said, then thought maybe it was best to not interfere any further, so she didn't continue with her questioning but instead continued with her embroidery work in silence.

"You don't understand what?" Christina said, placing her embroidery and spectacles on a table.

"I'm not sure if . . ."

"You can ask me anything, Glenda. What's bothering you?"

Glenda paused, then said, "Why is Rayburn in Honduras? Why is he working for a fruit company, when it's obvious he doesn't need to work. You have riches. Why isn't he here enjoying them?"

Christina rose and went to a liquor cabinet and

poured herself a glass of red wine. She turned to Glenda, holding the long-stemmed glass toward her. "Care for a glass?" she asked. Her face had paled and fine lines of wrinkles were making themselves known on her brow and around the perfect shape of her lips.

"No thank you," Glenda said. "I just can't like the wines and even the fancier drink that you call champagne. Champagne especially. It tickles my nose and then burns my throat."

Christina laughed silkily. She took a sip of the wine and began pacing the floor. "Rayburn left because of me," she said weakly. "He would have never traveled to Honduras had it not been for me. He thought the many miles being placed between me and Peter would be cause for me to forget Peter and the passions we shared. That's why. He felt the change in our lifestyle was what I needed. He had thought boredom to be the cause for me to welcome Peter's arms so eagerly. . . ."

"But it didn't work, did it?" Glenda said softly.

"It's strange, Glenda. . . ."

"What. . . ?"

"It is now that I find myself thinking of Rayburn . . . missing him," Christina said in her usual purr that Glenda had missed hearing . . . since . . . Honduras.

"You do miss him now?" Glenda said hopefully. Ah, to see Rayburn and Christina together again! It would be so nice. They had so seemed well suited for one another. Peter Grayson! He was a rogue . . . but yet . . . Glenda couldn't help but have special feelings for him. . . .

"Yes. I do. So very much," Christina said, settling back onto a chair. The wine or the speaking of Rayburn had caused color to rise in her cheeks again and a sparkle of sorts to shine in the blue of her eyes. "Rayburn, oh, wouldn't he be surprised to know that it was the return to our house that has caused my special, close feelings for him to swell inside me again? I suddenly need him. I . . . want . . . him. . . ."

Glenda leaned forward, a bit confused. "But, Peter. . . ?"

"I love him. Passionately. But I love Rayburn . . . gently. Oh, how hard a decision I now have to make."

"Then you are thinking of actively becoming Rayburn's wife again?" Glenda asked anxiously, eyes wide.

Christina sipped on her wine. "I truly don't know, Glenda," she sighed. "But there is no rush to my decision. Peter thought it best for me to stay here with you for a few days anyway. Maybe by the time I'm ready to return to New Orleans, I will have reached a decision."

"Will . . . uh . . . Rayburn take you back. . . ?"

"I'm not sure. Maybe he's even found another. . . ."

"Surely not in Honduras," Glenda giggled lightly.

Christina's eyes widened. "And why not?" she stated flatly. "It seems Peter Grayson and William Read deBaulieu had no problems."

Glenda's face paled of color. She quickly rose with a silken flutter of skirts and went to stare from the window. She had renewed feelings of shame. Not only for herself . . . but . . . for her mother. Had her mother willingly copulated with Peter Grayson? Oh! Would she ever get the courage to ask Peter about it all? She had known finding her father would be difficult. But it had become difficult in different ways than she had thought. She gave Christina a look of sadness through her lashes as Christina came and laced her arm around Glenda's waist.

"I'm sorry, sweet thing," Christina purred. "I know I shouldn't have said that. And what we both need is something to fully occupy our minds and time."

"What else could we do? We embroider. I love that."

"We can do more with our embroidery skills."

"For instance, what?"

"I've been thinking seriously of asking Peter to invest in a small shop for us on Bourbon Street."

Glenda's eyes widened. "What do you mean . . . shop?" she asked softly.

"A shop. A place to show and sell our embroidery pieces. It could busy our troubled minds. . . ."

"You're serious?"

"*Sí*," Christina teased, laughing.

"The two of us?" Glenda squealed.

"*Sí, sí!*" Christina teased further.

"How? When even?"

"There are many small shops in New Orleans. But I've yet to see one that displays beautifully embroidered dresses and skirts. We can do this. We can even have classes to show women the skills of sketching their own designs on the materials. It could be fun. Not work, Glenda. Do you agree?"

"Yes, yes," Glenda laughed. Then she scowled a bit as she moved from Christina's embrace. "But I can't," she murmured.

"And why not?"

"Because of Read. . . ."

"Read? What does he have to do with it?"

"I don't want him to know how to contact me," Glenda said icily. "I do not want him asking me to share

355

a bed with him again. I am not a whore."

Christina drew Glenda into her arms and hugged her as though her daughter. "Darling, it will be a shop for women. William Read would have no cause to enter."

"His wife? She might . . ."

"So? You would let me take care of her."

"And Read? What if he did find out?"

"You could also let me handle him," Christina said quietly.

"But if I see him, I know I couldn't stand it," Glenda said, feeling such an ache around her heart. "If he did have a chance to ask, I know I would follow him anywhere. Even to bed." She moaned deeply. "Oh, I *am* a whore. I *am*."

Christina caressed Glenda's back. "You are not," she purred. "You are sweet Glenda . . . a woman lost in love. I understand. Please try to understand yourself. And please say yes to this shop. It could be the answer for us both."

Glenda drew from Christina's arms and wiped a tear free from her eyes. "Yes. Let's see if we can do it," she said. "But you said you would ask Peter? Why not Rayburn?"

"I'm in no position to ask anything of Rayburn just yet," Christina murmured. "And I will see to it that Peter gets his money returned to him. Fully. One way or the other."

"Whatever you say, Christina. . . ."

Christina laughed softly and gathered her skirt in her arms as she began to race from the room.

Glenda followed after her. "Where are you going, Christina?" she said, watching Christina pull her silken flutter of a cape around her shoulders.

"To Peter's. I'm going to reveal our plans to him," she laughed and fled from the house, leaving Glenda to stare openly after her. Then Glenda went outside to the back terrace and began watching Nena again. Oh, feelings! Glenda had so many racing through her now and all of a different kind. . . .

The fragility of Harriett was hidden beneath a floor-length, smart, blue broadcloth cape, with its bottom flounce-stitched and trimmed with matching cording. Her hair lay in dark, sleek rivulets down her back and she was busy inching white gloves onto her long, thin fingers. "You really don't mind taking David with you this morning, do you, William Read?" she said, pleading with the soft flutter of her lashes over her dark velvet of eyes. "I do so need the time for a dress fitting. And David would much rather be with you, than left with servants."

Read had earlier slipped into a loose white cotton shirt opened at the throat and corduroy riding breeches, certainly not planning to babysit with his nephew. But when Harriett pleaded so with her eyes, ah, the world was lost to him.

He lifted the lid from a small, carved mahogany box and withdrew a fresh Cuban cigar from inside it. "If you won't take all day, Harriett," he said, smiling at David as he bounced into the room, attired in blue corduroy knee pants, white knee socks and a matching corduroy jacket, sporting a neat bow tie at the throat of his white cotton shirt. His golden hair reminded Read of Glenda, sending pangs of near anguish around his heart, but when David's brown eyes, wide and alluring, looked up

357

at Read, only David and his well-being could be considered. Oh, how David needed a father!

Read scooped David up into his arms, then threw him into the air playfully, warmed by David's giggles and shouts of glee.

"Seems you'll make it fine together," Harriett said beaming.

"Am I staying with Uncle William?" David said as Read lifted David to his shoulders, to let him position his legs around his neck. Though Read was holding tightly to David's waist, David was clinging much too tightly around Read's neck, causing him to choke a bit.

"Yes. And you be a good boy," Harriett laughed.

"Where are you going, Mother?" David persisted in a whine that he had acquired since his father's untimely death.

A look of near awkwardness showed by the sudden strain around Harriett's straight line of lips. She glanced at Read, then quickly back at David, blushing a bit. "Your mother needs some new dresses," she said softly. "So I'm going to be fitted for them. It's something little boys know nothing about, so don't bother yourself with it. Just go with Uncle William and mind his every word."

"Where are we going, Uncle William?" David shouted, squeezing harder around Read's neck.

"Nowhere if you insist on choking me so," Read laughed. He pulled his cigar from a front shirt pocket and placed it between his lips and lit it.

"Where are we going, Uncle William? Huh? Huh?" David persisted noisily, releasing his hold.

"To the riverfront, David," Read grumbled.

"What have you decided to do about the pleasure

boat, William Read?" Harriett asked, furrowing her brow. "I can't even believe you can change your mind so quickly about an investment. I've never seen you so wishy-washy. Not in my whole life. I most certainly wish I could understand you."

"It is my business, not yours, little sister," Read snapped, lifting David from his shoulders.

"Yes, maybe it is," Harriett sighed. "But it would be interesting to know what or who is guiding these decisions of yours. There for a while, you looked and acted like your old self. Then suddenly, you became withdrawn and uncommunicative all over again. God, William Read, if it's a woman causing you to be so confused with life, I hope I will one day have the opportunity to meet such a woman."

Read went to Harriett and gave her a gentle shake. "I've told you, there is no woman," he said darkly. "Do you hear me? No woman." He didn't like to be reminded of Glenda and the way she had suddenly decided to hide herself from him. He just couldn't understand it. And damn that Peter Grayson, he wouldn't even reveal to Read where Glenda could be found. No. He couldn't understand any of it. He had thought she loved him. But surely he . . . had . . . been wrong.

Harriett jerked free, eyeing him increduously. "All right," she murmured. "I hear you. You don't have to be so rough."

Read turned on a heel, combing his fingers through his hair. "Damn sorry about that," he grumbled. "Go on. Get your fitting over with. And if you return home before I do, don't fret. David and I will be at the riverfront. While there, I plan to make my final decision. . . ."

"Be sure and watch David closely," Harriett said,

fingering her gloves nervously. "I'm so afraid of water. Please watch him closely, William Read."

"You worry too much, Harriett," Read said, flicking ashes from his cigar into a crystal clear, cut glass ash tray.

"You must watch him," Harriett said, then rushed from the house and out into the waiting carriage. She directed the coachman, then settled back against the plush comforts of the cushioned seat, watching, yet not, the activities along the streets as the carriage maneuvered in and around other horse-drawn carriages and mule-drawn carts.

"I still can't believe he has asked me to his house," she sighed aloud, quickly forgetting her brother and son. She pulled the carefully folded note from inside her cape pocket and read it over again, feeling flutters of excitement tickling her insides. She read it aloud in silken whispers. . . .

Darling Harriett:

We are free now to meet in the privacy of my home. For a while at least we won't have to meet in the drab rooms of my building. You deserve to be stretched out on satin sheets. You deserve lace at your fingertips. We shall share the bubbles of champagne and let its effervescence guide us together to the sweetest joy of life . . . a joy only shared by two people as passionately in love as you and I.

Bring your love to me, darling. I am waiting. I will caress you until you are breathless. Until then
. . .

She ran her fingers over the silver-embossed wolf's head. The signature at the close of the note hadn't been needed. And now, after having read the words of passion, over and over again, she had to believe that her lover would soon be free to announce to the world their decision to wed. It had been so hard to meet in secret as they had, now as even before Jason's death.

Guilt had almost ruined their affair, though, with Harriett having felt that her husband's death had been a sure punishment for her infidelities.

"But I had only been unfaithful with one man, Jason," she whispered now. "And only because I truly loved him."

Her guilt had appeared to be that of mourning for her husband, which had worked out quite well for her. For because of this, it had been even simpler to go back to the man she loved without raising suspicions.

And now, my darling, are you truly prepared to make me wholly thine?" she said, tremoring with such thoughts of being able to share each precious night with him. The thoughts of this "other woman" being with him caused such a sick feeling to rise inside Harriett. She had thought that had been solved when the "other woman" had left the city with her husband. But when "she" had returned and had even moved in with Harriett's lover, Harriett hadn't understood at all.

"I have no choice, darling," he had said. "She has loved me for so long. What can I do? I simply cannot hurt her by rejecting her. Especially now, when she has chosen me over her husband. . . ."

"I so doubted your words," Harriett said, folding the note in fours. She brushed her lips against it softly. "But now? I am more sure of your love for me. We will have a future. We will."

The sweet breath of magnolia blossoms kissed her lips and nose as the carriage door swung open, where the coachman waited to assist Harriett. With a pounding heart and fever in her cheeks, she stepped out onto the flagstone walk and watched breathlessly as the heavy door on the Creole house swung open on solid brass hinges.

"Peter . . ." she whispered, seeing his tall erectness in the doorway, holding a hand out to her.

As though gliding, she reached her hand to him and sighed leisurely as he lifted it to his lips and kissed it, oh, so gallantly.

She eyed him quickly, seeing his loose, pale green silk shirt and snug tan breeches. She had never abhorred the cane and lame leg. They had intrigued her. They separated him from all other men she had known. The gray of his hair didn't even matter to her, nor did the difference in age. To her, he was the personification of man and would always remain ageless in her eyes.

"I'm so glad you could come, darling," Peter said, devouring her with his green cast of eyes. She made him feel younger. She made his blood warm in his veins. She was all women to him, and now that Christina was gone, somehow, damn it, he would see to it that she would stay gone. It was this young widowed thing that he was going to finally make his wife. The years. They were slipping by too quickly. Yes, he would miss Christina and her sweet charm, but she had become less than enough.

"I can't believe I'm really here," Harriett giggled, glancing around Peter, wanting to see his house . . . the house . . . she soon could also call hers. . . . "Pinch me,

Peter. Make me realize I am here with you."

He laughed gruffly as he led her by an elbow, on into the large drawing room. "My darling, I love the youthful way in which you show your pleasure," he said. "Here. Let's remove your cape."

Harriett swirled in a circle as she let him uncoil the cape from around her shoulders. She watched his eyes enlarge as he discovered what she wore beneath. "Do you like?" she laughed, straightening her back, letting the full figure of herself be revealed through the sheer, lacy chemise.

"Darling, you are full of surprises," Peter said huskily, already feeling the heat rising in his loins, feasting on her tiny waist, the velvet pink of her shapely thighs and the solid firmness of her well-rounded breasts.

"You said we would be alone," she said silkily, slinking toward him, then fitting her body into his. "I believed you. Was I right to?"

He put his full weight on his good leg and managed to use his cane to pull her even closer. "All the servants have been excused for the day," he said, breathing hotly against her lips as she stood on tiptoe to kiss him. "We are free to do anything of our choosing."

"Your bedroom. I must see your bedroom," she said, flicking her tongue across his lips. "The drawing room is lovely."

"I thought you were too busy to notice," he said, laughing. "You *are* quite a busy one."

"I can only stay a while," she said, drawing from him. She kicked her shoes off and pranced around barefoot, picking up, studying, admiring figurines, books, whatever, until he made his way toward the courtyard.

"And why a little while?" he said, reaching a hand, guiding her across the blue-gray flagstone walkway.

"It's William Read. He's in one of his nasty moods," she said, flipping her hair back from her eyes. "I think he's unhappy with the boat you sold him."

"Eh?" he said. "Why is that?"

"I think some woman problems have his brain all twisted in knots. I think he now desires to run a ship. One he can take to the sea."

Peter's face became shadowed with thoughts. He had never mentioned Glenda and Read's relationship to anyone . . . not even Harriett. When Read had persisted at asking where Glenda had disappeared to, Peter had felt like hell having to refuse him the truth . . . the answers Read wanted to hear. But a promise had been made to Glenda and, by God, some strange closeness he felt about her made Peter keep that word.

"Do you have a ship to sell to William Read, Peter?" Harriett asked, bending to pluck a purple petal from a wisteria vine. "I would most certainly like to see him with a smile on his face. It would be best for David. He is substituting his uncle for . . . a . . . a . . . father. . . ." She glanced quickly at Peter. David was the one big problem in their relationship. Peter was old enough to be David's grandfather. . . .

Seeing his smile quickly become erased by a frown, Harriett broke free from Peter and ran to the fountain, needing to draw his quick attention from her mention of David. She feared that David might cause a delay in her plans. She daringly stepped into the small pond of water, squealing with delight, oh, so a child herself when with the man she loved.

Mischievously, she bent and scooped water into her

hands and sent a spray of diamond splashes on Peter, laughing lightly when she saw an amused glint appear in the green of his eyes. He had confessed to her many times that it was her innocent youthfulness that he loved the most about her.

"You vixen," he teased. "If not for this damn leg, I would give chase to you."

"The leg shouldn't stop you," she encouraged, breathing hard from building excitement. "Come on, Peter. Come after me."

"There is not enough room for what I have in mind," he said. "And besides, the goldfish have had enough traumatic experiences as of late to last them a lifetime. I don't believe we need to add to their problems."

Harriett watched a few orange slivers dart on past her. "What do you mean, Peter?" she asked, stepping from the pond, shaking her feet free of water.

"The puma that was just recently in this courtyard. It had several feasts with my fish. There are only a few remaining."

Harriett laughed, then laced her arm through Peter's as he guided her up an outdoor staircase onto a balcony, then into the dark-shuttered shadows of a room. With the flip of a switch at the side wall, many lights sent golden rivulets around the room, touching a huge, canopied bed that displayed a cool-appearing pale blue satin sheet stretched neatly and tucked around the mattress and two satin pillows with yards of white gathered lace at all four sides. The pale blue antique satin draperies at the one lone window matched the plushness of the carpeting.

Sighing, Harriett inched on into the room. She knew that this room was meant for only one thing. For making love. The lack of other furnishings was just cause for her suspicions.

With the thrill of excitement causing her insides to tremor, Harriett turned to Peter and stretched her arms outward, inviting him to come to her. Suddenly she didn't feel like a giggling innocent. She was a woman, with womanly desires. "Love me, Peter," she said huskily, not sounding at all like her normal self. "The moments we're apart are torture. When I ache for you, I have only my remembrances of our times together to get me past those painful times."

With his free arm, Peter drew her roughly to him and devoured her lips with a reckless passion. With a fierceness, his head lowered and his teeth caught a nipple of a breast through the chemise and chewed hungrily.

Liking the feel of the heat of his breath and the pain being inflicted by his teeth through the silk of her attire, Harriett groaned sensuously and twisted her head from side to side. Her need for him was consuming her. She was beginning the slow drifting as ecstasy moved in and raged through her in fiery splashes.

"Darling, remove your damn garment," Peter grumbled, as he released his hold on her and began quickly shedding his own clothes. "We must not waste time. Our time together is gold. Let's savor every ounce."

With graceful, teasing movements, she soon stood nude before him, smiling hauntingly, seeing how his face had turned into a mask of hungry desire. When he stepped from his last garment, Harriett's eyes lowered and feasted on the part of him that was swollen with anticipated pleasure.

Then her gaze lowered, seeing the scar that revealed the need of his cane. He hadn't revealed to her the reasons behind such a wound, but truly didn't care. The scar didn't make him any less a man . . . and the man in him was what was causing her body to yearn for him so. She went to him and laced her body next to his, sighing luxuriously when she felt this hardness of his need pressing against her abdomen so warm . . . so pulsating. . . .

She touched him there and stood on tiptoe and teased him with feathery kisses on his lips . . . eyes . . . and then bent and bit one of his nipples, causing him to flinch with pain.

"God. You are a vixen," he growled then grabbed her by a wrist and wrestled her laughingly to the bed, where he then threw his cane onto the floor and began exploring the pink velvet of her flesh with quick flicks of his tongue.

She trembled beneath his caress of fingers and tongue, opening her legs to him when his head moved lower. His mouth was hot, burning her flesh with each assault. Her heart was pounding so, she could see colors of red throbbing as she pulled her eyes tightly closed, feeling the wondrous desire growing inside, so now caught up in a whirlwind of ecstasy's desire.

Peter's skin quivered from growing excitement as he continued to feast on the sweetness of her flesh. His tongue tasted and devoured and the smell of her was almost driving him over the edge. His fingers found both breasts and he cupped them as he moved his body upward and over her and entered her from below with one wild thrust.

His mouth then covered hers and he forced her lips

apart and let his tongue enter the sweetness of this cavern and probed and plunged with it, keeping a steady rhythm of his body thrusting in and out from below. His fingers entwined her hair as he forced her mouth even closer and kissed her strong and hard as the pressures were mounting inside him. He smiled to himself as she lifted her hips and more eagerly met his downward thrusts.

"My darling, you are my only love," Peter whispered, tracing her face with his fingertips.

"Peter, I have always loved you. From the moment I first saw you," Harriett sighed languidly, now almost mindless to the sweet pain he was inflicting upon her.

"I'm old . . . enough . . . to be your father," he grunted, still working his body.

Harriett placed a forefinger to his lips, sealing his words. "Shh," she whispered. "We love each other. Age means nothing. Nothing. . . ." Her eyes rolled back into her head as the pleasure burst loose inside her in magical beams of golden rays, rippling through her, mindless now of anything but pleasure . . . intense sweet, drowning pleasure. . . .

Peter felt her release and followed soon after with his own until they lay quietly spent in each other's arms.

"God. Sometimes I think you may be too much for this old body," he laughed, gasping a bit, aware of the fitfulness of his heart.

Harriett cuddled next to him, fingering the curls of his chest hair, having never been so content. "Please don't say that," she whispered. "Please. My love, I could never get enough of you."

He laughed again, turning to kiss her lightly on a breast. "Darling, that's exactly what I mean."

"I won't be as demanding of your body in the future if that's what you wish of me," Harriett visibly pouted.

He roughly jerked her to lie atop him, circling his arms around the smallness of her waist. Damn. Her body against his was causing the flames to rage in his loins again. "Darling, don't you ever say that again," he growled and reached his fingers to her head and crushed her lips to his. When she began to move her body seductively against his he couldn't help but become fully alive with added need. He thrust himself inside her and began moving with her again and in only moments they had shared another brief instant of heightened euphoria.

Again panting, Harriett slid from him and lay at his side, yet clinging. She had to possess him wholly while with him, to be sure he would hunger for her again. She would become his wife. She would. She loved him . . . she loved his money . . . and she now loved his house. She gazed around her, at this special room. She tried to close her thoughts to his having entertained other women there in the same fashion, especially his "kept woman" and instead began a soft conversation. "This room is beautiful," she sighed.

"Just for you," he said thickly, cupping a breast.

"You lie, Peter," she pouted.

"No, my love. No other woman has seen this room."

"Peter, I cannot believe that. . . ."

"It is true."

"You didn't make love to *her* here?"

"You can say her name," he grumbled. "Why can't you ever say her name? It's Christina, damn it. It's Christina. She is a person, not a thing."

Harriett's dark eyes flashed anger as she hopped from

the bed. She stood with legs apart and hands on hips. "You speak as though you are defending her," she hissed. "So her name is Christina. So what? To me she is nothing. What is she to you?"

Peter leaned up on an elbow, laughing. "Look in the mirror," he said. "See what a sight you make. You're even lovelier when angry."

Harriett glanced toward the mirror, seeing her full nude body and the stubborn stance she had taken, then giggled. "I have to try everything to keep your attentions," she giggled.

"Come here, vixen," Peter said, reaching, grabbing a wrist. "It's you I love. Believe me. You. Forever and ever."

Harriett sighed leisurely as he pulled her into his embrace and kissed her hard and long. She laced her arms around his neck and felt the familiar reeling of her head. "I love you, I love you, I love you," she whispered.

"We've become giddy and we've not yet even opened our bottle of champagne," Peter said, kissing each dimple of her cheek. "Shall I go rescue the bottle from ice?"

"Where is it?"

"In the library. I hadn't thought we'd make it so quickly to the bedroom."

"But, Peter you *should* have. . . ."

"Yes. Knowing you. I should have known better."

"I'd love a glass of bubbly," she said, scooting to sit cross-legged on the bed. She gazed at the brightness of the lights. "And, Peter," she added. "I love the electric lights you've installed. We still have the original gas lights in our Creole house."

"Gas lighting is more romantic," he said, kissing her

anew on the lips.

He rose from the bed and grabbed for his cane. Then leaning against it, he made his way toward the door.

Harriett muffled further giggles as she covered her mouth with her hands.

Peter swung around with a tilted eyebrow. "What's so damn funny?" he growled.

"You. . . ."

"Me . . . ?"

"You and that darn cane and you walking without any clothes on," she laughed further. "Are you actually going to go to the library like that?"

"There's no one here but a stray pigeon or two in the courtyard," he said matter-of-factly. "Why not?" He chuckled as he stepped out onto the balcony, enjoying the freedom, ah, the freedom. He whistled a cheerful tune as he sauntered into the library and just as he pulled the champagne bottle free from its bed of ice, he stopped, tensed, and listened. He felt a cold desperation rising inside himself as he heard footsteps drawing close. And when Christina appeared at the double doors, he dropped the bottle of champagne to the floor, shattering the bottle into a million pieces of glass. The sticky effervescence of the wine curled around Peter's toes as an iciness circled his heart. . . .

"Christina? Darling?" he gasped, teetering a bit. He watched her face pale and then her eyes slowly rake over him. He glanced down at his full figure and let out a mournful groan.

"Peter . . . what . . . ?" Christina said, reaching for a chair with which to support herself. She leaned her full weight against it, feeling suddenly ill. All feelings of love for Peter splashed through her and then left, leaving only a coldness in its place.

"Christina, what can I say?" Peter said, unconsciously covering the part of him that had only moments ago received and had given pleasure. . . .

"Who . . . ?" Christina hissed, straightening her back, getting composure of herself. . . .

A rush of bare feet into the room drew Christina around. Again she felt faint. The young woman standing so close to her . . . completely nude . . . and smelling of sex-play . . . was none other than William Read deBaulieu's *wife*. . . ! "You. . . ," Christina gasped, feeling a complete weakness of her knees.

Harriett recoiled, trying to cover herself, feeling her face burning with shock and shame. "Oh, God," she moaned. Her eyes moved desperately to Peter, seeing the complete humiliation in his eyes. "I heard . . . the crash . . . of the bottle," she said weakly. "I only came to . . ."

"That's all right, Harriett," Peter said clumsily. "But, please return to the . . . uh . . . bedroom. . . ."

Harriett felt tears surfacing as she glanced once more toward Christina, seeing how beautiful she was and understanding now how Peter had neglected breaking ties with her. She hung her head, weeping strongly now, and rushed to the bedroom, now wishing she had dressed appropriately so she could present herself in the proper fashion to Christina if a scene was going to be had. No matter what. If a fight for Peter was needed, a fight there would be! But how could one show dignity . . . in only . . . a chemise?

"Peter, I do not understand," Christina said. She was glad that Peter had worked himself to stand behind a high-backed chair. Seeing his nudity had so unnerved

372

her. "How long has this been going on . . . ?"

"Christina, now is not the time to discuss this. . . ."

She clenched her fists to her side. "Now *is* the time to discuss this," she shouted. "For you see, there will be no next time. I'm moving back to Rayburn's house . . . to be Rayburn's . . . wife. . . ."

"Because of what you've seen today. . . ?"

"Partly. . . ."

"Christina . . ."

"It's obvious you do not love me enough to remain faithful," she said flatly. "And though I'll always love *you*, I've discovered I still feel very deeply for Rayburn."

"And you came here today to tell me this? That you had decided to go back to Rayburn?"

Christina swung the fullness of her cape around and put her back to him. She couldn't help but ache for his arms . . . his lips . . . but had to conquer these feelings. It was over. "No," she murmured. "I did not."

"Then . . . why . . . ?"

Christina swung back around, strong-jawed. "To tell you of your daughter . . ." she blurted, then felt a deep remorse when she saw the shock distort his face so.

He forgot his nudity and moved to her and jerked her wrist to his chest angrily and held it there. "What's that you say?" he grumbled. "What about a . . . daughter . . . ? I have no daughter. . . ."

"The Bay Island woman you were in love with those many years ago? The wound you received because of her? She bore you a child. A white child. A daughter. There was only one white child born to a mestizo at that time. The child is yours. There is no doubt in my mind."

"How? There's no way. . . ."

"How? And, yes, there was a way I found out. This daughter? She is Glenda. Glenda Galvez. . . ."

"What. . . ?"

"She is you, all over again. You know it. You even wondered about the resemblance. The green of her eyes . . . the color of the hair that yours once was . . . her stately tallness . . . and her reckless, daring nature . . ."

Peter felt a wild thumping of his heart. He released her wrist and slumped down onto the chair. His shoulders sagged heavily. "All these years . . ."

"Yes. You've had a daughter. . . ."

"A daughter. My daughter. Glenda. . . ," he mumbled, as though testing the words.

"I will gather my things together and leave," Christina whispered. She could feel the crack widening in her heart. "I will leave you to your new lover, who is so even near the same age as your . . . own . . . daughter. . . ," she quickly added. She knew that she was leaving him at a vulnerable time. She hadn't meant to reveal such a truth, but the words had just slipped out. She could only think it was because she had wanted to inflict hurt upon him as he had just done to her. Her true reason for arriving this day was to not be spoken of. The shop . . . it would have to be forgotten. At least until Rayburn could assist her and Glenda in the adventure . . . even if he would.

Oh, God, how it hurt. How the knowing hurt. How could Peter have had another woman . . . and most likely . . . all along. . . ? She rushed from the room, weeping. . . .

Mindless of Christina and her fluttering around the house, gathering her belongings distraughtly, Peter rushed to where Harriett waited, pacing, for him. Closing the door behind him, he quickly drew her into his arms and comforted her. Oh, she was just like a child. His wounded, sweet child. "I'm sorry, darling," he murmured. "So very, very sorry. I wouldn't have had this happen in a million years. Forgive me?"

With a few labored sobs lingering, she gazed rapturously through her lashes upward at him. "I'd forgive you anything, my love," she said silkily. "My love, only hold me. Tell me I am yours."

With a fierce pounding of his heart, he held her to him, feeling the firmness of her breasts pressing into his chest. He wanted to kiss them each and lift her to the bed again, but he was too troubled to think of such pleasures. "You are mine, my darling," he whispered. "There will never be anyone else. What can I say . . . or do . . . to prove it?"

Quite boldly she blurted, "Make me truly thine, Peter. Make me legally thine. . . ."

He withdrew, eyeing her wearily. She didn't know he had a daughter . . . yes . . . a daughter almost her same age. Would she even understand? Did he even. . . ? Was . . . it . . . true. . . ? He had to go to Glenda . . . question her. But first he had to make up for Harriett's displeasure of only moments ago. He couldn't risk losing her. He had lost Christina. Forever. . . .

"Yes. We will wed," he said thickly.

Harriett swallowed hard. She felt a triumphant warmth seize her brain. "You *will* marry me, Peter?" she sighed. "You truly no longer love . . . *her*. . . ?"

He chuckled. "No. I no longer love *her*. . . ."

"When, then. . . ?"

"Soon. And if you wish, move on in with your things.

I'm getting too ancient to waste even one more day. . . ."

Her eyes wavered. "And . . . my son David. . . ?"

His face shadowed. He trembled a bit. He would be suddenly a father of a daughter . . . and . . . a son . . . after all the years of never having fathered anyone. . . ?

"Yes, and also David. . . ," he said quietly.

"Oh, Peter," she squealed. "How I do love you."

"Then love me enough to understand that I must leave you. Now. I have . . . uh . . . business to attend to. . . ."

Her lips curved into a pout. "It's nothing to do with her," she said. "Please tell me it isn't."

He began scooping his clothes up from the floor. "No. It's nothing to do with Christina," he grumbled.

"Then . . . what. . . ?"

"You will have to learn to trust me if you're to be my wife," he said flatly. "And now is a good time to begin such a trust."

"Yes, darling," she purred.

He looked at her, loving her, but also felt a small part of his heart leave him when he heard Christina walk past on the outside balcony. . . .

Chapter Seventeen

Releasing his grip from David's tiny hand, Read watched David begin running up and down the lowest deck of Read's paddlewheeler boat. Read checked the height of the railing, comparing it to David's, and felt safe enough to wander on away, to brood in silence. But Harriett's warnings of David's safety caused him to turn and cup a hand to his mouth. "David, you be careful and only explore where there is a side railing. Do you hear your Uncle William?" he shouted, watching how the steady breeze lifted David's hair and blew it about, looking as though corn silk, tangling.

David, teasingly, good-naturedly, mocked Read and lifted a hand to cup it to his miniature mouth. "Yes, sir, Uncle William," he shouted, then whirled around and was off. His clattering footsteps echoed up and down stairs, across one deck, then another, while Read went on to his private stateroom, where a bottle of claret waited, half-emptied. He poured himself a glassful and watched the sparkling reds winking back at him. He lifted the long-stemmed glass into the air, mimicking a toast. "And here's to you, Glenda Galvez, wherever you've chosen to hide," he said thickly, then tipped the glass to his lips and emptied it, coughing a bit as he moved the empty glass before his eyes to study the clear shine of the crystal. In a sudden burst of anger, he threw it against the far wall and laughed throatily, as its shattered fragments sprayed in every direction.

He couldn't help let the anger he felt almost suffocate him. Glenda's disappearance just didn't make any sense. First she was there, professing her love for him, and then she was gone, as quickly as she had materialized.

"I've got to get away," he grumbled. He kicked at a chair. "This paddlewheeler is not the answer." He had mainly invested in this gentler way of travel for Glenda's sake. He had thought to travel with her on many excursions down the Mississippi. It would have enabled them to never have to be separated again.

But the sea. Ah! The sea. Now that his ventures were to be made alone, the sea was luring him, like the temptress it was, all over again. If he couldn't have Glenda, he would accept the sea's bidding.

His face brightened. "That's my answer. I've been searching my mind for an answer, and by God, now I have found it," he said. "I shall deal with Peter Grayson again. I will make a trade. A ship it is for me. Not a tame river boat. I need excitement in my life to erase Glenda from my brain once and for all."

Turning on a heel, he rushed to the outer deck. He went to the rail and placed his back to it, looking down one length of the boat and then the other. "David! Come on," he shouted, squinting into the sun's rays as his gaze scanned the two upper decks. He tensed, lifting an ear to the wind, listening for the hastening of tiny footsteps, but hearing nothing.

"David, come on now. Don't play games with Uncle William," he shouted, letting annoyance creep into his words. "David? Damn it. I know you're playing hide-and-seek. But your Uncle William doesn't want to. I'm sick and tired of any games that have to do with hiding."

He watched and listened again, growing angry. He began moving along the deck, opening and shutting doors, checking behind deck chairs, but finding nothing. "Uncle William will take you to see some bigger boats, David, if you'll just come out of hiding."

He looked all around him again and listened even more closely, suddenly no longer angry . . . but . . . afraid. He felt something twisting his gut as he began running, up one flight of stairs, opening and shutting all the doors, then to the second deck, and then the third.

When every inch of the boat had been searched Read stood wild-eyed, panting, now knowing that David was nowhere on the boat. It was not a game. David . . . was gone. He swallowed hard as he wiped his brow clean of perspiration with the back of a hand, not able to control the nervous, frightened poundings of his heart.

He looked toward the wide expanse of the river, once more remembering Harriett's fear . . . of . . . the water. "Good Lord, no," he groaned, as he let his feet carry him to the boat's railing. Cautiously, he peered over the side into the gentle, lapping water of the muddy Mississippi River, looking for signs of his nephew who had been placed trustingly in his care.

"Nothing," he said, running his fingers through his

hair. He walked the full length of the boat, staring into the water, but still finding no signs of David.

"What am I to do?" he worried aloud. He felt deathly ill to his stomach, realizing that David's body might be beneath the muddy surface of the water. Like a madman, he tore his clothes from his body, down to his undergarments and dove headfirst over the railing. He took long, brisk strokes away from the boat, then began diving underwater, searching all around, seeing much discarded debris at the river bottom, but still no signs of David.

Gasping for air, Read popped his head to the surface, suddenly feeling the current grabbing at his chest and legs. He looked toward the boat and realized just how far away from it he had managed to swim and began struggling to keep from being washed away beneath the steady rushing of water. There had been no current closer to the boat. But if David had fallen overboard, could his body have moved by itself to where the current would tug and pull at him. . . ?

Letting tears roll from his eyes, Read finally won his battle with the water's force and began swimming back to the boat, never having felt so empty and forlorn. He swam around to where he could pull himself up on the gangplank and just as he began to reach upward, he saw the soft spray of gold hair . . . in . . . the mud . . . at . . . the river's . . . edge. . . .

"Oh, God, no," he cried, choking on emotions that were tearing him apart inside. From where David lay, face down, Read could tell that David had probably fallen from the gangplank face first, into only two feet of water.

"He can't be dead. Surely not in only that small

amount of water," he said, gasping for air as the tears fell in torrents and the strong sobs tore at his heart.

He hurriedly waded through ankle-deep mud and fell down next to David and turned him over and saw the peacefulness of his nephew's tiny-featured face. Feeling the grief working through him in painful stabs, he placed his fingers at the veins of David's throat. When there was no inkling of a throb, Read clutched David to his chest and let out a loud bellow of alarmed remorse.

He rocked David back and forth in his arms, placing his cheek next to his. Then his gaze settled on a dead fish that had been washed up into the mud, and had to conclude that David had seen this fish and had been reaching for it . . . to . . . rescue it. . . .

"Oh, David, sweet David," Read crooned. Then he forced himself to be brave and lifted David's limp figure into his arms and struggled up the slick slope of the river's edge, then took David to his carriage and gently placed him inside on the soft cushion of seat. Heavy-footed and head hung sadly, he went and returned to his clothes, then spat angrily over the boat's railing, cursing the river beneath his breath and went to the carriage and climbed aboard. He took the horse's reins and urged the horse gently onward, wishing it were he lying dead inside the carriage. Would this be a grief one could ever conquer?

"Oh, God, how do I even tell Harriett?" he worried aloud. "First she loses Jason and now . . . her . . . son? How will she be able to bear it?"

He wiped his eyes free of tears. "How will I be able to bear it. I am responsible. His death is my fault. I became careless. . . ."

He worked his way home, dreading having to face Harriett, but didn't expect her to be home just quite yet. Her fittings for dresses had in the past taken many hours. These hours this day would be a reprieve of sorts for Read . . . let him find the courage to face what had happened before having to face his sister with the sad, awkward truth. But as he made a turn in the road, his insides tremored, seeing Harriett's personal carriage standing at the edge of the public way outside the de Baulieu Creole house.

"I can't believe she's home so soon," Read murmured to himself. Then an eyebrow lifted when he pulled his own carriage next to Harriett's and saw the waiting coachman.

"She must have forgotten something," Read thought to himself. "Or why else the waiting coachman?" But no matter, her presence in the Creole house meant that Read had to confront Harriett much sooner than he had thought to have to do.

With weakened knees, Read climbed from his parked carriage, nodding a greeting to Harriett's coachman, then went and slowly opened his own carriage door and peered inward at the lifeless body. He choked on sobs, seeing how peacefully asleep David appeared to be. It was as though Read should be standing in David's bedroom at night, watching him, after prayers and goodnight kisses had been shared. But this wasn't David's bedroom . . . and David . . . was not . . . asleep. . . .

Read hung his face in his hands. He didn't know what do to. He just couldn't burst into the house with David in his arms to so suddenly thrust this horrible truth upon Harriett. No. He would leave David in the carriage for just a while longer and go ready Harriett before she would . . . see . . . him dead.

He closed the carriage door and cleared his throat nervously as he tried to straighten his hair to look more presentable. But he knew that nothing could erase the gloom etched onto his face. Surely Harriett would quickly understand that something terrible had happened before even words had to be spoken about it. Maybe it would even be easier that way.

Hurrying his steps, he went on into the house, thinking to meet Harriett face to face at any moment, but instead, found a house of silence. "Where is she?" he worried, then moved on up the staircase and moved through the sun-soaked parlor, through French doors, and on into Harriett's bedroom.

What Read saw drew a quiet gasp from between his lips. His gaze moved from one opened trunk on the bed, to another. Both were partially filled with neatly folded clothes, some of which were Harriett's and some of which were David's.

Harriett's back was to Read, not having heard him enter. She was busy emptying hangers of her dresses and gowns and tossing them anxiously . . . blindly . . . over her shoulder onto the bed next to the trunks. She was afraid to not hurry. What if Peter changed his mind? What if he stopped to calculate the true differences in their ages? What if he didn't wish to have a small child underfoot after all? He had never fathered a child. He had never wed before. Would he now? Truly? Why was she the exception? He surely had had many beautiful mistresses. Christina! Ah, how beautiful she was.

"What the hell are you doing?" Read said abruptly

from behind her, drawing her around with a start.

"William Read. . . ," she gasped. "You're home . . . already. . . ?" She saw his paleness and a look of strange confusion in his eyes. She had known to expect him to be shocked by her sudden decision to leave, since he hadn't even suspicioned her secret rendezvous with Peter. But for him to look so distraught without her having yet even told him the reason behind her packing both her and David's clothes just didn't make any sense. Had he known all along? Had he seen her with Peter. . . ?

Read walked hazily across the room, to the bed, and began picking dresses and gowns up, studying them, and then Harriett. "Where are you planning to go, Harriett? Why . . . are . . . you packing?"

He lifted a pair of David's corduroy breeches into his hands, remembering when he had last seen David wear this particular pair and how alive and electric he had been when he had run laughing around the courtyard. This particular day Read was now remembering, he had made a net for David, with which to catch butterflies. When David had managed to catch one lone monarch, with its lacy wings of black and orange, David's squeal of triumph had reverberated from wall to wall of the house's interior. . . .

Swallowing back a fast-growing lump in his throat, Read gently placed the breeches back on the bed, knowing there was no need, whatsoever, to pack them for any venture Harriett had so suddenly chosen to take.

He looked Harriett's way, quite aware that she had avoided his question. He went to her and clasped his hands firmly to her shoulders. "Harriett, what . . . are

. . . you doing?" he said thickly. Her packing had added to the stress of the moment. Why. . . ? Where. . . ?"

"I don't know how to tell . . . you. . . ," she stammered, lowering her eyes. She knew that he wouldn't approve. He would probably even try to force her to stay. He wouldn't want a sister whose reputation would be tarnished the moment she took one step across Peter Grayson's threshold, to become a willing part of his daily life, though a wedding date would soon be made to make it all quite legal and thus . . . respectable. . . .

"Tell me what, damn it," Read growled angrily, but realizing what he had to tell her would be even more difficult.

"David and I . . .," Harriett said softly, fluttering her lashes nervously. "We . . ."

He cut her words off by groaning a bit. He hung his head and dropped his hands to his side. "God, oh, God," he moaned. "David. . . ."

Harriett's heartbeat faltered. She placed a trembling hand on Read's arm. "David? What . . . about . . . David?" she whispered. Her head jerked as she looked on past Read. "William Read, where . . . is . . . David. . . ?" she murmured.

Read moved away from her and went to stare out the window, downward, seeing the stillness of the carriage. "David? He's . . . in the carriage. . . ," he replied in a near whisper.

Harriett laughed awkwardly, touching her brow with the daintiness of her fingertips. "Oh, you had me frightened for a moment," she said, going to resume packing. "So David is waiting for you take him someplace else with you? Well, William Read, you can go tell David to get into my personal carriage. We're going some place very . . . very . . . special. . . ."

Read swung around on a heel, ashen. "Harriett, I can't. . . ," he said, but she interrupted him. . . .

"And, William Read, yes, David and I *are* going some place special," she said, smiling, showing a renewed vigor, a confidence she hadn't shown moments earlier. She knew she had to tell her brother and felt it best to rush on through the chore. He could only shout for a little while and then he would have to accept the truth as it was.

"Ma chérie," Read encouraged. "You must listen. . . ."

She slammed the lid of a trunk down with a bang and secured its lock. "No, William Read," she said stubbornly. "It is you who must listen to what *I* have to say." She swung around, radiant, fluttering the skirt of her dress voluptuously. "I'm soon to be wed," she said proudly.

"Wed. . . ?" Read said, teetering a bit. Had his sister suddenly gone daft? There had been no mention of a man except for the man she had left the ball with that one night. No. It couldn't be him.

Harriett rushed to Read and took his hands in hers, searching his face with the dark velvet of her eyes. "William Read, this is something I want so badly," she said, pleading thick in her words.

"Harriett. . . ."

She silenced his words with the butterfly touch of her forefinger on his lips. "Shh, no words. Just listen. Then you can shout your anger to the rooftop, but now, please hear me out." She squeezed both his hands now, and spoke dreamily of her happiness . . . of whom it was she was to marry . . . of whom it was she was going to share a house with until the marriage. . . .

Read felt the anger rising in hot, spasmodic colors of red flashing before his eyes. He pulled his hands free and without thinking slapped Harriett on the soft pink of her cheek. "You bitch," he shouted. "You low-moraled bitch. I now realize the gossip of you and Jason before your marriage was not gossip at all but truth. You slept wantonly with him and now you are doing the same with another man . . . and not only a man . . . a man whose morals have also been questioned . . . a man old enough to be your father. How long has it been going on, Harriett? Huh? How long? All those dress fittings? You've been with him . . . giving your body freely . . . to . . . him!"

Harriett's tears tasted of salt on her lips. Her fingers tried to soothe the stinging of her cheek. She looked wild-eyed at Read, having never been struck by him before . . . having never been struck by anyone before. Not even her mother . . . or . . . father. . . .

"William Read, you're not yourself," she sobbed. "What I'm doing is my affair. There was no cause for such anger on your part. I'm in love with Peter and he is in love with me. There's nothing dirty or shameful about it and I shan't let you, my brother, interfere in my life."

He stared from the window at the carriage and closed his eyes and gritted his teeth. Then he swung around and glowered even more toward Harriett. "You say you don't want me to interfere in your life?" he said darkly. "All these weeks I've babysitted David?

I was even interfering then? It was on these occasions that you were free to go lift your skirts to Peter, am I not right?"

Harriett's face flushed crimson. She swung her skirt around and threw more clothes into the one open trunk. "I refuse to listen to any more of your insults," she said haughtily. "William Read, I will never ask another thing of you. Never. . . ."

"Harriett. . . ," Read said softly. "Harriett, I've been wrong to lose my tongue. This wasn't . . . the . . . time. . . ."

"Most certainly not," she said stubbornly. She lifted David's corduroy breeches and began to place them inside the trunk.

"You don't need to pack David's things," Read said, moving to her side, taking the breeches, touching the softness to his face.

"And why not?" she snapped, grabbing them from him.

"Because David won't be going to Peter Grayson's house with you. . . ."

Harriett groaned wearily. "Oh, William Read, will you please stop this nonsense," she said. She flipped the skirt of her dress angrily around and hurried toward the French doors.

Read's heart began to thunder inside him. He went to her and grabbed a wrist. "Where . . . are you going . . . ?" he said thickly.

She swung around with eyes snapping wildly. "To get my son," she said. "I am through playing word games with you."

"I have to tell you. . . ."

She yanked herself free and the echo of her footsteps on the staircase caused Read to gain full composure and dashed after her. But the sudden haunting reverberations of her screams stopped him at the bottom stair, where he froze and listened . . . and . . . listened. . . .

Christina entered her house in an angered flurry and searched and found Glenda standing peacefully next to the opened French doors of the library, sketching on a sheet of canvas that was resting on an easel. Stopping to silently study Glenda and the way her hair changed colors of goldens as the sun played on its waves, Christina was remembering whom she still thought to be Read's wife, stepping nude into Peter's library, where he had so leisurely been moving about, unconcerned that even he had been without a stitch of clothing.

The shock of discovery was now dissipating for Christina, realizing that her moments with Peter had most surely been numbered from the start. Peter was a man of the world and needed the taste of fresh flesh more often . . . than not.

Well, by his generous attentions to her, she at least had found that she was desirable to other men and at the same time had enjoyed the awakening of passion and feelings that had been gone for, oh, so long in her life. Yes, it had been time well spent.

But . . . Rayburn. . . ? Had she hurt him too deeply? And . . . Glenda. . . ? Should she be told about Read's wife? But, no. Let Read discover the infidelity and rid himself of her, then search Glenda out himself with the truth. . . .

Then she suddenly remembered the truth that had been revealed to Peter . . . that . . . Glenda was surely . . . his daughter.

Sensing eyes upon her, Glenda whirled around and smiled when she found Christina there. But her smile quickly faded when she saw the bright flush to Christina's face. And the look in her eyes! It was not one of peacefulness. She placed her pencil on the easel's tray and moved fluidly to Christina, taking her hands, squeezing them affectionately. "What's wrong? What's happened? Did Peter refuse you the money for the shop? You look so completely distraught," she said anxiously. "It truly doesn't matter, you know. It was only a dream . . . and I've learned that so many dreams do not come true."

"Dreams?" Christina murmured, gently easing her hands free, to lift one to Glenda's cheek. She smoothed her fingers across Glenda's face, as though memorizing it. "Sweet one," she added. "Each day one is granted breath on this earth is reason to believe dreams come true. Though life is full of ups and downs, anguish, and bitter surprises, one is blessed to have the honor of being a part of these mysterious feelings. You just continue to dream, Glenda. That is what makes for an almost magical sort of existence."

"Then what's the matter?" Glenda persisted, giving Christina a long, troubled look. "You do not appear to have experienced anything magical. What did Peter say? What did he even do. . . ?"

Christina gave a languid sigh as she reached to release the cape from her shoulders. When she was set free of it, she draped it across the back of a chair, and began nervously pacing the floor. She wrung her hands, shooting Glenda occasional glances through the thickness of her lashes. "I'm sure Peter will be arriving here," she said in a subdued voice. "And soon."

Glenda followed alongside Christina, the silken flutter of skirts filling the air. "Why is Peter coming here?" Glenda questioned. "He's never come since I've been here. You said it was because of Rayburn. . . ."

"Yes. This is not only my house, but also Rayburn's. And because of my relationship with Peter, I asked Peter to please not come. It would have been the same as doubling my infidelities with my husband."

"Then, I ask again, why?" Glenda persisted, swinging her arms into the air with compounded frustration.

Christina stopped abruptly and rescued the flailing arms and held Glenda's hands securely in hers. "Sweet thing, it seems my mission to Peter's house changed," she said in her silken purr. "Instead of discussing the possibilities of a shop for us, I, we instead, discussed other matters of the . . . uh . . . moment."

"What sort of matters?"

"I revealed to him our suspicions of you possibly . . . no, not possibly . . . I told him you were his daughter. . . ."

Glenda's heartbeat raced. She felt goosepimples rising on her flesh, causing her to even shudder, as though suddenly having felt a cold hand pressed to her brow. As long as Peter wasn't aware of the knowledge of her heritage, it had been easier to continue fantasizing about it. But now? It had to be met head on. "What did he say. . . ? Do. . . ?" she said in a near whisper.

"He didn't deny that you could be his. . . ."

Glenda moved from Christina and to a window, seeing the shadows lengthening beneath the monstrous, gnarled live oak trees. "So he had noticed our resemblance. . . ?" she said softly. "He is my true father, isn't he, Christina. . . ?"

The slamming of the front door and the sound of a cane and the dragging of a leg moved on into the library along with Peter. Christina swung around and held her head high. She had dreaded this next meeting, but somehow, being in Rayburn's house, feeling his presence with everything she saw and touched, she now felt only a strange remorsefulness for what she and Peter had shared, and an anxiety for when she would once again see Rayburn.

Yes! She had conquered her feelings and she was even a stronger person for having experienced this loss of a man that in truth was more gainful for her than . . . a . . . loss. . . .

She spoke in a cool and measured voice to him. "I shall leave you two alone," she said, glancing a warning to Glenda, then lifted the skirt of her dress and moved in a graceful glide from the room.

Glenda stood as though in a trance, seeing how his green eyes studied her so intensely. She studied him back. It was as though they were seeing one another for the first time. And weren't they? They were now . . . father . . . and daughter . . . having finally met. . . .

Ah, wasn't he yet so handsome, even with his thick head of gray hair? She could envision it as it must have been in his youth . . . the color of precious maize. His eyes, they were the color of emeralds . . . the color of the deepest waters of the Caribbean. His tall erectness hadn't been made any less by the steady use of the cane. Glenda swallowed hard . . . remembering once again . . . why . . . the cane.

He slowly approached her, in his impeccable attire of white silk shirt and snug black breeches. He wasn't as broad-shouldered as Read nor was he as muscular, but once again, Glenda was reminded of his age. "Hello, Peter. . . ," she murmured softly, busying her fingers at the gathers of her dress.

"Glenda, Christina said . . ."

"Yes," she said, lowering her eyes. "I know. . . ."

"It *is* possible? You were born of my love shared with your mother those many years ago. . . ?" he said thickly, reaching to touch her, then thought better of the gesture when her chin lifted quickly and he saw a silent rage in the depths of her green eyes.

"Don't speak of my mother that way," she hissed. "She did not freely share her body with you. She did not. You . . . raped . . . her. She said you raped her. . . ."

Peter's eyes wavered. "Then it cannot be the same woman," he sighed. "The beautiful, velvet-fleshed mestizo I made love to shared many embraces with me in the private surroundings of my ship's cabin while my ship was being repaired."

It was as though a knife had been plummeted into her heart. Either her mother had skillfully lied all those years or he knew the art quite well. She felt her heartbeats race when she inched her way toward him, studying him even closer. Looking into his eyes, was the same as looking into her own. There couldn't have been another ship's captain with such eyes . . . such hair. There couldn't have been two wrecked ships on Bay Island . . . there couldn't have been two men wounded in the same way that Peter had been, without a flurry of gossip in the small village, keeping the tale alive . . . from year . . . to year. . . .

"What was this mestizo's name?" she whispered, trembling.

"I never asked her last name. . . ."

Glenda's anger rose. "You know that I wish to hear the first name," she hissed. "The first name. I must know!"

"Glenda, I'm not sure. . . ."

"Tell me. . . ," Glenda shouted. She couldn't believe he would say. . . .

"Rosa," he said softly. "She was my sweet rose for such a short time. . . ."

Glenda swung around to place her back to him with tears now rolling from her eyes. She doubled her fists to her side and bit her lower lip, remembering Rosa and José's closeness . . . the intensity in which they had always made love. Had Rose shared the same with . . . a . . . stranger. . . ?

Oh, she hated the knowing! It shattered the image of her mother that she had always carried around in her heart, as though inside a precious locket, sealed away, from anyone but herself.

"Your mother's name, Glenda?" Peter said, turning her gently to face him, aching, seeing how the truth so hurt her.

"My mother's name . . . is . . . Rosa," she said, choking on tears. She had found a father . . . but in a sense . . . lost a mother. . . .

"Then . . . you are. . . ."

"Yes. I guess . . . I . . . am. . . ."

Peter felt a rush of warmth flow through him . . . a different sort of pleasure than he had ever experienced before. It was a beautiful feeling to know one's self to be a . . . father. . . . "May I hold you in my arms?" he murmured.

"Yes," she whispered. She let his free hand draw her gently to him. She placed her cheek on his shoulder, smelling him, knowing she would always remember this moment. "Peter, it is so much easier to let myself love you knowing that you did not rape my mother. I can relax around you now, knowing that I was conceived in love."

"And it was love, Glenda," he said, stroking her hair.

"But my mother," she sobbed. "How. . . ?"

"Don't be too harsh on her. She was young. She was reckless, like you, my . . . daughter. She was daring . . . and oh, had so much love for one woman. . . ."

"Yes. She's always given so much to my . . . uh . . . other father. I had thought they had always been in love."

"I had always hoped that after me, Rosa would remain faithful to her husband," he said. "In a sense, it would also be . . . to . . . me. . . ."

Glenda tensed a bit, remembering her old feelings. . . .

Peter continued speaking. "For you see, Glenda, I haven't been as faithful," he said quietly. "I've tried to drown my thoughts of Rosa with the oceans of other women's flesh. . . ."

"Christina. . . ?"

He laughed a bit nervously. "Yes, Christina," he

said. "But Christina . . . well . . . something has happened. . . ."

Christina moved back into the room in a silken flutter of skirts. "Yes, something has happened, Glenda," she said in a flat tone of voice. "Go on, Peter. What were you saying?"

Glenda tensed, seeing a cold shrewdness in the way Christina's jaw was set. She then glanced back at Peter, seeing a quiet apology etched across his face.

"I take it you didn't tell her," Peter said, leaning heavily against his cane.

"No. I felt other things were of more importance," Christina said icily. She moved to a chair and eased into it, glancing from Glenda, then to Peter.

"Well, then, I'll take my leave and let you two have a talk," Peter said weakly. He eyed Glenda intensely. "Glenda, would you consider living with me, since I am . . . your . . ."

Christina pushed herself angrily from the chair and flew to Glenda's side to drape her arm around Glenda's waist possessively. "She will not," she said angrily "I'm sure she wouldn't want to be a part of your . . . of your . . . way of life."

Peter was reminded of Harriett and his invitation to her to move in with him . . . and then his proposal of marriage to her. No. It would surely not work if Glenda was to accept his invitation. Glenda and Harriett under the same roof? It could be an awkward situation.

Then something grabbed at his heart. Should he even make a choice? Now that he had knowledge of a daughter, didn't she deserve first choice? But, God, he couldn't do it. He loved Harriett. Surely he couldn't live without her. . . .

"Christina, I plan to make things up to you," he finally blurted. "I don't like the bitterness I hear in the way you speak. I hate thinking that it was I who caused such a beautiful, feeling woman to become so full of bitter feelings. I *will* make it up to you."

"Don't bother," she snapped. "I can take care of myself."

"And, Glenda," Peter said further. "I will try and make things up to you. In some way. . . ." He slowly turned and began making his way toward the French doors, then stopped to say, "And you might want to know that the *Sea Wolf* is due to arrive at anytime now. I thought you might like to know it's to be the *Sea Wolf*'s last voyage."

He cleared his throat nervously, then added. "And, also, I've received word that Rayburn is giving up his post at El Progresso and will also be on his last voyage."

Christina's heart pounded nervously, so much so, she became breathless. "His . . . last. . . ?" she whispered.

"His last," Peter said, then stalked from the room, leaving Glenda and Harriett to look and wonder after him. . . .

Chapter Eighteen

Peter paced the balcony overlooking his courtyard. Had he ever known such silence? Had he ever known such emptiness? Had it been only days since Harriett had promised to be wholly his? Had it been only days since he had discovered who Glenda truly was?

"And, oh, God, to then discover David's death," he groaned, limping, even wobbling against his cane, feeling suddenly his age.

When he had returned home after having spoken with Glenda of his parentage, he had waited and waited for Harriett's arrival. But when she had not come, he had gone to her. When she refused to see him, locking herself in her bedroom with David, mourning and blaming herself, he had felt suddenly cut apart from any future he may have had with her.

David's funeral had been a private one, with few family even at his graveside. His grandmother and grandfather were still in France, leaving only William Read and Harriett to share this grief alone.

Peter had made sure neither the townspeople nor the newspaper heard of the accident. Gossip of where the child's mother had been at the time could have destroyed Peter's business relationships in New Orleans. Though most never talked of his amours, he knew that the people had to know and had just chosen to turn their heads, feeling it more important to remember what a dedicated businessman he was, and that he always quoted fair prices. But this latest amour of his could ruin him if word got around. David's death . . . he felt that even he . . . was responsible. . . .

"Maybe my latest investment will help ease my conscience about many things," he said aloud, finally able to smile. He could still see the excitement in Glenda's eyes when he had met with her and Christina at the vacant shop on Bourbon Street. Though Christina was still put out by him and the way in which he had treated her in the end, she still hadn't hesitated to send a note by messenger that an embroidery shop could be the best way to make things up to both her and Glenda.

"An embroidery shop?" he had laughed upon receipt of her note back to him. But then he had been so relieved to receive any sort of friendly message from Christina, he had promptly replied. . . . "It is the same as done. . . ."

Wondering about the time, not wanting to be late for his appointment with Glenda and Christina, to see just exactly how they had planned to stock the shelves of this shop, Peter wandered on into the parlor and looked toward the clock on the fireplace mantle. He nodded his head, then leaned more heavily against the cane as he began the slow descent down the stairs. He was anxious to leave the gloominess of his house behind him. He wasn't used to being alone. He had always had companionship. Always. But now, yes, he did feel so old . . . and even . . . a bit useless.

As he opened the door to leave, his heart raced, seeing Harriett standing there with arm raised, ready to knock. His gaze traveled quickly over her, seeing her frailty by the way in which her lace-trimmed silk dress hung loosely from around her waist. Her paleness and the anguish in the velvet brown of her eyes became pure torture for him.

"Harriett? Darling?" he said weakly.

"Peter," she murmured. "Darling, I couldn't stay away. I just couldn't bear being alone any longer. William Read? He's been gone for two full days and nights now. I don't know where. Peter, please? Can I be with you? I've missed . . . you . . . so. . . ."

Peter choked back a sob of relief and reached for her. When she stepped into his embrace, he buried his nose into the depths of her hair and held her, oh, so close, feeling her tormented sobs wracking both their bodies. She clung to him, long and hard, then he eased her away and guided her on into the privacy of his house.

Once more he drew her into his arms and held her, thanking God that she hadn't forgotten about him . . . through . . . her grief . . . that he held himself responsible for. Had they not made love that day, would David's life had been spared? But he couldn't . . . wouldn't think about that.

"Harriett, have you come . . . to . . . stay. . . ?" he found the courage to ask. If she said no, he would never allow himself to love so deeply again.

She looked upward and gazed rapturously into his eyes. "Do you still want me, Peter?" she asked, blinking droplets of tears from the tips of her lashes. She hadn't thought there were any tears left, but, yes, she still had some, that she had reserved for the man she loved. She could see how gaunt he had become since their separation. Did he love her so much, that her absence had caused him inner pain? She hadn't wanted to hurt him but her heart had been so full of her . . . David. . . .

"Need you even ask such a foolish question?" he said, lifting one of her hands to his lips. He kissed each fingertip, then held the hand to his cheek. "My darling, let me help you place all grief behind you. Our love is strong. I know that now. We will wed. Soon. I won't let any more harm come to you."

Harriett stood on tiptoe and kissed him gently on the lips. "My love, my only love," she whispered.

Hungrily, Peter laced his fingers through her hair and drew her lips fiercely to his and kissed her with such a passion, he seemed to force soft moans from deeply inside her. He so wanted to lift her into his arms to carry her to bed, but his damn leg had stopped those escapades long ago. Then he was reminded that Christina and Glenda were waiting. He had three women to keep happy now and suddenly he felt alive . . . needed . . . and could scoff at having felt so old only moments ago.

Gently, he withdrew from her embrace and straightened the lines of his shirt. "Harriett, my love, I have to know. Have you come to be a part of the rest of my life?" he asked, touching her cheek anew, relishing in its softness.

"Yes, yes," she said, leaning into his hand. "I must put all sadness behind me. I know this. And I can no longer blame us for what has happened. We were in love when together that day . . . as we are in love today. I have to be with you. I must. . . ."

He kissed her gently on the hand, then turned his back to her. He had left her once to go to Glenda. It had been on that day . . . that David. . . .

But damn it, he couldn't let Glenda down this day. She was his daughter. His *daughter*. He swung around and eyed Harriett with shadows darkening beneath his eyes. No. He should not yet tell Harriett. She wouldn't understand. The fact that she would soon have the title of "stepmother" thrust upon her? No. That could cause a sudden rift in the relationship that had just begun again between lovers. But he did have to go to Glenda. And he had to tell Harriett now. He only prayed that she would understand. . . .

"Darling, I am so glad that you have decided to be my wife," he said thickly. "And we will make it a reality. Soon. But today, I have an appointment. I was just getting ready to leave when you arrived. Would you. . . ?"

Harriett lifted her hands and framed his face with their softness. "Darling, from this day forth, I will be the adoring woman and will not keep you from your daily duties. I know that you are a busy man. I know you have a business to run. Yes, please do go on to keep your appointment."

"Will you stay here and wait for my return?"

"Yes. I will. I do so dread returning to the de-Baulieu Creole house. I need to get away from all the memories. I will wait here for you, my love, and while here, alone, I will let the thoughts of our shared love caress my inner soul."

402

Peter's insides warmed. He had thought he had lost her. But instead, he could see even a deeper love and commitment for him in her eyes. David's death had most surely caused her to think deeply on commitments . . . and she had chosen him as the only necessity in her life. "Then, I will return. Soon," he said. He drew her into his arms and kissed her gently, smelling and tasting her sweetness.

"I shouldn't say to hurry, Peter," she said softly. "I don't wish to nag. I know you must spend whatever time you must on your business. But I can't help it. I do want you to hurry back to me. It has been so long. I so need you. In every way. . . ."

The heat rose inside his loins. But he had to leave her for now. Their love would be rekindled fully later. Wouldn't it even put life into his walk again? Would Christina even see it in his eyes? "Until later, darling," he said and hurried on out and boarded the carriage and ordered Henry to take him to Bourbon Street.

He leaned his weight against his cane as the carriage traveled shakily over the cobblestone streets of New Orleans. He glanced out the window at the blossoming excitement of the city. He loved this city of great mansions, theatres and businesses. He was proud that they were thriving because of the seaport that seemed to keep the city alive.

The air was filled with the sweet fragrances from the profusion of flowers that were on every street corner and in every courtyard. Ah, there were the jasmine, the roses and the magnolia, which were his favorites.

The streets were busy with all varieties of activities, from the carts filled with vegetables and fruits headed for the open market, to the beautifully dressed women moving so gracefully along the walks. There was even a hustle of activity headed toward the banana wharf. The *Sea Wolf* was expected in. Oh, how it saddened Peter to know that this was to be its last voyage. But the last storm that it had encountered had weakened its bow and it was to be replaced by one of his newest, strongest vessels, one that had the refrigeration system installed, ready for using.

He was proud of this newest ship of his, but he would never, no, never love any the same as he had the *Sea Wolf*. But he wouldn't give the *Sea Wolf* up so easily. He had plans for it. He was going to leave it moored at the levee for visitors from other cities to board and explore, to see just what there was about such a ship to cause a man's heart to race with pride. Yes, it would be something worthwhile. He would make it a ship for showing. And his newest? He wondered just how many years it would be faithful to him. The *Sea Wolf* had been his faithful ally for twenty-one . . . long . . . years. . . .

The carriage drew to a halt in front of the shop Peter had just recently purchased. It was as all other shops along this busy thoroughfare with its lacy iron-work and balcony. But already at the front window, he could see that Christina and Glenda had been busy at work. Placed neatly on a display counter, one could see exhibited the finest of linen materials with many loops of colored threads draped across these. Then next to these lay beautifully embroidered pieces, which were household linens, handkerchiefs with embroidered monograms, and plump cushioned pillows, the same that Christina had even embroidered and had placed in his home.

He climbed from the carriage and moved on toward the door, pausing a bit to take a deep breath, knowing to see Christina again would be to cause some possible hurtful feelings. But yet, she had seemed eager to see Rayburn. Had she forgotten the shared moments so easily? She was a complex woman. So damn complex. . . .

Opening the door that led into the shop, Peter's attention was drawn to the tinkling from a bell that hang overhead. Glenda rushed from behind a velveteen curtain that separated the business area from the leisure area, then stopped and smiled nervously at Peter. She hadn't yet grown accustomed to his knowing the truth. She wasn't even comfortable with this truth herself. But he had accepted it and her. Wasn't the purchase of this shop proof enough of that?

"Hello, Peter," she said, extending a hand of friendship. She would never be able to call him father. She had truly only known one father. And as long as Peter accepted her calling him by his name, then that would be the way that it would remain.

"Don't you look lovely today?" Peter said, gazing up and down at her, remembering the times he had even lusted after her, not then knowing that she was of his own flesh and blood. Thank God, he had never made advances toward her.

His gaze raked her anew this day, thinking how elegant she looked, even in her plain white shirtwaist and her dark blue broadcloth skirt. Her golden hair was lifted from her shoulders and pulled back where it was secured behind her ears with combs. Her complexion was lovely and rosy and her smile was wide and sincere.

He took her hand and kissed it quite gallantly. "I see you have made progress in your new venture," he said, laughing lightly. He tensed as Christina moved from the back room. But when she smiled warmth back at him, attired in her black taffeta skirt and lowcut, white ruffled blouse, he felt a relief wash through him.

"Good morning, Christina," he said, even almost awkwardly. He felt as though it should be the same as all the years past . . . that he should grab her into his arms and devour her with his lips. But that was all behind him now. He had Harriett. Christina would surely have Rayburn. This was how it should be. . . .

"And how do you like what we've accomplished so far, Peter?" Christina said in a silken purr, lifting scissors and a wooden frame, to place them in a prominent place on display in the window.

"You do seem to have skills as businesswomen," he laughed gruffly. "But, first I guess I should ask if you have had any business thus far?"

"A few customers," Glenda giggled, flitting around the room, touching the softness of the threads and arranging them in rows of matching colors on the shelves along a side wall. "But once word travels, we shall have more women to do business with than to even count."

"And are you . . . even . . . happy. . . ?" he asked, going to Glenda, taking her hand in his. "I mean . . . really happy. . . ?"

A bit of hurt appeared in the green of her eyes. She hadn't been able to put Read from her mind. It had been too long now since having been with him. But each day . . . it became less and less agonizing for her. "Yes," she murmured. "I love what I do."

"Then I am happy," Peter said, kissing her fingertips. "If my daughter is happy . . . then . . . I am happy."

"Would you like to be shown some of our beautiful threads? See what you have so generously invested in?" Glenda asked anxiously, eyes wide.

"Yes. I would. That is why I came. To see you . . . and to check out my investment. . . ."

She laughed softly, watching Christina out of the corner of her eye and the way Christina seemed to be watching from the window. Christina had heard word of the *Sea Wolf*'s arrival this day. She had even watched the scramble of men headed for the banana wharf. Could Christina hold herself back and not rush to the banana wharf herself? Wouldn't Christina want to see Rayburn?

Glenda shook her head a bit, remembering Peter. She moved to a counter and began lifting threads into her hands. "This, Peter, is the loveliest of all threads that we plan to acquaint the women with in our shop," she said. "The golden silk. Isn't it beautiful?" she added quickly, sighing.

"Yes. Quite," he said, chuckling beneath his breath at her exuberance for what she was now a part of.

"Then there is the silver thread," Glenda continued. "Christina has already ordered white linen threads from Scotland and others from Russia. And then there are the floss silks, glass beads, and jewels we plan to offer for sewing onto a linen twill ground."

She flurried around the room, breathless. "And then there is the silk cord, the pearl and crochet cotton. We will offer designs predrawn, or teach the women how to capture designs from books illustrated with drawings of plants, flowers, trees or shrubs."

"And there is even more. . . ?" Peter laughed.

"So much more," Glenda said. "We shall offer our own color combinations and motifs. We shall teach women how to embroider family trees, stressing details. . . ."

Christina's gasp drew Glenda around suddenly. Glenda followed Christina's gaze and saw Rayburn . . . tall, handsome, gray-fringed, golden-haired Rayburn moving toward the door of the shop.

Peter also saw the familiar stance of the man and kissed Glenda swiftly on the palm of the hand. "I must go out the back way," he whispered. "I don't believe my presence here at this moment would be wise."

"But, Peter. . . ?" Glenda said softly.

"I had known of Rayburn's arrival. I had to come to see if he had received my message and would come to Christina. He did. He is smart. But it is time for me to take my leave." He kissed Glenda gently on the cheek, then moved swiftly from the room, leaving Glenda to stare openly after him, to realize what a decent, kind man he was. He had planned for Rayburn and Christina to meet. Though he had been a rogue, Peter was also a gentleman . . . someone she was proud to know as her father.

Watching Rayburn as he entered the shop, Glenda was reminded of the first time she had seen him. The rains . . . the way his carriage wheels had been stuck in the muddy paste of the streets at El Progresso . . . and the way in which he had eyed her so quizzically as she had also stood in this mud . . . drenched to the bone.

Yes. That's where it all had begun. From there her life had been continually changing. From one moment to the next. She loved him. He would always be special to her. She wanted to fly into his arms, but knew that Christina came first, so inched her way toward the velveteen curtain and slipped behind it, not wanting to listen, but too anxious for Rayburn and Christina to come to some sort of compromise, to not keep an ear to the curtain, knowing that her pulse was racing with anxiety. . . .

Christina's insides mellowed to mush when Rayburn stepped through the door. Yes, she loved him. Not in the way she loved Peter, but, oh, God, she loved him. But would he . . . could he . . . feel the same as before about her? Why was he here? How did he even know. . . ? The ship had to have only arrived. Did word travel that quickly?

"Rayburn. . . ?" she said softly. Her fingers trembled, yet she reached one hand to his arm. She touched it lightly, seeing the questioning in the blue of his eyes. She moved her fingers to his face, touching the angular lines and the familiar creases that age had gracefully given to him.

"Christina, I received word that you wanted to see me," he said, lightly brushing her hand away. He toyed with the collar of his blousy white shirt and flexed the muscles in his long, lean legs as he began moving around the room, studying it all. Then he suddenly swirled around and eyed her speculatively. "Are you all right? You aren't ill?" His gaze traveled over her, seeing her gracefulness and exquisite beauty. No. She wasn't ill. But there was something else. . . .

Christina lifted some pink cotton embroidery thread

to her fingers and began straightening it, pulling free any that had twisted. Her eyes now refused to look into his, not truly knowing what to say to him. She was a mass of wonder inside. She had not sent a message to Rayburn. Then who. . . ? She immediately thought of Glenda and smiled.

"No. I am not ill," she said in her silken purr. She would now seize the opportunity to speak her mind to him. Whoever had sent the message had done right by her. That would make it easier for her to confess her feelings to him.

"Then, why, Christina. . . ?"

"Rayburn," she said softly, dropping the embroidery thread onto a counter. She went to him and took both his hands in hers. "Rayburn, I have been a fool. A whorish . . . fool, if you even think that a better term for a wife who has done what I have done to such a fine husband as you."

A twinkle made an appearance in Rayburn's eyes. He had hoped . . . oh, damn he had hoped. . . ! "And so you feel I should label you as such, huh?" he said, trying to keep a serious tone to his voice. But inside, he felt suddenly triumphant. He knew that if he waited long enough, Peter would show his true colors.

Rayburn squeezed her hands. Ah, how he understood the reasons for Christina's having felt so reckless. There had been so little in her life. Only him . . . since age eighteen. She had never had the opportunity to taste of any other side of life. She had always been stifled by family . . . then husband. Yes. He understood and didn't love her any less!

"Do you think of me in such terms, Rayburn?"

Christina said, lowering her eyes. "If you do, I will understand. I will even understand if you turn your back to me and walk right out that door."

"Are you saying that . . . you are ready . . . to become my wife again?" he said, wishing that his heart would quit hammering so against his ribs. Might a rib even snap, the hammering was with such force?

"Rayburn, oh, Rayburn, if only you would forgive me," she said, now searching his face with the soft blue of her eyes. A quivering was at her lips and a tear at her eyes.

"And . . . are . . . you sure. . . ?"

"I have been living at our plantation house now . . . for a while," she murmured. "I had hoped you would also when you returned from your *Sea Wolf* voyage."

"It is my last voyage," he grumbled.

She didn't want him to know that she had already been told this by Peter. She didn't want to ever speak Peter's name again in Rayburn's presence. "Your . . . last. . . ?" she said, forcing a questioning . . . a surprise . . . into her words. "What does it mean, Rayburn?"

"You know that the only reason I went to El Progresso in the first place was because of you," he said, lifting one of her hands to brush his lips against the fingertips, then released both hands and began pacing the floor. "I had thought to give both of us a new way of life would erase the boredom from your days . . . and would help you to forget Peter Grayson. You know that I was damn happy at our plantation. But for you, I gave that up."

He swung around, facing her boldly. "But I couldn't stay at El Progresso without you. Each day

411

was a hellish torture for me. I thought if I returned home, then just maybe you might think of me being alone and would return also. If you are already there, waiting for me, it is more than I could ever have hoped for . . . or . . . prayed for. . . ."

"But I am," she purred. "And I do want you with me. The house? It is you. Every painting . . . every chair . . . every book. . . ."

"Then we *can* start all over again?" he said, moving to her, clasping into her shoulders.

"No. Not all over again. I don't ever want to be forced to put our earlier happier years behind us. Let's just let our future be an extension of the years we loved and shared. . . ."

He drew her into his arms and inhaled her sweetness. "That's beautiful, Christina," he said. He hated it when his voice broke a bit.

"But there is a change of sorts, Rayburn," Christina said, laughing silkily. She gently pulled away from him, showing a sort of mischief in the depth of her eyes.

"Hmmm. I'm not sure if I want to know," he chuckled. "I see that look you always get when up to something."

"But this something is very nice," she said.

"What . . .?"

"We have a house guest," she said. Then quickly corrected herself. . . . "We have two house guests. . . ."

"Damn it you say. . . ," he said.

"Yes. Glenda Galvez. Remember. . . ?"

"Glenda?" he exclaimed, then smiling widely. "I had heard about her stowing away on the ship. But I wasn't sure where she had settled after once arriving in New Orleans." But he had seen her, only moments ago. . . .

"Well, Rayburn, she is at our house," she said, then giggled a bit. "And our second house guest?"

"Yes. . . ?"

"It is a puma. An almost full-grown mountain lion. . . ."

His bushy eyebrows lifted. "What. . . ?"

"It's a long story," she laughed. "When we get home, I will tell you. . . ."

"Home? Ah, I can hardly wait," he laughed. Then his gaze moved to the curtain, seeing movement. "And, Glenda, you can come out here now," he said, walking toward it. He swung the curtain aside and gazed approvingly at her. "And so here is the *Sea Wolf*'s stowaway," he chuckled. "You have been the talk of El Progresso and Bay Island," he said further.

Glenda blushed a bit. "I have been?" she said, smiling awkwardly. "And what does everyone say?"

"Well, there has been gossip about the cat you also took aboard the ship," he said, then turned his laughing eyes toward Christina. "Yes, darling. I already knew. Such gossip had to travel to my ears. What does surprise me is that it is you who now have given the cat a place to live."

Glenda reached for Rayburn and touched his arm lightly. "Do you care?" she said in a strain. But whether he did or not, she knew that Nena's days were becoming shorter in New Orleans. If Rayburn didn't order Nena from the house, it was going to have to be she who made the decision that Nena would have to be taken back to her habitat. Yes, the time was drawing near.

"If my two women want to have a house pet, so be it," he laughed heartily.

Glenda and Christina exchanged quick glances. Then they both laughed together. "House cat?" Glenda exclaimed. "Rayburn, you have a surprise waiting for you."

Then Glenda drew serious. She took Rayburn's hands in hers and eyed him anxiously. "And, Rayburn, do you have any word of my family?" she said.

"If I had known I would be seeing you, I would have made special effort to speak to all of your family," he said. "But all that I can now tell you is that it seems fine with them all."

"My mother. . . ?"

"Doc McAdams has worked magic with her," he said. "She's up and active again."

"My brothers? My father?"

"Your brothers are still working with the bananas. Your one brother's tiny wife is with child, but I don't know much about your father. He keeps to Bay Island. With your mother. But all in all, your family is fine," he said. Then his brow furrowed. "There is only one thing," he added softly.

Glenda's pulse raced. "And what is that, Rayburn?" she said softly.

"There have been some uprisings in distant towns in Honduras," he said sullenly.

Something grabbed at Glenda's heart. She had always feared her brothers' having to fight. Was it truly going to happen? Oh, she would truly die for them. . . .

"There is to be an overthrow of the government of el Presidente Bonilla?" she said in a near whisper.

"All I can tell you is that some Salvadoran soldiers have attacked some towns. We at El Progresso could hear the booming of large guns in the distance. And there has been word of an assassination attempt on Bonilla's life."

Glenda swung her skirt in a silken flutter, throwing a fist to her mouth. "Oh, no. . . ," she murmured. "I feel I should be home. With family. Families should be together in times of trouble. . . ."

"Glenda, you are a woman. There is nothing you can do," Rayburn encouraged.

She swung around, her chin tilted haughtily into the air. "Yes. I am a woman," she snapped. "But a woman with spirit. If I was there, I would show those Salvadorian pigs! They wouldn't know what hit them!"

Rayburn laughed heartily. Even angry, Glenda was beautiful!

Glenda set her jaws tightly, now thinking to possibly become a stowaway again. Yes, she had loved the easy life with Christina. She had loved the beautiful threads and the shop her father had so generously given her. But the restlessness in her soul was causing reckless thoughts to surface.

Read? She had already lost him. The excitement . . . the thrill of his touch . . . and lips . . . were gone. She would find a way to have a similar excitement in her life again. She was now wondering about this new ship of Peter's that would be making its first voyage to El Progresso. Could she. . . ? Should she . . . sneak . . . aboard. . . ? She smiled coyly at Rayburn, then went to the window and looked toward

415

the river, already making plans. . . .

Feeling the nibbling of teeth along his flesh, Read grumbled as he awakened from another drunken night of restless sleep. He worked his tongue around the insides of his mouth, oh, God, feeling the dryness. It was as though someone had stuffed cotton there, absorbing all the moisture. He licked his parched lips and reached and scratched at the thick stubble of black whiskers on his face. With the continuing of nibblings along his chest, he grumbled a shallow "Hello," then said, laughing amusedly, "*Ma chérie*, Marissa, is there no end to your passions?"

Her full, dark liquid eyes looked upward at him. There was much mischief in their depths. And the wide, white flash of teeth when she suddenly broke into a smile caused Read to remember the many days and nights of being with her . . . trying to put behind him all tragedies . . . and . . . lonelinesses. . . .

"Marissa *has* warmed your blood. Yes?" she said devilishly, now sinking her teeth into one of his nipples, causing him to flinch with pain.

"Yes. You have," he said, laughing, brushing her away from him. "But I think it's time for me to get myself together and join the living again."

She sprang from the bed, nude, her beautifully rounded limbs as though dark velvet, as she placed her hands on her hips. "So you think you have not been with the living while with me?" she snapped. "How could you say such a thing? What if such news traveled from man to man? My reputation would be ruined. Do you hear! Ruined!"

416

Read moved from the bed and rescued his breeches from the floor. Every time Marissa spoke words that had been spoken the same by Glenda, it would only remind him of what he had lost. "I won't ruin your reputation," he grumbled, flashing her a long, lingering look as he pulled his breeches up and secured their buttons. "And I want to thank you for hiding me away as you have these past nights. Have I paid you enough? If not, just say the word. I will always be grateful. You see, I know I have kept many men from your door by occupying your bed while I was trying to drown my sorrows by both bottle and your exquisite flesh."

"Your skills at making love were reward enough," she said, forgetting her anger at him. Instead, she moved her body into his, touching him where he was so easily aroused. "Even now. I hunger so for you. . . ."

She slithered her body over his and let her fingers leave butterfly touches wherever they traveled, from his chest, down, to where they so skillfully worked beneath the tight confines of his breeches. "Please? Do not leave. No man will come knocking on my door until night. We have the full day. Please? Make love to me. Over and over again."

"Don't you ever get tired of it?" he asked, brushing her aside. "It seems your existence is only what a man can offer you. Don't you want anything more out of life?"

She looked blankly toward him. "*Señor*, is there more?" she said softly. "If so, I have never found it. I have only known the ways of my body since I knew there was such a thing as pleasure to be derived from the touch from a man."

Pity for her coursed through Read's brain, yet she was

truly no concern of his. He had used her. And now she was of no further use to him. It was his life that he was worried about. So far, he had been unable to fulfill his needs . . . his desires. But this day, he would start anew. Though whiskered and smelling of unbathed skin, he would go to Peter Grayson. Read had heard word of this new ship of Peter's. Well, it wouldn't be Peter's for long. Read was going to become the owner . . . and Peter . . . wouldn't have any choice but to comply with his wishes . . . demands. . . .

Marissa watched, wide-eyed as Read fully dressed. "You *are* leaving," she exclaimed. "Marissa has to say a goodbye to you?"

"Yes," he said, buttoning the last button of his shirt. He once again ran his fingers across the whiskers of his face, realizing that he had to be quite a sight, with his clothes also so rumpled and filth-laden. But this was suddenly of no concern to him. Haste in his footsteps was!

He went to the door and swung it open widely, bowing a bit and said a brisk, *Au revoir, ma chérie,"* and rushed on down the stairs, where his horse faithfully waited.

Squinting beneath the bright rays of the sun, he mounted the horse and began to move at a fast clip down the thoroughfare. He could see the excitement of people moving toward the levee and knew that the *Sea Wolf* must have docked. There wasn't much time. Damn, why had he waited so long to make the decision? But his drunken stupor had caused his brain to cease functioning.

Once again his tongue explored inside his mouth. He tried to spit, to remove the unsightly feeling from inside it, but no spittle would surface. Instead, he just swallowed hard and raced his horse onward until he found himself in front of Peter Grayson's house. He tensed a bit, seeing Harriett's personal carriage there. "She has apparently put her mourning for David behind her," he growled to himself as he dismounted and secured his horse's reins to a low oak limb.

He stared at the other carriage, recognizing it to be Peter's, glad that he had found him at home. Read hadn't wanted to go to Peter's place of business with his announcement. Loud words were planned to be spoken and Read preferred the privacy of a house in which to speak them.

"But, Harriett?" he grumbled, moving toward the door. "I hadn't thought she would be a part of this. I had thought she had learned her lesson. . . ."

He lifted the heavy brass knocker and let it drop with a loud thud, then waited. It was no surprise when Harriett opened the door. When she saw Read, her face paled and her shoulders drooped a bit.

"William Read. . . ," she said in a whisper.

Ma chérie, you have returned, I see," he grumbled, walking on past her, then seeing Peter move in through the French doors that led out into the courtyard. "And, Peter, ol' man, I see you've managed quite well to get my sister into your clutches for good."

He turned to Harriett and eyed her darkly as she in turn raked her eyes over his disarray. "I guess it's best this way, Harriett," he continued. "You couldn't sit behind doors the rest of your life. That wouldn't bring David back to you. . . ."

Harriett covered her eyes with her hands and let out a mournful gasp. "William Read. . . ," she pleaded softly. "Please don't."

Peter made his way across the room, leaning his weight heavily against his cane. "William, let her be," he said icily. "She has suffered way too much already. Isn't it enough that she has blamed herself along with me for letting such a thing happen to her son? Let her be. She is to be my wife. I will erase her nightmares from her life. Now and forever. I will make you a promise of that."

Read threw his head back, laughing. Then he sobered and glowered toward Peter. "You will, eh?" he said. "And how many women have you made these promises to, huh? I remember another recent woman companion of yours. Where is she now? Wasn't she good enough for you? Or is it that Rayburn had more drawing power in the end? Is she now with him, feeling even foolish for letting a one-legged son-of-a-bitch pull her away from the man who worshipped the ground she walked on?"

"I never promised Christina anything other than what she received from me," Peter argued. "We never talked of marriage. This is the difference between Christina and Harriett. I am going to marry your sister. I love her. I could never love another."

"And a child? Will you be capable of fathering a child for my sister, to bring another child into her life? Or are you too old? You are quite ancient, you know."

Peter doubled his free hand at his side. He gritted his teeth. "Please don't speak of children," he said sullenly. "Not now. Have a heart. . . ." He so often hated the weakness that his lame leg brought to him in times of having such a need to defend himself. But he had learned that money had taken the place of his muscles.

Whenever he needed something . . . needed to settle something with someone . . . he just had to hand over a large amount of "green" . . . and that would be the quick answer to any and all of his problems.

"Then there is something I do wish to speak openly of, Peter," Read grumbled, helping himself to one of Peter's expensive Cuban cigars. He lit it and inhaled deeply of its rich, manly fragrance.

"And what might that be?" Peter grumbled back, also lighting himself a tasty morsel.

"There will be no bargaining," Read said. "What I want, I plan to have and just as quickly as I can snap my fingers in your face."

Peter laughed a bit. His gaze raked over Read and the show of whiskers and wrinkled clothes. "I would think you are in no condition to bargain or demand anything of me," he said darkly. "Where have you been? Sleeping off a drunk down on the waterfront?"

"I've been where even you would give an eye tooth to know where," Read laughed, remembering the skills of Marissa. Surely Harriett didn't know of such skills, and Read was certainly not going to tell Peter where such pastimes could be found. Then his brow furrowed, thinking Peter probably already knew. He had probably had his fingers inside every single and married woman's breeches in New Orleans!

The thought of it angered him more, knowing that Harriett would in the end be hurt. But there was nothing he could do. Nothing. She had stars in her eyes . . . stars that had been gone for only a short while after David's useless death. . . .

"I don't think I even want to ask," Peter groaned, giving Read a look of utter contempt.

"Then hear this," Read said, going to Peter, speaking into his face. "I plan to have a new ship in which to travel the Caribbean . . . and this ship . . . is to be the one I've been hearing so much about. . . ."

Peter's face grew ashen. He spoke tersely. "And which ship is that?" He turned and flipped ashes from his cigar into the cold grate of the fireplace.

"The one you are to replace the *Sea Wolf* with," Read said, inhaling deeply from his cigar, lifting an eyebrow as he he saw the look of surprise jump into Peter's green eyes. . . . ah, green . . . the color of Glenda's. Funny, how they . . . Peter and Glenda . . . so resembled one another. . . .

"What. . . ?" Peter gasped, lifting his cane momentarily, swinging it into the air in protest, then leaned back against it, clutching tightly to the silver wolf's head. He laughed amusedly. "You, of course, are not serious. . . ."

Read leaned into Peter's face once more. "Damn serious," he stated flatly. "I will pay you top price plus give you back that flat personality of a paddlewheeler that I so stupidly purchased from you. I will have the money ready for you this afternoon after I get to the bank and withdraw it. Then I plan to board that ship and be the one handing orders out. I will be its owner *and* its captain."

Peter tossed his cigar into the fireplace, then threw his cane across the room in a dark fury. He crumpled down onto a chair, glaring. "And why do you act so sure of yourself?" he shouted. "Why in damnation would you think I would comply with anything as outrageous as that?"

"I demand it of you. Cut and dry," Read said. "You

have no choice. I will take my leave and then arrive shortly with the payment for the ship."

"Harriett, give me my cane," Peter shouted. When she scurried and rescued it for him, he pushed himself angrily from the chair and went to Read and gave him a shove. "Now you listen here, you bum, no way would I let that ship be yours. I've invested many years into that refrigeration unit aboard that ship and only I am going to give instructions as to who is in charge of the equipment and what is to be done on the ship. Only myself. And, yes, you will take your leave. Now. And don't show your whiskered face inside this house again. Leave me and Harriett be. She doesn't need you. And I most certainly don't want any part of you."

Read laughed huskily. "For a one-legged man, you do speak tough," he said. He had never liked making fun, knowing it was not the gentlemanly way to win an argument, but at this moment, he hated Peter and what he stood for with a passion.

"And you refuse to leave my house?" Peter shouted, eyeing the drawer where he kept his pistol.

"I mean to make you understand why it is that I will own your ship," Read said, seeing the way Peter's eyes were . . . settling . . . on the desk drawer. Read knew that most handguns . . . possibly even more powerful weapons . . . were kept within reach in most houses. But he could move much more quickly than Peter. Peter didn't have a chance. . . .

"To hell you will," Peter said, inching his way toward the desk. He jumped with alarm when Read placed himself between the desk and himself.

"Yes, I will," Read grumbled. "And now. I'm tired of wasting words with you. You see, Peter, I plan a sort of blackmail. I will tell everyone the circumstances behind David's death . . . that you were bedding up with his young mother that day . . . and weeks even before that. . . ."

Harriett flew to Read and grabbed his arm. "You wouldn't. . . ," she gasped.

Read shoved her gently away from him. "You stay out of this, Harriett," he said. "What I now do is for you as well as myself. . . ."

"How . . .?" she whined.

"You'll see. . . ," Read said softly.

"And what if I don't give a damn," Peter stormed. "What if I tell you to get that damn sister out of here and with it your threats. I have stability in this city. I know it. . . ."

Harriett felt the weakness in her knees as she crept toward Peter. Her face had grown a pale porcelain color. "Peter, do you realize what you just said? What you said . . . about . . .? she said in a near whisper.

"What . . .?" Peter said, teetering a bit against his cane.

"You called me William Read's damn sister," she said, sobbing.

"God, did I do that?" he boomed. With his free arm, he drew her into his arms and held her tightly to him. "I'm sorry. Darling, I am so sorry." He turned snapping eyes to Read. "Get out of here. Go and get the damn money. The ship is yours. . . ."

Read's lips formed into a relieved, wide smile. Not only had Peter agreed to sell Read his prized ship, but also had wholly proven his love for Harriett. Read now knew that Peter hadn't meant to curse Harriett. It was just a habit of men . . . to speak so loosely when angry. Peter's devoted affection he was now showing was proof enough for Read. Now he could leave Harriett behind as he traveled the high seas. In a way he was free . . . as free as he could be . . . knowing that forever he would be bonded to his deep love for Glenda.

"Until later, Peter," Read said, mock saluting with the flick of a wrist. When Harriett looked his way, Read winked at her and felt a warmth course through his veins when she smiled her sweet look of approval and understanding back at him. . . .

Chapter Nineteen

Glenda had reason to be both sad and excited. Her sadness was for Nena . . . her orphaned cub. The new ship of Peter Grayson's was to carry Nena back to Honduras this night to be set free among her own kind.

Then there was Glenda's reason for being excited. Her excitement stemmed from the fact that Christina was giving her first plantation party since Rayburn's return. As Glenda knelt on the terrace, hugging and loving Nena, she could hear the flurry of excitement in Christina's parlor. Many had already arrived. Christina had said that frolic even began with the trip itself, with so many arriving by large paddlewheelers from other cities along the wide range of the Mississippi River.

Dreamily, Glenda was reminded of her one time on board such a pleasure boat. It had been with Read. He had been so happy with his new purchase. She had been even happier to share his beautiful stateroom with him . . . until Peter had suddenly appeared and she had rushed away . . . to see only moments later . . . Read embracing another beautiful woman.

"So it is for this reason, among others, that I too will return to my lovely Honduras," she whispered into Nena's ear, caressing her sleek, tawny fur. Nena was stretched out on her side, watching Glenda with green, pleasant eyes, and purring gently. Her paws were thick and large and her teeth were sharp points of white. Glenda knew that in those jaws, there was the force of eight men, but never grew frightened of her. Not for even that one minute. Nena trusted Glenda . . . as Glenda trusted Nena.

Glenda leaned and kissed Nena on the tip of her black nose. "I too will travel on the new ship, but I cannot let anyone know," she whispered. "Again I will become a stowaway. If I could do it once, so shall I a second time."

Glenda knew that neither Christina nor Rayburn would approve of her returning to Honduras. In a sense, they had become as family. She had become the daughter they had never had and with this status, they had begun to be a bit overprotective of her. Her freedom was being stifled. She wasn't sure just how much longer she could have stood it.

Glenda caressed Nena some more, wondering if Nena had begun to feel this way also. She hadn't had any freedom since leaving her mother's side in the jungle. Was it possible that Nena in the end would have turned to extremes, to acquire freedom for herself?

"It could have happened, Nena," Glenda said softly. "This decision that I have made is best. You do need to be set free. But, oh, how I will miss you. . . ."

And then there was Glenda's family. She feared for

their safety. She wanted to be with them now during the threat of another revolution in her country. She would even fight to protect them if it became necessary.

"Glenda, come on inside and join the fun," Christina said as she glided out onto the terrace. As was Glenda, Christina was beautifully gowned in silk and lace with jewels and flowers in her hair. Diamonds sparkled at both their throats and wrists, and their dresses were low and revealing, causing a stir wherever they moved about.

Just inside the French doors, Glenda could see that Rayburn stood tall and proud of his two women. He showed no signs of having ever left the Taylor Plantation. The group of people arriving for the party acted as though they hadn't even known of the separation. It had been too long since Christina had entertained and all were willing to make this party a success, hoping that it would be the beginning of many more to come, as it had been those many years ago when Christina and Rayburn had shared happier times.

"Has he arrived yet, Christina?" Glenda said, once more stroking Nena.

"The jeweler? No. Not yet," Christina said, sighing heavily. "And are you even sure you want to do this, Glenda? Will it hurt Nena?"

"It will scare her a bit. But I surely do so badly want to be able to separate her from all the other pumas in Honduras. Maybe one day I will even be able to see Nena again. The earring would prove her identity to me."

Christina's eyebrows lifted. "But, Glenda, you won't even be in Honduras yourself," she said in almost alarm. "There truly won't be a need for such an earring. You are now a part of New Orleans. Think of the fun we are going to have together. We will have one party after another. I suddenly feel alive again. Why worry so much about Nena?"

Glenda felt her heartbeat hasten a bit. Christina would only have to believe that Honduras would not be a destination for Glenda in the near future. Christina did not know how to read Glenda's mind, to realize that Glenda would not be a part of New Orleans after this night. She hugged Nena tenderly. "Yes. I do worry about my orphaned cub," she sighed wearily. "The earring is quite necessary. It has to be done. Nena is like no other puma in the jungle. She will show them all that she is different. Yes. An earring is very necessary."

Christina turned a bit, staring at the hustle and bustle in the parlor. "But, Glenda, when my guests get one look at this puma, they may run for their homes, frightened to death," she said in a near whisper. "Surely you can coax Nena to leave the terrace. For a while at least."

"Not until we get the earring secured in Nena's ear," Glenda said stubbornly. "You see, Tom Andrews and another sailor are to come for Nena. Soon. I must see that she is truly prepared for the trip." Tears shone on the tips of her thick lashes. "Oh, Nena," she sobbed. "I shall so miss you. . . ."

Rayburn moved out onto the terrace with a short, thin man at his side, who was carrying a long, narrow black case. His dark eyes revealed an uneasiness in them and the narrow line of his lips showed a slight trembling.

"This is Mr. Black, the jeweler who has agreed to do the chore for you, Glenda," Rayburn said, patting Mr. Black on the back, possibly for reassurance, as Nena lifted her head and gave a slow, lazy hiss toward the intruders of the fast approaching night. The sunset showed orange slivers of light across Nena's back, making her look even more ferocious than ever. Once again she hissed, showing the wide expanse of her mouth and the sharp points of her fangs.

Glenda laughed a bit and began stroking Nena beneath her chin. A paw lifted lazily and then dropped to the floor as Mr. Black began to circle them. . . .

"Are you sure you wish to have this done?" Mr. Black asked in a strained, weak voice.

"Yes. It has to be done," Glenda snapped. "Surely Rayburn told you what was expected of you. If you had thought to not do it, you should have told Rayburn. He could have hired someone else. It has to be done tonight."

Rayburn placed a hand on Glenda's shoulder. "Honey, don't get upset," he said soothingly. "Mr. Black will do it. Just give him time to get used to the idea of Nena being so large."

"He is a bit large," Mr. Black said, clutching his case to his chest.

"Are you, or aren't you?" Glenda said, rising, placing her hands on her hips, thinking that Tom Andrews might arrive at any moment. She was relieved to know that this rusty-haired, gentle sailor had been given charge of her Nena for the full trip back to Honduras. She could remember his being gentle as he carried her from the *Sea Wolf* to

Peter's carriage that first night of her arrival to New Orleans.

Well, she would also rely on his kindness . . . gentleness . . . this night when even she would become a passenger on this new ship. She only hoped that she could sneak aboard. She only hoped that she could find Nena and Tom on the large expanse of the ship that she had traveled to the levee to see this very morning, to see if it was as great as all had spoken of.

She also remembered seeing painters painting the name of the ship on the side. They had just begun and had only painted two letters in bold black . . . the letters . . . N . . . E . . . .

She was curious to know what the rest would be. She was curious to know if the ship's owner had reason to name a ship a particular name? The *Sea Wolf*? She had never found out the true reason behind that name. Peter Grayson wasn't of the personality of a wolf now. But maybe in his youth . . . he had been. . . .

She was suddenly reminded of her mother and the truth that had been revealed to her. Oh, once with her mother, how could she act as though she didn't know. . .?

"Are you so certain this mountain lion won't attack me for inflicting some hurt on his one ear?" Mr. Black suddenly asked tremulously. "I'm not . . . I'm just not so sure."

Glenda turned on a heel, her green eyes flashing. "Oh, Rayburn," she sighed heavily. "Can't you do something? Please?"

Rayburn went to Mr. Black and jerked the case

from his clutches and opened it. He showed Glenda and Christina the inside velvet lining and the one, lone loop of a gold earring, and a few instruments required to place it on Nena's ear.

"The earring is beautiful," Glenda sighed, touching its smoothness.

"Pure gold," Rayburn said, then thrust the opened case back into Mr. Black's arms. "Do you hear what I say? I paid you well for that gold. Now you place it on this cat. If you don't, I shall make sure your future business will become nothing."

Glenda's eyes widened. She had never heard Rayburn threaten anyone. She smiled almost wickedly as the smaller man was quick to comply by lifting the earring from its bed of velvet.

"Please hold him tightly," Mr. Black said.

"Rayburn, will you assist?" Glenda said, moving to her knees, lifting Nena's head onto her lap. "Please just secure her hind legs, while Christina holds her front paws, if you will, Christina?"

All joined in and Glenda did tense a bit when she saw the smaller man at work. If his hands weren't trembling so, she would feel better about it. She was afraid that Nena would sense his fear. Then what? But it was done so quickly. Nena only let out a hiss of annoyance when the earring was secured and hung shining for all to see.

Rayburn moved to his feet, laughing. He patted Mr. Black quite hard on his back and walked him back into the parlor. "Very good, very good," Rayburn said. "Come. Let's have a brandy and a good cigar to celebrate."

Glenda let out a heavy breath of relief. She looked

toward Christina whose face had paled. "It is done, Christina," she said softly. "Now you can return to your guests without so much worry. I will stay with Nena until Tom Andrews and his associate arrive."

"He is here," Rayburn said, returning to the terrace with the rusty-haired, freckle-faced young man at his side. "No sooner did I get a glass of brandy lifted to my lips did he arrive."

Glenda rose and hugged Tom, as though a brother, not a stranger. "Tom. It is good to see you again," she said. She could see his eyes assessing her. Yes, she did look different than when he had last seen her.

"Glenda Galvez?" he said, laughing. "My how you have changed. But just as beautiful. . . ."

"Thank you," Glenda said, laughing also. Then she grew serious as she glanced back at Nena, who was now pacing back and forth, eyeing the added commotion nervously. "And the cage? You have brought it also?"

"It's out beside the back gate," Rayburn said. "Glenda, coax Nena from the terrace and out to the gate. Then we shall secure her inside the cage for the trip to the ship."

"I hate to watch . . . ," she murmured, tears near.

"Well, then, you get her to the gate, then leave the rest to us," Tom said, eyeing Nena with an eagerness. He wasn't afraid. She was tame. He had been convinced of this by Rayburn earlier in the day. Even the thick wad of bills thrust into his hand had helped to ease his worries. He was going to earn the generous amount of pay. If not for the puma itself, then for this beautiful Glenda Galvez. He only regretted his brief meetings with her. Would he ever get to be around her for a lengthier time? She was, ah, so sensuously beautiful!

"Rayburn, do you think that is all right if I do it in that way?" Glenda said, touching his arm lightly. "I do not wish to see Nena taken away. I do not wish to see her placed inside a cage. . . ."

"Glenda, I will do even more for you than that," Rayburn answered. "You give Nena her goodbyes now and I will coax her away from you. She has grown to trust me. I can do as well."

Glenda felt as though a traitor, not seeing Nena to the end, but yet, she could feel her heart breaking and wanted to now get her goodbyes over with as quickly as possible. "Yes. Please, Rayburn," she murmured. Then she eyed Tom quickly. "And when is the ship to leave? Soon? Or way later into the night?" she asked timidly.

She only hoped that she could participate in the party for a while at least, then leave, possibly while Christina was so crowded around by friends, Glenda wouldn't even be missed for hours . . . or at least . . . until the ship was so far out to sea, there would be nothing Christina could even do to stop her.

"There is quite some time left before leaving," Tom answered. "It's the new captain. Something to do with his delaying for a while."

Rayburn tensed, glancing quickly toward Glenda, hoping she wouldn't ask this new ship captain's name. It was best that she never see William Read deBaulieu again. Christina had confided the truth in Rayburn . . . in its entirety. It was then that he could have told Christina that William Read was not married . . .

434

that is was Read's sister who was to wed Peter. But Rayburn had thought it best that Glenda possibly find another man who was even more dependable. Yes, she would never know of William Read's investment in this grand ship. It was for her own future that he was thinking about.

Whisking Tom away from her, glancing back across his shoulder at Glenda and the confusion etched across her face for the abruptness, he said, "Now, Tom, you go on out to the gate, open it, and ready the gate. I'll get Nena to you as soon as I can."

Glenda fell to her knees once more and hugged Nena tightly around the neck, but knowing this wouldn't be the last time she would get to do so. But she had to make a good show. Everyone who was watching thought it would be her last time with Nena. Only she knew differently.

"Nena, my orphaned cub," she murmured. "I am doing the right thing. One day you will understand. You will now even be able to have many cubs of your own. How grand that will be."

"Glenda," Christina urged, touching Glenda lightly on a cheek. "Come. The guests. That will be the way to forget your sadness of goodbyes."

One more kiss on the tip of Nena's nose and Glenda rose and didn't look back. She swallowed back a lump in her throat, now making plans as to how she could leave this place of gaiety. She had to make sure she would get to the ship on time. . . .

"And isn't the parlor just breathtakingly beautiful?" Christina purred, clasping her hands eagerly in front of her, glancing around, so proud, so content now that she had decided just what she did need out of life

435

to be happy. She missed Peter . . . but Rayburn was quickly making her forget.

Glenda smiled warmly at all who danced around her as an orchestra played at the far end of the room. The orchestra had been brought out from New Orleans, and the house had been lavishly decorated with great masses of flowers. The staircase was garlanded with roses, and other blossoms filled vases strewn about tables and mantles. Candles in huge candelabras and also sparkling among the prisms of a crystal chandelier bathed the parlor and the dining room with golden light.

"Christina, your house couldn't look lovelier," Glenda finally answered. "And your guests seem to be enjoying it so much." The ladies were beautiful in plush gowns of silk and satins with their jewels sparkling invitingly as they would be drawn into the arms of their escorts, to accompany others around the glistening floor.

The men who weren't dancing were sipping a brandy or two while enjoying cigars and conversation of news of the city. Coffee, little cakes and steaming bowls of gumbo were placed invitingly on a table near the dining room entrance, but most of the crowd awaited the midnight supper where all would be served deftly, swiftly and generously by servants in the Taylor dining room.

Glenda felt suddenly awkward in these surroundings, not knowing any of the guests or the skills of how to mingle with proper talk with the other women. She felt even more ill at ease when a young gentleman with the blondest of hair came to her side and asked her to dance. She had never danced in her life. She

436

looked up into his sprinkling of gold dust eyes and saw his sincere friendliness, but had to refuse him. As he walked off in his neat black dress suit, she wanted to blink her eyes and make herself disappear.

"You should have tried, Glenda," Christina whispered, waving lightly to a friend who had just entered.

"You know I can't dance," Glenda murmured. She looked around for a fast escape, but felt trapped, so began forcing conversation with all who would stop to introduce themselves to her. She was relieved when Rayburn rescued Christina and began gliding her around the room in time with a pleasant waltz.

The hours seemed to be passing now, but Glenda had yet to find the right moment to escape without notice. When Christina wasn't dancing, she was by Glenda's side, and when Christina was dancing, she was watching, smiling toward Glenda. Glenda knew Christina was doing these things to make her more comfortable, but little did Christina know that she might in the end cause Glenda to not succeed at what she had wished for her own self. . . .

Glenda sighed with relief when word came that the midnight meal was being served. The guests were ushered into the dining room. Upon a huge oak table covered with elegant lace and silver and adorned with a tall epergne, filled with flowers from which ribbons traced a gleaming path to the bouquet at the place of each lady, was spread the array of food for which all plantations were famed. Here and upon sideboards and side tables were whole turkeys, roasts, cold ham, rich cheese, silver and glass bowls filled with salads, gelatins, cakes in richly iced pyramids, elaborately ornamented charlotte russe, thick custards and jellies and Mont Blanc of whipped cream.

Corks began popping gaily from champagne bottles, wines bubbled and sang as they gurgled from cut glass decanters, and all this would be followed with dancing until dawn, when servants would then reappear with silver trays of wine or punch, gumbo and black coffee.

Glenda had to force a smile as she was ushered next to Christina's seat. She eyed the food halfheartedly but took generous portions of all that was offered, then when the last bite of cake was eaten, was relieved when everyone began leaving the table. This was the time that she had waited for. Christina's face was rosy from the food, excitement and Rayburn at her side and didn't see Glenda when she slipped from the room.

Breathless now, Glenda rushed into her room and slipped out of her beautiful dress, lifted the jewels and flowers from her upswept hair, and chose a more comfortable attire to travel in. A black serge skirt and white shirtwaist, a change of clothes in her travel bag, and she was ready to slip out the back door. The next thing of danger was to secure a horse without drawing notice to herself. But Glenda had seen the servants carry out several trays of food and a decanter of wine to the stable hands, so she hoped they would be too busy to notice one horse being set free from the many. She had to make haste. Too much time had already been used up. What if she did miss the ship? She so wanted to travel with Nena, see to her safety along with Tom Andrews.

Stepping on tiptoe, she moved down the staircase

with her travel bag tucked into the corner of her left arm, stopping to glance quickly around her. When she saw that most still lingered in the dining room, standing, chatting, she flew out the back way, across the terrace, along the damp grasses of the lawn, and once she was through the gate and inside the stable, only then could she stop and get a deep breath.

Listening carefully to the sounds of voices at the far end of the stable, Glenda chose a sleek black stallion with which to make a swift escape to the levee, where she hoped most scurrying had ceased for the night. The ship's leaving wasn't as exciting as the ship's arrival. The bananas made all the differences in the world. When they were known to be on board, the whole city seemed to arrive to the levee, to take part in the excitement.

She mounted the horse and patted its mane and urged it out into the blackness of night. She smiled. The color of the horse was good. Even it looked a part of the night. The only thing that reflected around her was the whiteness of her blouse. She had chosen wrong. But maybe . . . maybe she would make it without notice.

She guided the horse in a soft trot until past the house, then once on the straight path of the road, gave the horse a quick flick of the reins and yelled a loud "Hahh" to it, so glad that Read had taught her the skills of riding a horse. She enjoyed the lift of her hair in the breeze and the aromas of the blossomed bushes and trees all around her. The moon was only a sliver in the sky and the stars twinkled as though sequins. But the shine of the Mississippi River beneath the soft moon's glow was even more welcomed. She followed its path until the levee came into view. Feeling threads of excitement weaving through her heart, she dismounted and secured the horse's reins next to another horse, hoping that surely someone would notice the deserted horse and lead it back to its rightful owner.

Then she moved slinkily through the night, avoiding any passersby as she worked her way onto the wharf. There were still a few loitering around, but made no notice of her. She let her gaze move from ship to ship, paddlewheeler to paddlewheeler, until she once again was looking upon this fine long ship with a smokestack looming into the air, all clean and waiting for its first blackening from soot.

Only a few lanterns were hanging, dimly lighted along the wharf, but there was enough light to read the name of the ship that was now fully painted in bold black on the ship's side. Glenda's heartbeat raced as she read the name . . . Nena. . . .

"What the. . . ?" she gasped. "Who would name their ship Nena . . . and . . . why. . . ?"

The approach of footsteps behind her drew her mind from her wonders and she then moved on toward the ship, glancing cautiously around her, then sped onto the gangplank and down steps, until she found herself alone in a dark corner of the ship. Panting, she unbuttoned the two top buttons of her blouse and blew down its front. Though a cool evening, her anxiety had caused her to become all a dither.

She wiped her brow free of nervous perspiration, then began searching around her. She couldn't see much. But she could hear a loud argument arising around the corner from where she stood. She listened closely, soon recognizing one voice to be that of Tom Andrews. Then she tensed and felt her heartbeat become erratic when she heard the other voice. It was . . . Read's. . . .

She put her hands to her mouth. Oh, how she ached to run to him. How long had it been? And, why was he on this ship? She would have expected him to be on his paddlewheeler, somewhere down the muddy strip of the Mississippi River. She took a step sideways, listening even more intensely, trembling now, remembering so much that had been shared with this man who was owned by another. . . .

Her eyebrows lifted when she heard the words. . . .

"You damn kid, tell me where you got this mountain lion," Read shouted. There was a strained silence, then Read spoke in a weakened voice. "You see, lad, this isn't only an ordinary puma. I know this cat. See how she lets you pet her? She is tame. There is only one such cat as this. . . ."

Tom Andrews said, "Yes. The cat is tame. But I cannot tell you where I got it. I was . . . uh . . . paid to keep my silence."

"If you value your position on this ship you will tell me," Read persisted angrily. "I am the ship's owner and captain. I shall order you from this ship and see to it that you don't board any other ship that docks at New Orleans. Do you understand? Do you?"

Glenda's mind was becoming a mass of confusion. She tried to put the pieces of the puzzle together that were being tossed around her. Who had paid Tom for his silence? Rayburn? Peter? And what did Read say about being this ship's captain and owner? He wasn't! Then her eyes widened as something else was remembered. The name of this ship. Nena. Read would be the one to use such a name. Hadn't he loved the puma . . . the orphaned cub . . . Nena . . . just as much as she had when first discovered in the thickness of the jungle?

But the ship's owner? This ship's captain? She suddenly felt the urge to flee. She no longer felt as though it was the best thing for her to be a part of a ship that was owned by the man she loved . . . since . . . this man wasn't free to love her back.

Feeling a tearing of her heart, she began to tiptoe back toward the gangplank, watching for any sudden movement around her. Luckily, it seemed that most were in the hold or boiler room, getting the ship ready for heading it out to sea. Then she felt a hand settle roughly around a wrist and jerk her back to the ship's deck. She looked anxiously around and saw a thickly bearded man glaring down at her with the darkest pools of eyes since . . . she had looked . . . into Read's. . . .

"Ma chérie. . .?"

Glenda recognized his voice. It *was* Read who was holding her so forcefully. It was Read well hidden behind this mask of beard! Oh, God, it was Read . . . so close . . . touching her . . . confusing her. . . .

"Read?" she said in a near whisper.

"What are you doing on this ship?" he said in a strained voice. "Why is Nena even on the ship? I don't have either of you listed on a passenger list. What is the meaning of this? Where in the hell have you been these past weeks? Nobody would tell me a damn thing. Why the damn mystery? I thought we had something special. What happened to kill that feeling between you and I? Damn it, Glenda, I need some answers."

"You are in no position to demand any answers from me," she forced herself to say. "Please release me. I have just changed my plans for this evening."

"Plans? What plans? Why are you on board this ship . . . my ship . . .?" Read shouted.

Glenda managed to jerk her wrist free, rubbing its soreness. "Your . . . ship . . .?" she said, then set her jaws firmly. "Like I said, *senor*," she hissed. "Nothing I do is of your concern."

Read drew her roughly into his arms and glared down at her with dark pools of passion. "*Ma chérie*, I sense there has been a misunderstanding somewhere in our relationship," he grumbled. "There is no reason for you to be treating me in such a cold manner. I have done nothing but love you from that very first day. . . ."

Glenda's heart raced. She swallowed hard. "Read, please. . . ," she said, squirming beneath his hold. Her insides ached for him. Hadn't she dreamed of his nearness? His touch . . .? But she had to remember . . . he was not hers any longer. Had he ever been? She knew the answer to that. The child that she had seen him embracing had to have been at least four years of age.

"Nena. Why is Nena on my ship? At least tell me that," Read persisted.

"Nena? Your ship?" she said, now as though in a daze because of his lingering closeness.

"Glenda, I no longer am the owner of a paddle-wheeler," he said, releasing his hold on her. His gaze shot around him, proud. "I now am the sole possessor of this fine ship." He whirled around and captured her devoted attention with his dark eyes. "A ship that I chose to name after something we shared for too short a time."

"Our . . . orphaned cub? Nena?" she said, softening now in her mood toward him. She was suddenly feeling as he had professed . . . that something had been misunderstood in their relationship. Surely soon what it had been would be revealed to them both.

"Yes. Nena," he said. He looked toward movement in the dark shadows. Then he clasped his fingers to her shoulders again. "Has Tom Andrews been instructed to take Nena back to Honduras?"

Glenda lowered her eyes. "Yes," she said. "It is time. She is too large and has shown signs of being restless."

"And you? Were you also planning to return? Travel once again as a stowaway? Are you . . . just . . . as restless . . . ?"

"Yes. . . ."

He quickly gathered her into his arms and held her tightly. "Glenda, Glenda," he said thickly. "I don't know what prompts you to do anything. You are a mystery to me. But you will not travel on my ship as a stowaway. If you must return to Honduras, you will do so in the privacy and comfort of my personal cabin."

His fingers combed through her hair, making his heart race with need for her. . . .

Glenda felt a shiver of pleasure rush through her. She lifted her eyes to his. "You would do this for me?" she whispered. "You do truly care. . .?"

His fingers worked to the nape of her neck and caressed her there. "Care?" he laughed. "I've never stopped caring. How could you have even thought I did?"

Her pulse raced. She didn't wish to mention a wife nor a child. She didn't want to break the spell they were becoming such a part of. It was as in the past . . . when in his arms . . . when being gazed upon by such penetrating eyes of pure passion . . . everything else was lost from her mind.

She laced her arms around his neck, almost purring she was so content to be with him again. Gently, she forced his face down until their lips were meeting, testing, then demanding as the world was placed behind them.

Tears surfaced as she continued to cling. A sob tore from her throat as the warm wetness of lips traced her face and he groaned noisily from the want and need of her building in a maddened heat in his loins.

"Oh, Read, I've missed you so," she whispered, touching him now on the lips, then giggling as the tips of his whiskers seemed to sting her fingertips. "Even bearded, you are so utterly handsome and desirable."

Read chuckled a bit beneath his breath, giving her a steady smile as he gently drew free from her. Then he glanced quickly around him when footsteps began increasing on all sides of them. He knew that this crew had finished checking out the refrigeration unit in the hold and had checked the boiler room to see if all the new equipment was well oiled and ready for its first true test at sea.

"The anchor will soon be lifting," he said, nervously

straightening his shirt. "You must go to my cabin and wait for me there."

"Nena? Where is Nena?"

"I will see to it that Nena will have the run of the cabin right next to mine. She won't have to be caged for the full trip."

"You did see her?"

"Yes. . . ."

"Isn't she a beautiful puma now, Read?"

He laughed nervously. "Big and beautiful," he said. "And what about Tom Andrews? Will it be safe for him to look after Nena if Nena is set free?"

"With me on board and able to move about freely myself, Tom's services won't even be needed," Glenda said. "If I had been only a stowaway and Nena would have had to have been caged for the full trip, only then would Tom's services be required."

"Then I will busy Tom with other duties," Read grumbled.

"Take me to the cabin where Nena is to be released," Glenda said. "Then once the ship is at sea, I shall leave her and come to you. . . ."

"*Ma chérie*, I never dreamed that I would be courting you and the sea together again," Read said, guiding her from the main deck, down a flight of steps and to where Tom still stood at the far end of the hallway, guarding Nena.

"Tom," Glenda sighed. She went to him and hugged him.

"Glenda?" Tom gasped, feeling awkward in her embrace. "What are you. . .?"

She drew from him, giggling. "What am I doing on board the Nena?" she said gaily. "I'm also traveling to Honduras."

"You are . . .?"

"Yes," she murmured, turning to cast Read a look of ecstasy through the thickness of her lashes. She no longer cared that he had a wife and a son. She would treasure these moments of pleasure with him. She just wouldn't deny herself of him any longer. How had she even . . . in . . . the past. . .? Oh, so many nights of love had been neglected. . . .

Chapter Twenty

The shimmerings of gold and purples from the stained glass of the skylight settled across Glenda's face, awakening her with a soft sort of nudge. She stretched lazily, then lifted her lips into a wide, happy smile when she let her gaze settle on Read sprawled out next to her on the wide expanse of his bed in the supreme privacy of his cabin.

Glenda slithered over next to Read and fitted her nude body next to his nudity, sighing pleasurably as he stirred in his sleep and unconsciously draped an arm across her back. Teasingly, Glenda began tracing the lines of his body, muffling a giggle as she watched his flesh ripple and become goosepimply along the path where her finger moved. Then she jumped with a start when he suddenly reached for her, laughing huskily, and soon had her pinioned against the mattress beneath him.

"Thought you could torment me forever, did you?" he said, forcing her legs apart with his knees.

"You were asleep," she said stubbornly, trying to release her wrists that were beginning a slow throbbing.

"Ma chérie, how could a man sleep while in your presence?" he said, then teased her with the hardness of his manhood between her outstretched thighs.

She let out a low moan as his mouth lowered over hers to seek hers with an almost wildness and desperation. She felt the urgency of his mouth and yielded herself to him, responding wantonly. She felt the sweet pain of his entrance and began the slow movement of her hips. She trembled as his lips continued to possess her and when his hands molded her breasts, she let out a small gurgle of contentment and let the passion mount inside her.

She was drowning in a sea of sensations, then cresting and riding high. His mouth continued to bear down with raw passion as his manhood worked furiously for completion. She had never felt so alive. Her whole body seemed to be tingling. She was clinging, desperate, wrapping her legs around him to bring him even closer to her.

"Ma chérie, oh, how I love you," Read whispered as he finally set her lips free. His mouth went to a breast and let his tongue worship the nipple, teasing it with quick flicks, then biting it, causing Glenda to writhe with the inflicted sweet pain of the continuing assault.

"How did I ever think I could live without you," Glenda sighed, feeling beads of perspiration breaking out across her brow.

Read framed her face with his hands, drawing his body to a quick halt. "And why even did you try?" he said, studying the green of her eyes . . . the gold of her hair . . . the rosy, sensual flush to her cheeks.

Glenda turned her face from him and closed her eyes. "Not now," she whispered. "Please . . . not

. . . now. . . ."

Read's eyebrows lifted at her reaction, but his body was agreeing that this wasn't the time. He reached beneath and lifted her even more into him and began a slow movement again, closing his eyes, feeling the sweetness of the pleasure he was sharing with her. He pressed his lips against the soft satin of her throat, then felt the giddiness begin inside his head as the quivering began in his body and together they shared a shattering, almost violent climax and soon lay panting next to one another.

"This is one damn way to run a ship," Read finally said, raising his arms above his head, resting his head in the palms of his hands. "Just lie around and taste of your sweet flesh. Yes, *ma chérie,* I could travel the sea forever with you as my companion."

He moved quickly to her side and laced his arm around her waist, drawing her gently to him. "Even as my wife? What do you say, Glenda? Marry me. Be my wife. I'll promise to be true, forever and ever. We would never have to be apart. Never again. I would then know you would have no just cause to flee and hide from me."

Glenda's heartbeat went wild. She stared upward at his eyes. They were darker than usual. There was a sincere, quiet pleading in them. She reached her hand to his face and let her fingers travel over the whiskers. Was he truly two people? Did a beard even make it so? Did he think he could have two wives at once? She then rolled away from him, stepping on the cold wood of the flooring. Their few days shared together on this ship were quickly drawing to a close. Why did he have to spoil it now? A few more hours . . . maybe not even that . . . and the ship would be inching its way into shore.

She looked around her, memorizing this room of love. She would always keep it inside her, forever and ever. The clean-smelling, fresh-paneled walls, the tan leather chairs and heavy oak tables and shelves. She and Read had shared not only sweet ecstasy of love, but many hours lingering over talk of her family . . . her true father Peter . . . her fears of a revolution in Honduras . . . the embroidery shop she still hoped to one day share with Christina . . . her fears for Nena . . . but yet . . . no mention of his family had been made. When she had asked if he had a brother or sister, he would only receive a pained look across his face and in his eyes and very skillfully change the subject. . . .

"Ma chérie," Read said, moving to her side. "What. . . ?"

Glenda silently ignored him and slipped into her black serge skirt and white blouse, draping her golden hair down her back. "I must go see to Nena," she said quietly. "I must see if her cage is ready for transporting from the ship. I must whisper many goodbyes to her."

Read jerked his breeches on, then went and blocked her way, refusing to let her leave. "Damn it, Glenda, you are not taking one step from this cabin until I have some answers," he grumbled. "Over and over again while we've talked, I've tried to pull answers from you. You must tell me now why you ran away from me before and why I have the distinct impression you are readying yourself for another such disappearance. I just asked you to marry me. Why would

451

you refuse? You profess to love me. Is your true reason for returning to Honduras not at all to see your family in your country's time of unrest, but to seek out that Ramón Martinez to now say vows with him?"

Glenda's eyes widened. Then she couldn't help but laugh. "Such a thought turns my insides to ice," she snapped.

"Then what is it?" Read demanded, running his fingers nervously through his hair. "Is your love for me not true? Is there something about me that you just do not like?"

Glenda's insides quivered from the warm wondrous desire she always felt for him. Couldn't he tell? Was he truly so blind? She touched his lips with a forefinger. "My darling, it is only you I love. Forever. Surely you know. . . ," she murmured.

He gathered her into his arms as she twined her arms around his neck. He sighed leisurely as his breath warmed her cheek. "Then you will, *ma chérie?* You will be my wife. . . ?"

"You know that I cannot," she said, tears near, yet clinging still. This could be their last moments together. She had to keep him near. But it was he who shoved her away. His eyes were a cold, dark anger. She bit her lower lip wonderingly.

He threw his arms into the air and began pacing. "No one ever told me that proposing to a woman could be such a feat," he grumbled, stomping heavily with each step taken. "This, my first woman to propose to, ever, and she refuses me, over and over again. *Mon dieu,* there will never be a second woman. I shall not humble myself before another woman. . . ."

Glenda's hands went to her throat. She was fully absorbing his words now. She was the first? Then how he managed to already . . . be . . . wed?

Read stopped abruptly and pointed toward the door. "Well?" he growled. "What are you waiting on? There's the door. You refuse to be my wife? I'll never pester you again or any other damn lady. I'm through! Do you hear? Through! I won't be humiliated. . . ."

Moving slowly toward him, Glenda reached her hand to him. She flinched as he took a step backwards. "Read, I must ask you something," she said, with a hammering heart.

"What else is there to say? Just leave, *ma chérie,*" he said, whirling around, grabbing a shirt, thrusting his arms angrily into its sleeves. "I've had enough. I've a ship to run. Step aside. . . ."

Instead, Glenda blocked *his* way. She was breathless from breathing so hard, so afraid that he might hit her. She had never seen him so angry. "Read, tell me about your wife and child," she finally grew brave enough to say.

Read's mouth opened and his eyes widened. He grasped her shoulders wildly. "What . . . did . . . you say. . . ?" he gasped.

Her knees weakened, feeling the hurt he was inflicting on her shoulders. She watched his labored breathing. Why would he be angry at her? It had been he who had kept the truths from her. . . . "Your wife and child," she murmured, swallowing hard. "I saw you with them. Christina . . . she also saw your wife. . . ." She hung her head. "I've been wrong to let myself enjoy another woman's man, but I fell in love with you before I knew. . . ."

Read laughed softly, then drew her roughly to him

453

and began to swirl her around, now laughing loud and victoriously. "Glenda, oh, *ma chérie,* you make me so happy," he shouted. He then held her still and showered her face with warm kisses.

"Read, I don't understand. . . ."

"Darling, all along, you've loved me. Now I do know how much," he said, lifting her into his arms, carrying her to the bed and easing her onto it. He stripped her gently, then himself, and lowered himself over her.

"Read, I am so confused," Glenda said, but already growing breathless from the fires being ignited along her flesh as Read began to consume her fully with the branding from his lips and tongue.

"You love me. You vixen, you love me," he said huskily. "And darling, what a surprise to now realize why you've avoided me."

She was clinging, floating, now almost mindless as his hands worked magic on her breasts, downward and then onto the satin of her thighs. She knew that she shouldn't. Especially now that he knew that she knew that he was already owned by another.

But something wicked inside her caused her to spread her legs and accept the warm full length of him inside her again. She sought his mouth with a desperate wildness. She arched and met his eager thrusts and felt the familiar spinning of the head, shuddered and cried out with her fulfilled climax just as he also shivered violently into her.

She turned her face from him and sobbed. "You've caused me to forget myself once again," she said. "I am no better than a whore. Even though you are the only man I've ever known in such an intimate way, I am no better than a whore."

He reached to frame her face between his hands and forced her gaze to meet his. *"Ma chérie, it is true? I am the only . . . man. . . ?"*

"Yes," she whispered. "Yes, yes. . . ."

"I cannot say you are the only woman I've taken to bed," he said softly. "But you are the only woman I've wanted to wed and have even proposed to. . . ."

"What. . . ?"

"Yes. I am not married," he said, chuckling a bit. He bent and placed a kiss on her lips, then saw her confusion was no less, so quickly added, "No, *ma chérie*, I am not married. The woman and child you saw me with? That was my sister and her son." His faced darkened as his eyes blinked back tears. "You see, I couldn't tell you about my sister and uh . . . nephew . . . these last few days when we've talked. It was too hard a subject for me to linger on. . . ."

Glenda was too thrilled to sense his uneasiness about anything! She had just discovered how foolish she had been to not have trusted and believed in him. She could now see a future for herself with Read. It had always been there and she had let it stray from her grasp. She swung her arms about his neck and pulled his lips to hers, kissing him more passionately than ever before. Then he laced her fingers through his hair and murmured, "Yes, my darling, I will be your wife. I love you, oh, how I love and adore you. . . ."

Ma chérie. . . ."

"But I must see to my family," she interrupted. "Should they need me. . . ."

"Should they need you, I will share you with them. . . ."

"You will do that willingly. . . ?"

"Anything," he said. "As long as you promise to never leave me again."

"I promise," she said. "But of course there will always be times. . . ."

"Oh?" he said, lifting an eyebrow.

"Like now," she murmured. "I must dress and go to be with Nena for a while before setting her free in the jungle."

"I can understand," Read said, then laughed as he rose and began to dress, as she also did. She was glad that she had chosen to not dress elaborately. She was to soon be with her family once more and they could feel a bit uncomfortable if she had dressed in lacy silk and with diamonds at her throat. And she was purposely going to leave her shoes behind. She could hardly wait to feel the warm, bleached-white sands beneath her feet, and smell the freshness that rippled outward from the depths of the forested jungle.

"I hope Nena will rush on into the jungle and quickly become a part of its habitat," Glenda said, already worrying about her orphaned cub's welfare.

With the last button secured on Read's shirt, he walked Glenda to the door and on to the next cabin's door. "Glenda," he said, taking her hands. "We must not let anyone know we've returned Nena to Honduras to set her free. It could cause quite a stir of excitement."

"But . . . Read. . . ."

"Not even your family, Glenda," he said firmly. "It's best for Nena. Believe me. Let's let her move on her own. Her own instincts will guide her to her own kind."

"You do believe so. . . ?"

"I know so. . . ."

She cast her eyes downward, already missing Nena. She stepped lightly next to Read as the cabin door was opened to a crack. A quiet hiss greeted them both as Read and Glenda stepped on inside.

"Nena. . . ," Glenda said, falling to her knees to wrap her arms around Nena's neck. She placed a cheek against Nena's mane, emitting a sad sigh. The voyage had awarded them many last moments together. Tom Andrews had not complained too much about having been freed from his duties to Nena. He still had the pocket of money that had so generously been paid him.

But Glenda had known that Tom Andrews had hated leaving her to Read. She suspected that he would have more than Nena with her. Ah! How funny it had been when Tom had discovered the intimacies shared between Read and Glenda. . . !

Read stood his ground. Nena just didn't appear that friendly to him. Nena's green eyes never left him. Not once. And when another small hiss emerged, followed by quite a showing of fangs, Read even worried about Glenda's safety. Nena was a wild animal, no matter if Glenda had raised her from a cub. A cat as large as Nena could turn on its owner if made nervous enough. Suddenly Read was anxious for land. "Glenda, do you . . . truly . . . feel safe. . . ?"he blurted. "She stares at me so. I don't feel so secure. . . ."

Glenda lifted a hand beneath Nena's chin and began to caress her there, causing a lazy purr to reverberate through the cabin's interior. "Don't you hear?"

Glenda said. "She is content. She loves me. She'd never hurt me. Why, I don't think she could ever harm anyone. . . ."

"Then I can leave you alone with her?" Read asked, massaging his whiskers nervously.

Glenda laughed amusedly. "Read, please go to your duties," she said. "I will tend to my own here. You see, as long as Nena is not set free, she is still mine. I've a duty to her. I have, since the day we found her in the jungle."

Read leaned and kissed Glenda, keeping eye contact with Nena. There was a touch of wildness there. He knew it. "I'll check in on you or have Tom Andrews do it. Real soon," he said, then turned and left the room, stopping outside the closed door, looking toward it, then shrugging his shoulders and hurrying to his duties. The horizon was no longer blues meeting blues, but he was now seeing sort of a dewdrop formation, sparkling. The sun was reflecting down upon what had to be Honduras. . . .

Glenda hugged Nena, then lifted a finger to the earring and touched it. "I will always know you, Nena," she whispered. "If in the jungle and you smell my presence and come to me, I will know it is you by the flash of the gold on your ear."

She lifted a paw and kissed it. "I always will miss you. I already miss you, my orphaned cub. I already . . . miss you. . . ."

The shallow draft boat scraped bottom at Bay Island as Read lifted the oars from the water. Glenda's eyes were sparkling from excitement. She had gone

458

patiently with Read to meet with El Progresso's division manager upon first arrival to the prosperous banana plantation. Shoeless and now even without underclothing, having chosen to leave even those behind on the ship, she had squirmed a bit uneasily through the close scrutiny of introductions with the impeccably attired man and wife who now occupied the house that for so short a time had been Christina's and Rayburn's.

Then once these formalities had been drawn to a welcome close, Read had accompanied Glenda to the house where Carlos, Marcos and Carlita lived. Glenda had been a bit horrified to see the change in Carlita. Instead of the petite person she had been, Carlita had seemed to have swollen into a round ball . . . a giggling, bashful round ball!

Ah, it had been so great being with brothers again and realizing that soon she would become an aunt!

But then happy thoughts were erased by sad. She could still see Nena hesitate at the edge of the jungle when first released from her cage. Then one bouncy spring and Nena was gone! Gone from Glenda's life almost as quickly as she had entered!

"Come, Glenda," Read said. "If I'm to meet my future mother and father-in-law, you will have to step from this boat and your dreams." He jumped over the side into the fizz of the lapping water's edge and held his arms out to her. "I'm truly sorry it's taken so long after docking to get to this island of your parents', but *ma chérie,* I had my duties."

"I understand," she said, realizing many hours had passed. But she had grown used to waiting. She had waited for a man like Read all her life and to think she almost lost him due to her ignorance! She laced her fingers through his and stepped over the boat's side. She smiled widely toward him, knowing she'd never make the same mistake again!

The water was icy cold to her feet and ankles, yet felt refreshingly good. She liked the feel of the wet sand between her toes and the way the effervescence of the water clung to her ankles as she moved on toward the pearl-white sands of the shore. When a small fish nibbled at the bubbles at her ankles, Glenda let out a squeal of delight and broke free from Read and rushed hurriedly onto the beach. She lifted her skirt and shook the water free from it, laughing at Read as he lifted one water-logged foot after the other until he was standing before her, laughing.

"Read, oh, Read," Glenda said, moving silkily into his embrace. "My love, I've never been happier."

He kissed her gently and then they moved onward together, holding hands, kicking their way through the sand. Glenda was aware of all eyes upon her and Read. The villagers who weren't on the beach or pier fishing, were hanging their heads from the windows of their houses, openly staring.

As the sun beat down upon Glenda, in its intensity, she was aware of her attire of jet black skirt and the heat it sucked in onto her body. She craved the looseness and lightness of one of her boldly flowered, gathered cotton skirts. She wanted to cast her long-sleeved, high-necked blouse aside to instead slip a low-necked, drawstringed blouse over her head. She lifted her free hand and began slowly unbuttoning the blouse and let the seabreeze move gently inside it to lift it partially away from her breasts.

Sighing, she lifted her head to the sun and shook her hair away from her face, to let it hang in gold rivulets down her back. She was home. She hadn't realized just how much she had missed the island and the sense of freedom it always afforded her. Then she suddenly remembered something else that always awaited her on this island! She slowed her pace and let her gaze travel around her, from man to man. Had Ramón heard of her return? Would he seek her out? A tremble soared through her. She draped her arm possessively through Read's and drew him close to her.

"*Ma chérie,* what is it?" he said, bending into her face. "You suddenly look as though a shadow has been cast over you."

She glanced quickly around her again, then pulled Read playfully from the beach to now lead him between a row of thatched-roof huts on high stilts and lazily swaying palm trees. "It is nothing," she laughed nervously. "It is nothing." Her heart skipped a beat when she saw the familiar house set at the far end of this road. Then her gaze traveled around it, seeing the well-kept garden and the tall stalks of maize that had predominance over all else that had been planted there. It was among these stalks that she caught her first glimpse of her father. He was straw-hatted, heavily mustachioed and round-shouldered as he was busily hoeing the furrows of ground.

"Papa," Glenda said in a low whisper. She broke free from Read and began running, lifting her skirt way above her knees, shouting, "Papa" over and over again. When he turned and saw her, he threw his hoe onto the ground and ran toward her with outstretched arms.

461

Weeping, she embraced José. She flipped his hat from his head and placed her cheek on the balding spot of his head, laughing inside, having almost forgotten how much taller she was than he. "Papa, how good it is to see you," she sighed. His arms were solid steel as he continued to hug her.

José then drew gently from her and studied her with dark, exploring eyes. "And how are you, my golden beauty?" he said as he clasped onto her shoulders. "What has brought you home? You don't look ill. . . ."

Glenda laughed amusedly. "No. I am not ill," she said. Her laughter faded away and her eyes wavered a bit. "I returned home for many reasons, Papa," she said further. "I had heard rumors of fighting in the cities. I had feared for my family. For my brothers," she said.

"No fear, Glenda," he said, dropping his hands to his side. He glanced upward at the sun, then stooped to recapture his hat and placed it back on his head at an angle. The sun's rays seemed to be baking his brain more with the loss of his hair. He knew that old age was quickly approaching and did not fear it, not with such a concerned, loving family as his. "It was just a few restless men causing troubles. It grew a bit worse after el Presidente Bonilla's assassination attempt," he quickly added. "But all is well now. We no longer hear guns in the middle of the night."

Glenda began fanning herself with the tail of her skirt. "Yes. Carlos and Marcos told me," she said. "I was so happy to hear such news. . . ."

"Your mother? She is another reason for your return?" José said, glancing toward the house, where smoke spiraled upward from a chimney. Ah, how proud he was to have given his sweet Rosa a new wood-burning cook stove. She cooked and cooked . . . and he ate and ate. . . . He smiled inwardly at his happiness.

"Yes. Mamma. How is she?" Glenda said anxiously, following José's stare of pride. Then she saw the chimney and knew! She smiled warmly toward José and gave him another quick hug. "Papa, how very nice of you."

"I made enough riches on the banana plantation for at least that one luxury," he boasted, squaring his shoulders. "Your mother? She loves her gift and she is quite well, Glenda. Quite well."

Read moved into view, having lingered behind to give father and daughter some private moments together. When Glenda turned and saw his approach, she ran to him and linked her arm through his, then almost dragged him to her father's side. "And here is another reason I've returned home," she said silkily. "To introduce you to the man I love and will marry."

At first, this hadn't been among Glenda's reasons for returning, but now it was. . . . She watched her father's expression of kindness turn to that of a dark brooding. Oh, why hadn't she thought to expect it? Didn't seeing Read bring so much to mind? Did José even know the full truth of his wife's relationship with the American sea captain of those many years ago? Surely not, or he would not have ever accepted her into his bed again!

Glenda took her father's hand, still holding one of Read's. "Papa, this is a very fine American named William Read deBaulieu," she said. She turned her attention to Read. "And, Read, this is my father, whom I've told you so much about."

Read extended his free hand in friendship. "Nice to make your acquaintance, sir," he said, smiling.

José slowly lifted his hand to Read's, frowning. Then his tongue twisted, almost comically, as he tried to pronounce Read's last name. "That is an American name?" he finally said, giving up his struggles with saying it.

Read laughed good-naturedly. "No. It is French. My family came by way of ship from France to America many years ago," he said. "Galvez is a much easier name to live with, I'm sure."

José liked this. He was proud of his name and to know that this American was showing his approval made José quickly decide to approve of Read. He gestured with the swing of an arm. "Come. Come and meet my Rosa," he said with his chopped English, another thing he had proudly acquired on the banana plantation.

Glenda sighed leisurely, seeing her father's approval, then raced on ahead of them and into the small house, where Rosa stood grinding maize. "Mamma?" Glenda whispered, only a silhouette at the opened door, against the backdrop of bright sky behind her.

Rosa swirled around and shadowed her eyes with the thick flesh of her left arm. "Glenda? Is . . . that . . . you. . . ?" she said, then threw her arms up into the air as Glenda stepped in out of the shadows.

"Mamma, yes, it is me," Glenda said, welcoming her mother's arms around her chest. She reached down and circled her arms around her mother's back,

464

again smiling because of towering so over her mother. She felt the heavy sobs against her surfacing from her mother, causing even herself to join in. What she had seen had been a healthy, contented mother, not ill and bedridden. Rosa had even added flesh to her bones. And as she was now looking up into Glenda's eyes with her dark eyes, Glenda could see a sparkle.

"You've returned to family?" her mother said. "Yes, Glenda? You have?"

"For only a little while, Mamma," Glenda said, both exchanging conversation in Spanish.

Rosa drew from Glenda and began wiping her hands on her apron. "What do you mean, for only a little while?" she said.

Glenda saw her mother's displeasure at this revelation, but this was the time to make her mother realize that life was many things and that family would always be of importance to her, but that she had her own family to begin now . . . with Read.

Her gaze raked over her mother, seeing the simplicity of her cotton dress, the coarseness of her black hair pulled back in a tight bun at the back of her head, and now wondering how she had looked when she had shared passionate moments with Peter Grayson. Had she smelled of spices and perspiration when Peter had embraced her as she now smelled?

Glenda blinked her eyes and shook her head a bit to clear her thoughts, not wanting to think of her true father. But wouldn't Rosa even want to know . . . if . . . she had found him. . . ? Did she ever dream of him and his tall handsomeness. . . ?

She swallowed hard and finally answered her mother. "I will return to New Orleans," she said softly. "I will return there to wed."

Rosa teetered a bit and leaned heavily against a chair. "You . . . are to wed. . . ?" she gasped. "To . . . an . . . American. . . ?"

"Yes, Mamma," she replied, then lowered her eyes. "Yes."

Rosa slumped down onto a chair. "To an American," she murmured softly. Her gaze flew upward. "Glenda, you know how I feel. . . ."

Glenda scooted onto a chair next to her mother and took her hand. "Mamma, yes, I know," she said. She would have to play this little game with her mother. Her mother would never know that the truth was now known. . . .

"And you still would. . . ?"

"Yes. I must. . . ."

Rosa began toying with a ceramic coffee cup, turning it round and round. "Glenda, while in America, did you succeed at finding. . . ?" she whispered.

Glenda's heart ached. She now knew her mother still thought of her own American love. . . . She cast her eyes downward. "No, Mamma," she said. "It is something I have decided to forget about." She would never, no, never mention a search for her true father again. Rosa did not need to know that the search had already been one of success. . . .

Rosa lifted her eyes to Glenda and a peacefulness was there. She smiled as she sighed. "I am so glad, Glenda," she said. "Truly, I am. . . ."

José directed Read on into the house where his nose was greeted by many aromas. There were spices . . . cooking pork. . . .

"And, Mamma, this is Read," Glenda said, rushing to his side. She beamed into Read's face. "And, Read, my sweet well mother. . . ."

Rosa's face flushed as she rose from the chair. Her heart pounded, remembering, oh, such another moment in her life. She was suddenly young, beautiful and highly spirited in her mind as Read's hand took hers in his. Yes, he was as Peter had been. She would always remember her sea captain . . . always. . . !

Chapter Twenty-One

Water was splashing over a high, gray rock formation, then swirling in clear blues into a lagoon that was laced by lush greenery at its banks. In its reflection were towering oaks, pine and palm trees, and spread out beneath these were smaller thorny trees, cacti and scrub brush, and then even more prominent the pageant of brilliance of the large beautiful orchids, begonias and varieties of roses.

Glenda tugged on Read's hand, urging him through the brush and then next to the shadowy blues of the lagoon. "See, I told you I'd find it," she said. "It's a special place. If things hadn't become so rushed when we were last together in this beautiful country, I would have led you here to show you where I've swum with only the water as my cover."

Read glanced around him, seeing streaks of green and yellows soaring through the air. Had he ever seen such magnificent colors as were on these quetzal birds and red and yellow macaws? The sound of the forest was soft around him as monkeys exchanged gossip and birds exchanged mating calls. "It is a paradise," he said, drawing Glenda next to him. He lifted an eyebrow as he burrowed his nose into the depth of her golden hair. "And you have swum, clothes shed, here, alone?"

"Yes, as you and I will now also do," she giggled, twirling around proceeding to unbutton his shirt. She paused long enough to trace his freshly shaven facial features. Without the beard, ah, he was her Read again.

"A sort of celebration, eh?" he laughed amusedly, lifting his arms as she now pulled a sleeve from each. He felt his heartbeats growing wild as her fingers now went to the buttons of his breeches and soon had even those eased from his legs. And when he was standing there nude, she worshipped his flesh with her lips, causing him to moan with lustful pleasure as she feathered kisses along his chest, lower then until she so lightly brushed her lips against where he was so hard and throbbing. But she teased him there for only a brief moment, then stepped back away from him and did a slow strip until she stood, silkily, motioning for him to come to her.

"Yes. A celebration of life," she purred. "Right at this moment, how could anything else be so perfect?"

"Yes . . . perfect . . . ," he said, inching toward her, but when she was within reach she splashed backward into the water, giggling, but still motioning for him to follow.

"I know just the place, darling," she said. "It will be as though we are on a cloud. . . ."

"*Ma chérie*, I do not like being teased," Read grumbled as he stepped into the water and lunged for her.

She stepped sideways, laughing as he fell face

forward into the water. Then she moved her body also down into the water and swam toward him. She reached for him and felt the velvet of his skin beneath the water and welcomed his touches as his fingers quickly found and captured her breasts.

Moaning throatily, Glenda fit her body into his. She felt full of the devil, oh, so very wicked as she laced her legs around him, causing his hardness to almost make entrance but just as his lips found hers in an almost frantic passion she broke free of him and swam farther away, watching the fury rising in the dark pools of his eyes.

Ma chérie. . . ."

"Darling, come here," she said. "My teasing is over. I've found the bed for our lovemaking. This is what I've been guiding us to. I'm sorry if I've frustrated you. . . ."

Read found the bottom of the lagoon with his feet, then followed her gaze to the most beautiful display of orchids he had yet to see. He could remember Glenda's earlier tale about orchids being called the Holy Ghost flower. This display of orchids was a bed of Holy Ghost flowers. A small smile lifted the corners of his lips. So this is what she had had in mind. He reached for her and guided her downward, stretching her out, and seeing how the orchids peeked out from all around her, she was a serene vision of loveliness. He gathered her into his arms and nuzzled the softness of her neck, causing a sexual excitement to ripple through him.

"Please. No preliminaries, Read," she whispered, already soaring and tingling with eager anticipation. She laced her arms about his neck and drew him into

470

her, surrendering herself seductively. As her hips strained upward, she welcomed his teeth at a nipple of a breast. She trembled as his mouth then found hers and began kissing her hungrily, causing her head to swim and her heart to pound. Desire threatened to drown her but soon found complete ecstasy as their passions became as one.

Breathless and spent now, Glenda leisurely plucked an orchid and placed it to her nose. "Lovely, so lovely," she sighed.

"You are more so," Read said huskily, stretching out on his back next to her. "Happy, *ma chérie?*"

"Yes, oh, yes, yes. . . ."

"Your family approved of me."

"Yes. . . ."

"Since my family is still a bit torn apart by grief for David, maybe you'd like to be married in your parents' house or church by a Bay Island priest instead of in New Orleans," Read said, leaning over her, devouring her with his eyes.

Glenda's heartbeat raced. Her eyes widened. She tossed the orchid into the air and threw her arms about Read's neck. "You mean it? Truly?" she shrieked.

"Yes, yes, *señorita,*" he teased, laughing throatily. "That is, if your mother wouldn't be too uncomfortable in my continuing presence."

"And why should she?"

"Maybe I remind her of her past relationship with Peter Grayson."

Glenda lowered her eyes. "Yes, Peter. . . ," she sighed. "My true father. . . ."

"Damn. I still can hardly believe it."

"It is true though. . . ."

"Peter gets around," Read grumbled.

"And your sister. As you finally confessed to me, she is not your wife but the one who now shares Peter's house. Christina was played for a fool. I hope your sister isn't also . . . such . . . a fool."

Read jumped to his feet and drew her up also. He looked at the lengthening shadows around him. "It is for Harriett to worry about. Not us," he said. "But it is the approach of night that should worry us. Come. Let's swim back to the other side of the lagoon, get dressed, and go back to our cabin on the ship. We don't have that much time before the loading of the bananas begins."

"And our marriage? When. . . ?"

"It will have to be one of quickly spoken words," he laughed. "Do you care. . . ?"

"Care?" she sighed. "Read, to be your wife? I would let words be spoken in any way that is needed, just as long as they are spoken."

"Then . . . so shall it be," he said. "But, darling, the bananas. Let's first get them aboard the ship . . . then we shall go to Bay Island for the ceremony."

"But the bananas. Won't they need to be quickly taken to New Orleans?"

"*Ma chérie*, have you forgotten the refrigeration unit on board? It won't hurt the bananas to wait a few hours longer."

"Will the refrigeration of your ship truly work?"

"Yes. It's been proven and ours is the beginning of many other such ships. I'm proud to be the owner of one of the first."

Laughing and splashing, they made their way to

their clothes and once they were dressed, they rushed on through the density of the brush. And when the powdery sand of the beach was reached, Glenda tensed, seeing Marcos rushing toward them.

When Marcos stopped before her, perspiring and panting wildly, Glenda could see a wildness in his dark eyes. She reached for his hands and clasped onto them. "What is it, Marcos?" she said, feeling her knees weaken with fear. "Is it Mamma? What . . .?"

"No," he panted. "It's Ramón Martinez."

Glenda's face flushed. Ramón had not yet approached her since her return. "What about Ramón?" she hissed, dropping her hands to her side, to circle them into tight fists.

"He is dead," Marcos said, wiping his brow with the sleeve of his shirt.

Glenda teetered a bit. "What? Did you say. . . ?"

"Yes. Ramón. He's been killed," Marcos blurted.

"How. . . ?" Glenda whispered.

"A puma," Marcos said excitedly. "A puma."

Read and Glenda exchanged quick glances. Then it was Glenda who spoke. "A puma?" she said, feeling her heart pounding frantically. Nena? No. Surely not. . . .

"Ramón was threatening me. He was demanding that I help him find a way for him to be with you, away from Read's presence," Marcos said quickly. "It was then that this puma appeared from the brush. It was as though it stood there studying Ramón for a moment, as though it knew Ramón from somewhere. Then suddenly it attacked and with one jerk had snapped Ramón's neck and broke it without even breaking the flesh of Ramón's skin."

"God. . . ," Read grumbled, running his fingers through his hair.

Glenda remained silent. She wasn't sad. She felt even a bit victorious. It was apparent that Ramón would have still been as much a menace to society as in the past. Yes, the world was better off without him.

"And, Glenda, something else," Marcos said. His eyes widened even further. "This puma. There was an earring . . . a gold earring on its one ear. . . ."

Glenda's hands went to her throat. "Nena. It is Nena," she said.

"Are you sure, Marcos?" Read said, circling Glenda's waist with an arm.

"I will always remember the flash of gold," Marcos reassured.

Fear crept up and down Glenda's spine. "Marcos, what happened to that puma?" she asked cautiously.

"It ran past me and into the jungle," he replied. "A lot of laborers got together and began trailing it, but we all decided from what we saw that it was headed for the mountains. It was just a crazy thing, him killing Ramón like that. You see, it could've also killed me. But we're saying it was just an accident that Ramón got in its way. We feel we don't have to worry about the puma. It wasn't after blood."

Glenda sighed. "Marcos, the puma? The earring? It was Nena. Nena? You know. The cub I rescued after Ramón shot its mother?"

Marcos gasped.

"We returned her to the jungle only yesterday."

"But you'd best not tell, Marcos," Read said thickly.

"Yes, sir," Marcos said meekly. He turned and

began moving back toward El Progresso. "I won't tell. I promise." He waved and disappeared into the brush.

Read took Glenda's hands. "And, *ma chérie,* how do you feel about this?" he said.

"Do you truly believe Nena will be safe?" she asked softly.

"Yes. I believe so," he said. "She has finally been able to get her revenge for her mother's death. I don't know how, but she did have the instinct to do this thing."

Glenda was remembering how Nena had stood watching Ramón try to rape her the one night on the beach. She smiled to herself. Somehow she knew that Nena had also had Glenda's welfare in mind when she chose to attack Ramón Martinez. . . .

"Then if Nena will be safe, I can only agree with what she was done," Glenda said. The day was now perfect. Her life was perfect. She looked toward the jungle and silently thanked her orphaned cub. . . .

ROMANCE FROM JANELLE TAYLOR

ANYTHING FOR LOVE   (0-8217-4992-7, $5.99)

DESTINY MINE   (0-8217-5185-9, $5.99)

CHASE THE WIND   (0-8217-4740-1, $5.99)

MIDNIGHT SECRETS   (0-8217-5280-4, $5.99)

MOONBEAMS AND MAGIC   (0-8217-0184-4, $5.99)

SWEET SAVAGE HEART   (0-8217-5276-6, $5.99)

Available wherever paperbacks are sold, or order direct from the Publisher. Send cover price plus 50¢ per copy for mailing and handling to Kensington Publishing Corp., Consumer Orders, or call (toll free) 888-345-BOOK, to place your order using Mastercard or Visa. Residents of New York and Tennessee must include sales tax. DO NOT SEND CASH.

ROMANCE FROM FERN MICHAELS

DEAR EMILY   (0-8217-4952-8, $5.99)

WISH LIST   (0-8217-5228-6, $6.99)

AND IN HARDCOVER:

VEGAS RICH   (1-57566-057-1, $25.00)

ROMANCE FROM HANNAH HOWELL